THE SECRET IS OUT

Robert Stanek is a pen name of bestselling author William Stanek, who is also the artist behind the scenes at World Galleries.

BW Fall Arrives at Multnomah Falls in Canvas Print with Floating Frame

Find his art at 360 Studios

360studios.pictorem.com

BW Extreme Closeup Tulips of the Netherlands 24 in the Art in Flowers Special Collection of William Robert Stanek

robertstanek.pictorem.com

Songbird in the Rain

A Novel

By Robert Stanek

Songbird in the Rain

Published by Big Blue Sky Press, Big Blue Sky and associated logos are trademarks and/or registered trademarks of Big Blue Sky Press.

Cover image licensed from Robert Stanek Studios.

Cover Design: Creative Designs Ltd.

Editorial Development: Andover Publishing Solutions

Copyediting: L & L Content Services

You can provide feedback related to this book by emailing the author at robertstanek@robertstanek.com. Please use the name of the book as the subject line. Learn more about the author at

robert-stanek.com

Acknowledgments

I would like to thank my writing group, my editors, and my publishers for their many years of support. A writer can't survive in this business without such wonderful support. I want to personally thank Jeannie, Tony, Frank, Ed & Holly, Patrick, Susan and everyone else who supported the journey and kept me on track with the writing. Your insights and assistance have always been much appreciated. I also want to thank Will, Jasmine, and Sapphire for always being the first readers to devour my work and come back hungry for more.

William Robert Stanek
40 Years of Writing - 35 Years of Books - 25 Years of Publishing

Dedication

To all those who dare to dream, even when the world tries to hold them back.

Epigraph

"You may encounter many defeats, but you must not be defeated. In fact, it may be necessary to encounter the defeats, so you can know who you are, what you can rise from, how you can still come out of it."

— Maya Angelou

Author's Note

Writing *Songbird in the Rain* has been one of the most meaningful creative journeys of my life. This story is a reflection of the powerful currents of change, love, and sacrifice that defined the 1960s—a time of great transformation in the history of the United States. But at its heart, it's also a deeply personal story about finding yourself in the face of overwhelming expectations.

I grew up not far from Janesville, Wisconsin, the setting of this novel. Like Lena, I've walked through those same streets and fields, felt the cold bite of a Midwest winter, and seen the slow unfolding of spring. This book is my way of bringing that world to life, a place where tradition and ambition collide, and where every choice feels like a turning point.

Songbird in the Rain is a love letter to the dreamers, the musicians, the rebels, and the romantics. It's about the push and pull of love—between what you want for yourself and what you're willing to give up for the people you hold dear. Lena's story is about longing for more while cherishing what you have, about the sacrifices we make, and the shadows of the past that linger even as we move forward.

Thank you for choosing to step into Lena's world. I hope her journey resonates with you and reminds you of the strength it takes to follow your dreams. And for anyone who has ever felt torn between the weight of responsibility and the pull of passion, this story is for you.

— Robert Stanek

1966

1

Lena sat cross-legged on her bed. The room around her was more than just a place to sleep—it was her sanctuary, a world apart from the narrow, constricting life she lived outside. The faint hum of the TV from downstairs blended with the muffled laughter of her parents, her father's low chuckle mixing with the canned laughter from *The Ed Sullivan Show*. The familiar sounds of their routine felt distant, like echoes from a life she no longer fully belonged to.

Her bedroom, however, was a world she had built for herself—a reflection of her growing, shifting identity. The worn wooden floors creaked beneath her as she shifted on her quilted bedspread, a patchwork of paisley and floral patterns that mirrored the earthy, bohemian style she had begun to embrace. Above her bed, posters of Bob Dylan and Joan Baez stared down at her, their eyes seeming to ask if she was ready to follow in their footsteps.

The dim light of her desk lamp cast shadows on the walls, where her handwritten lyrics hung on tattered pieces of paper. Her acoustic guitar waited patiently, a constant companion through the quiet struggles of her small-town life. Lena reached for it instinctively, her fingers grazing the smooth wooden body as she sat on the edge of her bed.

Her songbook lay open on her lap, the pages filled with half-formed ideas, scribbled lyrics, and notes that captured her thoughts, fears, and dreams. She glanced at the latest verse she had been working on:

The rain falls heavy, the skies turn gray
But I keep singing through the day...
The wind may howl, the storm may rage
But I've learned to dance on life's stage...

The words stared back at her, half-formed but already full of the emotion she was struggling to articulate. "Songbird in the Rain"—it was the beginning of something important. It wasn't just a song; it was a reflection of everything she was feeling. The weight of expectation from her family, her small town, and even from Tommy, who seemed so certain of the future they were supposed to have together. But Lena wasn't certain of anything anymore, except that she needed to keep singing, to keep writing, even if no one understood.

Outside, the rain tapped gently against the windowpane, a soft but persistent rhythm that matched the one in her heart. She had always loved the rain. To her, it wasn't just a backdrop to a gloomy day—it was cleansing, a reminder that even in the darkest moments, something beautiful could emerge. The rain seemed to echo her thoughts, offering comfort in its steady, soothing beat.

As Lena stared at the page, her thoughts drifted back to the conversation she had had with Tommy earlier that week. He had been so certain, so hopeful, when he asked her to wait for him. To build a life together when he returned from Vietnam. But Lena couldn't shake the feeling that waiting meant more than just passing time—it meant standing still, and she wasn't sure she could afford to do that anymore.

The words of their conversation replayed in her mind:

"I need you to wait for me, Lena. I need to know that when I come back, you'll be here."

"But Tommy, what if I'm not? What if I find something... out there?"

He hadn't understood, of course. How could he? Tommy loved her, and he loved the life they had grown up knowing. But Lena felt something pulling her away, something she couldn't explain, not even to herself. She didn't want to hurt him, but she also didn't want to live a life confined by other people's expectations—by her parents, her friends, even Tommy.

Lena ran her fingers along the guitar strings, the sound of the rain outside becoming a part of the melody forming in her mind. She closed her eyes and let her fingers find the familiar chords. It wasn't perfect yet, but the beginnings of "Songbird in the Rain" were there. Her voice was soft, barely above a whisper, as she hummed the first chorus under her breath:

I'm a songbird in the rain, I won't be denied
With every drop, I'm learning to fly...
Though the sky may fall, I'll spread my wings
And through the storm, I'll still sing...

Her fingers faltered for a moment, but then she picked up the rhythm again, determined to push through the uncertainty. The song was about resilience, about finding her voice in the midst of chaos and doubt. And she needed it more than ever. The song was her way of confronting the storms that threatened to drown her—the expectations of her parents, the pressure to conform to small-town life, and the weight of her relationship with Tommy.

As she sang softly to herself, she felt a sense of release. The rain outside was no longer just rain—it was her own storm, and she was the songbird refusing to be silenced by it.

From the living room, she could hear her parents talking, their voices low but steady. They were comfortable, settled, content. Her father's deep voice drifted through the walls as he commented on the TV show, and Lena wondered if he ever thought about what his life could have been, if he had dreams that went beyond the factory and the quiet routine of small-town life. Maybe he did once, before the world told him who he was supposed to be.

But Lena wasn't like them. She couldn't be. Every part of her rebelled against the idea of a life that was already mapped out for her—marriage, children, settling down in Janesville. There had to be something more. And her music was the only way she knew how to reach for it.

She turned back to her notebook and added another line to the verse:

The sky is heavy, clouds are thick,
I feel the weight of every drop.
Raindrops tracing paths on glass,
Each one a whisper, a silent plea.

The words felt right. The rain continued to fall, soft but steady, and Lena let the sound of it guide her as she strummed her guitar, lost in the melody of a song that was still taking shape. She knew she wasn't finished yet—there was so much more to say, so much more to feel. But for tonight, it was enough to know that her voice was still there, still fighting to be heard.

Lena placed the guitar back on its stand and stretched her legs out on the bed, pulling her songbook closer to her chest. Outside, the rain was slowing, but its presence lingered like a promise. She closed her eyes, imagining herself standing on a stage, her voice clear and strong, singing to an audience that understood. Someday, she told herself. Someday.

As the house around her fell into its familiar, comforting rhythm, Lena remained in her sanctuary, where her voice, her dreams, and her music could still take flight.

2

The sun barely peeked over the horizon as the dim light of dawn filtered through the kitchen window, casting long shadows over the linoleum floor. The soft clatter of dishes and the faint smell of coffee brewing filled the small kitchen. Lena sat at the table, her notebook from last night now closed and resting beside her. Her mother moved around the kitchen with practiced ease, frying eggs in a cast iron skillet while the percolator burbled quietly on the stove.

It was Friday morning, but it felt like every other morning in the Carter household—routine, predictable. Her father's heavy work boots thudded across the floor as he walked in from the hallway, straightening his faded denim jacket over his shoulders. His hair, still dark but graying at the temples, was slicked back with Brylcreem, and a thin layer of stubble clung to his jawline, catching the light.

"Morning, kiddo," her dad, Robert, muttered as he settled into his usual spot at the head of the table. His voice was low, gravelly, the kind that came from years of working long shifts in the factory. His presence in the room was solid and steady, much like everything about him. "How's school goin'?"

Lena shrugged, toying with the edges of the toast on her plate. "Same as always," she said softly, not meeting his eyes. The truth was, school was the least of her worries. Between her songs, her confusion about Tommy, and the constant pull to escape Janesville, the monotony of classes felt distant, almost irrelevant.

Her mother, Evelyn, bustled over with a plate of scrambled eggs and sausage, setting it down on the table with a practiced motion. She wore a soft floral apron over her house dress, her hair carefully curled at the ends, the way she wore it every day. There was a calm efficiency in everything she did, from wiping the counters to refilling Robert's coffee cup without him needing to ask. It was as if every movement had been rehearsed for years, and it probably had. The kitchen was Evelyn's domain, and she ruled it quietly, without question.

"Eat up, dear," her mother said gently, placing a small plate of scrambled eggs in front of Lena. "You'll need your energy."

Lena stared at the food for a moment, her appetite absent. Her thoughts were still stuck in last night's haze—her fingers brushing the strings of her guitar, the verses of "Songbird in the Rain" playing softly in her mind. The words felt raw and unfinished, much like her own life, but there was something in them that felt more real than anything else in this room.

Her father cleared his throat, breaking the silence. "Saw the news last night," he said, spooning eggs onto his toast. "More protests over the draft. Can't understand it. Boys should be proud to serve."

Lena's chest tightened. She could feel the unspoken conversation rising between them. The Vietnam War, the draft, Tommy—it was all a heavy cloud hanging over their family, especially since Tommy's deployment was drawing closer.

"I don't think it's about pride," Lena said cautiously, her eyes flicking up to meet her father's. She knew better than to push too hard, but the conversation in Mr. Benson's Civics class had stayed with her—about how the protests weren't just against the draft but the entire system of war, the loss of innocent lives. She had seen it in Joe's eyes, too, that restlessness, the same one that was growing inside her. "Some people just don't agree with the war."

Her father's fork clinked against the plate as he set it down a little too forcefully. "Agree or not, when your country calls, you answer. Doesn't matter what some kids in the streets think."

Lena bit the inside of her cheek and looked down at her food. There was no use arguing with him—her father's views were as solid as the house they lived in, built on a foundation of duty, loyalty, and hard work. His time in the service had shaped him, just as much as his years at General Motors had, and there was no room in his world for protest or rebellion.

Her mother, sensing the tension, quickly interjected. "Well, we're all proud of Tommy," she said with a nervous smile, glancing at Lena. "He's doing the right thing."

Lena's stomach twisted at the mention of Tommy. The same conversation echoed in her mind: *"Wait for me, Lena,"* he had said. *"We'll build something when I get back."* But waiting felt like a prison sentence, locking her into a future that didn't belong to her anymore. She had her own dreams, her own path to follow—and it wasn't in Janesville.

She pushed her plate away, suddenly unable to eat. Her father's gruff voice carried over the table again. "Speaking of Tommy, when's the last time you saw him?"

"Last week," Lena mumbled, her fingers tracing patterns on the table's worn surface. She could feel her parents watching her, waiting for her to say something more. They were always waiting, it seemed—for her to settle down, for her to fit into the mold they had carved out for her, for her to be like every other girl in town. But Lena couldn't do it. She wouldn't.

She thought of the song she had been writing, of the line that had echoed in her head all morning:

The world is loud with all its demands
Telling me I can't, but here I stand...
With my heart wide open, I face the pain
Like a songbird singing in the rain...

It was hard to feel like she was standing, though. Every morning felt like the same battle, and every conversation seemed to be a reminder of the life her parents expected her to embrace.

"Tommy's a good boy," her father said, as if trying to steer the conversation back to something more comfortable. "He's doing what he's supposed to, and when he gets back, you two can settle down. Start a family."

Lena stiffened. The weight of those words fell on her like a stone. Settle down. Start a family. The picture her father painted was a familiar one—one she had seen a thousand times in Janesville. Women her age getting married, working at the local shops, raising children, living the same life their mothers had lived before them. And while there was nothing wrong with it for some, for Lena, it felt suffocating.

She took a slow breath and nodded, though she said nothing. The idea of explaining her dreams—the music, the yearning for something beyond this small town—seemed impossible in this moment. Her father wouldn't understand. Not now, maybe not ever.

Her mother placed a hand on her shoulder, a gentle, fleeting touch. "You're quiet this morning, Lena. Is everything alright?"

Lena offered a small, tight smile. "Yeah. I'm fine." The words felt hollow, but they were all she could manage. The truth was too big to say out loud, too tangled in the chords of her songs, in the verses she scribbled late at night. How could she explain to them that what she wanted was out there—beyond the roads of Janesville, beyond the life they had planned for her?

The ticking of the kitchen clock filled the silence that followed. Her father stood, grabbing his lunchbox from the counter and giving her a brief nod. "Don't be late for school," he muttered, a familiar reminder as he headed out for another day at General Motors.

"I won't," Lena replied, her voice barely above a whisper.

As the front door closed behind him, the kitchen felt quieter, heavier. Lena looked at her mother, who was already clearing the dishes, humming softly to herself. There was peace in the mundane, Lena supposed. In routines. In expectations. But it wasn't enough for her.

She grabbed her notebook, slipping it into her school bag, and stood up from the table. "I'll see you later, Mom," she said, kissing her on the cheek.

Her mother smiled, her eyes soft with a quiet understanding that, even if she didn't fully grasp Lena's dreams, she sensed her daughter was wrestling with something big, something she couldn't yet name.

"Be careful out there," Evelyn said softly, turning back to the sink.

As Lena left the house, the fresh morning air hit her like a breath of possibility. She paused on the porch, closing her eyes for a moment as the faint melody of "Songbird in the Rain" hummed in the back of her mind. The world outside was loud with its demands, but here she was, standing tall, refusing to be washed away.

Lena Carter was learning to sing through the storm.

3

The air was crisp, with the scent of damp earth lingering from the rain that had fallen overnight. Lena kicked a pebble down the sidewalk as she made her way to school, her notebook tucked securely in her bag. The familiar streets of Janesville stretched out before her, neat rows of houses and picket fences, each one like the next. It was a town where everything felt static, where the weight of routine pressed down on her like a thick blanket.

Ahead, Lena saw Sarah stepping out of her house, her bright smile immediately cutting through the haze of Lena's thoughts. Sarah waved as she shut the front door behind her and started down the path toward the sidewalk. Her blonde hair was pulled into a high ponytail, and she wore a letterman jacket over her dress—Bill's jacket, of course. It was oversized on her, the sleeves falling past her wrists, but she wore it with pride.

"Hey!" Sarah called out, quickening her pace to catch up with Lena.

"Hey," Lena replied with a smile as Sarah fell into step beside her. The two had been best friends for as long as Lena could remember, growing up just a few blocks apart. Walking to school together had been their morning ritual since elementary school, a constant in a world that was beginning to feel anything but.

"So, ready for tonight?" Sarah asked, her voice full of excitement. "Sleepover at your place? I've got my mom to make those brownies you love."

Lena chuckled softly. "I can't say no to your mom's brownies. Of course, I'm ready. I could use a night to just... I don't know, forget about everything for a while."

Sarah tilted her head, giving Lena a look that was part concern, part curiosity. "Still feeling... weird about everything? Or is this about Tommy again?"

Lena sighed, glancing down at her feet as they walked. "A little bit of both, I guess. Everything's just... it's all moving so fast. I feel like I'm standing still, but everything around me is changing."

Sarah bumped her shoulder playfully. "Well, that's what the sleepover is for— no heavy thinking. Just brownies, gossip, and bad movies."

Lena laughed despite herself. "Okay, okay. I'll save the existential crises for later."

As they rounded the corner, the conversation naturally shifted to Sarah's favorite topic—Bill Thompson, her boyfriend and the school's star football player. Bill was well-liked by everyone—handsome, polite, and with a future laid out for him in Janesville, where he was expected to work for his family's business after graduation. In many ways, Bill represented everything that

Janesville stood for: stability, tradition, and the promise of a simple, predictable life.

"Bill's going to come over after practice tonight to say goodnight," Sarah said with a dreamy smile. "He's got a game tomorrow, so he won't be able to stay long. But, you know, I think it's kind of sweet."

Lena nodded, though her mind drifted for a moment. She'd always been happy for Sarah—Bill was a good guy, and he genuinely cared about her. They made sense together in a way that was as clear and solid as the sidewalk beneath their feet. And yet, the simplicity of it all—the idea of staying in Janesville, marrying your high school sweetheart, and living the same life as the generation before— felt like a weight around Lena's neck.

"That's nice," Lena said, her voice quieter now. "You two seem... perfect together."

Sarah grinned. "I think we are. I mean, Bill's not perfect, but he's everything I want. He makes me feel safe, you know? Like I know what my future's going to look like."

Lena nodded, though the pit in her stomach grew. Safe. That word lingered in the air between them, heavy with expectation. Was that what she was supposed to want too? She thought of Tommy, of the nights they had spent together talking about the future. Or rather, the future Tommy imagined for them— settling down after the war, building a family, living the same life everyone else did. The problem was, every time Lena tried to picture that future, it felt like a blurred image, something that didn't quite fit into focus.

"So... how are things with Tommy?" Sarah asked, breaking into Lena's thoughts.

Lena hesitated, unsure of how much to say. Tommy had always been a sensitive subject—he wasn't like Bill. He didn't belong to the high school world anymore, having graduated the year before. And now, with his deployment to Vietnam looming over them, everything felt uncertain. He had asked her to wait, to build a life with him after he came back, but Lena couldn't shake the feeling that waiting meant giving up on something—on herself, on her dreams, on the future she was struggling to envision.

"They're... okay," Lena said slowly. "I mean, it's hard, you know? With him getting ready to leave for Vietnam, everything feels so... up in the air."

Sarah's face softened, and she reached out to squeeze Lena's arm. "I can't imagine what that's like. I mean, I know it's tough for you. But Tommy loves you, right? That's got to count for something."

Lena forced a smile, grateful for Sarah's support even though it didn't feel like enough. "Yeah. It does."

But love wasn't the problem. It was everything else—the feeling that her life was on the verge of changing in ways she couldn't control. That her music was pulling her toward something bigger than Janesville, something bigger than the life Tommy had envisioned for them. But how could she explain that to Sarah, or to anyone, without sounding ungrateful or selfish?

The two of them passed the old red-brick church that stood at the corner of Main Street, the bells silent in the early morning light. Sarah kept talking about

Bill—about the upcoming game, about prom, about the future she was already planning. Lena listened, but her thoughts kept drifting to her own internal conflicts, the ones she didn't know how to talk about, even with her best friend.

"I wish I could be more like you," Lena said finally, her voice quiet but sincere.

Sarah raised an eyebrow, looking genuinely surprised. "Like me? Why would you want to be like me?"

"Because you're... sure of everything," Lena replied, glancing over at her friend. "You know what you want, where you're going, who you're going to be with. I don't know... any of that. Everything feels... messy."

Sarah's expression softened, and for a moment, the playful light in her eyes faded into something deeper, more understanding. "Lena, you've always been different. You've got... I don't know, this fire inside you. It's like, when you talk about your music or your dreams, I can feel it. I've always admired that about you."

Lena smiled faintly. "Yeah, but sometimes it just feels like a storm I can't control."

Sarah shrugged, a small smile creeping back onto her lips. "Storms pass. And when they do, you're still standing."

Lena blinked at her, struck by the unexpected wisdom in Sarah's words. It reminded her of the verse she had written just last night:

The rain falls heavy, the skies turn gray
But I keep singing through the day...

The wind may howl, the storm may rage
But I've learned to dance on life's stage...

Sarah had no idea, of course, but her words echoed the very heart of what Lena had been trying to express in her music—the resilience, the struggle, the way life could pull you in a million directions but still leave you standing. Maybe Sarah didn't fully understand the complexities of what Lena was feeling, but in her own simple way, she had hit on something true.

"Thanks," Lena said, her smile more genuine now. "That... actually helps."

As they reached the school, the building looming large ahead of them, Sarah spotted Bill standing with his friends near the entrance, tossing a football back and forth. Her face lit up, and she waved enthusiastically.

"I'll see you inside?" Sarah asked, already walking a little faster to meet Bill

"Yeah, see you then," Lena replied, watching as Sarah bounded ahead, her ponytail bouncing with each step.

Lena paused for a moment before heading inside, watching as Sarah and Bill greeted each other with easy smiles and laughter. It was a world Lena could have stepped into if she wanted—if she could let go of the questions gnawing at her, the restless pull of something beyond this town. But she couldn't.

With a sigh, Lena adjusted the strap of her bag and headed for the school doors. Another day in Janesville, another day of keeping her dreams tucked safely in the pages of her songbook. But for how much longer?

4

The bell rang, signaling the end of homeroom, and the hallway filled with the clatter of footsteps and chatter as students made their way to first period. Lena and Sarah walked together, navigating the crowded corridor toward the Home Economics room. The smell of freshly baked bread wafted through the air, a pleasant contrast to the usual scent of cleaning products that lingered in the school.

As they entered the Home Economics classroom, the familiar sight greeted them: rows of kitchen workstations, each equipped with an oven, countertop, and basic kitchen tools. Mrs. Helen Carver, a no-nonsense woman with a tight bun and a floral apron, was already at the front of the room, reviewing the lesson for the day. Her expression was as stern as always, but there was a warmth in her eyes that suggested she cared deeply for her students—even if she showed it through practical, tough-love lessons.

"Good morning, ladies," Mrs. Carver greeted them as they took their seats. "Today, we'll be learning how to make a basic pie crust. A skill every young woman should know—whether for a family dinner or a community bake sale.

Now, I expect you to follow the instructions carefully. A well-made pie crust is the foundation of any good dessert, and if you can't master this, you'll have trouble with more advanced recipes."

Lena exchanged a look with Sarah, who stifled a grin. Pie crusts weren't exactly at the top of Lena's list of priorities, but she had to admit there was something comforting about the routine of cooking. It grounded her, in a way that the rest of her life didn't.

Mrs. Carver handed out the recipe cards and began demonstrating the steps at the front of the class, rolling out the dough with steady hands. "First, you'll combine the flour, salt, and cold butter. Remember, the butter has to be cold— that's the secret to a flaky crust. Once the mixture resembles coarse crumbs, you'll slowly add cold water, just enough for the dough to come together."

Lena and Sarah moved to their assigned workstation, where the ingredients were already laid out. Lena grabbed the flour and began measuring it into the mixing bowl while Sarah reached for the butter.

"This seems easy enough," Sarah said, cutting the butter into cubes. "I think even Bill could handle this."

Lena chuckled softly as she sifted the flour into the bowl. "Yeah, but could he eat an entire pie by himself afterward? I bet he could."

"Oh, absolutely," Sarah laughed. "He's obsessed with cherry pie. His mom makes one every year for his birthday, and I swear he eats half of it before anyone else gets a slice."

The two girls laughed together as they worked, but Lena's thoughts drifted. This moment—baking in class with her best friend, talking about boyfriends, laughing over something as simple as pie—felt strangely disconnected from the rest of her life. It was like a scene from the life she was supposed to be living: learning homemaking skills to prepare for a future as a wife and mother. And yet, as comforting as it was, Lena couldn't shake the feeling that it wasn't her future.

As she added the cold butter to the flour and began working it into the mixture with her fingertips, her mind wandered back to the song she had been working on, "Songbird in the Rain." The lyrics from the night before echoed in her mind as she mixed the ingredients, the rhythm of her movements somehow syncing with the rhythm of the song.

I'm a songbird in the rain, I won't be denied
With every drop, I'm learning to fly...
Though the sky may fall, I'll spread my wings
And through the storm, I'll still sing...

She wondered if Mrs. Carver had ever felt the way she did—trapped between what was expected and what she really wanted. Had Mrs. Carver always dreamed of teaching girls to bake pies, or had she wanted something else once? Something bigger? The thought made Lena feel a little guilty, as though she were looking down on the life Mrs. Carver had built for herself, but it wasn't that. It was just... Lena knew deep down that she wanted more, needed more. The thought of settling down with Tommy after he returned from Vietnam felt like a pie crust that hadn't quite come together. It wasn't right—not yet, anyway.

"You're quiet today," Sarah observed, elbowing Lena gently. "What's going on in that brain of yours?"

Lena shrugged, not wanting to burden Sarah with her deeper anxieties. Sarah loved the predictability of life—Bill, high school football games, their small-town existence. She wouldn't understand why Lena couldn't seem to settle into it all as easily.

"Just thinking about tonight," Lena said, half-truthfully. "The sleepover."

Sarah smiled, rolling out the dough. "Yeah, it'll be fun. We'll pig out on my mom's brownies, watch some terrible movie, and maybe even do one of those hair masks we saw in Seventeen magazine. Nothing like a girls' night to fix everything."

Lena smiled, but it felt a little strained. Fix everything? She wasn't so sure anymore. Sleepovers and brownies wouldn't change the fact that she felt like she was standing on the edge of something much bigger than Janesville. Her music was pulling her toward a future that seemed far away, unreachable—but it was there, calling her all the same.

As the class continued their pie-making, Mrs. Carver walked around, peering over their shoulders and offering advice. She stopped at Lena and Sarah's workstation, watching them as they carefully rolled out their dough.

"Good, good," Mrs. Carver said, nodding approvingly. "Just be sure not to overwork the dough, girls. If you handle it too much, it'll get tough. Sometimes, it's best to let things be—don't force it."

Lena paused, her rolling pin still in hand. There was something in Mrs. Carver's words that struck her deeper than she expected. She glanced up at her teacher, wondering if she had meant more than just the pie crust.

Mrs. Carver noticed the pause and raised an eyebrow. "What's on your mind, Lena? You've been quieter than usual today."

Lena hesitated, not sure how to put her thoughts into words. "Just... thinking about the future, I guess."

Mrs. Carver gave her a knowing look, her expression softening just slightly. "Ah, yes. The future. Well, let me tell you something, dear. It's good to think ahead, but don't let it weigh you down too much. Life has a way of working out, even when it doesn't look like it will. Sometimes, you just have to trust that you'll figure it out as you go."

Lena blinked, surprised at the unexpected advice. For a moment, she wondered if Mrs. Carver could sense the storm brewing inside her—the tug-of-war between staying and leaving, between what was expected of her and what she wanted for herself.

"I guess so," Lena said softly, her hands resuming their work on the dough.

Mrs. Carver patted her on the shoulder. "You'll be fine, Lena. Just remember, don't overwork the dough. And don't overthink life. Both have a way of turning out better than you expect."

As Mrs. Carver moved on to the next group, Sarah gave Lena a sideways glance. "I think Mrs. Carver likes you," she teased, nudging her with her elbow.

Lena smiled, though her mind was still turning over Mrs. Carver's words. "Yeah, maybe."

Sarah stretched the dough over the pie tin, humming as she worked. "I'm telling you, Lena. You're too hard on yourself. Sometimes you just have to go with the flow. Look at me—if I worried about everything all the time, I'd go nuts."

Lena couldn't help but laugh softly. "You never worry about anything, Sarah."

Sarah grinned. "Exactly. You should try it sometime."

Lena shook her head, but there was affection in her smile. She admired Sarah's simplicity, her ability to find joy in the small things—Bill's football games, school dances, sleepovers. It was a kind of happiness that felt foreign to Lena, but she couldn't help but be drawn to it, even if she couldn't fully understand it.

But as the lesson came to an end and they slid their pie crusts into the oven, Lena knew that her own path would be different. It wasn't about ignoring the future or avoiding the hard questions. It was about facing them, about finding her voice in the storm of everything else.

The bell rang, signaling the end of class, and the girls wiped down their workstation before joining the rush of students heading to the next period. As they walked out of the room, the scent of baking pies lingered in the air—a reminder of the comfort of routine, of the life Lena was expected to embrace.

But as she stepped into the hallway, the melody of her song hummed in the back of her mind, reminding her that she was meant for something else—something beyond Janesville, beyond the pie crusts and sleepovers and simple futures laid out for girls like her.

And no matter how hard she tried to push it down, that song, like the rain, was always there—steady, persistent, waiting to be sung.

5

Lena made her way down the hall toward her Civics class. The energy in the school felt different here—more serious, more charged. As Lena stepped into the classroom, she noticed the usual seating arrangement: groups of students clustered together, some chatting about the latest school gossip, others already opening their textbooks. In the back of the room, slouched in his seat, was Joe Palmer, Lena's closest male friend and resident rebel of Janesville High.

Joe had always stood out, not just because of his unruly hair that constantly fell into his eyes or the way he dressed in faded jeans and beat-up leather jackets, but because of his attitude. There was a fire in him, a simmering discontent that set him apart from the others. While most of their classmates were concerned with prom or football games, Joe's mind was elsewhere—on protests, politics, and the bigger world outside of Janesville. He was the town misfit, and he wore that label with pride.

Lena caught his eye as she entered, and he gave her a small, knowing nod. She smiled faintly and slid into the seat beside him, placing her bag on the floor.

"You ready for another round of 'Benson vs. The System'?" Joe muttered under his breath as Mr. Richard Benson entered the room, holding his usual clipboard.

Lena chuckled softly. "Always."

Mr. Benson was in his early 40s, with graying hair at his temples and a habit of wearing tweed jackets with elbow patches—a look that made him appear both academic and approachable. He had a passion for civics that went beyond mere textbook lessons, and he wasn't afraid to talk about the tough issues: the Vietnam War, civil rights, and the changing political landscape. It wasn't the kind of class where you could sit quietly in the back and hope to go unnoticed. In Mr. Benson's classroom, everyone was expected to have an opinion, to engage with the world beyond their small town.

"Alright, class," Mr. Benson began, setting his clipboard on the desk and surveying the room with his sharp, thoughtful eyes. "Today, we're going to talk about something that's on a lot of people's minds—Vietnam. The draft, protests, and what it means for our democracy."

There was a quiet murmur in the room as he said the word Vietnam. The war was a topic that hung over everything, especially for students like Lena and Joe, whose friends and family were facing the reality of being drafted. Tommy was heading to Vietnam soon, and Lena could feel the tension of that fact settle into her chest whenever the war was brought up. But here, in Civics class, the conversation wasn't just about personal stakes—it was about what the war meant for the country, for the generation coming of age in the 1960s.

Mr. Benson moved to the blackboard, picking up a piece of chalk. "So let's start with a simple question. What is the role of the government in a time of war? Specifically, what is our role as citizens when it comes to supporting—or opposing—a war?"

He underlined the words support and oppose, then turned to face the class, his eyes scanning the room. "I want to hear from you. Should citizens always support their government during times of war, or is there a point where dissent is necessary? Where do we draw that line?"

There was a long pause. Mr. Benson often asked the kind of questions that made people uncomfortable. But in this room, uncomfortable was necessary—it was how you learned to think critically, to question.

Lena glanced at Joe, knowing this was his moment. Sure enough, Joe straightened in his seat, his rebellious energy barely contained. He raised his hand, though he didn't wait to be called on.

"I don't think the government always knows what's best for its people," Joe said, his voice steady but tinged with frustration. "And Vietnam? It's a perfect example of that. They're sending kids our age to die in a war that doesn't make sense, and for what? Some political agenda we had no say in? If anything, we should be fighting back, protesting—doing whatever it takes to stop it."

The room went silent for a moment. Joe's words hung in the air, bold and unfiltered. Some of the students shifted uncomfortably in their seats, while others nodded in agreement. It wasn't the first time Joe had voiced these opinions, but in a town like Janesville, where patriotism and support for the troops were ingrained, his views were still considered radical.

Mr. Benson, however, didn't flinch. He had always encouraged debate in his classroom, and he respected Joe's passion, even if it ruffled feathers.

"Alright, Joe," Mr. Benson said, pacing at the front of the room. "You've made your point. Dissent is one of the cornerstones of democracy. But what do you say to the argument that in times of war, especially a war like Vietnam, citizens have a responsibility to support their country, to support the soldiers who are risking their lives?"

Joe shrugged, leaning back in his chair. "I support the soldiers. I don't support the war. There's a difference."

Lena glanced at Joe, feeling the weight of his words. It was a sentiment she had heard from him before, but now, with Tommy getting ready to leave for Vietnam, it felt even more personal. She didn't know how to reconcile her love for Tommy with her growing unease about the war. She knew Joe was right in many ways, but it didn't make things any easier.

Lena raised her hand, hesitating for just a moment before speaking. "But what if... what if the soldiers themselves don't want to be there? I mean, a lot of them don't have a choice, right? They're drafted. Like Tommy." Her voice faltered slightly at the mention of Tommy's name, but she pushed on. "It's not like they're all fighting because they believe in the cause. Some of them just want to come home. So how do you support them without supporting the war?"

Mr. Benson looked at her thoughtfully, his expression softening. "That's a very good question, Lena. And it's a complicated one. The reality is, many of the men being drafted aren't given much of a choice. They're pulled into a conflict they may not understand or agree with, but they're expected to serve nonetheless."

He paused, addressing the class. "This is where things get tricky. As citizens, it's our job to hold our government accountable, to question decisions that don't align with our values. But at the same time, we can't forget that the men on the front lines are often victims of the system, too. Supporting them doesn't mean we have to blindly support the war."

Lena nodded, though the answer didn't make her feel much better. It was one thing to debate these ideas in class, to talk about supporting soldiers in the abstract. But when it came to Tommy—when it came to waiting for him, to knowing he could come back broken or not at all—there was no easy answer.

Joe leaned forward again, his frustration clear. "But what about the protests? People are marching in the streets for a reason. They're not just fighting for the soldiers—they're fighting to stop the whole machine. The government doesn't care about us, about our lives. We need to stand up before more kids are shipped off to die."

Lena glanced at him, feeling the fire in his words. Joe's passion was infectious, and sometimes, Lena found herself wishing she could share in his certainty. But she wasn't sure. About the war, about Tommy, about any of it. She admired Joe for being so bold, for speaking out when so many others stayed quiet, but for Lena, the world felt like one big question mark.

Mr. Benson nodded, acknowledging Joe's point. "You're right, Joe. Protests have played a huge role in shaping public opinion on the war. And they're part of what makes our democracy so unique—this ability to voice dissent, to demand change when we believe our government is wrong. But remember, change doesn't happen overnight. It takes time, effort, and a lot of voices."

He paused, glancing at the clock as the bell for the end of the period rang. "Alright, that's all for today. Over the weekend, I want you to think about what we've discussed—about the role of dissent in democracy, and about where you personally stand on the issues we've talked about. We'll pick this up on Monday."

The students began to gather their things, but Lena lingered for a moment, her thoughts still swirling. Joe shot her a look as they packed up.

"You good?" he asked.

Lena nodded, though she wasn't sure if she meant it. "Yeah. Just... thinking."

Joe smirked. "Well, don't think too long. Sometimes you just have to act."

Lena managed a small smile, but inside, the tension was still there—between her love for Tommy and her growing unease about the war, between her small-town life and the world Joe kept telling her about, the one outside of Janesville.

And somewhere, deep down, "Songbird in the Rain" was still playing in the back of her mind, each lyric pushing her closer to a decision she wasn't ready to make.

6

Lena made her way to fourth period English Literature, with Sarah chatting animatedly beside her about their sleepover plans and some local gossip. Sarah had a way of making even the most mundane details sound interesting, and while Lena nodded along, her mind was still lingering on the heavy conversation from Civics.

She spotted Joe just ahead, his usual swagger tempered by the lingering frustration from the earlier discussion on Vietnam. It wasn't easy for Joe to move on from things like that—he was a firebrand when it came to politics, and the war in particular seemed to light a fuse in him. But now they were moving into Mr. Joseph Hastings' domain, where the focus would shift from real-world conflicts to the world of literature.

As they stepped into the classroom, Lena felt a familiar sense of comfort. English Lit had always been a favorite of hers. Mr. Hastings was the kind of teacher who saw literature as more than just words on a page—he saw it as a way to understand life, society, and the human condition. He encouraged deep thinking, often asking students to draw connections between the texts they read and the world around them. For Lena, whose life felt like one long string of questions, this class was a rare opportunity to explore those questions in a safe space.

Mr. Hastings was already at the front of the room, leaning against his desk with his arms crossed, waiting for the class to settle in. He was in his mid-thirties, with messy brown hair that constantly fell into his eyes and a well-worn corduroy jacket that always smelled faintly of old books. His eyes were bright with enthusiasm, as though the subject matter of today's class was the most important thing anyone could ever discuss.

"Alright, class," he began, his voice warm and animated as he surveyed the students with a small smile. "Today, we're diving into a text that might feel a little familiar to some of you—but I promise, there's a lot more to it than meets the eye. We'll be continuing our discussion of F. Scott Fitzgerald's *The Great Gatsby*."

There was a collective rustling as students pulled out their copies of the book. Lena felt a little thrill run through her as she opened the worn paperback, the familiar pages filled with notes in the margins. The Great Gatsby had always resonated with her in ways that she couldn't quite explain. The story of longing, of chasing after something just out of reach—it felt like a reflection of her own life.

Mr. Hastings moved to the front of the room, pacing as he often did when he got excited about a topic. "So, we've been talking about Gatsby as a symbol of the American Dream—the idea that if you work hard enough, you can achieve anything. But I want to go deeper. What does Gatsby's dream—his obsession with Daisy—tell us about the nature of desire?"

He paused, looking around the room. "Is it about love? Or is it about something else?"

Lena's mind raced with thoughts. She had always seen Gatsby's pursuit of Daisy as something more than love—it was an ideal, something perfect in his mind that could never actually exist in the real world. It reminded her of the way she felt about her own dreams, about leaving Janesville, about her music. Was she chasing something that didn't exist? Was she trying to escape to a place that could never live up to the image in her head?

Joe, sitting next to her, raised his hand. He had his own take, as always.

"It's not love," Joe said bluntly. "Gatsby doesn't really love Daisy—he loves the idea of her, of what she represents. Daisy's just part of the dream. It's the same with the American Dream. People think they're chasing something real, but it's all a lie. It's just something to keep them distracted, something to chase so they don't realize how messed up everything really is."

Mr. Hastings nodded thoughtfully, leaning against his desk. "Interesting. So you're saying Gatsby's pursuit of Daisy—and by extension, the American Dream—is more about illusion than reality. That's definitely one way to look at it."

Joe smirked, pleased with himself, though his expression still carried a trace of the frustration from earlier. He always had a way of cutting through the romanticized view of things, digging right into the darker truths. Lena admired that about him, even though she wasn't sure she could always see the world in such stark terms.

Lena raised her hand, her voice more tentative but clear. "I think... I think Gatsby's chasing more than just an illusion. It's like... he knows on some level that Daisy isn't the person he's built her up to be, but he can't stop. It's not just about her—it's about needing to believe that there's something out there worth reaching for. Even if it's not real, the desire itself is real."

Mr. Hastings smiled at her, his eyes lighting up. "That's a very insightful point, Lena. Gatsby's desire for Daisy does seem to transcend the reality of who she is. It's like he needs her to represent something bigger—something that gives his life meaning. And in a way, isn't that what a lot of us do? We invest our hopes, our dreams, into something or someone, because the idea of it keeps us going, even if we know deep down it might not be what we think it is."

Lena felt a small surge of pride at his words, but also a pang of discomfort. What was she chasing? Was her dream of becoming a singer-songwriter just her version of Gatsby's green light? Was it something she had built up in her head, something perfect and unattainable?

Sarah, sitting next to her, raised her hand next. "But doesn't that mean Gatsby's setting himself up for disappointment? I mean, if he's chasing something that's not real, won't he always end up feeling empty in the end?"

Mr. Hastings smiled at Sarah, his tone gentle. "That's the tragedy of it, isn't it? Gatsby's dream is so deeply ingrained in him that even when it's clear Daisy isn't the person he's imagined, he can't let go. The pursuit becomes the thing that defines him, and in the end, it destroys him."

Lena exchanged a glance with Sarah, whose brow was furrowed in thought. For Sarah, who was happy and secure in her life with Bill, the idea of chasing something so uncertain probably seemed foreign. Sarah's world was stable, grounded in the reality of her relationship and her future in Janesville. But for Lena, the idea of giving up on her dream—of not chasing after something bigger than this town—felt like its own kind of tragedy.

Joe leaned forward again, unable to let the conversation drop. "But isn't that the whole problem with the American Dream? People get so obsessed with the chase that they lose sight of everything else. It's like they forget how messed up the system is because they're too busy trying to 'make it.' And what's 'making it,' anyway? A big house? Money? Who decided that's what life should be about?"

Mr. Hastings smiled, clearly enjoying the lively debate. "You're touching on one of the central critiques of the American Dream, Joe. The idea that success has been commodified—that it's been reduced to material wealth and status. And yet, for someone like Gatsby, that material success is inseparable from his personal dream. It's not just about the money—it's about proving to himself and to the world that he can transcend his past, that he can rewrite his story."

Lena thought about that—about rewriting your story. That was something she could understand. It was what she wanted, too. To break away from the small-town expectations of Janesville, to become someone different through her music. But like Gatsby, was she setting herself up for disappointment? Was she chasing something that could never live up to the image in her head?

As the class discussion continued, Lena found herself drifting into her own thoughts. Joe's cynicism and Sarah's practical optimism both swirled in her mind, contrasting with her own complicated feelings. Maybe there was truth in all of it—maybe she was like Gatsby, chasing an ideal that didn't exist. But she couldn't help but feel that the chase itself was worth something. The desire, the dream—it kept her moving forward. Even if she didn't know what she would find at the end of the road.

The lyrics of "Songbird in the Rain" surfaced in her mind again, the melody softly playing in the background of her thoughts. Then suddenly a new verse came to her:

They say the sky won't clear,
that it's foolish to keep waiting,
and yet I've learned to hold my ground,
even as it shifts beneath me.
I see the sun behind layers, deep,
like a memory or a promise,
and my heart keeps its rhythm,
steady, true to its path.

Was she chasing a dream that might ultimately disappoint her? Maybe. But she wasn't ready to stop. Like Gatsby, she needed to believe in something more, something bigger. Her dream wasn't just about music—it was about finding herself, about carving out a place in a world that didn't seem to have space for her yet.

The bell rang, pulling Lena out of her thoughts. Mr. Hastings clapped his hands together, signaling the end of the lesson. "Alright, everyone. For homework, I want you to think about how desire shapes our lives. Whether it's Gatsby's dream or your own, think about what keeps you going—and what you might be risking in the pursuit of that dream."

As students began packing up their things, Mr. Hastings approached Lena and Joe. "Good insights today, both of you. Keep thinking about it—it's not always about having the right answers, but about asking the right questions."

Joe gave him a casual nod, already shifting his bag over his shoulder. "I've got plenty more questions, Mr. Hastings. Don't worry."

Lena smiled at the exchange, her mind still buzzing with thoughts as she followed Joe and Sarah out of the classroom. She had plenty of questions too—questions about her future, about Tommy, about her music. But for now, all she could do was keep searching for the answers, one verse at a time.

As they walked down the hall, Lena's thoughts returned to her song. "Songbird in the Rain" wasn't just about resilience—it was about the chase, about daring to hope even when everything around you told you to give up. And no matter what, Lena wasn't ready to give up yet.

7

The cafeteria was buzzing with the usual noise—students laughing, trays clattering, and conversations blending together into a steady hum. Lena walked through the crowded room, tray in hand, scanning for Sarah, Joe, and Bill at their usual spot. She spotted them at a table near the windows, sunlight streaming in behind them, casting long shadows across the room.

Sarah was already there, her ponytail bobbing as she animatedly recounted something to Bill, who sat beside her, his broad frame hunched over his tray of food. Bill, the school's golden boy—handsome, confident, and easygoing— was the perfect counterpart to Sarah's bubbly energy. Across from them sat Joe, leaning back in his seat, poking at his food with a fork and wearing his usual look of detached cynicism.

Lena slid into the seat next to Joe, setting her tray down with a soft clatter.

"Hey, Lena," Sarah greeted with a bright smile, pushing her tray toward the center of the table. "You're just in time—Bill was telling us about the game tomorrow. It's gonna be a big one, right?"

Bill grinned, nodding as he took a bite of his sandwich. "Yeah, we're up against East High. It's gonna be tough, but we've got a good shot."

Lena smiled politely, though football had never been her thing. She admired Bill's dedication to the game—he was as passionate about football as she was about music—but it always felt like they were on opposite ends of some invisible spectrum. Bill's world was simple, straightforward: practice, play, win. Lena's world, on the other hand, felt tangled and uncertain, filled with questions she couldn't yet answer.

Joe scoffed, pushing his mashed potatoes around his tray. "Yeah, sure. Another night of watching guys slam into each other while the crowd cheers. Real intellectual stuff, Bill."

Sarah shot Joe a look. "Oh, come on, Joe. Not everything has to be about protests and politics. Some people actually enjoy football, you know."

Joe shrugged, a smirk playing on his lips. "Hey, I'm just saying. Seems like there's more important stuff going on in the world than a football game."

Bill, unfazed by Joe's usual banter, leaned back in his chair, crossing his arms. "Yeah, well, not all of us are trying to overthrow the government, Joe. Some of us just like a little competition."

Lena watched the exchange with quiet amusement. This was typical for their group—Sarah's optimism and Bill's easygoing attitude clashing with Joe's rebellious energy. They were an odd mix, but it worked, somehow. Sarah and Bill grounded things, while Joe kept them all thinking. Lena, caught somewhere in the middle, often found herself playing the role of observer, trying to balance the tension between wanting to break free like Joe and finding comfort in the familiar, like Sarah and Bill.

Lena picked at her salad, her mind still on the conversation from English class earlier. Gatsby's impossible dream, the endless chase—it had stirred something in her, something that made her think of her own life. She wondered if anyone else at the table felt that same pull toward something bigger, something beyond the narrow confines of Janesville.

"Hey, Lena," Sarah's voice broke through her thoughts. "You still on for tonight? I'm bringing all the good stuff—brownies, popcorn, the works."

Lena smiled. "Yeah, of course. I could use a distraction."

Bill, who had been focused on his food, chimed in. "Tommy coming by later tonight?"

At the mention of Tommy, Lena felt a familiar pang of anxiety. Everyone knew Tommy was shipping out soon, and it had become a quiet, looming presence in her life—something that everyone acknowledged but rarely talked about. Bill, however, had a way of bringing things up casually, like they were just another topic of conversation.

"Probably not," Lena said, her voice softer now. "He's busy getting everything ready."

There was an awkward pause at the table, the weight of Tommy's departure settling over them like a heavy cloud.

Joe, always quick to fill a silence, leaned forward. "You've gotta be thinking about leaving too, right, Lena? I mean, you've got bigger dreams than this place. You can't stay stuck here forever, waiting around for something to happen."

Sarah frowned slightly, giving Joe a gentle nudge. "Joe, don't start."

But Lena didn't mind. In fact, she appreciated Joe's honesty, even if it was blunt. He was the only one who ever really acknowledged her desire to leave Janesville, to go after her music. It wasn't something she could talk about with Sarah or Bill—they were content with their future here. For them, the idea of leaving was foreign. But Joe... he got it. He understood the need for more.

Lena shrugged, glancing down at her tray. "I've thought about it. New York, maybe. Or San Francisco. Somewhere where there's more going on."

Bill raised an eyebrow, looking genuinely curious. "But what about Tommy? He's gonna need you when he comes back. I mean, you guys have a good thing going, right?"

The question hung in the air, and Lena felt her stomach twist. Tommy did need her—or at least, he thought he did. But what about what she needed? She wasn't sure if she could put her life on hold, waiting for him to come back from a war that felt increasingly distant from her own dreams.

Joe, sensing her hesitation, jumped in again. "Tommy's not gonna want you sitting around waiting for him to come back to the same old life, Lena. You're better than that. Your music is better than that."

Lena bit her lip, unsure of what to say. Joe was right, in a way, but it wasn't that simple. It never was.

Sarah, ever the peacekeeper, broke the tension with a soft smile. "I don't think it has to be one or the other, though. You can still follow your dreams and, I don't know, figure things out with Tommy when the time comes. It's not like you have to make all the decisions right now."

Lena appreciated Sarah's optimism, but deep down, she knew it wasn't that easy. For Sarah, everything seemed to fall into place so naturally. Her future with Bill was already mapped out—a stable life in Janesville, marriage, kids, everything their parents wanted for them. But for Lena, the idea of staying here, of waiting for things to just happen, felt suffocating.

"Maybe," Lena said quietly, not wanting to dampen Sarah's mood. She knew Sarah meant well—she always did—but the more Lena thought about it, the more she realized that waiting around wasn't an option anymore.

Joe leaned back in his chair, crossing his arms. "Look, all I'm saying is, you can't let this town decide your future for you. There's too much out there— real change happening. People are waking up, protesting, writing songs that actually mean something. You've got the talent, Lena. You could be part of that. Or you could stay here and... I don't know, bake pies and watch football games."

Bill chuckled, shaking his head. "Not everything's a revolution, Joe. Some people just want a normal life."

"Yeah, well, 'normal' isn't all it's cracked up to be," Joe shot back, his voice taking on a sharper edge.

Lena glanced at Bill, who seemed unfazed by Joe's critique, and then at Sarah, who looked like she wanted to change the subject. But Lena couldn't help but think about what Joe was saying. There was a world beyond Janesville—a world of music, of protest, of everything she'd been writing about in her songs.

She had spent so much time scribbling lyrics in her notebook, dreaming of a life where her voice could actually be heard. And now, as Tommy's departure loomed closer, the question of what she wanted—what she really wanted—was pressing down on her harder than ever.

The bell rang, breaking through the tension at the table. Students began gathering their trays and shuffling toward their next classes. Bill gave Sarah a quick peck on the cheek before standing up, slinging his bag over his shoulder.

"See you after practice?" he asked her with a grin.

"Of course," Sarah replied, her smile soft and genuine.

Joe stood up next, his movements slower, more deliberate. He shot Lena a look, his expression serious. "Think about what I said, Lena. You've got something here," he said, tapping his finger against her tray for emphasis. "Don't waste it."

Lena nodded, though her thoughts were already swirling. She gathered her things and stood up, following Joe and Sarah toward the door, but her mind was elsewhere—back on her music, on Tommy, on the future that felt like it was slipping further out of her grasp with each passing day.

As they walked down the hall, Lena couldn't shake the feeling that something was about to change—whether she was ready for it or not.

8

The final bell rang, echoing through the hallways, and students flooded out of the classrooms in a rush to escape the day's routine. For Lena, the rest of the school day had passed in a blur—her mind still stuck on the conversation at lunch, thoughts of Tommy, and the unshakable pull of her music.

Beside her, Sarah chattered on, excitement bubbling about their sleepover that night. Lena smiled as they walked out of the front doors of the school, grateful for the distraction Sarah provided, though her thoughts were still tangled in the tension of her internal conflicts.

The cool afternoon breeze hit them as they stepped into the parking lot, the sun just beginning to dip behind the horizon, casting a warm, golden glow across the rows of parked cars. Lena and Sarah were heading toward the street when Sarah's voice suddenly perked up.

"Hey, look who it is!" she exclaimed, her voice filled with surprise.

Lena looked up, and there, leaning against the sleek frame of his 1957 Chevrolet Bel Air, was Tommy. The turquoise and ivory paint gleamed in the sunlight, the chrome accents catching the light and adding a bold contrast to the classic, polished exterior. The wide front grille, gleaming with chrome, and the tail fins that defined the era gave the car a presence that couldn't be ignored.

Tommy looked relaxed, leaning against the open driver's side door, one foot propped up against the car's frame. He wore a simple white T-shirt and jeans, his dark hair tousled and catching the breeze. His face broke into a smile as he spotted Lena and Sarah approaching.

"Well, well," Sarah teased, nudging Lena. "Looks like someone couldn't wait to see you."

Lena's heart fluttered at the sight of him. Tommy had a way of showing up just when she needed him the most, and though things had felt complicated lately, there was always something comforting about his presence. The sight of the car—his pride and joy—only added to the feeling. It was like a scene from a different time, from a world that felt both familiar and distant.

"Hey," Lena called out, her voice soft but warm as they approached.

Tommy pushed off the car and smiled, walking over to meet her. "Thought I'd give you a lift," he said, his tone casual, but there was a softness in his eyes as he looked at her. "Surprise."

Tommy opened the passenger side door of the car, motioning for Lena to get in. "What do you think?" he asked, his pride evident as he gestured to the car. "I got her cleaned up just for you."

Lena glanced at the car—the sleek, polished chrome, the iconic tail fins, and the two-tone paint job that gleamed in the sunlight. It was the kind of car that made people stop and stare, a relic of a different time, but still just as impressive. The Bel Air was more than just a car to Tommy—it was freedom, power, a way to escape. She could see it in the way he ran his hand over the doorframe, like it was something he was proud of, something that made him feel in control.

"It's beautiful," Lena said, meaning it. "You really take care of her."

Tommy grinned, clearly pleased with her approval. "She's smooth as ever. I've been working on her for weeks. Maybe we'll take a drive out to the lake later, huh?"

Sarah, who had been watching the exchange with a playful grin, chimed in. "We're not ditching our plans for you boys, though. We've got important sleepover business tonight, right, Lena?"

Lena laughed, grateful for Sarah's quick intervention. "Right. Brownies and bad movies. It's a tradition."

Tommy's face fell just slightly, though he quickly recovered. "Well, maybe we can steal you away for a bit before that? We're meeting Bill at the soda shop after his practice. You've got time for that, don't you?"

Lena hesitated for a moment, but Sarah was already nodding enthusiastically. "Come on, Lena. We've got time before the sleepover. Besides, I'm sure Bill would love to see me cheering him on after practice."

Lena smiled, feeling a bit of the weight lift from her chest. A quick trip to the soda shop wouldn't hurt. It was part of the routine, and though her mind was elsewhere, she knew it was important to Tommy—and to Sarah.

"Alright, you win," Lena said, slipping into the passenger seat of the Bel Air. The vinyl seats were cool against her legs, and the interior smelled faintly of the leather cleaner Tommy used to keep everything pristine. The dashboard gleamed with chrome accents, the large steering wheel and analog dials a reminder of the era the car came from.

Tommy got into the driver's seat, starting the engine with a low rumble that vibrated through the car. "Hop in, Sarah," he called out as he adjusted the rearview mirror.

Sarah slid into the back seat, her ponytail bouncing as she settled in. "I love this car," she said, leaning forward to look at Tommy. "Bill's always going on about how he wants a car like this one day."

Tommy grinned, shifting into gear and pulling out of the parking lot. "Well, tell Bill he's got good taste. Maybe I'll let him take it for a spin one of these days."

After the usual cruising around town, with the music playing loud and a few stops along the way, they pulled up to the local soda shop, a classic hangout spot just off Main Street, with a neon sign that blinked in pink and blue. The exterior was lined with glass windows, and inside, the booths were filled with other high school students sipping milkshakes and sharing baskets of fries. The air smelled like burgers and fries, a familiar scent that instantly made Lena feel like she was back in a different, simpler time.

Tommy parked the car, and they all got out, heading inside to claim their usual booth by the window. The vinyl seats squeaked as they slid in—Tommy and Lena on one side, Sarah on the other. They ordered milkshakes, fries, and burgers, the comfort food that always seemed to hit the right spot.

As they waited for their food, Tommy leaned in close to Lena, his hand brushing against hers on the table. "So, what's going on in that head of yours?" he asked, his voice soft, though there was a hint of concern. "Mr. Benson got you lost in Gatsby?"

Lena looked at him, her heart heavy with the weight of everything she couldn't say. She knew Tommy cared—deeply—but how could she explain the growing distance she felt, the way her music was pulling her in one direction while her life in Janesville, and with him, seemed to be pulling her in another?

"I'm just... thinking about stuff," she said, her voice trailing off as she glanced out the window. "About the future, I guess."

Tommy frowned slightly, his thumb brushing over the back of her hand. "We'll figure it out, Lena. You and me. I know things are crazy right now, with me leaving and all, but when I come back... we'll get back to where we were. I promise."

Lena swallowed, nodding, though the words felt heavy in her throat. She wanted to believe him—wanted to believe that when he came back from Vietnam, everything would fall back into place. But deep down, she knew that wasn't true. Too much was changing, and not just in the world around them. She was changing, too.

Just then, Bill walked in, still sweaty from football practice but grinning ear to ear as he spotted them. He made a beeline for their booth, sliding in beside Sarah and giving her a quick kiss on the cheek.

"Hey, everyone," he said, his voice full of that easy confidence he always carried. "Sorry I'm late. Practice ran long, and Coach was on us about the game tomorrow."

Sarah beamed at him, her hand resting on his arm. "You'll be great tomorrow. I'll be cheering for you, as always."

Bill grinned at her, then glanced across the table at Lena and Tommy. "So, what's the plan for tonight? You two coming to the game tomorrow, right?"

Lena smiled softly. "Of course. Wouldn't miss it."

The conversation shifted to football, milkshakes arriving at the table, but the mood was light. As they ate, Bill and Tommy started hinting about sneaking over to Lena's house later during the sleepover, their eyes gleaming with mischief.

"You know," Bill said, winking at Sarah, "we could always pop by later. Just to say goodnight."

Sarah rolled her eyes, though she was clearly amused. "No way. This is a girls-only night, Bill. You two can find something else to do."

Tommy grinned, his hand still resting on Lena's. "Come on, Lena. You can't deny us one last visit before we're stuck in football and war, right?"

Lena laughed, the tension lifting a little. "You boys can sneak by all you want. We're still having our sleepover, no interruptions allowed."

As the sun began to set outside the soda shop, the group laughed and talked over their burgers and fries. For a moment, everything felt easy—like it used to be before the weight of the world started pressing in. Lena let herself enjoy the moment, even as her thoughts kept drifting.

The world outside was changing, fast. But here, in the soda shop, surrounded by her friends, it felt like time had stopped—if only for a little while.

9

The 1957 Chevrolet Bel Air purred softly as Tommy pulled up in front of Sarah's house, the engine idling for a moment before coming to a smooth stop. The late afternoon sun had dipped behind the trees, casting long shadows across the quiet suburban street. The day was winding down, but there was a comfortable warmth in the air, a lingering reminder of summer not yet ready to give way to the autumn already unfolding.

Sarah leaned forward from the back seat, already unbuckling her seatbelt and reaching for the door handle. "I'll be quick. Just gotta grab the brownies and a few things for tonight," she said, giving Lena a bright smile. She slid out of the car, her movements quick and easy, but before she could take a step toward the house, Bill was already out of the car too, grinning as he caught up to her.

"I'll help you carry them," Bill offered, his voice warm, though there was a teasing lilt to it. "Can't have you breaking a nail."

Sarah rolled her eyes, but the smile on her face was unmistakable. "Oh please, as if I can't manage on my own."

The two of them shared a playful glance before heading up the path to Sarah's front door. Lena watched them go, her gaze lingering for a moment. Sarah and Bill made it all look so easy—the way they fit together, how natural it seemed for them to plan their lives around each other. Lena admired it, even as a part of her felt a quiet pang of something she couldn't quite name.

With Sarah and Bill momentarily out of sight, the car grew quieter, the hum of the engine now gone. Lena turned slightly in her seat, feeling the weight of Tommy's presence beside her. His hand was resting on the steering wheel, his fingers tapping absentmindedly against the leather, but his gaze was focused solely on her.

Tommy shifted, turning toward her more fully, his hand leaving the wheel to gently brush a strand of hair away from her face. "I missed you," he said softly, his voice low in the calm of the car. There was no accusation in his tone, just a simple, honest confession.

Lena smiled faintly, her chest tightening at his words. "I missed you too," she replied, her voice trembling slightly but sincere.

Tommy nodded, his thumb brushing lightly against her jawline before his hand dropped to take hers. "I know things have been tough lately," he said, his voice steady. "But we're going to get through this, Lena. You and me. No matter what."

Lena squeezed his hand, wanting to believe him, wanting to let herself feel comforted by his words. Tommy was always so sure of things—so sure of them, of their future, even when everything else around them felt uncertain. But as much as she loved him, there was still that nagging pull in her chest, the quiet hum of her music, of something bigger calling her away from this small town, away from this life.

"I don't want you to worry about me," Tommy added, his blue eyes searching hers. "When I'm over there… I need to know you'll be okay."

Lena's heart clenched at the thought of Vietnam, the reality of his deployment looming closer with each passing day. She didn't want to think about it—didn't want to picture him in a faraway place, in danger. She had written songs about the uncertainty of life, but none of them had prepared her for what it would be like to watch the person she loved leave for war.

"I'll be okay," Lena promised, her voice softer than she intended. "I'll be here… waiting."

Tommy gave her hand another squeeze, his smile returning, though there was something in his eyes—something Lena hadn't seen before. A quiet fear, maybe, hidden behind his usual bravado. "I'll be back before you know it. And when I am, we'll get out of here. Do all the things we've talked about. The road trips, the house by the lake…"

Lena nodded, though her chest felt tight. "Yeah," she whispered. "The house by the lake."

The front door to Sarah's house creaked open, and a moment later, Sarah emerged with Bill right behind her, balancing a plate of brownies in one hand and a small bag of snacks in the other. Bill followed closely, carrying a few more items Sarah had packed for the night.

"Alright," Sarah called as they approached the car. "Got everything we need for a perfect sleepover. Brownies, popcorn, and I even grabbed those face masks from the drugstore."

Lena let out a small laugh, grateful for Sarah's ability to keep things light. Tommy, sensing the moment had passed, gave Lena's hand one last gentle squeeze before pulling back, his usual smile returning as Bill opened the back door and stashed the snacks inside.

"Sleepover essentials," Bill said with a grin, giving Sarah a quick peck on the cheek before pulling back.

Sarah raised an eyebrow at him, smirking. "Don't even think about crashing our sleepover tonight, Bill."

Bill put his hands up in mock surrender. "Who, me? I wouldn't dare."

Tommy chuckled, leaning back in his seat. "We might sneak by for some brownies later, though. You won't even know we're there."

Sarah laughed, shaking her head. "You boys are the worst. But I'm telling you, no interruptions tonight."

Lena smiled softly, her gaze shifting between Tommy and Sarah, feeling a strange sense of calm wash over her. For now, everything felt okay—normal, even. But in the back of her mind, the questions lingered. What would things look like when Tommy left? When life wasn't so simple anymore?

Tommy made the short drive to Lena's. "We'll see you girls tomorrow, then," Tommy said, his eyes lingering on Lena for just a moment longer. "Have fun tonight."

Lena nodded, her voice catching in her throat. "You too."

Bill clapped Tommy on the shoulder as they both got back into the car. The engine roared to life, and the familiar purr of the Bel Air filled the air once again. With one last wave, Tommy backed out of the driveway, the car pulling away from the curb with that signature rumble. Lena and Sarah stood together, watching the boys drive off until the car turned the corner and disappeared down the street.

Sarah, always quick to break the silence, nudged Lena playfully. "You okay?"

Lena nodded, her smile small but genuine. "Yeah, I'm fine."

"You sure?" Sarah teased, linking her arm with Lena's as they started down the sidewalk, heading toward Lena's house. "Tommy looked like he didn't want to let you go."

Lena chuckled softly, though her heart still felt heavy. "Yeah. He's just... worried about the future, I guess."

Sarah's smile softened, and she gave Lena's arm a reassuring squeeze. "It'll be okay, you know. I mean, he loves you. That counts for something."

"I know," Lena said quietly. "I know he does."

But Lena's thoughts were miles away. She couldn't help but think about the future too. Her music was growing louder inside her, the lyrics of "Songbird in the Rain" taking shape in her mind with each step.

The rain can fall, the winds can blow
But I'm stronger now than you'll ever know
With every storm, I grow inside
No fear left, I've nothing to hide

"Hey," Sarah's voice cut through Lena's thoughts. "Don't think too much, okay? Tonight is about relaxing, not stressing."

Lena smiled, grateful for Sarah's easygoing presence. "Yeah, you're right."

As they approached Lena's house, the light in the windows glowed warmly, inviting them inside. Tonight would be about brownies, popcorn, and silly movies—just like they had planned.

10

As Lena and Sarah reached the front door of Lena's house, they could already hear the faint sound of music drifting through the windows. The familiar, warm melodies of Doo-Wop filled the air, a mix of The Platters and The Drifters, their harmonies sweet and nostalgic. It was a sound Lena had grown up with, something her mother always played when she was in one of her better moods—usually while preparing for an event, or, in this case, a special evening out.

Lena opened the door, and the music became clearer, the soft crackle of vinyl playing on the family's record player console blending with the scent of perfume and the familiar warmth of home. Evelyn Carter, Lena's mother, was standing in the small living room in front of a mirror, adjusting the pearl necklace around her neck. She was dressed in a simple but elegant light blue dress that cinched at the waist, with her hair pinned up in neat curls. She looked radiant, and there was a sense of excitement in the air—something Lena wasn't used to seeing in her mother.

"There you are!" Evelyn called out as she spotted the girls entering, her face lighting up with a smile. "You're just in time to help me finish getting ready."

Lena smiled at her mother, the tension from earlier in the day softening a little. Evelyn was often a source of pressure in Lena's life—her expectations for a more traditional path always clashing with Lena's dreams—but tonight, it was different. Tonight was about her parents, their 20th anniversary, and the excitement of something out of the ordinary.

"Wow, Mrs. Carter, you look beautiful!" Sarah chimed in, her eyes wide with admiration as she set the brownies and snacks on the kitchen counter.

"Thank you, dear," Evelyn replied, her voice full of warmth as she smoothed down her dress. "It's been a while since your father and I had a night out like this. Dinner and a movie—can you believe it?"

Lena stepped closer, smiling as she saw the genuine happiness on her mother's face. "You really do look great, Mom," she said, reaching for the pearl necklace to adjust the clasp.

Evelyn beamed, glancing in the mirror one last time. "It feels good to dress up. Reminds me of when we were young, going out to those fancy restaurants downtown. Your father, believe it or not, used to take me dancing." She let out a soft, nostalgic laugh, as if recalling a world far away from their quiet life in Janesville.

The girls worked together to help Evelyn with the finishing touches—Sarah carefully applying a bit of lipstick while Lena helped pin a loose curl back into place. The air was filled with the sound of Doo-Wop playing softly in the background, the music a sweet reminder of a simpler time, before life became all about routines and responsibilities.

"Can you believe it's been 20 years?" Evelyn asked, her eyes shining with affection as she thought about the evening ahead. "Twenty years of marriage... It feels like yesterday, and yet, so much has changed. But tonight... tonight will be special."

Sarah nodded, stepping back to admire her handiwork. "Twenty years is amazing! You two deserve a night out."

Evelyn smiled, the hint of pride in her eyes unmistakable. "We certainly do. And don't worry about dinner, girls. I've stocked up on your favorites— Swanson TV dinners. There's Turkey Dinner, Salisbury Steak, and Meatloaf, so take your pick. They're all in the freezer, just pop them in when you get hungry."

Lena and Sarah shared a look, both stifling a laugh. Swanson TV dinners were a staple in the Carter household—quick, easy, and nostalgic in their own way, but definitely not gourmet. Still, there was a certain comfort in the simplicity of it.

"You spoil us, Mrs. Carter," Sarah teased, grinning. "I think I'm going to go for the Salisbury Steak."

Lena rolled her eyes playfully. "I'll probably go with the Turkey Dinner. You know, for that classic touch."

Evelyn chuckled, clearly in high spirits. "Good choices, girls. And don't stay up too late watching those movies, alright?"

Just as they finished helping Evelyn, the familiar sound of the front door opening signaled Robert Carter's arrival. He stepped into the house, still dressed in his work clothes—faded jeans and a button-up shirt, his boots scuffed with the wear of a long day at the General Motors factory. There was a tiredness in his posture, but the moment he saw Evelyn, his expression softened, a rare warmth lighting his features.

"Well, would you look at that," Robert said, his voice rough but affectionate as he took in the sight of his wife. "You look just like the day I married you."

Evelyn blushed slightly, her smile widening. "Oh, stop it, Robert. You're going to make me cry before we even leave."

Robert chuckled, stepping closer to plant a soft kiss on her cheek. It was an unusual moment—Lena wasn't used to seeing her parents so... affectionate. They loved each other, of course, but their marriage had always seemed more practical, built on hard work and routine.

With a quick glance at the clock, Robert disappeared down the hall, calling over his shoulder, "I'll be ready in ten. You know us men, doesn't take long!"

True to his word, he returned moments later, dressed in pressed slacks and a button-up shirt, his usual no-nonsense demeanor softened by the occasion.

Seeing them like this, dressed up and looking forward to a night out, felt almost magical in its simplicity.

"You girls are alright here on your own?" Robert asked, turning his attention to Lena and Sarah, though there was no real concern in his voice. It was clear he trusted them.

"We'll be fine," Lena assured him, smiling. "Don't worry about us."

Robert nodded, his focus already shifting back to his wife. "Alright then. We'll be out late, but we'll be back before you know it."

Evelyn, now fully ready for her night out, turned to the girls, her eyes sparkling with excitement. "You two have fun tonight, okay? And don't forget to eat. There's more than enough food for you both."

"We'll be fine, Mom," Lena replied, her tone light as she gave her mother a quick hug. "Have a great time. You and Dad deserve it."

Sarah smiled warmly. "Yeah, have fun, Mrs. Carter. Enjoy your night out."

With one last glance in the mirror, Evelyn took Robert's arm, and the two of them headed toward the door. As they stepped outside, Lena and Sarah watched them go, the sight of her parents walking hand-in-hand down the front steps strangely comforting.

It wasn't often that Lena saw them like this—so full of life, so focused on each other. It made her wonder what their lives had been like before the factory, before the house, before Janesville had become their whole world. For a brief moment, she could almost see them as they might have been twenty years ago, young and in love, setting out to create a life together.

Once the door closed behind them, the house suddenly felt quieter, the Doo-Wop music still playing softly in the background but now just a gentle hum. Lena and Sarah exchanged a look, both of them smiling as the reality of their evening settled in.

"Your parents are so cute," Sarah said, breaking the silence. "I hope Bill and I are like that in twenty years."

Lena smiled, though her mind was already drifting back to Tommy. Would they still be together in twenty years? Would they even be the same people by the time he came back from Vietnam? She pushed the thought aside, focusing on the present.

"Alright," Lena said, clapping her hands together, "let's get this sleepover started. TV dinners first, then brownies."

Sarah laughed, clearly excited for the night ahead. "Sounds like a plan. I'll get the TV dinners going. You pick the first movie."

Lena smiled, feeling a sense of comfort in the familiarity of it all. Tonight was about brownies, silly movies, and the feeling of being young, with the whole world ahead of them.

11

Lena dashed up to her room. The familiar creak of the wooden floorboards under her feet as she moved through the hallway filled her with a sense of comfort, the house still buzzing with the music her mom had left playing softly in the background.

Her room was her sanctuary, her refuge, and she quickly headed straight for her small record collection, which was neatly stacked near her record player. She thumbed through her favorites—Bob Dylan, Joan Baez, and The Byrds—carefully selecting a few albums she thought would set the right tone for the night. After a brief pause, she also grabbed her Joni Mitchell record, something softer and a little more introspective for when the evening wound down.

Her acoustic guitar, leaning against the corner of her room, seemed to call out to her for a moment, and Lena's hand hovered over the strings, tempted to strum a few notes. But she resisted the urge. Tonight wasn't about playing music—it was about letting loose with Sarah, enjoying their sleepover before the weight of everything crashed back in.

Satisfied with her selection, Lena headed back downstairs to find Sarah already rummaging through the kitchen, preparing the Swanson TV dinners for the oven.

The girls settled into the living room, Lena placing her records by the family's large wooden record player console. The Doo-Wop tunes her mom had been playing earlier faded away as Lena carefully placed Joan Baez's album on the turntable. The soft strumming of Baez's guitar and her gentle, haunting voice filled the room, immediately setting a calm, introspective mood.

"Perfect," Lena said, smiling as she sank into the plush couch, tucking her feet underneath her. She reached for the TV Guide, which was sitting on the coffee table, its pages dog-eared and marked with small notes her mom had made throughout the week.

Sarah plopped down beside her, clutching a bowl of popcorn she'd popped while the TV dinners were cooking. "Alright, what's the movie lineup tonight? I vote for something romantic."

Lena flipped through the TV Guide, her eyes scanning the pages as she read out the options. "Okay, we've got Pillow Talk followed by Journey to the Center of the Earth on ABC. On CBS, it's East of Eden and then The Man Who Knew Too Much. And on NBC, there's North by Northwest followed by An Affair to Remember."

Sarah sighed dramatically, her eyes lighting up. "Oh my gosh, An Affair to Remember! That's the one where they meet at the Empire State Building, right? We have to watch that. It's, like, the most romantic movie ever!"

Lena chuckled, leaning back into the couch. "I don't know... North by Northwest is pretty great too. I love a good Hitchcock movie."

Sarah grinned, nudging Lena with her elbow. "You just want to watch Cary Grant run around in that suit. Admit it."

Lena laughed, shaking her head. "Maybe. But come on, East of Eden is on too. James Dean. It's a classic."

The girls debated back and forth for a while, tossing around ideas and laughing as they made their cases for each movie. Lena, despite her love for deeper, more introspective films, couldn't deny Sarah's enthusiasm for the romance of An Affair to Remember. There was something undeniably charming about Cary Grant and Deborah Kerr's fated love story, even if it did make Lena think of Tommy—and the uncertainty that clouded their future.

"Okay, okay," Lena conceded, tossing the TV Guide back onto the coffee table. "You win. We'll start with North by Northwest because it's a classic, but then we'll finish with An Affair to Remember. A little action, a little romance. Cary Grant running around in a suit. Cary Grant being the most charming man alive in a tuxedo on that ship."

Sarah clapped her hands together, clearly excited. "Deal. Plus, Bill would definitely approve of the action-packed stuff in North by Northwest. That crop-duster scene is crazy!"

At the mention of Bill, Sarah's smile softened, and she sank a little deeper into the couch, her mind clearly wandering. "Speaking of Bill..."

Lena raised an eyebrow, smirking. "Didn't we already tell them this is a girls-only night?"

"Yeah, but you know how boys are," Sarah replied, shrugging with a knowing grin. "He probably just misses me. We haven't really had much time together lately with him preparing for all those games."

Lena smiled, though she could feel a small pang of envy at how simple things seemed for Sarah and Bill. They had their future all mapped out—college, marriage, staying in Janesville. It was a certainty that Lena couldn't relate to.

As if on cue, Sarah shifted in her seat, her gaze softening as she turned toward Lena. "Things with Tommy look pretty good."

Lena hesitated, picking at the edge of a cushion, her mind still replaying the conversation they'd had earlier in his Bel Air. "I don't know," she admitted quietly. "I mean, things are good. He's... Tommy. He's always so sure of everything. But with him leaving soon, it's just... hard."

Sarah nodded, her face softening with understanding. "I get it. You've got a lot on your mind. He's going to war, Lena. That's a lot to deal with. I'd be freaking out."

Lena bit her lip, her fingers tracing invisible patterns on the armrest of the couch. "I am freaking out. But it's not just about him going to war. It's about... everything. My music, this town, our future. Sometimes I don't know if I can just... wait for him. You know?"

Sarah reached out, placing a gentle hand on Lena's arm. "Hey, it's okay to feel like that. You don't have to have all the answers right now. You're allowed to want more."

The oven timer beeped, and Sarah jumped up from the couch, excited to check on the TV dinners. She returned moments later, carrying trays with Swanson Turkey Dinner for Lena and Salisbury Steak for herself, complete with the signature mashed potatoes, gravy, and a small compartment of peas.

The girls settled in with their meals, the comforting taste of childhood in each bite. Lena smiled as the flavors brought her back to simpler times, back when life wasn't so complicated by the looming presence of war or the pull of unfulfilled dreams.

With Joan Baez's voice still softly playing in the background, the girls finally turned their attention to the TV, flipping the dial to NBC just as the opening credits for North by Northwest started rolling. Cary Grant's iconic figure filled the screen, and for the next couple of hours, Lena and Sarah let themselves get lost in the suspense and adventure, cheering and laughing at the action.

But as the evening wore on and North by Northwest gave way to An Affair to Remember, the tone of the night shifted. The romantic story unfolding on screen felt both comforting and bittersweet, a reminder of the love stories in their own lives—Bill and Sarah's, sweet and certain, and Lena and Tommy's, tangled and uncertain.

As Deborah Kerr's and Cary Grant's characters longed for each other on screen, Lena couldn't help but think of Tommy—of the promises he'd made, and the ones she wasn't sure she could keep.

12

The final notes of "An Affair to Remember" faded from the TV as the credits rolled, and Sarah stretched out on the couch, letting out a content sigh. The TV dinners were long finished, the trays now pushed aside on the coffee table next to an empty bowl of popcorn, and the living room was bathed in the soft glow of the lamp by the sofa.

Lena leaned back into the cushions, her legs curled up underneath her. The evening had been surprisingly calm, the warmth of Sarah's presence and the nostalgic comfort of the movies taking her mind off the usual weight of the future. Joan Baez's voice still lingered in the air, the soft strumming of the guitar from the record player adding a quiet melody to the night.

Suddenly, there was a faint knock at the window, almost drowned out by the music. Lena straightened, her brows knitting together in confusion.

"Did you hear that?" she asked, turning toward Sarah, who was already sitting up, her eyes wide with realization.

"Oh no," Sarah whispered, a grin spreading across her face.

Another knock, a little louder this time, came from the direction of the window near the side door. Lena and Sarah exchanged a look—equal parts amused and exasperated. They knew exactly who it was.

"Those idiots," Lena muttered, but she couldn't help the smile tugging at the corners of her mouth.

Lena got up from the couch and crossed the living room, pulling back the curtain to reveal Tommy and Bill standing outside, their faces lit with mischief. Bill was gesturing for her to open the door, while Tommy stood behind him, a smirk on his face as he shoved his hands into his jacket pockets.

Lena rolled her eyes and unlocked the door, letting it swing open with a playful scowl on her face. "What do you two think you're doing?"

Tommy stepped forward, grinning. "Just thought we'd check in, like we said we would. Can't let you girls have all the fun, now can we?"

Behind him, Bill chimed in, flashing Sarah a sheepish grin. "I swear, we'll be on our best behavior."

Sarah, leaning against the back of the couch with her arms crossed, raised an eyebrow. "You better be. We're in the middle of serious sleepover business."

Lena crossed her arms, pretending to be stern. "You're lucky my parents aren't home yet, or you two would be in trouble."

Tommy took a step closer, his grin softening as he looked at her. "I won't stay long anyway. Just wanted to see you."

Despite herself, Lena's mock frustration faded. "Well, you've seen me," she teased. "Now you better get going before my parents get home."

Bill and Sarah moved toward each other, their quiet laughter filling the room as they whispered back and forth, while Tommy reached out, gently taking Lena's hand.

"So, tomorrow…" Tommy began, his voice low. "You up for the lake? I figured we could spend the day out there, maybe go for a swim, have a picnic."

Lena smiled, the thought of a carefree day at the lake sounding like exactly what she needed. "Yeah, that sounds perfect. Sarah and I will be ready whenever you are."

Tommy's thumb brushed against her knuckles, his eyes soft as he held her gaze. "I'll pick you up around ten?"

"Ten it is," Lena agreed.

Bill, overhearing, turned toward Sarah, his grin wide. "Better pack a lot of snacks for tomorrow. You know how hungry I get after swimming."

Sarah laughed, swatting him playfully. "We'll bring enough food to keep you going, don't worry."

The four of them stood together for a time, their easy banter filling the air. Despite the weight of everything—Tommy's deployment, Lena's uncertainty—this was one of those rare moments when everything felt simple and right, when they could just be teenagers making plans for a day of fun without thinking too hard about the future.

But the moment couldn't last forever.

Lena glanced at the clock on the wall, suddenly reminded that her parents could be home at any moment. "Alright, you two better go. My parents could walk through that door any second, and I'm not about to explain why you're sneaking around at this hour."

Tommy's grin softened into something more sincere as he leaned in, brushing a soft kiss against her lips. "I'll see you tomorrow," he whispered, his breath warm against her skin. "Get some sleep."

"Yeah, yeah," Lena muttered, though her heart warmed at the gesture.

Bill gave Sarah a quick peck on the lips, his usual playful grin returning. "Don't let her boss you around too much tonight, Sarah."

Sarah laughed, shoving him lightly toward the door. "Oh, go on. I'll see you in the morning."

With one last glance and a wave, Tommy and Bill slipped back out into the cool night, heading for the Chevrolet Bel Air, their laughter fading as they disappeared down the street. Lena and Sarah stood in the doorway for a moment, watching them go, the warmth of the evening still lingering in the air.

Once the boys were gone, the house felt quiet again, the soft hum of Bob Dylan's voice playing faintly in the background. Sarah turned toward Lena, her grin wide. "They're so ridiculous, sneaking around like that."

Lena laughed, shaking her head as she closed the door. "They really are. But it was kind of sweet."

Sarah nodded in agreement, though her focus had already shifted back to their original plan for the night. "Okay, so... should we head to your room now? It's getting late, and I want to hear you work on that song you've been talking about."

Lena smiled, a hint of nervousness creeping in at the thought of sharing her unfinished song with Sarah. But at the same time, she trusted Sarah more than anyone. If anyone could help her make sense of her feelings, it was her.

"Alright," Lena agreed, leading the way upstairs.

Soon they were settled in Lena's room. The air thick with the smell of vanilla candles and the faint notes of Joni Mitchell's album playing in the background, Lena grabbed her acoustic guitar from the corner, her fingers brushing against the smooth wood as she tuned it.

Sarah sprawled out on the bed, propping herself up on one elbow as she watched Lena with anticipation. "You've been working on this for a while, right? I can't wait to hear it."

Lena nodded, feeling a knot of emotion tighten in her chest. This song— "Songbird in the Rain"—had been living inside her for days now, each lyric slowly piecing itself together in the quiet moments between her thoughts of Tommy, her music, and the future.

She strummed a few chords, the soft sound filling the room as she hummed the first few lines, her voice quiet at first but growing stronger with each note.

The rain falls heavy, the skies turn gray
But I keep singing through the day...

Sarah listened intently, her eyes soft as the melody carried through the air. The song was still unfinished, the lyrics only half-formed in Lena's mind, but the meaning behind them was clear. It was about resilience, about facing the storm that was coming and refusing to be silenced by it.

As Lena played, she felt the tension in her chest ease, the music offering her a kind of release that nothing else could.

When Lena finally stopped playing, her fingers still resting lightly on the strings, she looked up at Sarah, waiting for her reaction.

Sarah's eyes were shining, her expression full of warmth and admiration. "Lena, that was... beautiful. I mean, I don't know how you do it. You just capture everything in such a simple, honest way. It's perfect."

Lena smiled, feeling a sense of relief wash over her. "It's not finished yet," she admitted. "But it's close."

"Well, I can't wait to hear the rest of it," Sarah replied, her voice soft but full of encouragement. "You have a real gift, you know that?"

Lena shrugged, still unsure of how to accept compliments about her music. "I don't know… I just feel like I need to get it out, you know? Like if I don't, it'll just eat away at me."

Sarah nodded, understanding completely. "That's what makes it so special. You're not just writing songs—you're writing you."

Lena glanced down at the guitar in her lap, feeling the weight of Sarah's words settle in. Her music was more than just a hobby—it was her way of making sense of the world, of everything she was going through. And right now, that world felt more complicated than ever.

As the night deepened, Lena set her guitar aside, and the two girls settled in, the house quiet now except for the soft ticking of the clock on the wall.

The future still loomed large, with all its unanswered questions, but for now, Lena let herself drift off into the comfort of the moment—her music, her friendship with Sarah, and the promise of tomorrow's carefree day at the lake.

13

The soft morning light filtered through the curtains in Lena's room, casting a gentle glow across the floor. The air was still, the house quiet, except for the faint hum of a bird's song outside. Sarah was curled up next to her, still fast asleep, her soft breathing the only sound in the room.

But Lena was awake. She had woken with the full weight of her song pressing against her chest, the lyrics to "Songbird in the Rain" running through her mind as if they had been waiting for her all night. It was like the words had finally pieced themselves together while she slept, coming to life with a clarity she hadn't felt before.

Careful not to disturb Sarah, Lena slipped out of bed, her bare feet quiet against the cool wood floor. She reached for her music journal—the one that held all her unfinished songs, her lyrics, her thoughts—and settled at her small wooden desk by the window.

With the morning light streaming in, Lena flipped open the journal to a fresh page and quickly grabbed her pen. Her heart raced as she began to write, the words flowing from her as if they had been there all along, just waiting to be captured.

The pen glided across the paper, the bridge taking shape with each line:

The rain can fall, the winds can blow
But I'm stronger now than you'll ever know
With every storm, I grow inside
No fear left, I've nothing to hide
I'll stand my ground, I'll face the sky
With every song, I'm learning to fly
And when the morning light appears
I'll know I've conquered all my fears

Lena paused after finishing the final line, her heart pounding as she stared at the words. They were hers—her thoughts, her emotions, everything she had been feeling about Tommy, about her music, about the world beyond Janesville. And yet, they felt bigger than her, as if they were speaking to something universal.

The metaphor of the songbird in the rain wasn't just about resilience—it was about standing firm in the face of everything that told her to stay quiet, to fit into the mold she had been handed. It was about defying expectations, finding her voice, and holding on to her dreams even when the storm seemed too much to bear.

Lena set her pen down, her gaze drifting out the window as she let the moment wash over her. The sky outside was bright, not a cloud in sight, but the songbird perched on the telephone wire outside was still singing, filling the morning air with its cheerful melody.

A soft groan from behind her broke the quiet, and Lena turned to see Sarah stirring in her pile of blankets, her hand reaching up to rub the sleep from her eyes. She yawned, stretching out her arms before blinking up at Lena, her hair a tousled mess.

"Morning," Sarah mumbled, her voice thick with sleep. "You're up early."

Lena smiled softly, closing her journal. "Yeah, I couldn't sleep. I finally finished the bridge of my song."

Sarah sat up, her interest piqued immediately. "No way! Let me see."

Lena hesitated for a moment, then slid the journal across the desk toward Sarah. Sarah leaned forward, still wrapped in her blanket, and peered at the page. Her eyes moved across the lines, taking in the words carefully.

When she was done, she looked up at Lena, her face full of admiration. "Lena, this is… it's beautiful. You really have a way with words."

Lena blushed, the familiar wave of modesty washing over her. "Thanks. It just kind of came to me this morning. I couldn't get it out of my head."

Sarah smiled, standing up and crossing the room to Lena. "You're amazing, you know that? You're going to be famous one day, singing these songs to huge crowds."

Lena laughed softly, though the idea seemed far away and almost impossible. "I don't know about that. But I feel like I'm getting closer to something, you know?"

Sarah nodded, her expression serious for a moment. "I get it. You've got something real, Lena. Just keep chasing it."

A soft knock on the door interrupted their conversation, and Evelyn Carter's voice filtered in from the hallway. "Girls, breakfast is ready! Come down whenever you're hungry."

Lena smiled at Sarah. "Guess we should go eat before we head to the lake."

Sarah nodded, standing and stretching her arms again. "Yeah, I need fuel before Bill shows up and drags us into a day of swimming."

The two girls quickly freshened up and headed downstairs, the smell of bacon and eggs wafting through the air as they entered the kitchen. Evelyn was already setting plates down on the table, while Robert Carter sat at the head, reading the morning newspaper, his glasses perched on the bridge of his nose.

"Good morning, girls," Evelyn greeted them with a bright smile. "I made your favorite, Lena—bacon, scrambled eggs, and toast."

Lena sat down at the table, the warmth of the meal and the familiarity of the morning routine comforting her. "Thanks, Mom. It smells great."

Sarah sat across from her, grinning as she eyed the food. "Mrs. Carter, you always know how to make the best breakfasts. My mom's idea of breakfast is cereal."

Evelyn chuckled as she took a seat. "Well, I figured you girls need a good meal. You'll need your energy."

The kitchen was cozy, filled with the soft sound of forks clinking against plates and the occasional rustle of Robert's newspaper as he turned the page. The conversation was light, with Evelyn asking about their plans for the day.

"So, Tommy's picking you up?" Evelyn asked, glancing at Lena.

Lena nodded. "Yeah, we're heading out to the lake. Bill and Sarah are coming too. Just a day to relax before…" Her voice trailed off, the unspoken reality of Tommy's departure lingering in the air.

Robert, sensing the change in tone, folded his newspaper and set it aside. "Well, you two have a good time today. Be back before it gets too late, alright?"

"We will, Dad," Lena promised, though her thoughts were already drifting toward the day ahead—toward the lake, toward Tommy, and toward the future that seemed to loom closer with each passing moment.

After breakfast, Sarah stood and stretched, giving Lena a playful nudge. "Alright, I'm gonna head home and get ready for the lake."

Lena nodded, smiling. "Sounds good."

Sarah grabbed her things and waved goodbye to Evelyn and Robert as she headed for the door. "Thanks for breakfast, Mrs. Carter!"

Evelyn smiled warmly. "Anytime, dear. Have fun today."

As the door closed behind Sarah, Lena felt a quiet settle over the house once again. She stood in the kitchen for a moment, her mind still on the verse she had written earlier that morning. It was coming together, piece by piece. But there was still so much she hadn't figured out—about her music, about Tommy, about what would come next.

14

It was just before 10:00 AM when Lena heard the familiar low rumble of Tommy's Bel Air as it pulled into the driveway. The sun was already casting long shadows across the neat front lawn as Lena stood at the window, watching the car's sleek turquoise and ivory frame roll to a stop. A flutter of excitement and nervousness danced in her chest as she smoothed her hair, still feeling the weight of the verse she had written earlier that morning.

Downstairs, she heard the front door creak open, followed by her father's familiar, deep voice. Robert Carter was already outside, greeting Tommy before Lena had even made it down the stairs. She grabbed her bag—packed with the essentials for a day at the lake—and hurried out to the front porch, where her father and Tommy stood by the car.

Robert clapped Tommy on the shoulder, his grip firm and fatherly. "Good to see you, Tommy," he said, a hint of pride in his voice. "It's not every day we get someone like you around here. Doing your part for the country and all."

Tommy smiled modestly, his hand resting on the Bel Air's polished hood. "Thanks, Mr. Carter. Just doing what I have to, I guess."

Lena could see the quiet pride in her father's eyes as he nodded at Tommy. Robert, a man who believed in hard work and responsibility, clearly appreciated Tommy's sense of duty. "You've always been a good kid. Your father would be proud too."

The mention of Tommy's father—who had fought in World War II—seemed to soften something in Tommy's expression. He nodded, but there was a shadow of something unspoken behind his eyes. "Thanks. That means a lot."

Lena shifted on her feet, sensing the gravity of the moment. Her father's approval of Tommy was obvious, and while it made her heart swell to see them bond, it also deepened the weight of the choices that lay ahead—choices she wasn't sure Tommy fully understood yet.

Robert turned to Lena, his voice lightening as he smiled at his daughter. "You two be careful out there. Stay out of trouble."

Lena smiled back, grateful for his warmth. "We will, Dad."

With that, Robert stepped back, watching as Tommy opened the passenger door for Lena. She slid into the Bel Air, the familiar scent of vinyl and gasoline filling her senses as Tommy climbed in beside her, the engine rumbling to life as they pulled out of the driveway. "Figured I'd swing by a little early, thought we'd hit Main just the two of us before picking up Sarah and Bill."

For a few moments, the only sound between them was the low hum of the engine and the wind rushing past as they drove down the familiar streets of Janesville. Lena watched the town pass by outside the window, the quaint, tree-lined streets she had known her whole life, and felt a strange mix of comfort and restlessness.

Tommy, always attuned to her moods, glanced over at her, his hand resting casually on the steering wheel. "Good sleepover?" he asked, his voice soft but filled with something unspoken.

Lena smiled faintly, though her thoughts were far away. "Yeah. Just thinking."

Tommy raised an eyebrow, a knowing smile tugging at the corners of his mouth. "Thinking about what?"

Lena hesitated, her mind still wrapped around the song she was working on—the way the words had come so easily, and yet how they seemed to say everything she couldn't quite articulate out loud. "I guess... about the future. About everything that's coming."

Tommy nodded, his gaze shifting to the road ahead. "I think about it too," he admitted, his voice quieter now, more thoughtful than usual. "It's hard not to, with everything going on."

There was a pause, the silence between them heavy with unspoken thoughts. Lena knew that for Tommy, the future was more immediate, more urgent. Vietnam loomed large, casting a shadow over everything. But for Lena, it wasn't just about the war—it was about her music, her dreams, and the feeling that something bigger was waiting for her, something beyond Janesville and beyond the life they had planned.

"You ever wonder what things will be like when you come back?" Lena asked, her voice tentative. "If things will be... different?"

Tommy glanced at her, his expression soft but serious. "I don't know," he said honestly. "I try not to think too much about that part. I just keep telling myself that when I come back, everything will fall back into place. Like it's supposed to."

Lena bit her lip, nodding, though a part of her wasn't so sure. Could things really go back to the way they were? Would they still be the same people by the time the war was over? The world was changing so fast—her world was changing—and Lena didn't know if she could put everything on hold, waiting for things to fall back into place.

"I guess I just hope..." Lena trailed off, unsure of how to finish the sentence.

Tommy reached over, gently placing his hand on hers. "Whatever happens, Lena... we'll figure it out. You and me. We always do."

Lena smiled softly, but the knot in her chest didn't loosen. She wanted to believe him—to believe that love and loyalty were enough to weather whatever storms lay ahead. But as the road stretched out in front of them, leading to places she wasn't sure she was ready for, the future seemed more uncertain than ever.

As they neared Sarah's house, the conversation drifted back to lighter things— the lake, their plans for the day. By the time they pulled into Sarah's driveway, Lena felt a bit of the heaviness lift, though the questions still lingered in the back of her mind.

Sarah and Bill were already waiting on the front porch, bags slung over their shoulders and wide grins on their faces. Bill, as always, looked eager for adventure, while Sarah gave Lena a playful wave as they approached the car.

Bill hopped into the back seat first, slapping Tommy on the shoulder as he did. "Ready for a good day, man? I've got the football packed, and I'm not going easy on you today."

Tommy laughed, glancing back at him through the rearview mirror. "You wish. I'll take you down just like last time."

Sarah climbed in after Bill, settling in beside him as she shook her head, laughing at their boyish competitiveness. "You two are ridiculous. It's a day at the lake, not the championship."

Lena smiled, glad to see Sarah's easygoing energy filling the car. She turned in her seat to look at her best friend. "You ready for some sun?"

Sarah grinned. "Absolutely. Let's just hope Bill doesn't hog the picnic blanket like last time."

"Hey, I was tired!" Bill protested, earning a playful shove from Sarah.

15

The day was perfect for the lake—blue skies stretched endlessly overhead, and the sun was warm but not oppressive as Tommy's Bel Air rumbled down the highway. The cool breeze whipped through the open windows, tousling Lena's hair as she leaned back in the passenger seat, lost in thought. In the back seat, Sarah and Bill were already buzzing with excitement about the day ahead, talking over each other about swimming, the picnic, and, of course, football.

By the time they pulled into the dirt parking lot near the lake, the shimmering water stretched out before them, the trees casting dappled shadows along the shore. The air smelled of fresh grass and sunscreen, and the quiet lapping of water against the rocks added to the sense of peace.

As they stepped out of the car, Sarah immediately peeled off her summer dress, revealing a bold bikini beneath—a bright floral pattern in shades of pink and yellow, the high-waisted bottoms accentuating her slim figure. She smoothed out the fabric with a grin, her excitement evident.

"Last one in the water is a rotten egg!" Sarah teased, glancing at Lena with a playful glint in her eye.

Lena chuckled softly, slipping out of her own light cotton shorts and striped T-shirt to reveal a more modest one-piece swimsuit. It was a classic navy blue with a sleek, form-fitting design that still felt comfortable and allowed her to move easily. She'd never been one for the boldness of bikinis, preferring the simple elegance of her one-piece.

Tommy, ever the gentleman, leaned against the car, watching Lena with an easy smile. His eyes followed her movements, a soft admiration in his gaze. "You look great, you know that?" he murmured as she adjusted the straps of her swimsuit.

Lena blushed slightly, giving him a playful nudge. "You say that every time."

"Because it's true every time," he replied, his grin widening as he tossed his T-shirt into the back seat of the car, revealing his lean, athletic frame. The sunlight caught his tan skin, and for a moment, Lena allowed herself to forget everything else—the war, the uncertainty—just focusing on this moment.

They claimed a small spot near the shore, spreading out blankets and towels. Bill immediately started rummaging through the picnic basket that Evelyn Carter had packed for Lena and Sarah, pulling out sandwiches, sodas, and a big bag of potato chips.

"We're eating later, Bill!" Sarah laughed, tugging the bag of chips out of his hands. "We just got here!"

Bill shrugged, unbothered, as he grabbed a football from the back of the car. "Fine, but after I wipe the floor with Tommy in football, I'm gonna need all the snacks."

Tommy, not one to back down from a challenge, smirked as he stretched his arms. "You wish. You still haven't gotten over that last game, huh?"

At the mention of football, Sarah perked up. "Speaking of games, have you guys heard about that new AFL-NFL Championship they're setting up? My dad was talking about it the other day."

Lena raised an eyebrow, glancing at Sarah with mild interest. "Isn't that the thing they're calling the 'world championship' or something?"

Sarah nodded, clearly more excited than Lena about the topic. "Yeah, it's supposed to be this huge deal—combining the two leagues. My dad thinks it's going to change football forever."

Bill, always quick to jump into sports talk, grinned as he tossed the football lightly in the air. "It's about time they had something like that. Can you imagine? The best of the AFL against the best of the NFL? Finally, we get to see who's really better."

Tommy, standing nearby with his arms crossed, laughed. "I'm guessing you're betting on the NFL?"

Bill shrugged, catching the football in one hand. "Of course. The AFL's good, but the NFL's got the history. It's going to be a bloodbath."

Tommy raised an eyebrow, clearly enjoying the debate. "I don't know, man. The AFL's got some serious players. They might surprise you."

The conversation circled back to football intermittently as they continued setting up their spot by the lake. Sarah threw in her own thoughts from time to time, and even Lena—who wasn't as into football as the others—found herself listening more closely than she expected.

Once everything was set up, they wasted no time heading for the water. Sarah was the first to sprint toward the lake, laughing as she dove into the cool water with a splash. Bill followed close behind, already shouting about how he was going to beat everyone to the middle.

Lena was more cautious, walking slowly into the water, her toes sinking into the cool mud and rocks at the bottom. The cold water hit her legs, but she welcomed the shock, letting it wake her up fully. She glanced over at Tommy, who waded in beside her, his smile soft and easy as always.

"You waiting for the water to warm up?" he teased, splashing her lightly.

Lena laughed, splashing him back. "I'm coming, I'm coming. Don't get impatient."

They swam out a little ways, joining Bill and Sarah in the deeper part of the lake. The four of them splashed and played, diving under the water, racing back and forth, and enjoying the feeling of the sun on their faces.

As they rested on the shore later, drying off in the sun, Bill tossed the football in the air again, unable to let go of the AFL-NFL talk. "I'm telling you, this game is gonna be historic. You mark my words. Years from now, people will be talking about the first one."

After a while, the boys took off to throw the football back and forth on the beach, leaving Lena and Sarah lying on their towels in the sun. Sarah pulled out a pair of sunglasses and sighed contentedly, the warm rays soaking into her skin.

"I love days like this," Sarah murmured, half-asleep as she stretched out on the blanket. "No drama, no stress. Just fun."

Lena smiled, propping herself up on her elbows. "Yeah, it's nice. I needed this."

She glanced over at Tommy, who was tossing the football to Bill on the beach. His carefree laughter echoed across the sand, and for a moment, Lena's heart clenched. Days like this were precious—moments where everything felt normal. But they were fleeting, and Lena knew it.

She sighed, letting the thought drift away as she focused on the present.

As the sun began to dip lower in the sky, casting long shadows over the beach, the group finally gathered their things, tired but happy. They packed up the picnic, leaving behind nothing but footprints in the sand.

"Alright," Tommy said, tossing the last of the towels into the trunk of the Bel Air. "What's the plan for the rest of the weekend?"

Bill, still tossing the football lightly in his hands, grinned. "How about we hit up the diner tomorrow? Get some burgers before school starts again?"

Sarah smiled, slipping her arm through Bill's. "Sounds good to me."

Lena nodded in agreement, though her mind was already drifting back to her music journal at home.

"Yeah, that sounds fun," Lena said, climbing into the car beside Tommy.

As they drove away from the lake, the car filled with easy conversation, Tommy's laughter mixing with the hum of the engine, Lena let herself enjoy the simplicity of the day. Tomorrow could wait. Today was for them—just friends, laughter, and the promise of more days like this.

16

By the time the Chevrolet Bel Air rolled to a stop in front of Bill's house, the sun was casting a warm, golden glow over the quiet neighborhood. Bill was still buzzing with energy from the day, tossing the football lightly in his hands.

"Alright, you two," Bill said with a grin as he climbed out of the car. "Don't have too much fun without us."

Sarah laughed, rolling her eyes as she gathered her things. "We'll see you tomorrow."

Bill waved to Tommy and Lena, giving Tommy a friendly slap on the shoulder. "Good luck with her tonight," he teased, nodding toward Lena with a wink. "Don't let her talk you out of being at the open mic."

Lena flushed at the mention of the open mic night, her stomach doing a small flip. She had nearly forgotten about it during the day at the lake, but now that it was looming in front of her again, the nerves came rushing back.

As Sarah got out of the car, Lena leaned out the window, her voice soft but insistent. "Hey, don't forget. I need you at the café tomorrow night for the open mic."

Sarah smiled warmly, her eyes full of reassurance. "Of course, I'll be there. You'll be great, Lena."

Lena smiled, but she couldn't shake the nervous energy building inside her. "I'm not so sure about that," she admitted. "I think I'm too nervous for Bill and Tommy to be there too... I don't want to screw up in front of everyone."

Tommy, who had been quiet for most of the exchange, raised an eyebrow, glancing over at her. "You don't want me to come?" His voice was soft, not hurt, but curious.

Lena bit her lip, turning to face him. "It's not that I don't want you there. It's just... I don't know. I'm already so nervous, and I just—" She sighed, feeling the weight of her anxiety pressing down on her chest. "I don't want to mess up."

Sarah leaned into the window, resting her arms on the frame. "You're going to be amazing, Lena. And hey, if it makes you feel better, I'll sit right in the front row and make faces at you the whole time."

Lena couldn't help but laugh, grateful for Sarah's lightheartedness. "Alright, deal."

With Bill and Sarah safely dropped off, Tommy and Lena pulled away from the curb, the hum of the engine filling the quiet space between them. The golden light of the setting sun bathed the streets in a soft glow, and as they drove, Tommy's hand found its way to Lena's, resting lightly on her knee.

"You really don't want me there?" Tommy asked after a moment.

Lena sighed, glancing out the window. "It's not that, Tommy. I just... I don't know if I can handle the pressure of having everyone I know there, watching me."

Tommy nodded, his thumb tracing small circles on the back of her hand. "I get it. But, you know, I'd be proud of you no matter what. You're talented, Lena. You've got something real."

Lena smiled softly, her heart warming at his words. Tommy tried to be supportive of her music, even if he didn't fully understand it. But there was still a part of her that felt like he didn't quite see the bigger picture—didn't see how much she needed her music, how it was more than just a passion. It was her path to independence, her way out of the small-town life she felt so confined by.

As they reached a quiet spot on the edge of town, Tommy slowed the car and pulled over to the side of the road. They had done this countless times before—parking somewhere quiet to talk, to be alone. The world seemed to slow down in moments like these, with just the two of them and the fading light of the day.

Tommy turned off the engine, the silence between them now filled with the soft rustling of the wind through the trees. He looked over at her, his eyes full of the quiet love that had always been there, steady and unwavering.

"You know I believe in you, right?" Tommy said, his voice low and sincere. "I know how much you love your music. I'll be there for you... whatever happens."

Lena met his gaze, her chest tightening at the sincerity in his voice. "I know you believe in me, Tommy. I just..." She hesitated, struggling to find the right words. "I just don't know if you understand how important this is to me. My music—it's not just a hobby. It's my way out."

Tommy frowned slightly, confused. "Way out? Of what?"

Lena sighed, turning to look out the window, her eyes distant. "Out of this. Out of Janesville. Out of... everything." She paused, the words hanging in the air between them. "I want more than this, Tommy. I want to see the world. I want to make something of myself, not just... settle down."

There it was—the heart of the issue. Lena knew Tommy loved her, that he wanted a future with her, but his idea of the future was so different from hers. He saw marriage, a home, a family... and while she loved him, she wasn't ready to give up her dreams. The thought of settling down in Janesville, of becoming a wife and mother while her music took a back seat, filled her with dread.

Tommy was quiet for a long moment, his brow furrowed as he processed her words. "I didn't realize you felt that way," he admitted softly. "I mean... I always figured once we got married, you'd keep doing your music, but, you know, we'd have a life here."

Lena's heart ached at his innocence, his assumption that marriage wouldn't change anything. But she knew better. She had seen it happen to too many women—how their dreams were swallowed up by the responsibilities of home and family. She couldn't let that happen to her.

"I don't know if I can stay here, Tommy," she said quietly, her voice barely above a whisper. "I love you, but I can't give up on my music. It's the only thing that feels like mine."

Tommy looked at her for a long moment, his expression unreadable. He was trying to understand, she could see that—but there was a part of him that just couldn't grasp it. His world was simple, structured. He had always seen their future as something solid, something that didn't involve the kind of uncertainty Lena craved.

"I'm not asking you to give it up," he said finally, his voice careful. "But... I guess I thought you'd do it here, with me. We'd get married, and you'd still have your music, but we'd have a life too."

Lena closed her eyes for a moment, the weight of his words sinking in. She wanted that life too—she wanted Tommy, wanted the love they shared—but she wasn't sure if she could have both. Not the way he imagined it.

"I don't know if I can have both," she whispered. "Not the way you want it."

Tommy's jaw tightened slightly, but he didn't argue. He just sat there, staring out the windshield, the silence between them heavy and full of things they couldn't say.

After a long pause, he turned back to her, his voice soft but resigned. "I guess we'll figure it out when the time comes."

Lena nodded, though her heart felt heavy. She wasn't sure if they could figure it out—not without one of them giving up something important. But for now, they were here, together, and that would have to be enough.

In the quiet of the car, with the fading light casting shadows on their faces, Tommy leaned in, gently cupping Lena's face in his hands. His touch was soft, familiar, and Lena closed her eyes as his lips met hers in a slow, tender kiss.

For a moment, all the uncertainty melted away, replaced by the warmth of his love, the steadiness of his presence. In this moment, it was just the two of them, no future, no past—just the now.

When they finally pulled apart, Tommy rested his forehead against hers, his breath warm against her skin. "Whatever happens, I'll always be here for you, Lena."

Lena smiled softly, though her heart still ached with the weight of everything unsaid. "I know. Thank you."

They sat there for a while longer, the car parked on the side of the road, the world outside quiet and still. Eventually, they would have to go back—back to Janesville, back to the reality of their lives. But for now, they held on to each other, not ready to let go of the moment just yet.

17

The soft, pale light of the early Sunday morning filtered through Lena's curtains, casting gentle shadows on the floor. The house was still, with only the faint sound of birds chirping outside, and Lena slowly stirred awake, her mind already buzzing with fragments of lyrics. She lay there for a moment, letting the words roll over her, piecing themselves together like a melody waiting to be sung.

The third verse of "Songbird in the Rain" had been dancing just out of reach for days now, but as she blinked the sleep from her eyes, it clicked into place with startling clarity. She reached for her music journal on the nightstand, grabbing her pen and flipping to the page where she had scribbled the first verse.

With a deep breath, she began to write, her fingers moving quickly, as if the words were pouring out of her all at once:

The thunder rolls, but I won't hide
I've got a fire burning deep inside
The world may say I'm not enough

But I'm made of dreams, I'm built from love
The road is long, and the nights are cold
But I've found my voice, and it's strong and bold
Through every tear and every ache
I'm the songbird no storm can break.

She sat back after the final line, her heart racing with a quiet sense of satisfaction. The verse was raw, a reflection of her inner strength and determination. It wasn't just about resilience anymore—it was about power, about finding her voice in the midst of everything that was trying to keep her silent. Tommy, the war, her family's expectations... none of it could stop her if she stayed true to herself.

With a soft smile, Lena closed the journal and placed it carefully back on the nightstand. Today was going to be a long day, but at least she had these words to hold on to.

Downstairs, the familiar smell of bacon and fresh coffee greeted Lena as she padded into the kitchen, her feet cold against the linoleum floor. Evelyn Carter was at the stove, flipping pancakes while humming along to a song playing softly on the kitchen radio—something by Perry Como or Dean Martin, one of her usual favorites. Robert Carter sat at the table, his coffee cup in one hand and the Sunday newspaper spread out in front of him, reading the headlines about the Vietnam War and the latest political debates.

"Morning," Lena said softly, sliding into her usual seat at the table.

"Good morning, sweetheart," Evelyn replied with a warm smile, glancing over her shoulder as she flipped the last pancake onto the plate. "Did you sleep well?"

Lena nodded, though her mind was still on the song. "Yeah, pretty well. Thanks."

Her father, without looking up from the newspaper, took a sip of his coffee. "Big day today—don't forget we've got church, and your mother's social this afternoon."

Lena's stomach twisted slightly at the reminder. The church social was the last place she wanted to be. Her friends—Sarah, Tommy, and Bill—were planning to grab lunch at the diner after the service, and she had hoped to join them. The social meant an afternoon of small talk with the same churchgoers she'd known her whole life, endless discussions about housework, recipes, and future plans that didn't include music or independence. Just the thought of it made her feel trapped.

Evelyn turned back toward the table, setting down a plate of pancakes in front of Lena. "It'll be good for you," she said, her voice kind but firm. "Maybe Missy will be there too."

Lena hesitated, poking at her pancakes with her fork. "Actually, Mom, I was thinking... Sarah and I were planning to meet Tommy and Bill at the diner for lunch."

Her mother's smile didn't waver, but there was a slight shift in her eyes, a subtle tightening that Lena recognized all too well. "Lena, we've talked about this," Evelyn said gently. "The church social is important. It's part of your responsibility to the community, and it's good practice for when you're older— when you'll have your own home and family to take care of."

Lena swallowed the lump in her throat. Responsibility. Practice for the future. Her mother always framed it that way, as if Lena's life was already mapped out—marriage, a home in Janesville, raising children, and attending endless church functions. There was no room in that vision for music, for independence, for the life Lena truly wanted.

"I know, Mom," Lena said carefully. "But it's just lunch."

Evelyn sighed softly, sitting down across from Lena and pouring herself a cup of coffee. "Lena, you're seventeen now. You need to start thinking about the future. These socials aren't just for fun—they're part of building a life here. You'll be meeting people, making connections. The sewing circle is starting up again next week, and I think it would be good for you to join. It'll help you prepare for being a wife and mother one day."

Lena felt her heart sink at the mention of the sewing circle. Every week, it was the same—her mother's quiet insistence that Lena needed to learn the domestic skills that would make her a good wife. Cooking, cleaning, sewing, hosting... all the things Evelyn had devoted her life to, and that she expected Lena to follow in her footsteps.

But Lena wasn't her mother. Her future wasn't here in Janesville—it was out there, somewhere bigger, somewhere where she could be free to chase her dreams, to make music, to live a life that wasn't confined by these expectations.

"I'll think about it," Lena said quietly, though the words felt hollow. She wasn't going to join the sewing circle, but she didn't have the energy to argue.

Evelyn smiled, patting Lena's hand. "Good girl. Now, eat your breakfast before it gets cold."

The rest of breakfast passed in relative silence, with only the clinking of silverware and the occasional rustle of Robert's newspaper breaking the stillness. Lena's mind was elsewhere, her thoughts drifting back to her song and the upcoming open mic night. Tonight was her chance—her opportunity to step into a world that felt like it was hers, even if only for a few minutes on stage.

After breakfast, the family got ready for church. Lena slipped into a simple dress—nothing fancy, just something that her mother wouldn't fuss over—and grabbed her purse. As she stood in front of the mirror, fixing her hair, she thought about how different her life could be. Would she be able to make her own choices one day? Or would she always be caught between what her heart wanted and what was expected of her?

When she came downstairs, her mother was already in her Sunday best, adjusting her hat in front of the hall mirror. Evelyn turned to her with a smile. "You look lovely, Lena. Don't forget to remind Sarah about the potluck."

Lena forced a smile. "I won't."

As they headed out the door, Robert locked up behind them, his Bible tucked under his arm. "Come on, ladies, let's not be late."

18

The church bells tolled softly in the distance as Lena and her parents made their way through the small crowd gathered outside the stone church. The weathered brick walls stood tall, casting long shadows across the lawn, while families dressed in their Sunday best lingered, exchanging pleasantries. The familiar routine of Sunday mornings—the walk, the greetings, the small talk—felt heavier today, weighed down by the thoughts swirling in Lena's mind.

As they reached the entrance, Lena spotted Joe leaning casually against a low stone wall near the side of the church, his hands shoved deep into the pockets of his leather jacket. He stood out in stark contrast to the sea of pressed suits and floral dresses, his rebellious posture a quiet act of defiance against the expectations of the small town. Joe wasn't one for church, and Lena hadn't expected to see him here. But there he was, watching her with a knowing look.

Lena turned to her parents, offering them a quick smile. "I'll be right in. I need to talk to Joe for a minute."

Her mother, Evelyn, gave her a gentle nudge, her voice soft but firm. "Don't be long, Lena. The service is starting soon."

Lena nodded and made her way over to Joe, feeling the weight of her parents' eyes on her as she left. The chatter of the congregation faded behind her as she approached him, and when she was close enough, Joe gave her his usual crooked grin.

"You clean up well, Carter," he teased, his eyes flicking over her dress.

Lena smirked, leaning against the wall beside him. "Didn't expect to see you hanging around a church. What's up?"

Joe shrugged, glancing at the ground before meeting her eyes again. "I just wanted to catch you before you went inside. I know this whole family values, small-town stuff gets to you. Figured I'd make sure you're alright."

Lena sighed, grateful for Joe's perceptiveness. "It's fine, I guess. Just... feels like everyone's always pushing me toward a life I'm not sure I want."

Joe's eyes softened, and he leaned in closer, lowering his voice so only she could hear. "Lena, you don't have to follow the same path as everyone else. You've got your music. You've got dreams. Don't let them tell you otherwise."

Lena nodded, though her chest felt tight. "I know. It's just hard when it's my family, you know? They want what's best for me, but..."

"They want what they think is best for you," Joe finished, his tone sharp but understanding. "Not what you want."

Lena bit her lip, the truth of his words settling in. Before she could respond, the church bells rang again, louder this time, signaling the start of the service. She glanced back at the entrance, where her parents were waiting just inside the doorway.

"I should go," she said softly, though a part of her didn't want to.

Joe gave her a quick nod. "Yeah, don't let me keep you. Just... don't forget what we talked about."

"I won't," Lena promised, offering him a small, grateful smile before turning back toward the church.

As she walked away, Joe's words echoed in her mind—don't forget what we talked about. It was easy for him to say, standing on the outside of it all, detached from the expectations and the weight of family. But for Lena, the pressure was constant, pulling her in two different directions.

The air inside the church was cool and still as Lena slipped into the pew beside her parents. The familiar scent of old wood and incense lingered in the air, mixing with the faint murmur of voices as the congregation settled in for the service. Lena clasped her hands in her lap, staring at the altar but lost in her thoughts.

As the service began, Father Michaels stood before the congregation, his voice steady and warm as he welcomed them. His sermon was on family values—a common theme in their small Midwestern town, where traditions ran deep and change was slow to come.

"Today, I want to speak to you about the foundation of our community—the family," Father Michaels began, his hands resting on the wooden pulpit. "The family is the cornerstone of society. It is within the family that we learn love, respect, and responsibility. It is through the family that we grow in faith, and it is the family that binds us together in times of joy and hardship."

Lena listened, though her mind was only half-attuned to his words. She had heard this sermon—or versions of it—countless times before. Family as the foundation. Family as the bedrock of society. It was the message that had been drilled into her since childhood, and yet, each time she heard it, it felt more distant from her own life. She loved her family—of course she did—but the idea of building a life around only family, of staying in Janesville, settling into the same routine... it didn't feel like enough.

Father Michaels continued, his voice rising with conviction. "In these times, when the world seems uncertain, when our young men are being sent off to war, it is more important than ever to hold tight to the values that unite us. As we pray for the safety of those who serve, we must also remember the role of the family in supporting one another, in guiding our children, and in living a life that honors God's teachings."

Lena's stomach twisted at the mention of the war. Tommy, always in the back of her mind, felt closer now. She thought of him sitting next to her in the pew, how much he respected these values, how much he believed in the life they were expected to build together. But did he truly understand how much she wanted something different?

Father Michaels concluded with a call to action. "As we leave here today, let us recommit ourselves to our families, to our faith, and to the strength that comes from living a life of love, respect, and responsibility. Let us support our young men as they prepare for the future, and let us always remember that it is through God's grace that we find our way."

The final hymn began, and Lena stood with the rest of the congregation, though her heart wasn't in it. The words of the sermon clung to her like a weight—family, responsibility, duty—the very things that were pulling her away from her dreams. As the song filled the church, Lena found herself longing for the freedom to chase her music, to break away from the mold that had been cast for her.

The bright midday sun greeted them as they left the church, the warm air a welcome contrast to the cool stillness inside. Families mingled on the steps, exchanging pleasantries and making plans for the afternoon. Evelyn and Robert were already talking with friends, their voices filled with the easy familiarity of small-town life.

As Lena scanned the crowd, she spotted Bill and Sarah, standing a few feet away. They were both dressed in their Sunday best, Sarah's floral dress flowing in the breeze while Bill tugged at the stiff collar of his shirt, clearly uncomfortable.

Sarah caught Lena's eye and smiled, waving her over. "Hey, you!" she called. "What'd you think of the service?"

Lena shrugged, walking over to join them. "Same as always. Family values, duty, all that."

Bill rolled his eyes good-naturedly. "Gotta love it."

"Right," Sarah added with a playful smirk. "Because last week's sermon was any different. All about honoring your father and mother, right?"

Bill groaned. "Don't remind me."

Lena chuckled, though her mind was still elsewhere—on Joe, on Father Michaels' sermon, on the open mic night coming up. As the three of them stood together in the sun, talking about plans for the afternoon, she couldn't help but feel the familiar pull of expectation tugging at her. The life that waited for her here in Janesville felt so different from the one she wanted, and yet it seemed inescapable.

19

The sun had started to set, casting a soft orange glow through the thin curtains of Lena's bedroom. The day was slipping away faster than she'd realized, and with it, her time to finish the song she would perform at open mic night. The anticipation, the anxiety, the crushing weight of wanting to succeed—it all crowded around her like a storm brewing on the horizon. Her heart pounded in her chest, her fingers hovering uncertainly over the music journal that lay open on her bed.

Lena sat cross-legged on the floor, her acoustic guitar resting on her lap. The first three verses of "Songbird in the Rain" had come to her in bursts of inspiration, but now, with the pressure mounting, the rest felt elusive. She had been struggling with the final parts of the bridge and second chorus for what felt like hours, picking through the words, trying to make them fit together like the final pieces of a puzzle. But nothing seemed to work.

She stared down at the half-written lines, frustration tightening her throat. Then it hit her that verse 2 wasn't quite finished. She added:

So here I stand, amidst the storm,
Not broken, just weathered by time.
Every gust, every flash of lightning feels like a call,
A song rising from the depths of pain.

Lena sighed, running a hand through her hair. The words felt hollow, unfinished. She scribbled out the last line with a hasty stroke, starting again from the top. But no matter how many times she rewrote it, the song felt too big, too ambitious. Who am I kidding? she thought, her stomach twisting with doubt. I'm not ready for this.

The more she worked at it, the more impossible it seemed. The song had to be powerful, it had to mean something—but right now, it was just a jumble of words that didn't seem to say enough.

Lena bit her lip, her eyes welling with tears of frustration. She had signed up for this open mic night thinking it would be a chance to prove herself, to show everyone that her music mattered. But now, sitting in her room with half a song and no confidence, it felt like a terrible mistake. What if I make a fool of myself?

The thought gnawed at her, the fear sinking deep into her chest. Maybe Tommy was right. Maybe music was just a hobby, something she should do on the side while she focused on the real parts of life. Marriage, a family, a house. That was the life laid out for her—the one she was supposed to want.

But that life felt too small for the songbird inside her.

She picked up the guitar again, her fingers absentmindedly strumming a few soft chords. The melody came to her easily now, but the words... they were the struggle. She closed her eyes, trying to lose herself in the music, to let the melody guide her. Slowly, she began to piece together the final part of the bridge, finding a rhythm, a flow that matched the emotion she was desperate to convey:

Through the haze, I see the light,
A beacon guiding me forward.
No longer afraid of the rain,
I embrace the strength it brings.

The lines came out shaky at first, but with each repetition, they grew stronger, the rhythm taking shape under her fingers. It wasn't perfect, but it was something. It was hers.

But she wasn't done yet. There was still the final chorus and outro—the moment where the song needed to soar, where she needed to push past everything holding her back and let the music carry her.

Lena frowned, biting her lip as she thought. The final parts of the song had to be about growth, about overcoming fear and doubt. It had to show that no matter what the world threw at her, she wouldn't break. With a shaky breath, she began to scribble the lines into her journal:

I'm a songbird in the rain, chasing the light
With every note, I'm holding tight
I'll rise above, I'll find my way
Singing through the rain, come what may
As the rain begins to cease,
I spread my wings and take flight.
A songbird soaring through the calm,
Leaving behind the stormy night.

Her hand shook as she wrote the last line, a quiet sense of triumph filling her chest. She played through, her fingers stumbling over the chords at first, but the more she played, the more it felt right. It wasn't perfect, but it didn't have to be. It was enough for now.

But as soon as the final chord rang out in her room, the self-doubt crept back in. What if it's not enough? What if I freeze up on stage?

She buried her face in her hands, feeling the weight of the night ahead pressing down on her. Why did I sign up for this?

A soft knock on her bedroom door startled her from her thoughts. Lena looked up, her heart pounding. Before she could say anything, the door creaked open, and Sarah's familiar face peeked through.

"Hey, you ready for your big night?" Sarah asked with a grin, stepping into the room without waiting for an answer.

Lena let out a shaky laugh, wiping her eyes quickly before Sarah could notice. "I don't know about that. I'm kind of freaking out."

Sarah plopped down on the bed beside her, glancing at the open journal with curiosity. "You've got this, Lena. I know you're nervous, but seriously, your songs are amazing. You're amazing."

Lena sighed, running a hand over the strings of her guitar. "It doesn't feel amazing right now. It feels... terrifying. I keep thinking I'm going to get up there and forget all the words. Or my voice will crack. Or—"

"Stop," Sarah interrupted, putting a hand on Lena's arm. "You're going to do great. And even if you mess up, which you won't, it's not the end of the world. This is just the beginning for you. Trust me, everyone at the café is going to love your song."

Lena smiled faintly, though the nerves still buzzed in her chest. "You really think so?"

"I know so," Sarah said confidently. "And I'll be right there in the front row, cheering you on. You're not doing this alone."

Lena felt a small weight lift off her shoulders at Sarah's words. She wasn't alone. Even with all her fears, even with the uncertainty of what would happen tonight, she had her best friend by her side. And maybe that would be enough.

"Thanks, Sarah," Lena said softly, her voice filled with gratitude.

Sarah grinned and jumped up from the bed, grabbing Lena's hand and pulling her to her feet. "Come on, let's get you ready. You've got a song to sing, and the world needs to hear it."

As Lena stood there, looking at herself in the mirror, guitar in hand and lyrics in her heart, she knew Sarah was right. This was her chance—her moment to step into the spotlight and let her voice be heard.

The fear was still there, but underneath it was something stronger: hope. She was a songbird in the rain, and no storm could silence her.

20

The evening air was cool and crisp as Lena and Sarah stepped out of Lena's house, the sky fading into soft hues of purple and pink. Lena had her guitar slung over her shoulder, its familiar weight both comforting and nerve-wracking. Her hands felt clammy, and her heart was pounding in her chest, but she forced herself to keep moving, focusing on the steady rhythm of their footsteps as they headed toward the café.

"You ready for this?" Sarah asked, glancing sideways at Lena.

Lena nodded, though she didn't fully believe her own response. "Yeah. Just... nervous."

Sarah smiled warmly. "You've got this. Just think of it as another practice. Except with more people."

"More people who could watch me mess up," Lena muttered under her breath.

"Stop," Sarah teased, nudging her lightly. "You're going to kill it tonight."

Lena's heart skipped a beat when she saw Tommy's familiar Bel Air parked at the curb in front of her house. The car's sleek turquoise-and-ivory frame gleamed in the fading light, and then she saw Tommy leaning against the hood, arms crossed, waiting.

Lena exchanged a quick glance with Sarah, who raised an eyebrow but said nothing. The sight of Tommy filled Lena with a mixture of warmth and dread—part of her was glad to see him, but another part of her knew this wasn't going to be a smooth conversation.

As they approached the car, Tommy pushed off from the hood and straightened up, his usual easygoing smile tugging at the corners of his mouth, though his eyes seemed more serious than usual.

"Hey," he greeted them, his gaze lingering on Lena. "I was hoping I'd catch you before you left."

Lena shifted her guitar on her shoulder, glancing at Sarah before meeting Tommy's gaze. "Hey. Didn't see you at church today."

Tommy shoved his hands into his pockets, his smile faltering slightly. "I thought maybe we could hang out tonight. Just the two of us. I know you've got this... open mic thing, but I figured we could skip it and do something fun. Go for a drive or grab dinner."

Lena blinked, her heart sinking a little. She had been hoping Tommy would understand how important tonight was to her, that he would show up to support her—not to pull her away. The quiet tension between her desire for independence and Tommy's expectations flared up again, and she felt the weight of it settling over her.

"Tommy, I can't," she said softly, trying to keep her voice steady. "I'm performing tonight. I've been practicing for this. I can't just... skip it."

Tommy's brow furrowed, his hands tightening in his pockets. "It's just one night, Lena. You've got plenty of time for this music stuff. I thought maybe we could spend some time together. I haven't seen you much lately. I really need to talk to you about something."

Lena swallowed, feeling a mix of frustration and guilt bubbling up inside her. She understood where Tommy was coming from—he was trying, in his way, to be there for her. But this wasn't just a "music thing" for her. This was everything. She had poured her heart into this song, and she couldn't turn away now, not when she was so close.

"I know," Lena said, her voice firmer this time. "But this isn't just a hobby, Tommy. I've been working on this for weeks, and tonight's important to me. I need to do this."

Tommy's jaw clenched slightly, and he glanced away, staring at the ground for a moment before looking back at her. "I get that you're into this, but... I don't see why it has to be tonight. We could do something special instead. Just us."

Lena's frustration flared, and she shook her head, feeling a tightness in her chest. "It's not about tonight, Tommy. It's about you not taking this seriously. This is more than just some passing interest for me. I want... I need to do this."

There was a beat of silence, the tension thick in the air between them. Sarah, standing off to the side, glanced between them, clearly feeling the strain of the conversation but staying quiet.

Tommy let out a slow breath, running a hand through his hair. "Lena, I'm trying to be here for you. I just thought maybe we could—"

"Be here for me by supporting me, Tommy," Lena interrupted, her voice sharper than she intended. "I'm not asking you to do much. Just let me have this. Let me have tonight."

Tommy's shoulders sagged slightly, the frustration melting into resignation. He looked at Lena for a long moment, and she could see the hurt behind his eyes, the quiet misunderstanding of what this meant to her.

"Alright," he said finally, his voice low. "If it's that important to you, I'll take you."

Lena exhaled, feeling both relief and sadness in equal measure. She knew Tommy was trying, but a part of her wondered if he'd ever truly understand her dreams. She nodded, her voice softer now. "Thank you."

Sarah, sensing the shift, smiled and stepped forward. "Alright, let's go then! We don't want to be late."

Tommy opened the passenger door for Lena, and she slid into the seat, her guitar resting against her legs. Sarah hopped into the back, still buzzing with excitement, while Tommy rounded the car and climbed into the driver's seat.

As they drove toward the café, the tension between Lena and Tommy lingered in the air, unspoken but clear. The hum of the engine filled the silence, and Lena stared out the window, her thoughts racing. She knew tonight wouldn't solve everything—there were still so many things between them that felt unsettled, unspoken—but at least for now, Tommy was here. He was taking her to the café, even if he didn't fully understand why it mattered so much.

When they arrived at the café, the parking lot was already buzzing with activity. People milled about, chatting in groups, while the soft strum of acoustic guitars drifted from inside. Lena's stomach flipped at the sight—this was real now. In just a little while, she'd be up there, singing her song in front of everyone.

Tommy pulled the car to a stop near the entrance and cut the engine. He turned to Lena, his expression soft but still shadowed with a hint of frustration.

"Good luck tonight," he said quietly, his voice sincere despite the tension from earlier.

Lena smiled faintly, appreciating the effort he was making. "Thanks. I'll see you inside?"

Tommy hesitated for a moment, then nodded. "Yeah. I'll be there."

Sarah leaned forward from the back seat, giving Tommy a playful nudge. "You better be. She's going to blow everyone away."

Tommy chuckled softly, though the smile didn't quite reach his eyes. "I know she will."

Lena's heart swelled at his words, even though part of her still ached with the unresolved tension between them. But for now, she pushed those thoughts aside. She had a song to sing—a song about resilience, about standing strong in the storm.

And no matter what happened tonight, she was going to sing it.

21

The café buzzed with the energy of a small-town crowd eager for entertainment. The low hum of conversations and the clink of coffee cups filled the air as people gathered around small wooden tables, eyes fixed on the makeshift stage at the front of the room. The dim lighting and exposed brick walls gave the place a cozy, intimate feel—perfect for an evening of music, but for Lena, it felt suffocating.

Her heart pounded as she stood just offstage, her guitar slung over her shoulder, the weight of the instrument a constant reminder of what was about to happen. The room felt smaller than she remembered, and the faces in the crowd—Bill, Joe, Tommy, and a few classmates she recognized—blurred together in a haze of anticipation and nerves.

"Are you ready?" Sarah whispered beside her, giving her a quick squeeze on the arm. Her eyes were full of encouragement, but Lena could tell Sarah knew how much was riding on this for her.

"I... I think so," Lena whispered back, her voice shaky.

"You've got this," Sarah said with a confident smile. "Just remember why you're doing it. It's your moment."

Lena swallowed hard, her throat dry despite the cup of water she had barely touched. She wasn't sure she did have it. Not with Tommy and Bill sitting in the back, their quiet presence adding to the pressure. Not with Joe in the front, watching her with that intense, expectant look he always had when he was pushing her to be more. And certainly not with Sarah, her best friend, her biggest cheerleader, waiting for her to prove she could do it.

The host called her name—"Next up, we have Lena Carter!"—and the room quieted.

Lena took a deep breath, the sound of her name ringing in her ears as she stepped onto the small stage. The spotlight above her felt too bright, too warm, and she blinked against it as she adjusted the guitar strap over her shoulder. She could feel the weight of every eye in the room on her, each one expecting something, even though none of them knew how hard she had worked for this moment.

She sat down on the stool in the center of the stage, her fingers trembling slightly as they rested on the strings of her guitar. Her heart was racing, her pulse loud in her ears. She glanced briefly at Tommy, who gave her a small, reassuring smile from the back of the room, and then to Sarah, whose face was lit with encouragement. Joe sat forward in his seat, arms crossed, a slight smirk on his face, as if daring her to prove herself.

This was it. Her song.

She strummed the first few chords of "Songbird in the Rain," her voice soft and shaky as she began to sing. The room was so quiet that she could hear her own breath between the notes, and that silence made it all the more terrifying.

The rain falls heavy, the skies turn gray
But I keep singing through the day
The wind may howl, the storm may rage
But I've learned to dance on life's stage

Her voice wavered slightly on the second line, and a surge of panic rushed through her. What if I mess this up? The question hung in her mind, taunting her. The next chord slipped out of her fingers wrong, the note landing awkwardly, too harsh against the melody.

She faltered, her breath catching in her throat as the mistake echoed in the air.

Her eyes darted nervously to Tommy and Bill, who were both watching her intently. Tommy gave her a small nod, as if telling her to keep going, but the pressure only made her fingers tremble more. She wasn't supposed to fumble like this. This was her moment to shine, but all she felt was fear tightening around her throat.

For a terrifying moment, Lena thought she might not be able to continue. Her mind was blank, her hands numb, and her voice had almost disappeared. But then, she looked at Sarah, sitting there in the front row, beaming with quiet encouragement. Joe, too, had that look in his eyes—the one that said I believe in you.

She took a deep breath and forced herself to keep going, even though the next few lines came out shaky:

The world is loud with all its demands
Telling me I can't, but here I stand
With my heart wide open, I face the pain
Like a songbird singing in the rain

Her voice was thin, the words fragile, but she pushed forward, her fingers slowly finding their rhythm again on the guitar strings. The melody began to steady itself, even if her confidence hadn't quite caught up.

The first verse was behind her now, and as she moved into the interlude and chorus, she tried to let herself go—tried to let the song carry her, even as her nerves clung to her every movement.

The sky is heavy, clouds are thick,
I feel the weight of every drop.
Raindrops tracing paths on glass,
Each one a whisper, a silent plea.
I'm a songbird in the rain, I won't be denied
With every drop, I'm learning to fly
Though the sky may fall, I'll spread my wings
And through the storm, I'll still sing...

The chorus came out stronger than the verse, and Lena felt a small flicker of hope in her chest. *This is what I'm here for.* She could feel the song starting to take shape, feel the audience leaning in, waiting to see what she would do next.

By the time she reached the bridge, her fingers had stopped shaking. The fear hadn't gone away entirely, but something inside her had shifted—something that told her she couldn't stop now, not when she had come this far.

Her voice grew steadier, clearer:

They say the sky won't clear,

that it's foolish to keep waiting,
and yet I've learned to hold my ground,
even as it shifts beneath me.
I see the sun behind layers, deep,
like a memory or a promise,
and my heart keeps its rhythm,
steady, true to its path.
So here I stand, amidst the storm,
Not broken, just weathered by time.
Every gust, every flash of lightning feels like a call,
A song rising from the depths of pain.

The words felt like they were coming from somewhere deep inside her, each line pulling her further away from the fear that had gripped her earlier.

Like a songbird, I'll soar through the pain
With my melody, I'll call the sun again
No matter the storm, no matter the strain
I'll keep singing—this songbird in the rain.
The thunder rolls, but I won't hide
I've got a fire burning deep inside
The world may say I'm not enough
But I'm made of dreams, I'm built from love
The road is long, and the nights are cold
But I've found my voice, and it's strong and bold
Through every tear and every ache
I'm the songbird no storm can break.

Her voice rose with the emotion behind the lyrics, and as she sang the final lines of the bridge, she felt a surge of strength she hadn't expected:

I'll stand my ground, I'll face the sky
The rain can fall, the winds can blow
But I'm stronger now than you'll ever know
With every storm, I grow inside
No fear left, I've nothing to hide

I'll stand my ground, I'll face the sky
With every song, I'm learning to fly
And when the morning light appears
I'll know I've conquered all my fears
Through the haze, I see the light,
A beacon guiding me forward.
No longer afraid of the rain,
I embrace the strength it brings.

Lena could feel the eyes of her friends—Sarah, Joe, Bill, and Tommy—all fixed on her as she neared the end of the song. She had fumbled her way through parts of it, and the panic had nearly overtaken her, but now, in this final moment, something clicked. This was her song, her voice, her truth.

I'm a songbird in the rain, chasing the light
With every note, I'm holding tight
I'll rise above, I'll find my way
Singing through the rain, come what may

The last chords filled the room as she sang the outro, her voice clearer, stronger than it had been at the start:

As the rain begins to cease,
I spread my wings and take flight.
A songbird soaring through the calm,
Leaving behind the stormy night.

As the final note faded into the silence of the café, Lena let out a breath she hadn't realized she'd been holding. Her fingers stilled on the guitar strings, and for a moment, she just sat there, unsure of what would come next.

The silence lingered for a beat too long, and Lena's heart sank. Had she really messed it up that badly? Had they all noticed how shaky she had been, how she had nearly fallen apart halfway through?

But then, slowly at first, the sound of applause filled the room. Sarah was the first to clap, her smile wide and proud as she stood, urging others to join in. Joe, with his usual laid-back smirk, clapped along, nodding his approval. Even Bill was clapping, leaning back in his chair with a grin, though it was clear he didn't quite understand what the big deal was.

And then, from the back of the room, Tommy stood, clapping softly, his face a mixture of pride and something Lena couldn't quite read.

She had done it. It wasn't perfect, but she had made it through. She had sung her song.

22

The small soda shop just off Main Street was a familiar haunt for Lena, Sarah, Joe, Bill, and Tommy. It was the kind of place where the booths were lined with vinyl cushions, the floors gleamed with black-and-white checkered tiles, and the air always smelled faintly of fried food and sugary milkshakes. The jukebox in the corner was playing something light and breezy—probably The Supremes or The Beach Boys—though the song seemed distant to Lena, lost in the buzz of conversation around her.

The gang had gathered around their usual booth, each with a milkshake or soda in front of them. Sarah and Bill were deep in conversation about the upcoming football season, their voices filled with easy laughter. Tommy sat beside Lena, close but quiet, while Joe leaned back in his seat across from her, his usual half-smile tugging at his lips as he observed everything with his sharp, knowing eyes.

But for Lena, the room felt like it was spinning. She still hadn't shaken the nerves from her performance, the way her voice had wavered, the way her fingers had stumbled over the chords. The applause had been polite, supportive even, but in her mind, it hadn't been enough. It wasn't what she had hoped for, and the sting of imperfection still sat heavy in her chest.

She absentmindedly stirred her milkshake with the straw, the thick chocolate swirl barely moving. Tommy, sensing her unease, leaned in closer, his voice low and soft.

"Hey," he murmured, his hand brushing lightly over hers. "You were great tonight."

Lena forced a smile, glancing up at him. "Thanks," she said quietly, though she didn't quite believe it.

"I mean it," Tommy insisted, his brown eyes sincere. "You've got real talent, Lena. Everyone saw it tonight."

But before she could respond, Tommy's tone shifted, his voice taking on a slightly more serious edge. "But, you know, it's just one night. There'll be other chances. You don't have to let it get to you."

Lena frowned, pulling her hand away slightly. "It's not just about tonight, Tommy. This... this is what I want to do. I've been working on this song for so long."

Tommy's smile faltered, and he glanced around the room as if searching for the right words. "I know, and it's great that you have something you're passionate about. But... it's not everything, right? I mean, we've got a future to think about too. When I get back from Vietnam, we'll have our whole lives ahead of us. You'll still have your music, but... we'll have other things to focus on."

Lena's chest tightened. There it was again—the subtle dismissal, the quiet assumption that her music was something she'd eventually set aside for something more "practical." Something more normal. She swallowed the frustration rising in her throat and forced a smile, though her heart wasn't in it.

"Yeah," she said, her voice soft. "I guess so."

Tommy, thinking the conversation had settled, gave her hand another reassuring squeeze. "I'm proud of you, though. Just don't let it stress you out too much. We've got bigger things ahead."

Lena nodded numbly, though inside, her thoughts were a whirlwind of doubt and frustration. Bigger things. Was that how he saw their life? A future that didn't include the one thing she truly cared about?

After another few minutes of idle conversation and forced smiles, Lena felt the walls of the soda shop closing in on her. The noise, the clatter of dishes, the laughter of other patrons—it all felt too much. She needed air.

"I'm just going to step outside for a minute," she said quietly to the table, standing up before anyone could question her.

The cool evening air hit her as she stepped out into the quiet street. The sky was a deep navy now, stars just beginning to peek through the darkness. She took a deep breath, letting the calm settle over her as she walked a few steps away from the entrance, her guitar still slung over her shoulder, a constant reminder of the night.

As she leaned against the brick wall, staring out at the dimly lit street, she heard the sound of footsteps behind her. Joe.

"You alright?" he asked, his voice cutting through the silence. He stepped up beside her, hands stuffed in his jacket pockets, that familiar casual stance that always made him seem so at ease with the world.

Lena let out a small, bitter laugh. "Not really."

Joe nodded, as if he understood more than she was saying. "You didn't crash and burn like you think you did, you know."

Lena shook her head, her eyes still focused on the empty street. "It felt like I did. I was shaking the whole time. I couldn't get the chords right. I almost stopped in the middle of the second verse."

"But you didn't stop," Joe pointed out. "You finished the damn thing. That's more than most people would do. And you had some strong moments. The end was solid."

Lena sighed, finally glancing over at him. "It didn't feel that way. I just... I don't know. I don't know if I'm cut out for this."

Joe's smirk softened into something more serious, more thoughtful. "Listen, I've known you for a long time, Lena. And I've seen you pour yourself into this. You've got something real here. You just need to stop holding back."

Lena frowned. "What do you mean?"

Joe leaned against the wall beside her, his eyes scanning the street before landing on her again. "I mean, your song was good. Really good. But you've got more in you than just... that. You're singing about the rain and rising above, but what about everything else you feel? Everything going on in the world? You've got a voice, Lena. Use it."

Lena hesitated, feeling the weight of his words sink in. Joe had always pushed her to be more political, to be bolder with her music. He was the one who made her read books about civil rights and protest movements. He believed music was more than just personal expression—it was a tool for change. But Lena wasn't sure she was ready for that.

"I don't know if I can do that, Joe," she admitted, her voice quiet. "It's hard enough just to get up there and sing about my own stuff."

Joe shrugged, his expression unbothered but his eyes intense. "Then start with that. But don't stop there. You've got a platform—use it. The world's changing, Lena. People like us... we need to speak up, or nothing's ever going to change. You think these songs about love and heartbreak are the only thing you can write about? You've got bigger things to say."

Lena was quiet for a long moment, staring at her feet. Joe always made it sound so simple, so easy. But it wasn't that easy for her. She wasn't like him—she wasn't ready to stand up and shout about the war, about injustice, about all the things that scared her.

But maybe... maybe she could get there. Maybe she could start small and find her way.

"I'll think about it," Lena said finally, her voice soft but sincere.

Joe nodded, seeming satisfied with that. "Good. You've got something to say, Lena. Don't waste it."

The two of them stood in silence for a while, the quiet of the night settling over them. Inside, the hum of the soda shop continued, but out here, the world felt bigger, quieter, and full of possibility.

23

The night was still as Tommy's 1957 Chevrolet Bel Air rumbled down the dirt road leading to the lake, the soft hum of the engine the only sound in the quiet darkness. Lena sat in the passenger seat, her hands clasped tightly in her lap, her mind swirling with thoughts she couldn't quite untangle. The moon hung low in the sky, casting a pale light over the trees, while the headlights of Tommy's car illuminated the narrow path ahead.

The drive had been mostly quiet, a quiet that felt natural settling between them after the bustle of the soda shop. But now, as they neared the lake, Lena's heart began to beat a little faster. She had been out here with Tommy before—plenty of times—but tonight felt different. There was a weight in the air, something unspoken hanging between them.

As the car rolled to a stop near the edge of the lake, Tommy killed the engine, and the night fell into a soft, almost eerie silence. The water stretched out in front of them, calm and dark, reflecting the stars above. It was beautiful—peaceful, even—but Lena's mind was anything but calm.

Tommy glanced over at her, a small, quiet smile tugging at his lips. "You okay?"

Lena nodded, though the lump in her throat made it hard to speak. "Yeah, just... thinking."

Tommy reached over, his hand resting gently on hers. "About what?"

Lena hesitated, her eyes drifting out to the lake. She wasn't sure how to put into words what she was feeling. There was so much swirling inside her—excitement, fear, love, uncertainty. This night, this moment, felt monumental, like a turning point she couldn't quite see past.

"I don't know," she said softly, her voice barely above a whisper. "Everything, I guess."

Tommy turned his body toward her, his brown eyes searching her face. "I've been thinking too," he said quietly. "I don't know how much time I've got left before they send me out. It could be soon."

Lena's heart tightened at the mention of his leaving soon. Tommy had talked about Vietnam before—his fear, his uncertainty—but tonight, the reality of his leaving felt more immediate. More real. The draft was looming over them both like a storm cloud, and though Tommy tried to stay strong, Lena knew the weight of it hung over him constantly.

"I know," Lena said, her voice catching slightly. She didn't want to think about Tommy leaving, didn't want to imagine him halfway across the world, facing danger she couldn't protect him from. But that was their reality now.

Tommy squeezed her hand a little tighter. "That's why tonight... I don't know, I just wanted it to be special. I wanted it to be... us. Before everything changes."

Lena's breath hitched in her throat. She knew what he meant, what he was asking. The unspoken tension between them had been there for weeks now, growing stronger each time they were alone together. But tonight was different. Tommy's uncertainty about the future, about when he'd be shipped off to war, had brought everything into sharp focus.

This could be the last time they had together like this.

Lena turned to face him fully, her heart pounding in her chest. "Tommy, I..." She hesitated, her words faltering as she tried to make sense of the thoughts racing through her mind.

He reached up, gently tucking a strand of her hair behind her ear. "We don't have to, Lena. Not if you're not ready. I just... I wanted to be with you tonight."

Lena felt a rush of emotion, her throat tightening as tears pricked at the corners of her eyes. She loved Tommy—she did—but there was so much more to consider. This wasn't just about being with him physically; it was about everything that came with it. The expectations, the changes, the unknown future.

In 1966, small-town values still held strong. She knew what people would think if they knew—what her parents would think. But then there was the other part of her, the part that was growing louder every day. The part that wanted to break free, to make her own choices, to live her life on her terms.

She glanced down at their intertwined hands, feeling the warmth of his skin against hers. Tommy was here, now, and he loved her. And she loved him. But even as the thought settled over her, the future felt impossibly distant and uncertain.

"Tommy," she whispered, her voice shaky. "I'm scared."

His expression softened, and he leaned in closer, his forehead resting gently against hers. "I know," he said softly. "Me too."

They stayed like that for a long moment, the only sound the quiet rustle of the wind through the trees and the soft lapping of the lake against the shore. Lena closed her eyes, letting the warmth of his presence steady her, letting the love she felt for him wash over her. But behind it all was the nagging question—is this the right time?

"Everything's changing so fast," Lena murmured, pulling back slightly to meet his eyes. "I don't know what's going to happen, with you... with us."

Tommy's hand cupped her cheek, his thumb brushing gently across her skin. "I don't either. But I know I love you, Lena. I've loved you for a long time. And I want to be with you, whatever happens."

Lena's heart swelled at his words, but the doubts still lingered. She wanted to be with him, but she also wanted to hold on to the part of herself that wasn't just Tommy's girlfriend, the part that was chasing something bigger. Her music, her independence, her dreams. Could she be both? Could she give herself to him fully tonight, knowing everything that lay ahead?

"I love you too," Lena whispered, her voice trembling with emotion. "But..."

Tommy leaned in, pressing a soft kiss to her lips, cutting off her words. It was gentle, tender, and filled with all the love he couldn't put into words. Lena kissed him back, her heart racing, but even as their lips met, her mind was still spinning. Was this really what she wanted?

After a moment, she pulled away, her breathing uneven, her eyes searching his. "I'm scared of losing myself, Tommy," she admitted quietly. "I'm scared that if I give you everything, there won't be anything left for me."

Tommy's brow furrowed, his expression confused but soft. "You're not going to lose yourself, Lena. This is just us. It doesn't change who you are."

But to Lena, it felt like more than that. She knew that once they crossed this line, things would change. She didn't know how, but they would. And the part of her that longed for independence, that wanted to chase her music and her dreams, wasn't ready to let go.

"I don't know if I'm ready," Lena whispered, her voice breaking slightly. "I thought I was, but... I don't know."

Tommy's expression softened, and he pulled her into his arms, holding her close. "It's okay," he said gently. "We don't have to do anything you're not ready for. I love you, and that's enough."

Lena let out a shaky breath, resting her head against his chest. The weight of the decision lifted slightly, but the uncertainty still lingered. She loved Tommy—that much was true—but she also needed to hold on to the parts of herself that weren't ready to be defined by him. She was more than just someone's girlfriend, more than just a future wife. And tonight, even with all the love between them, she wasn't ready to let that go.

24

The moon hung low in the sky, casting long shadows over the empty road as Tommy's Chevrolet Bel Air rumbled quietly through the night. The headlights cut through the darkness, illuminating only the narrow stretch of road ahead. Inside the car, Lena sat silently in the passenger seat, her thoughts swirling like the night air outside, the weight of the evening pressing heavily on her chest.

Tommy kept his eyes on the road, one hand on the wheel and the other resting on the seat between them. He didn't say much—he didn't need to. The tension from earlier, the conversation by the lake, still lingered in the space between them, heavy and unspoken. Lena's mind replayed the moment over and over, trying to make sense of her own emotions.

She loved Tommy. She knew that. But tonight had left her feeling more conflicted than ever. The thought of Vietnam—of him leaving, of the uncertainty of his return—made her heart ache. Yet the idea of losing herself, of giving up the part of her that longed for something more, terrified her even more.

Tommy glanced over at her once, his gaze soft, searching for some kind of reassurance, but Lena couldn't bring herself to meet his eyes. She offered him a small, tight smile instead, one that didn't quite reach her eyes.

As the car pulled into her driveway, the soft rumble of the engine died away, leaving an almost oppressive silence in its wake. The house was dark, save for the porch light her parents always left on for her. Tommy shifted in his seat, turning slightly toward her.

"Hey," he said quietly, his voice breaking the stillness. "Are we okay?"

Lena nodded, though the uncertainty in her chest felt heavier than ever. "Yeah," she whispered. "We're okay."

Tommy studied her face for a moment longer, his brow furrowing slightly, as if he wanted to say more. But instead, he leaned in and kissed her gently on the forehead. "I'll call you tomorrow," he said softly.

Lena gave him another small smile, the weight of the night still pressing down on her. "Goodnight, Tommy."

"Goodnight, Lena."

She slipped out of the car, the cool night air brushing against her skin as she walked quietly toward the house. Tommy waited until she was safely inside before pulling out of the driveway, the sound of his car fading into the distance as she closed the door behind her.

Lena moved through the dark, familiar hallway with practiced quiet, trying not to wake her parents. The house was still, save for the soft ticking of the clock in the living room. She tiptoed up the stairs, her hand gliding along the wooden banister, her mind still swirling with everything that had happened at the lake.

She had nearly made it to her room when she heard the soft creak of a door opening behind her. Turning, she saw her mother, Evelyn, standing in the doorway of her bedroom, her robe wrapped tightly around her as she squinted into the dim light.

"You're home late," her mother said softly, her voice carrying the warmth of concern.

Lena felt her heart sink slightly. She hadn't expected her mother to be awake, and part of her just wanted to disappear into her room and sleep off the weight of the night. But she couldn't ignore the gentle worry in her mother's eyes.

"Yeah, we were just out at the lake," Lena said quietly, trying to keep her voice light. "Nothing crazy."

Her mother stepped out into the hallway, her slippers shuffling softly against the wooden floor. "Everything alright?" she asked, her gaze searching Lena's face. "You look... troubled."

Lena hesitated, biting her lip. Her mother had a way of sensing when something was off, even when Lena tried to hide it. There was no point in pretending everything was fine.

"I'm just... thinking," Lena admitted, her voice barely above a whisper.

Evelyn crossed her arms, leaning slightly against the doorframe. "About Tommy?"

Lena nodded, but her thoughts weren't only about Tommy. They were about everything—her music, her future, the expectations everyone seemed to have for her. It all felt like too much to handle, and tonight, it had come crashing down on her all at once.

Evelyn studied her daughter for a long moment, her face softening with quiet understanding. "You know, Lena," she said gently, "it's okay to not have everything figured out. You're young. You've got time."

Lena looked down at her feet, her throat tightening. "I know. But... it feels like everything is happening so fast. Tommy's leaving soon, and... I just don't know what I'm supposed to do."

Her mother's gaze softened even more, and she stepped forward, placing a gentle hand on Lena's shoulder. "You don't have to know all the answers right now. Life has a way of sorting itself out, even when it feels impossible."

Lena's chest tightened at her mother's words. Life sorting itself out—it was the kind of thing her mother always said, the kind of comfort that was meant to ease the burden of uncertainty. But to Lena, it felt like an expectation to just go with the flow, to let things happen instead of actively shaping her own path.

"I just don't want to let anyone down," Lena whispered.

Evelyn squeezed her shoulder gently. "You're not going to let anyone down, Lena. You're smart, and you're capable, and you've got a good heart. Whatever you choose, it'll be the right decision."

Lena nodded, though the words didn't fully settle in. She appreciated her mother's reassurance, but it didn't make the weight of her choices any lighter.

"Thanks, Mom," she said softly, managing a small smile.

Her mother smiled back, leaning in to press a soft kiss to her forehead. "Go get some rest. You'll feel better in the morning."

Lena nodded again and turned toward her room, her footsteps quiet on the wooden floor. She slipped inside and closed the door gently behind her, the familiar comfort of her room wrapping around her like a soft blanket.

The room was dark, save for the faint glow of moonlight filtering through the curtains. Lena moved over to her bed, setting her guitar down gently against the wall before sinking onto the mattress. She stared at the ceiling for a long moment, her mind still racing with everything that had happened tonight.

The lake, Tommy, her mother's words—all of it swirled together in a tangled mess of emotions she couldn't quite unravel. She loved Tommy, but tonight had made her realize just how much she still needed to figure out about herself. She wasn't ready to be anyone's everything—not yet.

She reached over to her bedside table and grabbed her music journal, flipping it open to the page where she had written the final lines of her song earlier that day. The words stared back at her, a reflection of her own conflicted heart from the middle chorus:

Like a songbird, I'll soar through the pain
With my melody, I'll call the sun again
No matter the storm, no matter the strain
I'll keep singing—this songbird in the rain.

Her fingers traced the ink on the page, the meaning behind the lyrics resonating more deeply with her now than ever before. She was that songbird, standing in the middle of a storm, trying to find her way through the chaos. She wasn't ready to give up her song—not for Tommy, not for anyone. But she wasn't sure yet how to balance that with everything else.

As Lena curled up under the blankets, the quiet of the night settling around her, she closed her eyes and let her thoughts drift. Sleep came slowly, her mind still filled with half-formed melodies and the weight of unanswered questions.

25

The morning sun filtered through the pale curtains of Lena's bedroom, casting soft rays of light across the room. Lena lay in bed, blinking at the ceiling, her mind already humming with a melody that seemed to have followed her from her dreams. It was different this time—not just a soft, personal song like the ones she'd written before, but something bigger, something with more power behind it.

She could hear the words forming, the faint echoes of the social changes she had been reading about, watching unfold on the news, and hearing in Joe's fiery conversations. The protests, the marches, the calls for equality. It was all bubbling up in her, and somehow, it had found its way into her music.

"A change will come," she murmured to herself, the lyrics beginning to piece together in her mind.

For a moment, Lena stayed in bed, her heart swelling with the possibility of this new song. It wasn't fully formed yet, but she could feel it—this would be different from anything she'd written before. It wasn't just about her; it was about everything happening around her, about the world breaking free of its old chains, just like she wanted to.

The smell of bacon and eggs wafted through the house, pulling Lena out of bed. She quickly scribbled down the first few lines of the song in her music journal before throwing on her clothes and heading downstairs.

In the kitchen, her mother, Evelyn, was already at the stove, flipping bacon in the pan while her father sat at the small table, the morning newspaper spread out in front of him. The familiar scene of their quiet, conservative life greeted Lena with a sense of comfort, but this morning, she couldn't shake the feeling that the world outside her home was changing faster than her parents could understand.

"Morning, sweetie," her mother greeted without turning around. "Grab a plate, the bacon's almost ready."

"Morning," Lena mumbled, still distracted by the half-formed song running through her mind. She grabbed a plate and slid into her usual spot across from her father, her fingers tapping lightly on the table as her thoughts swirled with melody and lyrics.

Her father, Robert, glanced up from his newspaper, his reading glasses perched low on his nose. "You're looking awfully thoughtful this morning," he remarked, his voice gruff but not unkind.

Lena shrugged, glancing down at her plate. "Just... thinking about school," she lied. The truth felt too complicated to explain right now.

Her father grunted, turning the page of the newspaper. "You keep those grades up. Not much longer till you graduate." He took a sip of his coffee before adding, "Factory's looking to hire some new folks soon, might be something there for you after graduation. Good steady work."

Lena felt a pang in her chest at the thought. The General Motors factory, where her father worked, represented everything solid and traditional about their town—stability, hard work, and a life that followed a predictable pattern. But the thought of working there, of settling into that routine, felt like a cage.

She forced a smile. "I'll think about it."

Evelyn placed a plate of bacon and eggs in front of her husband, then sat down beside him. "You've got plenty of time to figure things out, Lena. We just want what's best for you."

"I know," Lena said, though her mind was far from the conversation. She picked at her food, the tune of her new song running through her head like a persistent whisper.

Her mother glanced at the clock, wiping her hands on her apron. "You'd better get a move on if you don't want to be late for school."

Lena nodded, glancing at the clock as well. She quickly ate a few bites, though her appetite was diminished by the swirl of thoughts and emotions. She was itching to write down the rest of the song, but school was calling, and her journal would have to wait.

Her father stood, stretching as he folded his newspaper. "Alright, I'm off. Long day ahead," he said with a sigh. He kissed her mother on the cheek, then turned to Lena. "You have a good day, kiddo."

"Thanks, Dad. You too."

She watched as he grabbed his lunch pail and headed out the door. The sound of his truck starting up in the driveway was a familiar hum, one she had heard every morning for as long as she could remember. But today, as the truck pulled away and disappeared down the street, it felt like a symbol of everything she was trying to move away from. The factory. The routine. The life that had already been written for her.

Lena stood by the kitchen window, staring out at the empty street. Her mother had already moved on to cleaning up from breakfast, humming softly to herself as she worked, unaware of the quiet revolution stirring in her daughter's heart.

The song wouldn't stop echoing in Lena's mind, its words pushing their way to the surface. She grabbed her journal and quickly flipped to the next blank page, scribbling furiously.

The world is shifting, it's breaking free
Voices rising, fighting to be seen
In the streets, we march for peace
Dreaming of the day when the wars will cease

The first verse poured out of her like a flood, the words rushing to capture the feeling of change, of revolution, both in the world around her and inside herself. She could feel it—the unrest, the desire for something more than what her small town could offer. It was in the music she listened to, in the conversations she had with Joe, and even in her quiet defiance of the path her parents expected her to follow.

Her fingers tapped out a soft rhythm on the kitchen table as she scribbled the next few lines:

From every corner, a new dawn breaks
You can feel the ground beneath us shake
The time has come to stand as one
And know that change has just begun

It was about more than just the Vietnam War, more than just the civil rights movements happening across the country. It was about freedom, about breaking free from the chains that had held people down for so long—chains of tradition, of expectation, of fear.

Lena barely noticed when her mother turned to her, a questioning look on her face. "You alright, honey? You've been scribbling away for the past five minutes."

Lena looked up, startled. She hadn't realized how absorbed she had become. "Yeah, just... writing something for class," she said quickly, closing the journal and standing up. "I better get going."

Her mother gave her a knowing smile, though she didn't press further. "Alright, but don't forget—we've got the church potluck on Wednesday. And the sewing circle this weekend."

Lena nodded absentmindedly as she grabbed her bag, her mind still fixed on the words she had just written. The idea of the sewing circle—another one of the things her mother thought would help prepare her for a future as a wife and mother—felt like it belonged to another world. A world she was slowly but surely stepping away from.

"Yeah, I won't forget," Lena said, though part of her knew she'd have to find a way out of it. She had other things to focus on now.

26

Lena stepped out into the crisp morning air, her guitar case slung over her shoulder, her journal tucked safely in her bag. The melodies of her new song, "A Change Will Come," were still swirling in her mind. She couldn't stop thinking about it—the words, the music, the message. It was all coming together, slowly but surely, and as she walked down the familiar streets of Janesville, she felt a new sense of purpose rising within her.

The quiet streets were beginning to come alive with the sounds of a small-town morning—cars starting, birds chirping, neighbors calling out to one another. Sarah's house was just a few blocks away, and Lena quickened her pace, eager to see her best friend before the day officially began. She caught sight of Sarah stepping off her front porch just as she reached the corner.

"Hey, you!" Lena called out, waving.

Sarah turned, her face lighting up when she saw Lena. "Lena! Morning! You seem... chipper," she said, falling into step beside her.

Lena smiled, though her thoughts were still miles away, tangled in lyrics and melodies. "I've got a new song in my head. It's driving me crazy—I can't stop thinking about it."

Sarah chuckled, shaking her head. "I should've known. You've always got some song stuck in your head."

They walked in comfortable silence for a moment, the familiar routine of the morning settling around them. Lena loved this part of her day—walking with Sarah, talking about anything and everything before school took over their lives for the next several hours.

"By the way," Sarah said, breaking the silence, "Bill wants to know if we're still on for Saturday night. You know, hanging out after the football game?"

Lena nodded absentmindedly. "Yeah, of course." But in truth, her thoughts were far from football games and Saturday nights. She was more focused on the upcoming open mic night at the local café, where she was planning to debut her new song. But she didn't want to bring that up with Sarah just yet. She wasn't sure she was ready.

As they approached the school grounds, Lena felt a wave of nervous energy wash over her. The song was taking over her thoughts, and she wasn't sure how she was going to focus on her classes today.

The smell of flour and butter filled the Home Economics classroom, where Mrs. Helen Carver stood at the front, explaining the intricacies of baking a pie crust. Her voice was as steady and no-nonsense as ever, her apron tied neatly around her waist as she demonstrated how to knead the dough.

"Now, girls," Mrs. Carver said, her sharp eyes scanning the room, "the key to a good apple pie crust is cold butter and gentle hands. If you overwork the dough, it'll be tough. And no one likes a tough pie crust."

Lena stood at her station next to Sarah, her hands working the dough as her mind drifted back to her song. She could still hear Mrs. Carver's voice in the background, but her focus was elsewhere—on the cultural revolution, on the idea that change was coming, not just in the world, but for her too.

Sarah nudged her, snapping her out of her thoughts. "You're spacing out again," she whispered, a teasing smile on her lips.

Lena blinked, shaking her head slightly. "Sorry. Just... thinking."

"About your new song?" Sarah asked, her voice soft and curious.

Lena smiled. Sarah knew her too well. "Yeah. It's been stuck in my head all morning."

"Well, you'd better start thinking about this pie crust before Mrs. Carver notices," Sarah said with a wink. "You don't want to end up with detention for making a 'tough' pie."

Lena laughed quietly, trying to focus on the task at hand, but it was hard. The song kept creeping back into her mind, like a melody that wouldn't let go.

The Civics classroom was filled with the quiet hum of students flipping through their textbooks as Mr. Richard Benson stood at the front, his tweed jacket and elbow patches giving him the air of a man who took his job very seriously. His voice was passionate as he lectured about the importance of civic duty and the role of the government in maintaining order.

"Today, we're discussing the role of the Supreme Court in shaping the laws that govern us," Mr. Benson said, his eyes scanning the room. "The Bill of Rights is a living document, and it's up to us as citizens to understand it, to question it, and to use it to protect our freedoms."

Lena sat in the back row next to Joe, who was, as always, a little too relaxed in his seat, his arms crossed as he listened with a smirk playing on his lips.

Mr. Benson was in full swing, talking about civil rights cases, about the Vietnam War protests and the First Amendment, and how freedom of speech was being tested in the face of growing unrest across the country.

Joe leaned over to Lena, his voice low. "You should write a song about this."

Lena glanced at him, raising an eyebrow. "About what? The Supreme Court?"

Joe shrugged, that familiar rebellious glint in his eyes. "No, about fighting for something bigger than yourself. You know, like these protests. You've got a voice, Lena. Use it."

Lena's thoughts flickered back to her new song—about the change that was coming, about the fight for freedom and justice. Joe wasn't wrong. This was the kind of thing she had been thinking about, the kind of song she wanted to write.

"I'm working on something," she said quietly, though she didn't elaborate.

Joe nodded, satisfied. "Good. Just don't let people like Benson tell you what to think. Figure it out for yourself."

Lena smiled. Joe's constant push for her to be more outspoken, more political, was always on her mind. But she wasn't quite ready to be as bold as he was. Not yet.

The Business Math classroom was as structured and orderly as ever, with Mrs. Mabel Price at the front, writing out equations on the chalkboard. Her voice was steady and serious, her tone a stark contrast to the passionate debates of Civics.

"Today, we'll be calculating interest rates and understanding how to budget for a business," Mrs. Price said, her sharp eyes focused on the board. "It's important to understand these concepts, especially if you're planning on running a household or a business one day."

Lena sat near the middle of the room, her notebook open but her mind elsewhere. She could feel Bill's presence a few seats away, his focus entirely on the lesson. He was always good at this sort of thing—practical, straightforward math that had a clear answer. Joe, on the other hand, was less interested, slouched in his chair as if he couldn't be bothered.

Lena scribbled the beginnings of another verse in the margin of her notebook, her mind still on the song she had been working on that morning.

We're breaking chains that held us down,
Tearing walls that shut us out...
The future's calling, can't you hear?
The sound of hope, the end of fear...

She glanced up at the board, trying to focus on the math problem Mrs. Price was explaining, but the lyrics kept pulling her back in. The cultural shift, the fight for freedom—it was all there in her mind, waiting to be put into song.

From Selma's streets to city squares
There's power in the love we share
Together, we'll rise, we'll make it known
We'll carve a path to freedom's throne

The English Literature classroom was a sanctuary for Lena, a place where words and ideas flowed freely, and where Mr. Joseph Hastings encouraged his students to think deeply about the world around them.

Today, they were discussing *The Catcher in the Rye*, and Mr. Hastings stood at the front of the room, his hands gesturing wildly as he spoke about Holden Caulfield and his search for meaning in a world that seemed phony and hollow.

"Holden's struggle is a universal one," Mr. Hastings said, his voice filled with excitement. "He's trying to figure out who he is in a world that's constantly telling him who he should be. And that's something we can all relate to, right?"

Lena nodded along, feeling a deep connection to the character. She, too, was searching for her place in the world, trying to figure out who she was amidst all the noise and expectations around her.

Beside her, Joe was doodling in the margins of his notebook, but she could tell he was listening. Sarah, on the other hand, was fully engrossed in the discussion, raising her hand to offer her thoughts on Holden's rebellion against the adult world.

"He's fighting to hold onto his innocence," Sarah said thoughtfully. "But at the same time, he knows he can't stay innocent forever. He has to grow up."

Lena listened, her mind drifting back to her own struggles—her fight to hold onto her dreams while the world around her expected her to settle down, to follow the path that had been laid out for her. In many ways, she felt like Holden, standing on the edge of the world, unsure of what came next.

27

The school cafeteria was filled with the hum of students talking and the clatter of trays as Lena and her friends settled into their usual spot at a table near the windows. The early autumn sun filtered through, casting soft light across the room. Lena sat beside Sarah, her guitar case leaning against the wall behind her, while Joe and Bill took seats across from them, their trays laden with cafeteria food.

As usual, the conversation started casually—school gossip, classes, and weekend plans—but it quickly shifted to the subjects they all cared about in different ways.

"So, what are you working on now, Lena?" Joe asked, spearing a piece of meatloaf with his fork and glancing at her with that familiar spark of curiosity. He always seemed more interested in her songs than anyone else.

Lena hesitated for a moment, then shrugged. "Just a new song... It's not finished yet, but it's about... change. You know, everything going on right now—civil rights, Vietnam, people standing up for what's right."

Joe's eyes lit up. "That's what I'm talking about! You're finally writing something real, something that matters."

Lena smiled, though she felt a twinge of nervousness. Joe had been pushing her to be more political with her music, and while she admired his passion, sometimes it overwhelmed her. "It's not exactly finished yet," she said, her voice soft. "But yeah, it's something I've been thinking a lot about."

"Everyone's talking about it," Sarah chimed in, picking at her salad. "The protests, the marches—it's all over the news. My mom can't stop talking about how the world's going crazy."

Joe snorted, leaning back in his chair. "The world's not going crazy—it's waking up. People are finally standing up for themselves. For once, things are changing."

Bill, who had been mostly quiet, looked up from his tray, glancing between Joe and Lena. "That's all well and good, but some things don't need changing," he said, his voice casual but firm. "Like football. That's one thing that's never gonna change. You should come out and watch the game on Friday, Joe. You're missing out."

Joe rolled his eyes. "Yeah, because watching you guys bash each other's brains in is exactly how I want to spend my time."

Bill grinned, shaking his head. "You say that now, but wait till you see me nail that quarterback on Friday. You'll be hooked."

Sarah laughed, nudging Lena with her elbow. "You should come too, Lena. It'll be fun. We can all hang out after."

Lena smiled, though her thoughts were elsewhere. She appreciated her friends' support, but she was more focused on her music—on the song that had been growing in her mind. Still, she nodded. "Yeah, sure. I'll be there."

Joe shook his head, still grinning as he turned back to Lena. "Don't let Tommy distract you. You've got something good with that song. Stick with it."

Lena appreciated the encouragement, though she wasn't sure how much more she could take of intensity. There was always a sense of urgency with him, a need to push harder, to go further. Sometimes, she just wanted to write music for the sake of music, not to make some grand statement.

The sound of sneakers squeaking on the polished gym floor filled the air as Lena and Sarah stood with the rest of their classmates, waiting for Coach Robert "Bob" Clark to finish his instructions. The coach, a former athlete with a gruff but fair demeanor, paced back and forth in front of them, a basketball spinning casually in his hands.

"Alright, ladies," he said, his voice booming. "We're running drills today. Get into teams, and let's get moving. And no slacking, understood?"

Lena and Sarah exchanged a glance, then joined a few other girls to form a team. Sarah was always more enthusiastic about P.E. than Lena, but Coach Clark had a way of making even the most reluctant students get involved.

As they jogged across the gym, Lena's thoughts drifted back to her song, her mind half-focused on the drills and half on the melody that kept looping in her head. The idea of change—not just in the world, but in herself—kept bubbling up. She wanted to capture that feeling in the song, but it was hard to find the right words.

"Hey, Lena, you're spacing out again," Sarah called, dribbling the basketball past her. "Come on, focus!"

Lena laughed, shaking her head as she tried to snap back to the present. "Sorry, just... thinking."

"You've been doing that a lot today," Sarah said, tossing her the ball. "What's going on?"

"Just working on something," Lena replied, though she didn't elaborate. Sarah knew how important her music was, but there were some things Lena liked to keep to herself until she was ready.

The rest of the class passed quickly, and by the time they finished, Coach Clark gave them his usual gruff nod of approval. "Good work today, ladies. Now hit the showers."

The Art Room was a sanctuary for Lena—a place where she could let her creativity flow without the pressure of grades or expectations. Ms. Alice Davis, with her free-spirited approach to teaching, always encouraged the students to express themselves, no matter how unconventional their ideas might be.

Today, the room smelled of paint and charcoal, with students spread out across easels and tables, working on their own projects. Lena sat beside Sarah and Joe, a paintbrush in her hand, staring at the blank canvas in front of her.

"Alright, everyone," Ms. Davis said, her voice soft and calm, "I want you to think about change today. How does change shape us? How does it challenge us? Use that as your inspiration."

Lena glanced at Joe, who was already sketching something bold and abstract. He always had a clear idea of what he wanted to create—sharp lines, rebellious images that challenged the status quo. Sarah, on the other hand, was painting something soft and familiar—a landscape, probably. Something peaceful.

Lena dipped her brush into the paint. Change. It was everywhere—in the world, in her life, in the way she was starting to see things differently. She didn't know what to paint, but she let the brush move across the canvas, creating shapes and colors that felt right, even if they didn't make sense yet.

"Let yourself be free," Ms. Davis said, walking past her. "Don't think too much. Just feel."

The final class of the day was Music Appreciation, and for Lena, it was the perfect way to end the day. Mr. David Morgan, with his easy-going nature and love for all things music, was always excited to share new records and ideas with his students.

Today, he stood at the front of the room, a vinyl record in his hands. "Alright, class," he said, "we're going to listen to something a little different today—Bob

Dylan. I want you to think about how his music has changed over time. What does his music say about the world he's living in?"

Lena's heart skipped a beat at the mention of Dylan. He was one of her biggest inspirations, and the idea of discussing his music in class felt like a dream.

As the opening notes of "The Times They Are a-Changin'" filled the room, Lena closed her eyes, letting the music wash over her. The lyrics hit her in a way they hadn't before, resonating deeply with the song she had been working on.

The class was quiet as they listened, but when the song ended, Mr. Morgan asked, "What do you think Dylan's trying to say here? How does this song reflect the changes happening in the world?"

Lena raised her hand, surprising even herself. "He's talking about how we can't stop change," she said, her voice steady. "It's happening, whether we like it or not. The world is shifting, and we have to move with it, or we'll be left behind."

Mr. Morgan smiled, nodding. "Exactly. And that's something we're all grappling with right now—how to navigate a world that's changing faster than we ever expected."

Lena felt a sense of pride in her answer, but more than that, she felt the song growing stronger in her mind. "A Change Will Come". It wasn't just about the world—it was about her too. She was changing, just like everything else, and maybe that wasn't such a bad thing.

28

The school hallways were slowly emptying as students headed home, their voices echoing down the long corridors. But for Lena, Monday afternoons meant one thing—Music/Guitar Club. It was the part of the week she looked forward to the most, a sanctuary where she could be herself and focus entirely on her music.

As she made her way back to the Music Room after talking with Sarah, her guitar case slung over her shoulder, she felt a familiar excitement rising inside her. Today's club meeting felt particularly important, especially with the new song, "A Change Will Come," still swirling in her mind, its verses not yet fully formed but growing stronger with each passing hour.

When she entered the room, Mr. David Morgan, the club advisor and music teacher, was already setting up. His laid-back demeanor and passion for music made him a favorite among the students. A few of her fellow club members were already there, tuning their guitars and chatting quietly about what they had been working on.

Lena took her usual seat, resting her guitar on her lap as she quietly strummed a few chords.

Mr. Morgan looked up from his stack of vinyl records, smiling warmly at the group. "Alright, everyone. Let's get started."

The meeting began like most others, with the group sharing the songs they had been working on and discussing different techniques. But as the conversation deepened, Mr. Morgan turned his attention to something more personal.

"So, I've been thinking a lot lately," he began, his voice thoughtful. "About what it means to really find your voice. Not just as a musician, but as a person. I think that's something we all struggle with at different points in our lives."

Lena's heart skipped a beat. His words felt almost tailored to what she had been going through recently—the inner conflict between who she was and who the world expected her to be.

Mr. Morgan glanced around the room, his eyes settling on Lena. "What about you, Lena? You've been writing a lot lately, haven't you? How are you finding your voice in all of it?"

Lena hesitated, her fingers lightly grazing the strings of her guitar. She wasn't sure how to put into words what she had been feeling, but she knew this was the moment to try.

"I guess... I've been thinking a lot about change," Lena said slowly, her eyes focused on the guitar in her lap. "Not just in the world, but in myself. I've been writing this new song, and it's about everything that's happening—civil rights, the war, everything that feels like it's breaking apart and coming together at the same time. But it's also about me, about... finding my place in all of it."

The room fell quiet as Lena spoke, her fellow club members listening intently. Mr. Morgan nodded, a small smile playing on his lips.

"That's exactly it," he said softly. "Music is a reflection of who we are, and who we're becoming. It's not just about making something sound good—it's about telling the truth. Your truth."

Lena felt a surge of emotion at his words. She had always known, deep down, that her music was more than just a hobby. It was the way she made sense of the world, the way she processed her feelings and tried to carve out her own path. But hearing Mr. Morgan say it out loud made it feel real, like she had permission to fully embrace that part of herself.

"You should play the new song," Joe, who had been sitting quietly in the back of the room, suddenly spoke up. His voice was casual, but there was a seriousness in his eyes. "We've heard about it all day. Let's hear it."

Lena hesitated, glancing down at her guitar. The song wasn't finished yet. It still felt rough, incomplete. But part of her knew this was the perfect place to test it out—to see if the emotion behind it resonated with others.

"I don't know if it's ready," Lena admitted quietly. "But I'll give it a try."

She took a deep breath, positioning her fingers on the frets as she strummed the opening chords. The room fell silent as the gentle, melodic sound filled the space. Lena closed her eyes for a moment, letting herself sink into the music, the words coming to her slowly but surely.

The world is shifting, it's breaking free
Voices rising, fighting to be seen
In the streets, we march for peace
Dreaming of the day when the wars will cease.

Lena's voice was soft at first, a little uncertain, but as she moved through the verse, she felt the power of the song taking hold. The lyrics were raw, born out of the emotions she had been grappling with. Change. Revolution. Freedom.

From every corner, a new dawn breaks
You can feel the ground beneath us shake
The time has come to stand as one
And know that change has just begun

When she reached the chorus, her voice grew stronger, the words echoing the feeling of hope and determination that had been growing inside her:

A change will come, I feel it near
A brighter day is drawing clear
The winds of revolution blow
And in my heart, I know, I know
A change will come for the world, for me
I'm breaking free, I'm learning to be
The woman who can stand and fight
For her own dreams, for what is right

Lena played through the first verse and chorus, her nerves slowly dissipating as she connected more deeply with the message of the song. By the time she finished, her heart was pounding, her fingers trembling slightly from the intensity of the performance.

The room was silent for a long moment, and Lena wasn't sure what to expect. But then Joe nodded, a small smile tugging at his lips. "That was good," he said simply, but there was a weight behind his words.

Mr. Morgan smiled as well, his expression thoughtful. "It's powerful, Lena. You're tapping into something real there."

Lena felt a sense of relief wash over her, but also something more—a quiet pride. The song wasn't finished yet, but it was on its way. And for the first time, she felt like she was truly finding her voice, not just as a songwriter, but as a person.

After the performance, the club fell into a deeper discussion, one that felt more urgent and meaningful than their usual talks about chord progressions and technique.

"Music has always been a force for change," Mr. Morgan said, leaning against the piano as he addressed the group. "Think about Woody Guthrie, Bob Dylan, Joan Baez—they used their voices to speak out against injustice, to push for something better. That's something you all can do too."

Joe leaned forward, his arms resting on his knees. "That's what I've been saying. Music isn't just about love songs and feel-good stuff. It's about fighting back. It's about using your voice to change the world."

Lena glanced at Joe, feeling a mixture of agreement and hesitation. She admired his passion, but she also knew that not every song had to be a battle cry. There was room for both—the personal and the political, the quiet and the loud.

"But it's also about connection," Lena said softly, her eyes meeting Joe's. "Music brings people together. It's not just about fighting—it's about healing too."

Joe shrugged, though he didn't argue. "Sure. But sometimes you have to break something apart before you can put it back together."

Mr. Morgan nodded, clearly pleased with the direction of the conversation. "You're both right. Music can do all of that. It's up to you to decide how you want to use it. Whether it's to fight, to heal, to express yourself—whatever it is, just make sure it's honest."

Lena thought about that as the meeting drew to a close. She knew that "A Change Will Come" was about more than just revolution—it was about her own journey, about finding her place in a world that felt like it was shifting beneath her feet. And as she packed up her guitar and said goodbye to her friends, she felt more certain than ever that her music had the power to shape not only her future, but maybe even the world around her.

29

The church basement was filled with the familiar smells of casseroles, pot roasts, and baked goods, as Lena moved between tables, helping her mother set out the last of the dishes for the evening potluck. The clatter of dishes and the murmur of conversation provided a comforting backdrop, but Lena's mind was elsewhere, caught up in thoughts of her music and the slow, growing anxiety she hadn't yet identified.

She had spent most of the day in a blur, going through the motions of school while "A Change Will Come" continued to take shape in her mind. Now, she found herself lost in those thoughts again as she arranged a tray of brownies, her hands working automatically.

Her mother, Evelyn, bustled beside her, ever the picture of efficiency and warmth. "Lena, could you help Mrs. Mitchell with the coffee? And don't forget, we'll need to refill the lemonade soon."

Lena nodded, forcing a smile. "Sure, Mom."

But even as she crossed the room, she couldn't shake the feeling that something was about to happen, something she hadn't quite prepared for.

As Lena walked toward the kitchen, her gaze drifted toward the windows facing the street. Outside, under the dim glow of the streetlight, Tommy was leaning against his 1957 Chevrolet Bel Air, his hands shoved deep into his pockets. His silhouette was familiar, comforting, yet somehow... different tonight.

Her heart skipped a beat. He had tried to talk to her earlier, but with all the preparations for the potluck and helping her mother, she hadn't had a chance to give him much attention. But now, seeing him waiting for her like this, she knew something was off.

She quietly slipped out the side door of the church, leaving behind the bustle of the potluck. The cool evening air hit her as she approached Tommy, her footsteps soft against the gravel.

"Tommy," she called, her voice low. He looked up, his face tense and serious, more so than she had ever seen.

"Hey, Lena," he replied, his voice carrying an edge of urgency.

"What's going on?" Lena asked, crossing her arms against the chill in the air. "You've been... off today. Is something wrong?"

Tommy let out a long breath, pushing himself off the car and turning toward her. For a moment, he didn't say anything, just stared at her like he was trying to find the right words.

"I got my draft orders," he said finally, his voice rough.

Lena's stomach dropped. She knew this was coming—everyone knew it was coming. But hearing him say the words out loud made it real in a way she hadn't fully prepared for.

"When?" she asked, her voice barely above a whisper.

"Tomorrow," Tommy said, running a hand through his hair. "I have to report for pre-induction in Madison. I'll be leaving for basic training soon after that."

The words hung in the air between them, heavy and unmovable. Lena's heart pounded in her chest, the weight of the situation sinking in. Tomorrow. It was happening tomorrow, and he hadn't told her until now.

"Why didn't you tell me sooner?" Lena asked, her voice tinged with hurt.

"I didn't know how," Tommy admitted, his eyes pleading with hers. "I didn't want to ruin things. I thought maybe... maybe if I ignored it, it wouldn't feel so real."

Lena blinked, trying to process the information. Tomorrow. It felt like the world was spinning out of control, like everything was happening too fast.

"I want you to come with me," Tommy said suddenly, stepping closer. "To Madison. I have to leave early, but I want you there with me. We can spend the day together... before everything changes."

Lena stared at him, her mind racing. She didn't want to be there when it happened; didn't want to see the light and hope disappear from his eyes. "You want me to skip school? To go with you to Madison?"

"Yeah," Tommy said, his voice soft but insistent. "I don't know when we'll get another chance to be together like this. They still haven't told me anything. I might ship out the day after. Some guys have... I'll be in basic training, and then... who knows where I'll be."

Lena felt torn, a storm of emotions swirling inside her. She wanted to be there for Tommy—of course she did. But everything felt so rushed, so sudden. She didn't know if she was ready for this, for the war, for what it meant for their future.

"I don't know, Tommy," she said, her voice trembling. "I don't know if I can..." That was a lie, and she knew it. She looked away. The truth was she couldn't be there when it happened. To see him put on yet another brave face for her when she knew he was being torn apart on the inside. It would kill her on the inside, just as it had been slowly eating away at her insides since he'd shown her the draft notice.

"Please, Lena," Tommy said, his eyes searching hers. "I need you with me tomorrow. Just... just for one day."

The draft was looming over them both like a shadow they couldn't outrun People were dying in Vietnam. It was on the news every day, and every day the tallies of killed and missing in action grew. The draft wasn't just unfair; it was unjust. Rich families' sons weren't dying over there. Sons from families in towns just like Janesville were. They were dying by the tens, hundreds and thousands.

"I don't know if I can just leave everything," Lena said, her voice breaking. "What about my parents? School? They'll notice I'm gone."

Tommy stepped closer, his hands reaching for hers. "Just for one day, Lena. I need you with me. After tomorrow... I don't know when we'll see each other again. Please."

Lena swallowed hard, her eyes filling with tears she didn't want to shed. She wanted to be strong for Tommy, but the weight of the decision felt like too much. How could she say no to him? How could she refuse him when tomorrow, everything could change?

But at the same time, how could she walk away from her own life? From school, from her parents, from the small piece of stability she had left?

The decision Tommy was asking her to make was monumental. Lena felt torn between her loyalty to Tommy and the fear of stepping out of the routine she had clung to for so long. The war was no longer an abstract concept—it was here, staring her in the face, and it threatened to take away everything she held dear. She didn't want to face the truth of it; she couldn't.

She looked into Tommy's eyes, searching for some kind of reassurance, but all she saw was uncertainty, the same fear she felt reflected back at her. Seeing fear in his eyes was crushing. But then she saw that brave face—the one that terrified her more than if he just let his emotions out for once. She knew it was for her, so she wouldn't know how torn up inside he was. He might as well have stabbed a dagger into her chest. It hurt just as much.

"Okay," she said, her voice a whisper that barely reached him. "I'll go with you."

Tommy exhaled, relief washing over him. He pulled her into a tight hug, holding her close like he never wanted to let go. "Thank you," he whispered into her hair. "Thank you, Lena."

But as Lena stood there, wrapped in Tommy's arms, she couldn't shake the feeling that everything was about to change. Tomorrow, they would drive to Madison, and after that... nothing would ever be the same again. She held back tears, but just barely, as his words echoed in her thoughts: *I might ship out the day after. Some guys have...*

30

The sky was still a deep, inky blue as Lena quietly shut the front door of her house behind her, the cool air of the early morning hitting her face. Her heart pounded in her chest, a mix of nerves and anticipation swirling inside her. She paused for a moment on the porch, her eyes darting toward her parents' bedroom window, hoping they wouldn't wake up. It wasn't like her to sneak out, but this wasn't just any morning.

Waiting at the curb, leaning against his 1957 Chevrolet Bel Air, was Tommy. The car's chrome accents gleamed faintly under the dim glow of the streetlights, and the soft rumble of the engine hummed in the background. Tommy straightened when he saw Lena, his expression tense but softened by the faintest hint of a smile.

Lena glanced over her shoulder once more before hurrying down the front steps and slipping into the passenger seat. As she closed the door, the weight of what they were doing hit her all at once. Tommy's march toward Vietnam had begun. Tomorrow, everything would be different.

"You ready?" Tommy asked quietly, his hands gripping the steering wheel as he looked over at her. There was something fragile in his voice, like he wasn't just asking about the drive.

Lena nodded, though her throat felt tight. "Yeah, I'm ready."

Without another word, Tommy pulled away from the curb, the familiar streets of Janesville passing by them in a blur of shadows and soft morning light.

The car was filled with the steady hum of the road beneath them, the Chevrolet Bel Air gliding smoothly along the highway. The sun hadn't fully risen yet, and the landscape was still bathed in that strange pre-dawn quiet. Lena stared out the window, watching as the open fields stretched out before them, the occasional farmhouse or silo breaking up the horizon.

For the first few miles, neither of them spoke. There was an unspoken understanding between them, a recognition of the enormity of what lay ahead. Tommy was leaving. He was being drafted. And after today, things would never be the same.

Lena finally broke the silence, her voice soft. "When were you going to tell me?"

Tommy glanced over at her, his jaw tightening. "I wanted to, but I didn't know how."

Lena's heart twisted. She understood why he hadn't told her, but it didn't make it hurt any less. "You should've told me, Tommy. I could've been there for you."

"I know," he said, his voice low, regret seeping into his words. "I just... I didn't want to make it real."

The quiet stretched between them again, heavy and uncomfortable. Lena didn't push further. She knew Tommy wasn't the type to talk about his fears, not openly. But she could feel it in the air—the weight of everything that was unsaid.

She'd been distant at times lately because she didn't know how to process what was happening. And because sometimes it hurt just to look at Tommy knowing what was coming. But now, it was here, and there was no avoiding it or pretending it hadn't been coming from them all along.

As they drove farther from Janesville, Lena tried to focus on the here and now, not on the unknown future that loomed ahead of them. The thought of him being drafted, sent off to basic training and then to Vietnam, felt too overwhelming to hold in her mind all at once. So instead, she shifted the conversation.

"Have you thought about what you'll do when you're there?" Lena asked, keeping her voice steady, even though the question weighed heavily on her heart.

Tommy shrugged, his eyes fixed on the road ahead. "Not much to think about. Basic training's gonna be tough. They'll probably try to break us down, then build us back up again."

"And after?" Lena pressed, feeling a knot form in her stomach. "When you're... you know, out there."

Tommy's grip tightened on the steering wheel, and Lena saw his shoulders tense. He didn't answer right away, and the silence between them felt like it was growing. When he finally spoke, his voice was quieter, more unsure than she had ever heard it.

"I don't know, Lena. I don't know what it'll be like. But I'm not... I'm not gonna let it change me."

Lena turned to him, her eyes searching his face. She wanted to believe that— wanted to believe that Tommy would come back the same person he was now. But deep down, she knew that wasn't how it worked. War changed people. It broke them, sometimes in ways that couldn't be undone.

She swallowed hard, forcing herself to stay composed. "I'll write to you. Every day."

Tommy smiled softly, though it didn't quite reach his eyes. "I'll look forward to that."

After that, the conversation lapsed again, the weight of their words hanging in the air. The silence was different now—deeper, more profound. Lena stared out the window, her mind racing with thoughts she couldn't quite pin down.

The road stretched on ahead of them, long and empty, flanked by the fields that marked the edge of towns and the open countryside beyond. The sun was beginning to rise, casting a warm, golden light over the landscape. It should have been beautiful, peaceful even, but all Lena could feel was the ticking clock, counting down the hours until everything changed.

Tommy reached over, his hand finding hers. His grip was firm but gentle, and in that moment, Lena felt a surge of emotion she wasn't sure she was ready for. She didn't know how to say what she was feeling—didn't know how to tell him that she was scared for him, scared for what their future might hold.

Instead, she squeezed his hand, letting the simple gesture speak for her. Tommy glanced over at her, his eyes softening, and for a moment, it felt like everything was okay. Like they were just two people on a drive, with no war hanging over them, no deployment notice waiting at the end of the road.

As they neared Madison, the buildings growing larger on the horizon, Lena knew the moment was coming when they would have to face what was happening. Tommy would go to the Military Entrance Processing Station, and when he came out, he would officially be a part of the military. After that, there would be no turning back.

"I keep thinking about the future," Lena said quietly, breaking the silence again. "About what happens when you get back."

Tommy turned to her, his brow furrowed. "When I get back?"

"Yeah," Lena said, her voice small. "What happens then? Do you... do you still want to settle down? Do all the things we talked about before?"

Tommy's face softened, and he gave her hand another squeeze. "Of course, Lena. I still want that. I want to come back, get a good job, marry you, and have a family. That's what I've always wanted."

Lena felt her heart twist again. She wanted to believe him, wanted to believe that everything would go back to the way it was before. But deep down, she knew she couldn't. Not really.

"But what if..." Lena's voice cracked, and she had to swallow her fears before continuing. "What if things don't go the way we plan?"

Tommy looked at her, his eyes serious. "We'll figure it out. Together."

Lena nodded, but the words didn't comfort her as much as she wished they would. She knew Tommy meant well—knew he loved her—but there was a part of her that couldn't shake the feeling that she was losing him, that the war was pulling him away from her in ways neither of them could control.

As they reached the outskirts of Madison, the city came into view, its buildings and streets coming to life as the sun climbed higher in the sky. The weight of the moment settled heavily over them, and Lena felt a lump form in her throat as they neared the Military Entrance Processing Station.

Tommy pulled the car into a parking spot, the engine idling for a moment before he turned it off. They sat there in silence, the world around them moving on as if nothing had changed, even though everything was different now.

"Are you sure you want to wait here?" Tommy asked, his voice soft. "You don't have to, you know."

Lena turned to him, her eyes filled with unshed tears. "I want to. I want to be here when you come out."

Tommy nodded, his jaw tight as he leaned over and kissed her forehead gently. "I'll be back soon."

Lena watched him get out of the car, her heart pounding as she saw him walk toward the building. She wanted to run after him, to stop him, to hold onto him for just a little longer. But she knew she couldn't. All she could do now was wait.

As Tommy disappeared through the doors, Lena sat back in her seat, staring out at the city around her. She knew that this was just the beginning—that after today, there would be more goodbyes, more waiting, more uncertainty. But for now, all she could do was hold onto the hope that somehow, they would make it through.

Lena let herself cry then. Tears she'd been holding back for so long. Tears that streamed down her cheeks just as hard as she'd fought to hold them back so no one—not her parents, not Sarah, and certainly not Tommy—would know how afraid she was. For him. For her. For everything.

Love wasn't supposed to hurt this much. But it did. It hurt so damn much and so damn deep her body convulsed over and over and over, as tears flowed in a stream broken only when it hurt so bad it seemed there was nothing but pain—that there had never been anything but pain. An eerie calm found her then, as if she'd cried all the tears that would ever be inside her.

31

The car sat quietly in the parking lot of the Military Entrance Processing Station in Madison, its engine turned off, and the world around it slowly waking up as the city came to life. Lena sat in the passenger seat, her hands balled into fists, her guitar case in the backseat behind her, though she hadn't touched it since they'd arrived. She wasn't sure if she could. Not with everything swirling inside her head.

Tommy had been inside for over two hours now, going through the pre-induction physical exam. The weight of the situation pressed down on her, suffocating in both its uncertainty and certainty. She leaned back in her seat, staring out at the people passing by on the street, wondering how they could all just go about their lives when hers felt like it was being torn apart.

Her thoughts were a tangled mess of emotions—fear for Tommy, for what the war might do to him; frustration at the helplessness of it all, that he had no choice in the matter; and the slow-growing dread that their plans for the future, the life they'd dreamed of, might never happen.

And then there was her music.

It was always there, humming in the back of her mind, like a steady pulse that wouldn't let her go. Was she holding on so tight to it because she couldn't—wouldn't be able to—hold on to Tommy? Was it the one thing grounding her?

"A Change Will Come" played in her thoughts, the lyrics she'd been piecing together suddenly taking on a deeper meaning. The change she'd been writing about wasn't just the cultural revolution happening in the world—it was personal, too. The world was shifting beneath her feet, and she wasn't sure she knew how to stand on solid ground anymore.

Lena felt the notebook in her bag calling to her, the blank pages waiting to be filled with the emotions swirling inside her. But she hesitated. Could she put it all into words? Could she capture this moment, this overwhelming sense of being caught between two worlds—the life she wanted with Tommy and the dreams she had for herself? Or would her life forever after feel like it was on hold, waiting for her to be able to take a breath?

She ran her fingers through her hair, her eyes drifting closed for a moment as she tried to calm the storm inside her. She wished she could be strong for Tommy, like she had promised. But the truth was, she wasn't sure she could handle this. She wasn't sure she could watch him leave, knowing he might not come back the same, knowing he might not come back at all.

Putting distance between herself and Tommy lately had been about more than uncertainty or anything Tommy said or did. She knew that now. It had been about not wanting to feel what she felt right now. She'd let herself care too much, fall too deep. She knew right then that if he told her he loved her and she said it back one more time—*one more time*—there would be nothing left of her heart to give to him or anyone. For the whole of her heart would be his. Forever. Always.

The sound of the car door opening snapped Lena out of her thoughts. She blinked, sitting up straighter as Tommy slid into the driver's seat, the weight of the morning written all over his face.

"Hey," he said quietly, his voice thick with exhaustion. He didn't look at her right away, his hands gripping the steering wheel as if he needed something solid to hold onto.

Lena swallowed hard, her heart pounding in her chest. "How did it go?"

Tommy let out a long breath, finally turning to look at her. "I'm 1-A," he said simply, his eyes searching hers for some kind of reaction. "Fit for duty."

Lena felt the air leave her lungs, even though she had been expecting it. 1-A. It was the classification that meant he was healthy and ready to serve. "Did they…?" She paused, couldn't let herself say the words. "Did they say when?"

Tommy shook his head, his frustration evident. "No one in there could tell me anything. It's all just... up in the air."

Lena's mind spun. "But... you don't know when that will be?"

"A phone call or a letter," Tommy continued, his voice flat. "That's when I'll know where and when I have to report for official induction."

Lena sat back in her seat, processing the information. As she'd waited in the car, she had prepared herself for the worst—that Tommy would be leaving today, that they'd have to say goodbye right there. But now, they had more time than they thought. Time they weren't sure they'd have.

Tommy ran a hand over his face, letting out a small, humorless laugh. "I thought I'd feel relieved, you know? Knowing I've got more time. But it's just... hanging over us now."

Lena nodded, understanding exactly what he meant. The uncertainty wasn't a relief—it was a delay, a brief reprieve that didn't change the fact that their lives were still on the edge of something irreversible. The war was still waiting, looming just out of reach.

Tommy started the car, pulling out of the parking lot and onto the road. They drove in silence for a while, the tension between them thick, like a wall they couldn't quite break through.

Lena stared out the window, her mind racing with thoughts of what they should do with this time they'd been given. Should they try to pretend everything was normal? Should they make the most of every moment, knowing it might be the last time they had together before the war took him away?

"Maybe we should go somewhere," Lena suggested quietly, not looking at him. "Just... get away for a little while. Spend the day together."

Tommy glanced at her, a small smile tugging at the corner of his mouth. "Yeah? Where would we go?"

Lena shrugged. "I don't know. Somewhere quiet. Somewhere... just us."

Tommy was quiet for a moment, his fingers tapping lightly on the steering wheel. "That sounds nice. But..."

Lena turned to look at him, her heart sinking at the hesitation in his voice. "But what? We've been so busy pretending, but knowing this was coming. Now it's happened... happening. And all I want to do is go back to yesterday."

Tommy sighed, shaking his head. "I don't know, Lena. It's like... no matter what we do, this thing is always gonna be there. Hanging over us."

Lena felt her chest tighten. She knew he was right. No matter how hard they tried to escape it, the draft and the war were always there, lingering just out of sight, waiting to pull them apart.

"I don't want it to ruin everything," Tommy said softly, his voice breaking slightly. "I don't want this... hanging over us every second. But I don't know how to stop it."

Lena reached out, resting her hand on his arm. "We don't have to figure it all out right now. We don't have to... fix everything today."

Tommy nodded, though the tension in his body didn't ease. "But we should make the most of this time, right? Before... before everything changes?"

Lena hesitated, her mind swirling with the enormity of what he was saying. Make the most of the time. The words echoed in her head, and she wasn't sure what they really meant. Were they supposed to act like nothing was wrong? Like they could just keep going as if the war wasn't looming over them?

Or was it all just... too much?

"I don't know," Lena admitted quietly, her voice barely above a whisper. "I don't know if I can do that."

Tommy's grip on the steering wheel tightened, and for a moment, Lena thought he might get angry. But instead, he just sighed, his shoulders slumping in defeat.

"Yeah," he said softly. "Me neither."

Lena leaned her head against the window, watching the landscape pass by, her heart aching with the weight of everything she couldn't say. They had more time than they thought. But time wasn't the issue. It was the uncertainty, the fear, the knowledge that nothing they did would or could change what was ahead.

Just outside Madison, Tommy pulled over to the side of the road and turned off the engine. "Lena..."

She turned to look at him, her eyes meeting his. He looked lost, like he was searching for something, anything to hold onto.

"I love you," he said quietly, his voice raw. "You know that, right? I love you so damn much it hurts."

Lena nodded, her throat too tight to speak.

Tommy leaned in, resting his forehead against hers. "I just... I don't want to lose you."

Lena closed her eyes, feeling the warmth of his skin, the familiar scent of him surrounding her. "You won't, Tommy," she whispered, though the words felt hollow because they weren't the three words she wanted to say back to him.

They stayed like that for a long time, neither of them moving, neither of them speaking. Just holding onto the moment, knowing that no matter how hard they tried, the war would come for them both eventually.

When Lena finally opened her eyes and looked at Tommy she saw tears in the corners of his eyes. She knew the tears weren't for himself, but for her. For everything that could have been—would have been—without the draft, without the war. "I love you, Tommy," she finally told him. "I don't want you to leave. I want you to stay. I want to be here with you. In this place. In this moment. Turn the car around. Let's go back to Madison. Let's have the day we should have had all along."

32

The late morning sun was starting to warm the streets of Madison, casting a golden light over the quaint shops and cafés lining State Street. Tommy guided his Bel Air down the lively road, the sound of street chatter, the hum of pedestrians, and the occasional honking of cars filling the air.

Next to him, Lena sat quietly, her thoughts a jumble of emotions. They had more time—Tommy's induction wouldn't be immediate, but the reprieve wasn't the relief she thought it would be. There was still a clock ticking over them, and she wasn't sure how to make the most of this extra time they'd been given.

Tommy, sensing her tension, glanced over. "Hey, I know it's been a heavy day. How about we try to enjoy the rest of it, huh?"

Lena forced a small smile, appreciating his effort to lighten the mood. "Yeah, let's try."

As they drove further down State Street, a record shop caught Lena's eye. The vibrant vinyl-covered windows and large sign—MadCity Records—beckoned to her like a siren's call. Tommy noticed the way her eyes lingered on it, and before she could say anything, he pulled over and parked.

"C'mon," he said with a grin, "let's go check it out."

The bell above the door jingled as they stepped inside, the rich smell of old vinyl and new music washing over them. The walls were lined with records, their covers bursting with color, and the soft hum of a Peter, Paul and Mary song played in the background. The shop was dimly lit, with narrow aisles and crates full of records that seemed to stretch back into another world.

Lena's eyes widened as she looked around, her fingers already itching to flip through the stacks of albums. Her heart swelled a little. Music had always been her escape, her way of processing the noise in her head. Being here felt like finding a moment of peace in the middle of the storm.

Tommy leaned against the counter, watching her with a soft smile. "Take your time. I'll see if I can get the lowdown on what else we can cram into today."

Lena nodded, already drifting toward the nearest stack of records. As her fingers danced across the covers, she found herself lingering over familiar names—Bob Dylan, The Byrds, Joni Mitchell—artists whose music had shaped her own songwriting and fueled her dreams.

She picked up a Bob Dylan album and held it in her hands, tracing the familiar cover art. The lyrics to "A Change Will Come" floated through her mind, and she thought about how much change was coming not just in her life, but in the world around her. The Vietnam War, the growing protests, the shifting role of women—it all felt like a wave they were barely keeping up with.

The song playing overhead changed to "There But For Fortune," Joan Baez's melancholy voice echoing through the shop. Lena closed her eyes for a moment, letting the music wash over her. She felt the lyrics settle into her bones, the familiar ache of wanting more than the life laid out in front of her.

Tommy returned, smiling wide as he tapped her on the shoulder. "You ready to have an unforgettable day in Madison?"

Lena looked up, her eyes softening at his attempt to pull her out of her thoughts. "Yeah, I think I am."

"Great! I talked to the guy at the counter, and he gave me the scoop. First, we'll walk State Street, check out the shops, maybe grab some lunch. Then we can head up to the Capitol for a bit—he said the view is great from up there. And after that... I thought we could check out Picnic Point for some peace and quiet."

Lena smiled. "That sounds perfect."

Tommy grinned, pleased with himself. "And tonight, I'm taking you to the Memorial Union Terrace. They have live music by the lake—figured that'd be right up your alley."

The thought of sitting by the lake, listening to music, felt like just what she needed. "It is."

As they walked down State Street, hand in hand, the bustling energy of Madison wrapped around them. The street was full of life—students milling about, couples window-shopping, and groups of friends grabbing coffee or ice cream at small cafés. The eclectic mix of shops was an invitation to explore, and Lena found herself getting lost in the sights, sounds, and smells of the city.

They stopped at a small diner for lunch, the conversation light and easy. Tommy seemed to relax, the weight of his draft notice momentarily pushed aside. Lena watched him as he laughed at something the waitress said, his face softening, and for the first time all day, she felt a flicker of hope. Maybe they could still find happiness in the time they had left.

After lunch, they made their way to the Capitol. The grand white dome rose above them as they walked up the steps, the architecture imposing and beautiful. Once inside, they wandered through the halls, taking in the intricate details of the building. The rotunda was awe-inspiring, its painted murals telling the story of Wisconsin's history.

Tommy led them to a balcony, where they could look out over the city. From this vantage point, Madison felt endless—the streets stretching out in all directions, the lakes glimmering in the distance, the university campus bustling with life.

Lena leaned against the railing, taking it all in. "It's beautiful," she whispered.

Tommy nodded, his arm around her. "Yeah, it is."

For a moment, the world felt still, like the weight of the future didn't matter. Lena closed her eyes, letting herself breathe in the moment, savoring the peace while it lasted.

The drive to Picnic Point took them away from the city and toward the edge of Lake Mendota, the landscape becoming more serene as they neared the water. When they arrived, they parked the car and walked down one of the trails, the sound of the lake lapping against the shore in the distance.

Picnic Point was quiet, secluded—a stretch of land that jutted out into the lake, surrounded by trees and nature. The peace of the place enveloped them as they found a spot near the water to sit.

Lena kicked off her shoes, letting her toes sink into the soft earth. Tommy sat beside her, his hand brushing against hers.

"I wish we could stay here forever," Lena said softly, her eyes on the water.

"Me too," Tommy replied, his voice low. "But we can't, can we?"

Lena shook her head, the reality settling back in. "No, we can't."

For a while, they sat in silence, watching the water ripple in the gentle breeze. The weight of everything—the draft, the war, the uncertain future—hung in the air between them, but for now, they were together. And that was enough.

As the sun began to set, they made their way to the Memorial Union Terrace, where the iconic terrace chairs sat scattered along the shore of Lake Mendota.

The air was cool, but the atmosphere was alive with the sound of live music, the twang of guitars and the soft rhythm of drums filling the space.

Lena and Tommy found a spot near the edge of the lake, sitting close together as the band played. The sun was sinking lower, casting a golden glow over the water, and the sky was painted in hues of pink and orange.

The music wrapped around them, the melodies blending with the soft murmur of conversation around them. Lena rested her head on Tommy's shoulder, her heart swelling with both love and sadness. This day—this perfect, fleeting day—was a gift. But it was also a reminder of what was waiting for them.

"I'll remember this," Lena whispered, her voice soft. "No matter what happens, I'll remember today."

Tommy pressed a kiss to her temple. "Me too."

They stayed like that until the sun disappeared below the horizon, the music still playing, the lights of the terrace twinkling in the evening air.

For a few more hours, they pretended that the world wasn't about to pull them apart.

33

The soft glow of the library's lights greeted them as Tommy and Lena walked toward the grand doors of the Memorial Library at Library Mall, the final stop on what had been a magical day in Madison. The day had been full of everything—music, quiet moments, laughter, and now this. Books. Tommy had remembered, as he always did, that Lena's love of books ran deep, maybe even as deep as her love for music.

"I know how much you love books," Tommy said, smiling softly as he led her inside. "I figured it was the perfect way to end a perfect day."

Lena's heart swelled at the thoughtfulness behind it. Tommy, with all his focus on the future, had still carved out space for her dreams—her music, her love of learning, her curiosity about the world. She squeezed his hand as they stepped through the library doors, the quiet, scholarly atmosphere immediately embracing them.

The smell of old paper and leather-bound volumes greeted Lena as they walked past the towering shelves. The vastness of the space made her feel like they were stepping into another world, one where the pressures of draft notices and war didn't exist.

Lena drifted toward the section on music theory and songwriting, her fingers gently brushing the spines of the books as she walked by. Titles like "The Art of Folk Music" and "Protest Songs of the 20th Century" caught her eye, reminding her of how intertwined her personal dreams were with the shifting landscape of the 1960s.

She pulled one of the books from the shelf and flipped through its pages, her mind whirling with new ideas. Music was more than just an escape for her—it was her way of processing the world, of finding her voice in a society that often didn't value the voices of young women like her. The book spoke of how songs could be a force for change, a way to protest injustices and rally people together.

Her thoughts drifted to her unfinished songs, especially the one she had been working on since that morning—"A Change Will Come." It wasn't just about her anymore. It was about the world she lived in, the wars being fought, both at home and overseas. It was about the shift she felt happening around her, the revolution brewing beneath the surface.

Tommy leaned against the bookshelf, watching her as she flipped through the pages, a soft smile playing on his lips. "Find something good?"

"Yeah," Lena said, her voice distant as she thought about everything the day had given her. "This one's really good."

For a moment, everything felt perfect. The way the world outside seemed to pause while they were in the library, how the day had been filled with little pieces of what made their relationship work—his strength, her dreams, their love for each other. Lena tucked the book under her arm, ready to check it out.

"Thanks for this," she said, meeting his eyes. "It really is the perfect way to end the day."

Tommy smiled wider, stepping closer to her. "I just want you to be happy, Lena. Even if..."

Lena reached out and took his hand. "I am."

When they left the library, the calm of their perfect day was shattered almost immediately by the sound of raised voices. Chanting. Drums. The rumble of a crowd's energy filled the air as they stepped out into the cool night. Across Library Mall, a large group of protesters was gathering, marching toward the Capitol.

Lena's stomach clenched as she recognized the tone of the chants. "No More War!" echoed through the street, and she could see people carrying signs that read things like "End the Draft" and "Bring Our Boys Home."

Tommy stiffened beside her, his body going rigid as he took in the scene. The crowd was growing, their voices loud and angry as they moved toward the heart of the city, their signs bobbing in time with the rhythm of their chants.

Lena swallowed hard, glancing at Tommy. She knew what the protests meant to him—how much he hated being caught between his sense of duty and the rising tide of anti-war sentiment. Tommy had always been the All-American boy, proud of his country, proud of his family's service. But now, he was facing a future that he didn't want, a war he didn't believe in, and the protesters only made that harder.

As the crowd moved closer, one of the protesters—a man in his early twenties—caught sight of Tommy's short, clean-cut hair and squared shoulders. The man sneered as he passed, shaking his head. "Another soldier-boy ready to die for the machine," he spat, loud enough for Tommy to hear.

Lena tensed, her heart racing as she looked at Tommy, hoping—praying—that he wouldn't take the bait. But she could see the anger building in his eyes, the way his jaw clenched tight.

"Tommy, let's just go," she urged quietly, tugging on his arm.

But it was too late. Another protester shouted, "How does it feel knowing you're just cannon fodder for a war that doesn't mean shit?" The words were like a match to a fuse, and before Lena could stop him, Tommy turned toward the voice, his face hard with fury.

"What did you just say?" Tommy growled, stepping forward.

The protester smirked, clearly enjoying the confrontation. "I said, you're just a cog in the machine, man. They're gonna send you off to fight their dirty war, and you'll be lucky if you come back in one piece."

Lena's stomach dropped as she watched Tommy's fists clench at his sides. She could see the war raging inside him—the pull of his pride, the anger at being put in this position, and the helplessness of knowing he had no real choice.

"Tommy, don't," Lena whispered, stepping in front of him. "Please. Let's just go."

But Tommy wasn't hearing her anymore. His anger had taken over, and he pushed past her, shoving the protester in the chest. "Say that to my face again."

The protester stumbled back, his eyes flashing with surprise before narrowing in defiance. "You wanna fight, soldier boy?"

Within seconds, a shouting match had broken out, drawing the attention of other protesters. The crowd began to close in, their chants rising in volume as tension crackled in the air. Lena's heart pounded in her chest as she watched, panic surging through her. This wasn't how the day was supposed to end.

A small group of protesters began to push against Tommy, their voices rising with angry taunts. "You're just a pawn! Stop playing their game!" one shouted.

Tommy's fists clenched, his muscles taut, ready to swing.

"Tommy, please!" Lena shouted, grabbing his arm again, pulling him back. She could feel the heat of the crowd, their anger, their energy. It was overwhelming.

But this time, Tommy heard her. He looked down at Lena, his chest heaving with adrenaline, his eyes still burning with anger. Slowly, he stepped back, his hands still balled into fists at his sides. "Let's go," he muttered, his voice tight with barely controlled rage.

Lena nodded quickly, her heart racing as she led him away from the crowd. The protesters kept chanting behind them, but Tommy stayed silent, his jaw clenched as they hurried back to the car.

When they finally reached the car, Tommy slammed the door shut, his breathing still heavy as he gripped the steering wheel. Lena sat beside him, her own heart pounding from the tension of the encounter.

For a long time, neither of them spoke. The perfect day they had shared felt like a distant memory, swallowed up by the chaos of the protest and the harsh reality of the world they were living in.

"I hate this," Tommy muttered, his voice low and full of frustration. "I hate feeling like I'm just... stuck."

Lena looked at him, her heart aching for the boy she loved. "I know," she whispered. "But fighting them won't fix it."

Tommy let out a bitter laugh. "Feels like nothing will fix it."

They sat there in silence for a while, the only sound the distant chants of the protesters fading into the night. Lena reached over and took his hand, holding it tightly in hers. They had more time, yes—but that time was still overshadowed by everything they couldn't escape.

"I'm sorry," Tommy said quietly, his voice cracking. "I just... I couldn't listen to them talk about it like that."

Lena nodded, understanding. "It's okay."

But even as she said the words, she knew that nothing about this was okay. The war was pulling them apart, even when they were together, and the world was changing faster than either of them could keep up with.

For now, all they could do was hold on to each other—and hope that somehow, it would be enough.

34

Lena awoke to the soft glow of the early morning sun filtering through her curtains, but the warmth of the light did nothing to quell the tension she felt brewing. The house was too quiet, the kind of silence that came before a storm. She knew what was waiting for her downstairs. Her father always left for work early, but today, he hadn't left yet.

They know.

She took a deep breath and sat up, feeling the weight of the previous day still hanging over her. The ride to Madison, Tommy's pre-induction exam, the day they had spent trying to hold on to something that was slipping through their fingers—it was all catching up to her now. And her parents had found out.

The moment her feet hit the floor, she could hear the faint murmur of voices downstairs. Her mother's softer tones were unmistakable, but her father's voice—usually so steady and controlled—sounded sharper than usual. They were talking about her. She knew it.

She got dressed slowly, trying to gather herself for whatever conversation lay ahead. There was no use in putting it off.

Lena stepped quietly into the kitchen, the smell of coffee and freshly made toast wafting through the air, but the usual comfort of breakfast felt heavy and foreign today. Her father stood by the table, already dressed in his work clothes, his lunch pail resting beside him. Her mother was bustling near the stove, but Lena could see the tension in her shoulders.

Her father turned the moment he saw her. His face was hard, his expression unreadable, but his eyes were heavy with disappointment.

"Lena." His voice was steady but clipped, as if he were holding back the full force of his emotions. "The school called yesterday. You weren't there. Your mother had to find out from them that you skipped. Care to explain where you were?"

Lena's stomach knotted. She had known this was coming, but standing here now, under the weight of her father's stern gaze, it felt overwhelming. She swallowed hard, trying to find her voice.

"I... I went to Madison," she admitted quietly, her eyes flicking from her father to her mother, who had turned around, her face a mixture of concern and quiet frustration.

Her father raised an eyebrow. "With Tommy, I'm guessing?"

Lena nodded. "Yes. He had his pre-induction exam yesterday, and he asked me to go with him."

Her father's expression darkened. "And you didn't think it was necessary to tell us?"

"I... I didn't want you to worry," Lena replied, her voice small. "It was important to him, and... I wanted to be there."

"You didn't want us to worry?" Her father's voice grew harder, more incredulous. "So instead, you decided to skip school, lie to your mother and me by omission, and leave without a word?"

Lena felt her throat tighten. "I didn't mean to lie."

"But that's what you did," her father shot back, his tone cutting through the air. "You're about to graduate. You've got your future to think about, and skipping school like this is no way to go about it."

Her mother stepped in then, her voice softer but firm. "Your father and I are concerned, Lena. We know how much you care about Tommy, but you have your own life to live, your own responsibilities. You're going to have to figure out where your priorities are."

Lena's chest ached as her mother's words sank in. Where your priorities are. They didn't understand. Tommy was leaving—soon, maybe too soon—and she had wanted to be there for him. But now she was left wondering if she was sacrificing too much of herself for something that was slipping out of her control.

"I'm sorry," Lena said, her voice thick with emotion. "I just... I wanted to be there for him. He's scared. I'm scared. And it all feels so... uncertain."

Her father's gaze softened ever so slightly at her admission, but his voice remained firm. "I get that, Lena. But running off to Madison without a word isn't the answer. We've raised you to be responsible, to think about your future. You can't let Tommy's situation throw everything off course."

Lena bit her lip, her heart heavy with the weight of her father's words. Her future. It was a constant pressure, something everyone seemed to have mapped out for her—but it wasn't her map. Her dreams, her music, they were so often brushed aside in the face of what others expected of her. But how could she explain that? How could she make them see?

The tension hung in the air, thick and stifling, until suddenly, a knock echoed from the front door.

Her mother, grateful for the distraction, wiped her hands on her apron and went to answer it. A moment later, Sarah's familiar voice floated in from the hallway, bringing a small sense of relief to the room.

"Hey, Lena!" Sarah called out, her voice cheerful as ever, though it softened when she saw Lena's mother standing by the door. "I just wanted to check in on you. You weren't at school yesterday, and I got a little worried."

Lena exhaled, the tension loosening its grip on her chest. Sarah always had a way of showing up at just the right time, like a ray of sunshine cutting through the darkest clouds.

"I'm okay," Lena said, walking over to her friend. "Just... a lot going on."

Sarah looked at Lena's parents, sensing the tension in the air. "I can see that," she said gently. "Mind if I steal her for a bit?"

Lena's mother, grateful for the reprieve, nodded. "Go ahead, girls. But Lena, we'll talk more later."

Lena knew the conversation wasn't over, but for now, she could escape. She grabbed her jacket and followed Sarah out the door, the fresh air a welcome change from the heavy atmosphere inside the house.

The two girls walked in silence for a few minutes, the crisp morning air filling their lungs. Lena kept her eyes on the pavement, her mind still reeling from the confrontation with her father. Sarah glanced at her, concern etched on her face.

"Do you want to talk about it?" Sarah asked gently, her voice full of understanding.

Lena sighed. "I went to Madison with Tommy yesterday. He had his pre-induction exam. I didn't tell my parents, and now they're pissed."

Sarah nodded, her expression softening. "That's a big deal, Lena. The pre-induction exam, I mean. I'm not surprised you went with him."

"Yeah, well, my dad doesn't exactly see it that way," Lena muttered, kicking at a stray rock. "He thinks I'm throwing my future away by running off with Tommy. And my mom... she just wants me to be some perfect little housewife."

Sarah frowned. "I'm sorry. That's a lot of pressure."

Lena shrugged, her frustration bubbling to the surface. "It's just... I don't know what to do anymore. I love Tommy, but everything's happening so fast, and I don't even know who I'm supposed to be in all of this. My music... my dreams... it feels like I'm losing myself."

Sarah stopped walking and turned to face her friend, her expression serious. "You don't have to choose, you know. You can love Tommy and still go after your dreams. It doesn't have to be one or the other."

Lena blinked, surprised by Sarah's words. "You really think that?"

Sarah smiled. "I know that. You've always been someone who's known exactly what you want, Lena. Don't let anyone—Tommy, your parents, even yourself—make you forget that."

Lena felt a lump rise in her throat, a mixture of gratitude and emotion welling up inside her. Sarah always had a way of grounding her, reminding her of who she really was.

"Thanks," Lena said softly, her voice full of gratitude. "I needed to hear that."

Sarah wrapped an arm around her, pulling her into a quick hug. "Anytime. Now, let's get you through today without any more drama, okay?"

Lena smiled for what felt like the first time that morning. "Deal."

And with that, the tension of the morning began to ease, though the weight of the choices ahead still lingered in the back of Lena's mind. She knew there were hard decisions to make—about Tommy, about her future—but for now, she had her friend by her side, and that was enough.

35

The familiar scent of fresh dough filled the air as Lena and Sarah entered the Home Economics classroom, where the tables were already prepped for a bread-making lesson. Large bowls of flour, measuring cups, and yeast packets were set out at each station, and Mrs. Carver, their stern but knowledgeable teacher, was already demonstrating how to knead the dough on the large prep table at the front of the room.

Mrs. Carver, her hair pulled tightly into a neat bun, didn't waste any time getting to the lesson. "Ladies, today we'll be baking homemade bread. A skill every woman should have in her repertoire. Bread baking requires patience, attention to detail, and care—just like managing a home." She gave a pointed look around the room as if to remind them that these were life skills they needed.

Lena glanced at Sarah, who was already eyeing the ingredients on their table, ready to start. "This is one of my favorite lessons," Sarah whispered excitedly. "There's something so comforting about fresh bread, don't you think?"

Lena offered a small smile, but her heart wasn't really in it. Her mind was still tangled up in the events of the past few days—Tommy's pre-induction exam, the tense morning with her parents, and the conflict she felt growing inside her. She reached for the flour, mechanically measuring it into the bowl as Mrs. Carver continued her instructions.

"Be sure to measure accurately," Mrs. Carver said, pacing around the room. "Bread making is an art, but it's also a science. Get the measurements wrong, and your dough will either rise too much or not at all."

As Lena and Sarah mixed their ingredients, Lena's thoughts wandered. Tommy was on her mind, as he always seemed to be lately, but more than that, she felt an increasing tension between the life everyone expected her to live and the life she wanted to live. She stirred the flour into the water and yeast mixture, watching as the dough began to form.

"Everything okay?" Sarah asked softly, glancing at Lena as she kneaded her dough.

Lena shrugged, her hands working the dough more aggressively than necessary. "Just... a lot on my mind."

Sarah didn't push, but she gave Lena a sympathetic look. "Well, if you need to talk, I'm here."

Mrs. Carver passed by their station, inspecting their work with a critical eye. "Lena, don't overwork the dough," she said, her voice stern but not unkind. "You need to be gentle, or the bread won't turn out the way you want it to."

Lena paused, staring down at the dough beneath her hands. Gentle. That's what everyone wanted her to be. Gentle. Obedient. Predictable. But the tension building inside her didn't feel gentle—it felt like a storm, like something that was about to break free. She forced herself to ease her grip on the dough, taking a deep breath as she did.

By the time Civics class rolled around, Lena was feeling even more restless. As she slid into her seat next to Joe, she found herself scanning the classroom, her mind still heavy with thoughts of Tommy, the war, and the uncertainty of everything that lay ahead.

Mr. Benson, their passionate and sharp-minded teacher, was already at the front of the room, scribbling today's lesson on the chalkboard. The words "The Vietnam War: Policy and Protest" stood out starkly against the chalkboard, sending a fresh wave of anxiety through Lena. This was the last thing she wanted to talk about today.

"Alright, class," Mr. Benson began, turning to face them. "Today, we're going to be discussing the political climate surrounding the Vietnam War. Specifically, we'll be looking at how U.S. policy has evolved over the last decade and the growing anti-war sentiment both at home and abroad."

Joe nudged Lena gently, his expression serious. "Looks like today's going to hit close to home."

Lena nodded, her stomach twisting as Mr. Benson continued. She had always admired Mr. Benson's willingness to challenge authority and encourage critical thinking in his students, but today, the topic felt too personal, too raw.

"The draft has been one of the most contentious issues surrounding the war," Mr. Benson said, pacing in front of the class. "Many young men are being sent to fight in a war they don't understand, while back home, protests are growing louder. People are asking hard questions—why are we fighting this war? What are we fighting for?"

Lena felt Joe's eyes on her, but she kept her gaze fixed on her notebook. She could feel the weight of the room, the tension that had been building in the country for years now, creeping into the classroom.

"What do you think?" Joe whispered, leaning in slightly. "About the war?"

Lena hesitated, the words choking in her throat. She wanted to support Tommy—he was doing what he thought was right, after all. But everything about the war, the violence, the uncertainty, and the way it was tearing people apart—it didn't feel right to her.

"I don't know," Lena whispered back, her voice tight. "Yesterday, Tommy had his pre-induction exam, and... it's just all so much. He's scared. I'm scared. But what am I supposed to do? Just sit here and watch him get shipped off to fight in a war neither of us understands?"

Joe's expression softened, the usual fire in his eyes dimming for a moment. "You're not supposed to just sit here. You've got your music, Lena. Use it. Speak up."

Lena shook her head. "It's not that simple. I want to support him. I want to be there for him, but I also want to... I don't know, express myself, I guess.

Through my music. But it feels like no matter what I do, someone's going to be disappointed."

Before Joe could respond, Mr. Benson's voice cut through the room again. "Many people argue that this war is unnecessary. That we're fighting for reasons that don't align with the values we claim to uphold as a country. Others, however, believe that it's our duty to fight for freedom, to protect democracy abroad."

The class was quiet, the weight of the topic pressing down on them.

"I want you all to think about this," Mr. Benson continued. "What does freedom mean to you? And how far are you willing to go to protect it? Whether that's through military service, protest, or something else entirely."

Lena's heart raced. Freedom. That word had been echoing in her mind for days now, but she wasn't sure what it meant to her anymore. Was it freedom from the expectations of her parents? Freedom to chase her dreams and make music? Or was it the freedom to live a life where she didn't have to worry about the war taking away the people she loved?

She glanced at Joe, who was watching Mr. Benson intently, his brow furrowed in thought. Joe had always been vocal about his opposition to the war, but for Lena, it wasn't so clear-cut. She wanted to be brave like him, to speak out through her songs, but she also didn't want to alienate Tommy or disappoint her parents. It felt like she was caught between two worlds—one pulling her toward her music and self-expression, and the other anchoring her to the life she had always known.

After a long moment of silence, Mr. Benson called for an open discussion. Students hesitated at first, but eventually, a few brave souls began to share their thoughts. Some spoke about their family members who were serving, others voiced their fears about the draft. The room buzzed with quiet conversation, but Lena couldn't bring herself to speak up.

Instead, she turned to Joe, her voice barely a whisper. "What if I don't know where I stand yet?"

Joe leaned in, his voice low but encouraging. "That's okay. You don't have to have all the answers right now. But you do have to find your voice, Lena. Whether it's through music or something else, you can't stay silent forever."

Lena felt a knot in her chest. She knew Joe was right. She couldn't keep living in the shadows of other people's expectations. She had to start figuring out what freedom meant for her, even if it meant disappointing some of the people she loved.

36

The classroom for Business Math felt like a world away from the swirling emotional intensity of Civics. The walls were lined with charts displaying interest rates, compound interest formulas, and neat examples of household budgets. At the front of the room stood Mrs. Mabel Price, her steely gaze sweeping across the students as they filtered in.

Lena slipped into her seat between Bill and Joe, her mind still buzzing with the conversation from Civics. The stark contrast between discussing the fate of the world and learning how to balance a budget felt almost surreal.

"Alright, class," Mrs. Price said in her usual brisk tone. "Today, we'll be diving into compound interest. This is something you'll all need to know, especially if you ever plan on taking out a loan for a car or a house. It's a life skill, not just a math problem."

Joe rolled his eyes and leaned over to whisper to Lena, "Because what I really need to know right now is how to calculate the interest on a car loan when half of us are about to get drafted."

Lena stifled a smile but stayed focused on the lesson. Despite the monotony of the subject, Mrs. Price had a way of keeping the class in line. Her approach was firm, her voice sharp, and she didn't tolerate distractions. "You might find this boring now," Mrs. Price continued, "but when you're in the real world, you'll be glad you learned it."

As she wrote a series of equations on the board, Lena glanced over at Bill, who was already scribbling down the formulas with ease. Business Math seemed to come naturally to him, a boy with a clear path laid out before him—football, work at his father's business, marry Sarah, settle down. Bill represented the security and certainty that felt so distant to Lena right now.

Joe, on the other hand, wasn't even pretending to pay attention. His notebook was open, but instead of taking notes, he was doodling the same anarchist symbols he always scrawled in the margins. Joe's mind was somewhere far away from interest rates and savings plans.

Mrs. Price called on Bill to solve a problem at the board, and he walked up confidently, solving the equation without breaking a sweat.

"That's the future businessman of Janesville right there," Joe muttered under his breath. "Meanwhile, I'll be off burning my draft card."

Lena gave him a sideways glance. "You really think that's going to make a difference?"

Joe shrugged. "Better than sitting around doing nothing."

The shift to English Literature was a welcome one for Lena. The room was brighter, the posters on the walls less about math and more about words—famous quotes from writers like F. Scott Fitzgerald, Emily Dickinson, and J.D. Salinger. Mr. Joseph Hastings stood at the front of the class, his hair wild and his tie slightly askew, his usual look of being deep in thought, even while teaching.

"Alright, everyone, let's continue our discussion on *The Catcher in the Rye*," Mr. Hastings said, his voice full of enthusiasm. "Holden Caulfield. The eternal rebel. The kid who feels out of place in a world that keeps trying to force him into a mold. Sound familiar to anyone?"

Lena sat up a little straighter. If there was a character she could relate to right now, it was Holden Caulfield—lost, misunderstood, searching for some kind of meaning in a world that felt fake and constricting. Her eyes flicked over to Joe, who was also sitting up, a rare occurrence for him in any class other than Civics.

"So, why do you think Holden spends so much time searching for authenticity?" Mr. Hastings asked, looking around the room. "What is it about the world around him that feels so... fake?"

Joe raised his hand, and Mr. Hastings nodded to him. "Holden's pissed off because he sees through all the bullshit," Joe said, leaning back in his chair. "Everyone's pretending. They're all phonies. And Holden's trying to find something real."

Mr. Hastings smiled. "Exactly. Phoniness. It's everywhere for Holden. He's looking for something genuine in a world that's full of masks."

Lena felt a twinge in her chest. Wasn't that what she was feeling too? Torn between who she was supposed to be—Tommy's girlfriend, the good daughter, the girl who never broke the rules—and who she wanted to be, the girl who wrote songs that made people feel something.

"Lena, what do you think Holden's really looking for?" Mr. Hastings asked, pulling her out of her thoughts.

She hesitated, then said, "I think he's looking for... a place where he belongs. Somewhere that makes sense. But it's hard to find that when everyone around you is telling you what you should be."

Mr. Hastings nodded, clearly pleased. "Well said, Lena. Holden's searching for a place where he can just be himself, without the world forcing him into a role he doesn't want to play. I think that's something a lot of us can relate to."

The cafeteria was buzzing with the usual lunch chatter as Lena sat down at the table with Sarah, Joe, and Bill. The clatter of trays, the low hum of voices, and the faint smell of cafeteria food filled the air as they began unpacking their lunches.

"So," Bill said, leaning back in his chair, "how are your songs coming, Lena? You got any new ones for us?"

Lena shrugged, feeling a little self-conscious. "I'm working on something, but it's not ready yet."

Sarah smiled encouragingly. "I'm sure it's going to be great. You've been on fire lately."

Lena felt her face warm under the praise. The truth was, she hadn't finished "A Change Will Come" yet. The words were swirling in her mind, but every time she tried to write them down, they slipped through her fingers like water.

Joe shifted the conversation. "You see the lineup for the first AFL-NFL Championship Game?" he asked Bill, his tone a little sarcastic. "They're calling it the 'Super Bowl.' Can you believe that?"

Bill grinned, leaning forward. "Man, I can't wait for that game. It's going to be huge. Think about it, the best of the AFL and the NFL going head-to-head. What more could you ask for?"

Joe smirked. "Yeah, except it's just a way for the owners to make more money. Doesn't mean the game won't be good, though."

Lena watched as the boys bantered back and forth, their conversation veering into talk of football stats, upcoming games, and the players they admired. The usual chatter. It was comforting, in a way, to hear them talk about something so normal in the midst of all the chaos and uncertainty surrounding them.

But even as she listened, Lena's mind wandered back to the music she was working on, the unfinished songs that were trying to take shape. The tension she had been feeling all day was still there, gnawing at the edges of her thoughts. She wanted to be like Holden Caulfield—rebellious, unafraid to challenge the phoniness of the world. But unlike Holden, she didn't want to just run away from it all. She wanted to change things.

After lunch, Lena and Sarah headed to P.E. with Coach Clark, the afternoon sun spilling through the windows of the gymnasium. Today, it was volleyball day, and the girls changed into their gym uniforms, joining the rest of the class on the polished wooden floor of the gym.

Coach Clark blew his whistle. "Alright, team up! Let's see some good, clean games today. Work together and have fun!"

Lena wasn't particularly athletic, but she enjoyed the team spirit that came with volleyball. The game was fast-paced, and it was a nice distraction from the weight of everything else on her mind. As the game progressed, Lena found herself getting into the rhythm, laughing as Sarah dove for a ball and missed spectacularly.

"Nice try, Sarah!" Lena called, grinning.

Sarah laughed, brushing herself off. "I'll get the next one!"

In Art class, Lena found her mind settling into a different kind of rhythm. Ms. Davis had set up paints and canvas boards for today's lesson, encouraging them to express themselves through abstract art. As Lena sat down beside Sarah and Joe, she found herself staring at the blank canvas in front of her, her mind still swimming with thoughts of Holden Caulfield, Tommy, and her unfinished songs.

"Just paint what you feel," Ms. Davis said, walking between the tables. "Don't overthink it. Art should come from your emotions."

Joe smirked as he dipped his brush into the bright red paint. "Well, in that case, I'm painting my rage against the system."

Sarah rolled her eyes but smiled. "Of course you are."

Lena smiled faintly as she picked up her brush, her mind wandering. As she made broad strokes across the canvas, she felt some of the tension begin to release. Art, like music, was a way for her to express the things she couldn't always put into words.

The day ended with Music Appreciation, which had become one of Lena's favorite classes. Mr. Morgan always brought an eclectic mix of music to class, and today was no different. He stood at the front of the room, flipping through records.

"Today, we're going to listen to a little bit of everything," Mr. Morgan said with a grin. "We've got some Dylan, some Ella Fitzgerald, and even a little Beethoven. Music spans time and genres, so I want you to really listen today. Think about how music expresses emotions and ideas across different eras."

As the music played, Lena closed her eyes, letting the sounds wash over her. The lyrics, the melodies, the emotions—they all swirled together in her mind, mingling with her own thoughts and feelings.

Her songs—her unfinished, imperfect songs—were still there, waiting to be written, waiting to find their voice.

Just like her.

37

The Soda Shop was alive with the usual hum of laughter and conversation, its neon lights flickering through the light fog settling outside. Inside, the smell of hamburgers and fries mixed with the sweetness of milkshakes, a comforting combination that made the place feel like a second home for Lena and her friends. The small jukebox in the corner played soft rock, and students, all decked out in their weekend best, filled the booths and counters.

Lena, Sarah, Tommy, Bill, and Joe were crammed into their usual booth near the back, where they could talk freely but still catch snippets of the conversation and laughter swirling around them. Tommy's arm rested casually across the back of Lena's seat, while Bill sat with his back straight, eyes lit with the excitement of tomorrow's championship game. Sarah was tucked into the corner next to Lena, practically buzzing with pride and anticipation.

Across from them, Joe slouched with his arms crossed, a teasing smirk on his face as he looked at Bill.

"You think we're gonna win tomorrow, man?" Joe asked, his tone mock-serious, but the edge of a grin giving him away.

Bill chuckled and flexed his hands like a fighter prepping for a bout. "We've been killing it all season. Tomorrow's just another win in the books," he said confidently.

"Always so cocky," Joe shot back. "But hey, I'll give it to you—you've been on fire lately. Just... don't blow it under pressure, Thompson."

Bill grinned, unfazed by the jab. "Please. You're gonna eat your words tomorrow."

Sarah nudged Lena. "You're coming to watch, right? I'll need someone to sit with while I'm screaming my lungs out for Bill."

Lena smiled, nodding, but her mind was elsewhere. She wanted to be in the moment, to join in on the banter and the laughter that filled the booth, but her thoughts kept drifting to her performance tomorrow night—the second time she'd ever step foot on that stage. The first time had been a shaky, nerve-wracking mess, and despite the encouragement from Sarah and Joe, the memory of fumbling her way through that song haunted her.

Her fingers traced the rim of her milkshake glass absentmindedly, the melody of her latest song "A Change Will Come" playing over and over in her mind like a mantra she couldn't quite lock down.

"What about you, Lena?" Bill asked, breaking her out of her reverie. He leaned forward, his expression curious. "You excited for open mic? Got that new song ready to go?"

Lena hesitated, her hand pausing on the glass. She glanced at Tommy, whose expression was unreadable, then back to Bill and Sarah, who were both watching her expectantly.

"I've been working on it... but I don't know," Lena admitted, her voice soft. "It still feels... unfinished."

Sarah's brow furrowed, concern knitting her features together. "Unfinished? Lena, you've been working on that song for days now. I'm sure it's amazing."

Lena shrugged, the weight of her own self-doubt pulling her shoulders down. "Maybe. I don't know. I just—" She bit her lip, unsure how to put it into words. How could she explain that the song wasn't just a collection of notes and lyrics? It was a piece of her heart, a reflection of everything she'd been feeling, and that made the idea of performing it even more terrifying.

Tommy, who had been unusually quiet all night, finally spoke up. His voice was calm, steady, but there was something in his tone that made Lena's stomach tighten. "You're gonna do fine, Lena. But maybe you're overthinking it. It's just a song, right?"

Just a song.

Lena felt a flicker of frustration rise in her chest, hot and sharp, but she swallowed it down before it could surface. Just a song? No, it wasn't just a song.

It was everything she was struggling to say, everything she wanted to scream into the world. It was her voice, her soul, her way of figuring out where she stood in all the chaos around her.

But instead of snapping back, she forced a smile, nodding like she agreed. "Yeah, maybe."

The conversation moved on, the focus shifting back to football and the excitement of the big game, but Lena was barely listening. Her mind was swirling with doubt, fear, and anticipation, all coiling together until it felt like she could barely breathe.

Tommy had been distant lately, not in the physical sense—he was always around, always close—but emotionally. There was a wall between them that hadn't been there before, and Lena couldn't quite put her finger on when it had started to rise.

As the conversation bounced between Joe's sarcastic jabs and Sarah's gushing excitement about Bill's chances in the championship, Lena felt Tommy shift beside her. He leaned in, lowering his voice so that only she could hear.

"You're really nervous about tomorrow, huh?" Tommy asked, his eyes searching her face.

Lena nodded, glancing down at her hands. "Yeah. I guess I am. I just want it to go well."

"It will. You've been practicing enough," Tommy said, though his tone carried a slight edge—like he didn't quite see why it mattered so much.

"I've been practicing because I want it to be perfect," Lena said quietly, her voice tight. "This song... it's important to me."

Tommy was silent for a moment, his brow furrowing as if he didn't quite get it. "I know it's important, but... it's not the end of the world, you know? If it doesn't go perfectly."

Lena pressed her lips together, the frustration bubbling up again. It wasn't about perfection. It was about feeling heard, feeling like she was finally saying something that mattered. But Tommy didn't see it that way. To him, the future was clear-cut—they'd get through this draft stuff, he'd go to Vietnam, come back, and they'd settle down. Simple as that.

But Lena's future wasn't that simple anymore.

The rest of the night at the Soda Shop was filled with the usual laughter and chatter, but Lena couldn't shake the heavy feeling settling over her. Her nerves about the performance were getting worse, and the tension between her and Tommy was a thread that she couldn't stop pulling at. Slipping into their old patterns was easier than facing the reality of their situation.

Joe, noticing her unease, leaned over during a lull in the conversation. "You good, Lena? You've been quiet."

Lena offered a weak smile. "Yeah, I'm just... in my head, I guess."

"You'll be great," Joe said, his tone genuine. "Don't let it get to you. Besides, you know half the crowd is gonna be there for Bill's big win. You've got an audience already built-in."

That brought a small smile to Lena's face. Joe always knew how to lighten the mood, even when the weight of her own thoughts threatened to pull her under.

But as the night wore on and they all eventually headed out into the cool night air, Lena couldn't help but feel like the performance wasn't the only thing hanging over her head.

There was Tommy, there was the war, there was the question of what came next. And through it all, the song—her song—was waiting for her, ready to be sung.

Saturday dawned with the crisp promise of autumn, the kind of day that seemed tailor-made for football. By the time afternoon rolled around, the entire town buzzed with excitement, the stadium already filling with the hum of voices and the shuffle of feet on concrete. Lena, Sarah, and Joe wove through the crowd to the bleachers, the tantalizing aroma of popcorn and sizzling hot dogs mingling with the cool breeze. Bill's team was moments away from taking the field for the state championship, and the anticipation crackled like static electricity.

The roar of the crowd hit a fever pitch as Bill and his teammates jogged onto the field, their cleats pounding the ground in rhythmic unison. Bill, the local hero and football star, looked every bit the part, with his broad shoulders and confident stride. Friday night at the Soda Shop had only been a prelude to this—the big game, the one the whole town had been waiting for.

Lena could feel the energy all around her, but her mind was elsewhere. While Sarah clapped enthusiastically beside her, practically bouncing, Lena sat more quietly, her fingers nervously tapping her knees in rhythm with her thoughts.

Tommy was there, sitting close enough that his warmth radiated next to her, his arm slung casually around her shoulders. But there was a distance between them—an invisible wall that had slowly been building.

The crowd erupted as Bill's team took the lead early in the game. Bill's throws were crisp, his passes hitting their mark like they were scripted, and the crowd cheered with every successful play. Sarah, watching intently, cheered louder than anyone.

"He's unstoppable today," Sarah said, grinning at Lena as Bill completed another pass.

Lena nodded, forcing a smile, but her mind drifted to the song she had been working on for days. "A Change Will Come." It wasn't just a song anymore—it was her anthem, the lyrics swirling in her head, unfinished and raw. The world was changing, and so was she, and yet, the gap between who she was and what she was supposed to be felt wider every day.

The game was nearing halftime, and it was intense. The score was tied, the other team had picked up momentum, and the crowd was tense with every down. Bill's team needed a big play, and everyone knew who it was going to come from. The cheerleaders were chanting and bleachers were filled with fans clapping in unison, urging the team on.

Joe leaned forward, grinning, his eyes never leaving the field. "Bill's gonna pull something out of the bag. He always does."

Sure enough, as the quarterback called the play, Bill streaked down the sideline like a bullet, arms pumping. The ball arced through the air, spiraling perfectly toward him. The crowd collectively held their breath.

"He's got it!" Sarah screamed, clutching Lena's arm.

Bill leapt up at the last second, snagging the ball just as two defenders closed in on him. With a quick spin move, he dodged them both, then broke into a full sprint down the field. The stands went wild.

"Go, Bill, GO!" Joe shouted, jumping to his feet.

Lena stood, her heart racing not with excitement for the game but with the weight of everything that was about to change in her life. Bill crossed into the end zone, and the crowd erupted into cheers that shook the entire stadium.

The whistle blew for halftime, and the atmosphere in the stands was jubilant. Sarah was practically floating as she talked about Bill's play.

"He's going to win this whole game for them!" she gushed, still riding the high of the touchdown. "Can you believe it?"

Lena smiled weakly, nodding along. She felt Tommy shift beside her, his hand resting on her leg, a gesture that felt less comforting than it used to.

"Great game," Tommy said, his voice low, trying to catch her eye.

Lena blinked, coming back to the present. "Yeah... Sarah's in her element that's for sure—and Bill, this is his day. He'll be walking on air if they win this."

Tommy grinned. "I'm glad I came today. I'm glad we're here together."

"Me too," Lena said softly, and she meant it. The big game was raging and the town was in celebration mode. She squeezed his hand, held it close to her. "Sorry, I've been so much in my head lately."

As the second half began, the opposing team came out with newfound energy, driving the ball down the field with fierce determination. The game became a battle of wills, each play more brutal than the last. The once lighthearted energy in the stadium turned tense as both teams fought for control of the game.

Bill's performance was still stellar, but the other team was matching him play for play. Each tackle felt harder, each cheer more desperate.

Joe leaned over to Lena. "You know, I've been thinking... football's like a microcosm of life, right? It's all strategy, all about playing the right moves."

Lena arched an eyebrow. "Football? Life?"

Joe smirked. "Think about it. Bill's got a plan. But so does the other team. They counter each other until someone cracks."

Lena gave a soft laugh despite herself. "You always find a way to make everything philosophical."

Joe shrugged. "Hey, football's about as close to modern-day gladiators as we get. You could probably write a song about it."

Lena smiled, but the weight in her chest remained. Her mind was still far away, on Tommy, on her music, on the future that felt uncertain.

The final quarter of the game was a nail-biter. The score was tied again, and both teams were playing with everything they had. Bill was out on the field, sweat pouring down his face, determined to bring the victory home.

The clock was ticking down—just two minutes left, and Bill's team had possession. The coach called a timeout, and the crowd buzzed with nervous energy. Everyone knew the ball was going to Bill again.

"This is it," Joe muttered. "They've got one shot."

Lena held her breath as Bill's team took the field. The quarterback called the play, and once again, Bill sprinted down the sideline. The ball was snapped, and the quarterback launched a perfect pass.

Bill caught it mid-stride and made a break for the end zone, weaving between defenders like they weren't even there. The crowd was on its feet, everyone screaming as Bill charged toward the goal line.

He dodged one last tackle and leapt forward, crashing into the end zone just as the clock hit zero.

The stadium erupted into chaos. Bill's team had won.

The field was a frenzy of cheers, hugs, and celebration. Bill was hoisted onto his teammates' shoulders, the hero of the hour. Sarah was grinning from ear to ear, waving excitedly as Bill caught sight of her in the stands. Even Joe, who usually scoffed at anything remotely conventional, couldn't help but smile.

Lena cheered too, swept up in the excitement. As the team celebrated on the field, Tommy turned to her, his voice low in her ear. "Want to take a drive? I need to feel the open road."

Lena nodded, though her heart felt heavy. As they made their way out of the stadium and into the cool night air, Tommy seemed distracted. He had been supportive of Lena's music, but something was clearly bothering him.

"Lena," he said quietly as they walked toward his car, "I know tonight's a big deal for you, but... I don't know if I'll ever understand why you're so hung up on this. It's just a hobby, right?"

Lena stopped in her tracks, her eyes narrowing. "Just a hobby? Tommy, this is more than that. It's everything I've been feeling—about you, about us, about the world."

Tommy's jaw tightened, and he sighed. "I just don't want you to lose sight of what's important."

"What's important to you isn't necessarily what's important to me," Lena said softly, her voice laced with frustration.

And with that, the tension between them was laid bare. Tonight would bring more than just a performance. It would bring decisions—about her future, her dreams, and whether or not Tommy would be part of them.

Tonight was Lena's moment. And she had to make it count.

38

The café was packed, the energy still riding high from the day's football victory, where Bill's team had clinched the state championship. Lena stood backstage, her guitar clutched tightly in her hands as she peeked through the curtains. The room was filled with familiar faces—Sarah, sitting up front with an encouraging smile, Joe leaning back with a look of quiet support, and even Bill, basking in the afterglow of his win, his arm draped over Sarah's shoulders.

But it was Tommy, sitting alone by the window, that drew Lena's gaze and held it fast. He stared out into the darkened street, his face caught between shadow and light, his expression unreadable but heavy. The tension between them had been brewing ever since Madison. Ever since the protests, the shouts of *soldier boy* and *cannon fodder* hurled like stones at his pride. She hadn't realized then, but it had shaken him—shaken her, too. The nightmare she tried to forget still lingered at the edges of her mind: Tommy in a flag-draped coffin, his face cold and still. Her stomach tightened at the thought. How had she missed how much it had wounded him? How much pain he must be carrying alone? His presence tonight was a double-edged sword—comforting in its familiarity but sharp with the unspoken truths between them. He was a reminder of the life she was supposed to want, the path everyone expected her to walk. But those expectations felt as suffocating as the small-town walls she was desperate to escape.

Maybe he was pushing her away on purpose. The thought flickered in her mind, uninvited but persistent. Tommy wasn't one to talk about his fears, but she'd seen it in his eyes lately—the quiet resignation, the distance he was building between them. Maybe he thought he was protecting her, sparing her from the grief that could come if he didn't make it back from Vietnam. Or maybe it was something deeper, a realization that their paths had already started to diverge. She could feel the weight of his choices, the heavy burden of duty he'd been taught to carry since childhood. Maybe he thought letting go now would hurt less than holding on. But in trying to shield her, he was only adding to the ache that already gnawed at her.

Taking a deep breath, Lena stepped out from behind the curtain. The applause that greeted her was polite but distracted, the crowd still buzzing from the game. This performance wasn't for them, though. Tonight wasn't about applause or approval. This was for her—for her music, her voice, and the truths she needed to pull into the light. The pressure coiled in her chest, taut and fierce, but she held onto it. This time, it wouldn't shatter her. Not tonight.

She settled onto the wooden stool, her guitar resting on her knee. With a quick glance at Sarah, who gave her an enthusiastic thumbs up, Lena strummed the first chord of her song. The quiet murmur of the café began to hush, the crowd slowly turning their attention toward her.

Lena took one last calming breath, closed her eyes, and then let the words flow.

Her voice started soft, almost tentative, the weight of her thoughts and emotions pressing down on her chest.

The world is shifting, it's breaking free
Voices rising, fighting to be seen
In the streets, we march for peace
Dreaming of the day when the wars will cease
From every corner, a new dawn breaks
You can feel the ground beneath us shake
The time has come to stand as one
And know that change has just begun

The lyrics hung in the air, wrapping themselves around the audience. Lena could feel the nerves pulsing through her fingertips as they brushed the strings, but she didn't let it stop her. This song wasn't just for her anymore—it was for everyone who felt like they were on the cusp of something bigger, something beyond the walls they'd been taught to accept.

The first few lines wavered, but she pushed through, her voice growing stronger as she hit her stride.

Crowded streets pulse with restless energy,
Faces blur into a sea.
Voices rise, blending into a chorus of hope,
Each step forward writes a new chapter.

She glanced at Tommy, who still hadn't turned to look at her. His expression was distant, as though his mind was somewhere else entirely. It stung, but Lena forced herself to keep going. The words were hers, and she wasn't going to let anything—not even the tension between them—pull her focus now.

As she launched into the chorus, the familiar swell of confidence rose within her. This was the moment she had been building toward for weeks. She had fumbled her first performance, but this time was different. This time she felt like the song was carrying her, lifting her voice as it rose above the noise of the café.

A change will come, I feel it near
A brighter day is drawing clear
The winds of revolution blow
And in my heart, I know, I know
A change will come for the world, for me
I'm breaking free, I'm learning to be
The woman who can stand and fight
For her own dreams, for what is right

The audience was leaning in now, their earlier chatter forgotten. Lena could see the way they were hanging on her words, their expressions a mix of curiosity and something deeper. They were hearing her. She was no longer just the girl from the small town of Janesville. She was becoming someone else—someone with a voice that mattered.

By the time she hit the second verse, Lena's voice had steadied, her fingers moving effortlessly over the strings. The tension she'd felt earlier began to dissolve, replaced by a newfound strength.

We're breaking chains that held us down
Tearing walls that shut us out
The future's calling, can't you hear?
The sound of hope, the end of fear
From Selma's streets to city squares
There's power in the love we share
Together, we'll rise, we'll make it known
We'll carve a path to freedom's throne

This was her declaration, not just for herself but for the world she saw changing around her. The protests in Madison, the war looming over everyone's future, the conversations she'd had with Joe about standing up and being heard—it all came crashing together in this moment.

In the stillness of the night, plans are made,
Underneath the stars, commitments are laid.
We're the architects of tomorrow's dawn,
With every step, the old is gone.
Whispers turning into roars on the ground.
With every heartbeat, a promise ignites,
A future shaped by our collective might.

She sang these words with conviction, her eyes drifting across the crowd until they landed on Joe, who gave her a small nod of approval. He understood. He always understood. Tommy, however, remained unmoved, his gaze still fixed somewhere out the window. The gulf between them was becoming impossible to ignore.

A change will come, I feel it near
A brighter day is drawing clear
The winds of revolution blow
And in my heart, I know, I know
A change will come for the world, for me
I'm breaking free, I'm learning to be
The woman who can stand and fight
For her own dreams, for what is right

Lena's voice soared through the bridge, her confidence now fully realized. She wasn't just singing a song—she was making a statement.

I've felt the chains, I've known the weight
But now I rise, now I create

A future where my voice is strong
Where I belong, where we belong
The world is turning, can't you feel?
The truth is rising, the wounds will heal
In every heart, a fire ignites
We're marching toward those better nights

The crowd was with her, their quiet attention a testament to how deeply her words were resonating. Lena felt the rush of adrenaline, the thrill of performing something that mattered. Her voice carried through the room, each note filled with passion and purpose.

A change will come, I feel it near
A brighter day is drawing clear
The winds of revolution blow
And in my heart, I know, I know
A change will come for the world, for me
I'm breaking free, I'm learning to be
The woman who can stand and fight
For her own dreams, for what is right

The final outro came, and Lena's voice, though a little shaky from the emotional weight of it all, remained steady.

A change will come, it's in the air
For every heart that dares to care
In every soul, in every hand
We'll build the future, we'll take a stand
As dawn breaks, we stand united,
A testament to what's been ignited.
Change will come, it's our time to shine,
Building a world where dreams align.

As the last chord echoed through the room, the café went completely silent. For a moment, Lena feared she had misstepped—that perhaps the song had been too much. But then, almost in slow motion, the applause began. It started with Sarah, clapping wildly and beaming with pride. Joe joined in, his slow clap building in intensity until the rest of the café followed.

The room erupted in applause, cheers filling the air. Lena let out a shaky breath, her heart racing, her fingers trembling slightly as she held her guitar close. She had done it. She had made it through.

But even in the midst of the applause, Lena's eyes found Tommy. He was clapping, but it was half-hearted. His expression hadn't changed. The distance between them hadn't been bridged by the song—it had widened.

After the applause died down, Lena stepped off the stage, her heart heavy despite the praise. Sarah rushed to hug her, Joe offered a congratulatory slap on the back, and even Bill was grinning and nodding in approval.

But Tommy was silent.

As the crowd began to disperse, Tommy finally stood, walking over to Lena. There was something tight in his expression, a mixture of pride and frustration.

"That was... good, Lena," he said softly, his hand resting awkwardly on her shoulder. "You really put everything into it."

Lena forced a smile, searching his eyes for something more. "Thanks. It felt good to sing it."

Tommy nodded, but the weight of his next words was heavy in the air. "I'm proud of you, you know. But... I just don't understand why you're making this music thing such a big deal. It's not gonna change anything, Lena. The world's still gonna be the way it is."

Lena's heart sank. This was what she had feared—that no matter how much she poured into her songs, Tommy would never fully understand. She loved him, but it was becoming clearer that the path she was walking wasn't one he could follow.

"I just want to express myself," Lena said softly, her voice trembling. "I need to do this. It's not just a hobby for me."

Tommy sighed, his hand dropping to his side. "I know, but... I guess I just don't get it. I'm sorry."

Lena nodded, the unspoken distance between them growing more tangible by the second. The applause was fading, and with it, the illusion that everything would be okay between them.

Later, as the café started to empty out, Joe found Lena standing near the back door, her guitar case slung over her shoulder. The night air was cool, and she had stepped outside to clear her head after her conversation with Tommy.

"Hey," Joe said, stepping up beside her, his hands shoved into his jacket pockets. "You did good tonight."

Lena smiled faintly. "Thanks. I wasn't sure how it would go."

Joe nodded, glancing back toward the café. "Look, I know Tommy doesn't get it. But that doesn't matter. What you're doing... it's important. You've got a voice, Lena. And people need to hear it."

She looked up at him, her chest tight with emotion. "But... do you really think it's enough?"

Joe shrugged. "I think it's a start. And if you keep going, if you push yourself to be even bolder... I think you can make people listen."

Lena let out a breath she hadn't realized she'd been holding. Joe's words hit her in a way that no one else's had. He believed in her music—truly believed in it. And as much as she cared for Tommy, it was Joe who understood her in this moment.

"Thanks, Joe," she whispered, feeling the weight of the night lift, if only a little.

Joe gave her a lopsided smile. "Anytime. Just... keep going, okay? Don't let anyone tell you your voice doesn't matter."

As Lena stood there, guitar in hand and the cool night breeze brushing against her skin, she realized something: this was her path. It might not be easy, and not everyone—Tommy included—might understand it, but it was hers. And she was ready to keep walking it, no matter what.

39

The applause had long since faded, and the bustling energy of the open mic night was just a faint hum in Lena's mind as she stood outside the café, still clutching her guitar case. Tommy was waiting by the door, his hands shoved deep into his jacket pockets. He had offered to take her home, but his earlier words still echoed in her mind—"It's not gonna change anything, Lena."

Lena's chest tightened at the thought. She loved Tommy, she really did, but they were on different paths. The gap between them was widening, and tonight, it felt like she was standing at the edge of something she wasn't ready to face.

Tommy glanced at her, his eyes soft but laced with confusion. "You ready to go?" he asked, his voice gentle, like he was trying to smooth over the tension from earlier.

Lena hesitated, her fingers tightening around the strap of her guitar case. She could feel Sarah watching from the corner of the café, waiting to see what she would do. But something inside Lena was pulling her in another direction—a quieter, deeper voice telling her she needed to think. To breathe. To figure out what all of this meant for her, and for them.

"I think... I think I need some time," Lena said softly, her voice barely above a whisper. She looked up at Tommy, and saw the uncertainty in his eyes, the flicker of realization that maybe things weren't as simple as they had once seemed.

"Time?" Tommy repeated, his brows furrowing. "Lena, what do you mean? We've got time... don't we?"

Lena's throat tightened, but she forced herself to nod. "I just... I need to think, Tommy. I'll talk to you tomorrow, okay? But tonight... I just need to be alone."

Tommy's expression softened, though hurt flickered behind his eyes. He didn't argue, though. Instead, he let out a slow breath and nodded. "Alright," he said quietly. "I'll call you tomorrow."

With that, Tommy gave her a brief kiss on the cheek—so familiar and warm, but distant—and turned to walk to his car. Sarah, sensing the tension, gave Lena a questioning glance but didn't push. She, too, said a quick goodbye and hurried after Bill, leaving Lena standing alone outside the café.

Lena had just started to walk down the dimly lit street, the night air cool against her skin, when she heard footsteps behind her. Turning around, she saw Joe catching up to her, his hands casually shoved into his jacket pockets. His expression was unreadable, but there was something in the way he moved that told Lena he wasn't just here to walk her home.

"Hey," Joe said as he reached her, falling into step beside her. "You okay?"

Lena shrugged, not sure how to answer. "I don't know," she admitted. "It's just... a lot. You know?"

Joe nodded, his usual cocky grin absent. "Yeah, I get it. Tommy...?"

"Tommy," Lena repeated, her voice softer. "And the music... and everything. It's like... I don't even know who I'm supposed to be anymore."

They walked in silence for a moment, the only sound the soft shuffle of their footsteps on the pavement and the distant hum of passing cars. The cool night air was refreshing against Lena's flushed cheeks, but her thoughts were still a swirling mess of doubts, fears, and hopes.

Joe glanced at her, his eyes thoughtful. "You know... you're not the only one trying to figure things out, Lena."

Lena frowned, surprised by the vulnerability in his voice. "What do you mean?"

Joe let out a breath, his gaze drifting up toward the night sky. "I mean... everyone thinks I've got it all figured out. Like I'm just this rebel who wants to piss off the whole town. But that's not it. Not really."

Lena looked at him curiously, her heart softening. She had known Joe for years—he had always been the guy who pushed boundaries, who questioned everything, who never seemed satisfied with small-town life. But this side of him—this quiet vulnerability—was something she hadn't seen before.

"I've never thought you were just trying to piss people off," Lena said softly. "You've always... been searching for something, haven't you?"

Joe glanced at her, a small, rueful smile tugging at his lips. "Yeah. I guess I have. This place... Janesville, it's not where I'm supposed to be, you know? I've been dreaming about getting out for as long as I can remember. Going somewhere where I can actually make a difference."

Lena nodded, understanding the feeling all too well. "Where do you want to go?"

Joe shrugged. "Somewhere bigger. Berkeley maybe. Or D.C. I don't know. I just... I want to be part of something that matters. All this talk about the war and civil rights... it's like everything's changing, and I don't want to be stuck here watching it happen from the sidelines."

Lena's heart ached at the words. She understood the desire to be part of something bigger, to find her place in a world that felt so vast and uncertain. She had always admired Joe for his passion, for his fearlessness in standing up for what he believed in, even when it made him an outsider.

"You've always been the brave one," Lena said quietly, her voice full of admiration. "You've never been afraid to say what you feel."

Joe smiled, but there was a sadness in his eyes. "Maybe. But I've been afraid of something, Lena."

"What?"

Joe hesitated, his gaze flickering over her face before he looked away. "Afraid of losing people. Of pushing too hard and making people walk away."

Lena's heart clenched. She knew what he was talking about—how he sometimes rubbed people the wrong way, how his relentless questioning of everything could make him feel like he didn't belong. But Lena had never felt that way about him. To her, Joe had always been someone who challenged her, who made her think more deeply about the world.

"I'm not going anywhere, Joe," Lena said softly. "You've always been my friend. And you've always been more than just the town rebel to me."

Joe glanced at her, and for a brief moment, the weight of his feelings flickered in his eyes—too brief for Lena to fully understand, but enough to leave something unspoken between them. "You've always been different, Lena. From everyone else here. I think you know that."

Lena swallowed, her thoughts a jumble of emotions. She had always felt different, but hearing Joe say it made it real. Made her realize that maybe she wasn't as alone as she sometimes felt.

"You'll figure it out, Lena," Joe continued, his voice low and full of certainty. "You're gonna find your way. And I'll be there. Whether it's here or somewhere else, I'll be there."

They walked in silence for a while longer, the night stretching out before them like a blank canvas waiting to be filled. Lena's heart felt lighter, her thoughts less tangled. Maybe Joe was right. Maybe she would find her way, one step at a time. And she wouldn't have to do it alone.

As they neared her house, Joe stopped, giving her a gentle smile. "Get some sleep. You've had a hell of a night."

Lena nodded, smiling back. "You too, Joe."

She turned and walked up the path, glancing back just once to see him standing there, watching her go, his silhouette outlined against the dim streetlights. She waved, and he waved back, his movements slow, as if reluctant to let her disappear.

And as she closed the door behind her, Lena felt a warmth she couldn't quite name. She didn't notice the way Joe lingered on the sidewalk for a moment longer, his gaze fixed on her house before he finally turned and walked away into the night, his shoulders heavy with feelings he couldn't say aloud.

40

Lena opened the front door softly, stepping inside the familiar warmth of her home. The dim glow of the television cast flickering shadows across the living room. Her parents sat on the couch, her father reclining with a cigarette, her mother knitting absentmindedly, their eyes fixed on the screen.

The familiar sounds of The Ed Sullivan Show filled the air, a comforting hum of laughter and music from the small black-and-white TV set perched on the wooden console. Lena took a moment to steady herself, the weight of the evening still clinging to her shoulders, but she knew she couldn't avoid this forever.

Her mother glanced over, her eyes brightening as she noticed Lena. "You're home late, sweetheart."

Lena forced a small smile, shrugging off her jacket. "Yeah, just walked back with Joe."

Her father, still focused on the television, gave a grunt of acknowledgment. "Good game today, wasn't it?" he said, referring to the earlier football championship where Bill's team had won.

Lena nodded, moving into the room and sitting down on the armrest of the chair across from her parents. "Yeah, Bill did great."

Her mother gave her a gentle smile, though there was something curious in her eyes. "How was your performance? Sarah called earlier to say she was excited for it."

Lena hesitated, her fingers brushing against the fabric of the chair. "It went... okay," she said, not wanting to dive into the complexities of how she really felt. "Better than the last time."

Her mother's smile widened, but it was a soft, knowing smile. "That's wonderful, Lena. You've always had such a gift for music. It's nice to see you sharing it with people."

Lena's father grunted again, his eyes glued to the screen as Johnny Carson made a quip about some celebrity. "As long as you don't forget about the real world," he muttered, the cigarette perched between his fingers. "Music's fine, but it ain't gonna pay the bills."

Lena swallowed, her smile fading slightly. The familiar tension crept in—her father's quiet disapproval of her dreams always hovering over her like a shadow. "I know, Dad."

Her mother shot him a gentle look, placing her knitting down. "She's young, Robert. Let her enjoy this time."

Her father just waved his hand dismissively, focusing on the TV again. Lena stood, not wanting to get into it. "I'm gonna head upstairs," she said softly, grabbing her guitar case and starting toward the stairs.

Up in her room, Lena felt the familiar comfort settle over her. Her sanctuary. She gently placed her guitar against the wall, her eyes wandering over the posters of Bob Dylan and Joan Baez on her walls. They had always been her silent mentors, the voices that guided her through the confusion of growing up in a town where she never quite fit in.

Her notebook lay open on her desk, a few scattered pages with half-finished lyrics and melodies. She ran her fingers over the paper, the edges worn from hours of scribbling and erasing. The words for "A Change Will Come" had spilled out of her like a river, but now, in the quiet of her room, they felt both powerful and fragile.

Lena sat down on her bed, picking up her acoustic guitar and strumming a few chords absentmindedly. She replayed the night in her head—her performance, the way the audience had responded, and, of course, the tension with Tommy. She sighed, trying to push it all out of her mind, but it lingered like a stubborn weight.

Her fingers drifted over the strings, and as she closed her eyes, a melody began to form in her mind, something new and tentative. But before she could follow the thread, the phone on her nightstand rang, startling her out of her thoughts.

Lena placed her guitar down and picked up the receiver, pressing it to her ear. "Hello?"

"Lena?" It was Sarah's voice, soft and full of concern. "Hey, I just wanted to check on you... You seemed kind of off earlier."

Lena let out a breath, leaning back against her pillows. "I'm okay," she said, though even she wasn't sure if it was true. "Just... a lot on my mind."

There was a pause on the other end, and then Sarah's voice came through again, gentle but insistent. "Do you... want me to come over? We can just hang out, talk girl stuff or whatever. I don't want you to be alone if you're feeling down."

Lena smiled, warmth flooding her chest at the thought of Sarah's unwavering friendship. "Yeah," she said softly. "That'd be nice."

"I'll be there in fifteen," Sarah replied, her voice brightening. "I'll bring some snacks."

Lena laughed softly. "You're the best, Sarah."

"Of course I am," Sarah teased. "See you soon."

After hanging up the phone, Lena sat for a moment, letting the quiet settle back in. She picked up her notebook again, flipping through the pages of her past songs, her eyes lingering on the newer lyrics that had begun to take shape. "A Change Will Come" had felt like a breakthrough, a way for her to express everything she had been feeling about the world, about herself, and about her relationship with Tommy.

But even though she had finished the song, there was still a part of her that felt incomplete—like there was something else waiting to be said, something she hadn't yet found the words for.

She wasn't sure what was going to happen with Tommy, or with her music, or even with the uncertain future that loomed ahead. But for tonight, she was grateful for the simplicity of girl talk with her best friend—and maybe that would be enough to carry her through the rest of the weekend.

As Lena gathered herself and headed downstairs to greet Sarah, she knew that while the world around her was full of uncertainty, she could always count on her friends to keep her grounded—and that, at least, was something she could hold onto.

Lena had just made it downstairs when she heard the light tap on the front door. She hurried over, opening the door to find Sarah standing there with a bag of snacks and her usual bright smile. But even in the dim light of the porch, Lena could see that Sarah's energy was slightly more subdued than usual—like she, too, had something weighing on her.

"Hey, you," Sarah greeted, stepping inside and kicking off her shoes by the door. "I come bearing chocolate and potato chips—two essential food groups."

Lena chuckled, grateful for the distraction. "You know me too well."

"Of course I do," Sarah grinned, but there was an underlying softness in her expression, like she was reading between the lines of Lena's forced smile. "Come on, let's head up. You look like you need a good vent session."

They climbed the stairs together, making their way to Lena's room, where the soft glow of her bedside lamp cast a warm light over the space. Lena sat cross-legged on her bed, while Sarah flopped onto the rug, setting down the snacks on the floor between them. The easy quiet stretched between them for a moment, the kind that only best friends shared—no need to fill every gap with words, just being together was enough.

"So," Sarah finally said, tearing open a bag of chips, "what's on your mind? I could tell earlier at the cafe that you were... I don't know, kind of off. Did something happen with Tommy?"

Lena sighed, running her fingers through her hair. She leaned back against her pillows, staring up at the ceiling as she tried to put her thoughts into words. "I don't know, Sarah. It's... everything, I guess. Tommy... he just doesn't get it. I thought tonight was about my music—about the song and what it means to me—but to him, it's like I'm just playing pretend. Like it doesn't matter."

Sarah munched on a chip, nodding in understanding. "Guys can be clueless like that sometimes. They just don't think the same way we do."

"I know," Lena agreed, her frustration bubbling to the surface. "But it's more than that. He just assumes that once we get married—or once he comes back from Vietnam—that I'll... I don't know, fall into place. Be the girl everyone expects me to be. And I don't want that, Sarah. I want something more."

Sarah bit her lip, her expression thoughtful. "Does he know that?"

Lena shrugged. "I'm not sure if he even wants to hear it. Every time I try to talk about my music, or my dreams, he brushes it off like it's just a phase. I love him, but... what if we want different things?"

Sarah gave her a sympathetic look. "I get that, Lena. I really do. But..."

Lena noticed the hesitation in Sarah's voice, the way her eyes flickered with uncertainty. She tilted her head, curious. "What is it?"

Sarah let out a soft laugh, leaning back against the foot of the bed and crossing her legs. "It's just... Bill and I. We've been getting... serious."

Lena's eyebrows shot up in surprise, though a part of her had suspected it. "Serious?"

Sarah nodded, her cheeks flushing slightly. "Yeah. I mean, he's been talking about the future—about getting married. Maybe even right after graduation."

Lena's stomach did a small flip, and she sat up straighter. "Wait—married? Sarah, that's... huge."

"I know!" Sarah exclaimed, a mixture of excitement and nerves in her voice. "I mean, I love Bill. He's great. But... is it too fast? Or is this just the natural course of things?"

Lena studied her best friend, noting the uncertainty in her eyes. "Do you want to get married right now?"

Sarah hesitated, her fingers fiddling with the edge of her shirt. "I think so... I mean, we've been together for years. Everyone says it makes sense, right? He's already talking about getting a job at his dad's business after football, and he's got everything planned out."

"But what about you?" Lena asked gently, her voice soft but firm. "What do you want?"

Sarah's gaze dropped to the floor, and for a moment, she was silent. When she spoke again, her voice was quieter, more vulnerable. "I don't know. I guess... part of me just thinks it's what I'm supposed to do. Settle down, get married, have kids. It's what my mom did, what everyone expects."

Lena nodded, understanding the pressure all too well. "But does it feel right? Deep down?"

Sarah looked up, her eyes searching Lena's for reassurance. "I don't know if it does, not yet. I mean, I love Bill, and I can see myself with him, but... I also wonder if I'm ready. Like, what if there's more I want to do first?"

Lena reached out, placing a hand on Sarah's knee. "Then you should take your time, Sarah. Don't rush into it just because it's what people expect. This is your life. You should live it on your terms."

Sarah's eyes filled with gratitude, and she gave Lena a small smile. "You always know what to say, you know that?"

Lena smiled back, though her own thoughts were swirling. She understood the pressure Sarah was feeling all too well—they both did. But while Sarah's struggle was about whether or not she was ready to settle down, Lena's was about something deeper. She didn't just want to settle down—she wanted to soar.

The moment stretched, quiet but not awkward, as they munched on snacks and reflected on the weight of their decisions. Sarah shifted slightly, her voice softer now. "Do you think... you and Tommy will get married?"

Lena stared at the ceiling, the question hanging in the air. "I don't know," she said honestly. "I love him, but... I don't know if we're meant to want the same things."

Sarah reached for another chip, her voice equally contemplative. "Sometimes I feel like the whole world is moving faster than I can keep up."

Lena sighed, the truth of those words settling deep within her. "Yeah. Me too."

As the night went on, their conversation drifted from light topics—gossiping about boys at school, joking about their teachers and the latest trends in music and fashion—to deeper, more reflective thoughts about the future. They were both at a crossroads, standing on the precipice of adulthood and trying to figure out where they were supposed to go.

"I mean, what if we go off and get married right after graduation?" Sarah mused, her eyes unfocused as she stared at the ceiling. "Will we be like our parents? Just... work, raise kids, and that's it? I'm scared I'll wake up one day and feel like I missed out on something."

Lena turned to look at her, her voice soft but steady. "Then don't let that happen. You have a choice, Sarah. We both do."

Sarah blinked, her eyes widening a little as if realizing it for the first time. "Yeah... I guess we do."

Lena leaned back against her pillows, her heart full of uncertainty but also a strange sense of clarity. "We've got time. We don't have to figure it all out tonight."

Sarah nodded, a small smile tugging at her lips. "Thanks, Lena. I needed this. You always know how to make me feel better."

Lena grinned, though her thoughts were still clouded. She wasn't sure how things would play out with Tommy, or what the future held, but she knew one thing for certain: she wasn't going to settle for less than what she truly wanted.

As they both drifted off into lighter conversation and laughter, the future felt a little less overwhelming, at least for now. And sometimes, a night of girl talk with your best friend was enough to keep the uncertainty at bay—even if just for a little while.

41

The sun had barely begun to rise when Lena awoke with a jolt, her heart racing as the remnants of a vivid dream lingered in her mind. But it wasn't just a dream—it was a song, one that was swirling around her head like a freight train, loud and insistent.

She blinked groggily, the words and melody pressing against her consciousness, demanding to be let out. It was the first time she had woken with such a rush of inspiration, as though the song had been waiting in the wings, ready to emerge fully formed. Her fingers itched for her notebook, the lyrics already on the tip of her tongue.

Lena hurried to her desk, flipping open the worn pages of her journal, and began scribbling down the lines that had come to her:

Fragments scattered in the wind,
Lost reflections deep within.
Torn between the past and dreams,
Nothing's ever as it seems.

Her pen flew across the paper, the lyrics flowing effortlessly.

I've been living in between
Who they want and who I dream.
Every day, I wear a different face,
But none of them fit, none feel like a place.
My heart is pulled in every way,
Torn apart by what they say.
Should I stay or should I run?
Is there a road where I'm the only one?

It was as if the song was coming from somewhere deeper than usual—deeper than the surface-level feelings she had about Tommy, her parents, or even her music.

In the quiet corners of my mind,
Fragments of who I am drift and collide.
Each piece a story, a moment in time,
Trying to find where they all align.

This was about her—her fragmented sense of self, the conflicting roles she was expected to play, and the person she was still trying to figure out how to become.

The lines she was writing reflected the tension she felt every day: between the expectations of her family and society, and the burning desire she had to be something different, to be a songwriter, a musician, a voice.

I'm searching for the pieces of me
Scattered like leaves on a windblown field
Trying to find where I fit in
In a world that tells me I don't belong
But I'll gather every piece I've lost
No matter the price, no matter the cost

I'll build myself from what's been torn
And find the woman I was meant to be born

She paused for a moment, her hand stilling as she read over the words she had written. They were raw, filled with the kind of emotion she had been bottling up for weeks. This song was different from anything she'd written before—it was an anthem of self-discovery, an ode to the journey she was just beginning to understand.

She didn't have the whole song yet, but the pieces were coming together, just like the lyrics said.

After capturing the core of the song, Lena set down her pen and glanced at the clock. It was still early, but she needed to get ready for school. With a sigh, she closed her notebook and picked up her guitar, strumming a few quiet chords as she hummed the melody to herself.

The sound of her guitar was soft, almost a whisper in the quiet morning, but it was enough to remind her of what lay ahead. 7th period Music Appreciation with Mr. Morgan—that was the class she always looked forward to. Today especially, she couldn't wait to get there and talk about this new song.

But it wasn't just Music Appreciation she was excited for. Guitar Club after school was where she could really dive into her music, surrounded by people who understood what it meant to feel something so deeply it had to be put into song. Joe would be there too, and despite everything, he always seemed to push her to dig deeper, to challenge herself.

Lena threw on her clothes, grabbed her guitar case, and headed downstairs for a quick breakfast. She still had time before school, but her mind was buzzing with the possibilities this new song represented. She knew she had something special—something that felt like a turning point.

The school day seemed to stretch on forever, each class blurring together as Lena's thoughts kept drifting back to her song. She'd scrawled a few more ideas in the margins of her notebook during English Literature and couldn't help but tap her fingers against the desk in rhythm, her mind composing the melody that would bring the lyrics to life.

Verse 2:
There's a voice inside that calls my name
But the world outside is not the same
They say to follow, they say to stay
But I feel the music pulling me away.
I'm caught between the girl I know
And the woman I've yet to show.
The path is blurred, the lines aren't clear
But somewhere in the shadows, I'll appear.
Scattered pieces, floating in the breeze,
Searching for the one that sets me free.
In the chaos, I find my ground,
Piecing together what's always been mine.

By the time 7th period rolled around, Lena was practically bouncing in her seat with anticipation. Music Appreciation with Mr. Morgan was her safe space, where she could talk about Joan Baez, Dylan, and the deep, poetic connection between music and the world. She couldn't wait to get his feedback on the song running through her mind.

When the final bell rang, Lena was already halfway back to the music room after talking with Sarah and Bill at their lockers. Guitar Club was her real sanctuary—her chance to play with others, to bounce ideas off Joe and the rest of the group, and to really push the limits of what she could do with her music.

Joe was already in the music room, casually tuning his guitar. He gave Lena a nod as she walked in, his usual air of rebellion softened by the guitar resting in his lap. For all his talk about politics and protests, this—the music—was where Joe's real passion lay.

"Hey," he greeted, strumming a few chords as Lena sat down beside him. "You look like you've got something on your mind."

Lena smiled, setting her own guitar case down and pulling out her acoustic. "Yeah, I've been working on something. A new song... it feels different this time."

Joe raised an eyebrow, intrigued. "Different how?"

Lena paused, trying to find the words. "It's about me. I mean, really about me—who I am, or... who I'm trying to figure out I am. It's like I'm... piecing myself together through the lyrics. I don't know, it's hard to explain, but it feels important."

Joe's eyes softened with understanding. "Sounds like you're finally starting to get to the good stuff, the real stuff."

Lena smiled at that, feeling the weight of his words settle in. "Yeah... I think I am."

As Mr. Morgan called the group together, the room filled with the quiet hum of tuning guitars and whispered conversation. The atmosphere felt charged with the usual post-school energy, a comfortable buzz of creative excitement. But for Lena, there was an extra layer of anticipation humming beneath her skin. She couldn't wait any longer.

With her guitar resting lightly in her lap, Lena took a deep breath and strummed the opening chords of her new song, "Pieces of Me." The gentle vibrations of the guitar strings echoed through the room, and as soon as she began to sing, the space around her seemed to fall silent, all eyes and ears on her.

The notes wrapped around her like a protective shield, their familiar comfort allowing her to focus on the lyrics. She let the words flow naturally, unfiltered, straight from the deepest corners of her heart:

Fragments scattered in the wind,
Lost reflections deep within.
Torn between the past and dreams,
Nothing's ever as it seems.
I've been living in between
Who they want and who I dream.
Every day, I wear a different face,
But none of them fit, none feel like a place.
My heart is pulled in every way,
Torn apart by what they say.
Should I stay or should I run?
Is there a road where I'm the only one?
In the quiet corners of my mind,
Fragments of who I am drift and collide.
Each piece a story, a moment in time,
Trying to find where they all align.

Her voice wavered only slightly at first, but as she continued, the words seemed to carry her forward, each note a little stronger than the last. Joe had stopped fiddling with his own guitar, his eyes fixed on Lena with an intensity that suggested he knew this was different—special. Even Mr. Morgan, usually quick to give feedback or guidance, remained silent, his gaze transfixed by the unfolding performance.

I'm searching for the pieces of me
Scattered like leaves on a restless sea
Trying to find where I fit in
In a world that tells me I don't belong
But I'll gather every piece I've lost
No matter the price, no matter the cost
I'll build myself from what's been torn
And find the woman I was meant to be born...

Lena poured herself into the song, the confusion, the self-doubt, and the hope all woven into the melody. By the time she reached the second verse, the nervous energy that had gripped her had dissolved, replaced by something far more profound:

There's a voice inside that calls my name
But the world outside is not the same
They say to follow, they say to stay
But I feel the music pulling me away.
I'm caught between the girl I know
And the woman I've yet to show.
The path is blurred, the lines aren't clear
But somewhere in the shadows, I'll appear.
Scattered pieces, floating in the breeze,
Searching for the one that sets me free.
In the chaos, I find my ground,
Piecing together what's always been mine.

She poured herself into the bridge that came to her as she sang:

I'll stitch together every scar
Every dream that's wandered away.
From the ashes, I will rise
With the truth reflected in the stars.
And though I stumble, though I fall,
I'll keep searching, through it all.
For in the pieces, I will see
The woman that's been waiting in me.
Through the storms and through the calm,
I navigate with an open heart.
Every fragment, every scar,
Guides me closer to where we are.

And followed it with the chorus:

I'm searching for the pieces of me
Scattered like leaves on a restless sea
Trying to find where I fit in
In a world that tells me I don't belong
But I'll gather every piece I've lost
No matter the price, no matter the cost
I'll build myself from what's been torn
And find the woman I was meant to be born...

As the final chord echoed, the room sat in stunned silence for a moment, as if the song's raw power had taken their collective breath away. Then, the spell broke, and a murmur of awe spread through the group.

Joe, sitting closest to her, leaned over with a small smile and whispered, "That's the best thing you've written yet, Lena."

Lena's heart swelled, but it wasn't just pride—it was something more, something bigger. For the first time, she felt like the words she had sung truly belonged to her. This song wasn't about love or the war, or about someone else's story—it was hers.

Mr. Morgan, standing in front of the group, cleared his throat, drawing their attention back to him. "That was... exceptional, Lena," he said, his voice unusually solemn. "I think you're starting to find your voice."

Lena blushed at the praise, glancing down at her guitar. "Thank you," she murmured, trying to process the gravity of his words.

Conversation and music flowed as the group lingered, bouncing ideas off one another. Joe played a few protest song riffs, his fingers moving with practiced ease, while another student attempted a jazzy improvisation. Lena joined in, harmonizing here and there, her confidence growing with each note. There was an unspoken connection in these moments, an easy rhythm that made the room feel alive with possibility.

Joe leaned over to her at one point, his voice low enough that only she could hear. "You've got them hooked, you know. That song? It's gonna stick with people. It's sticking with me."

Lena flushed, caught off guard by the sincerity in his tone. "Thanks, Joe. That means a lot."

"You should keep playing it," he added. His gaze lingered on her, serious now. "Not just here. People need to hear it, Lena."

She nodded, unsure how to respond. Joe had always been her biggest supporter, even if he didn't always say it outright. But there was something in his eyes this afternoon—something unspoken, heavy with meaning—that made her heart skip a beat. She pushed the thought away, focusing on the music.

As the group began packing up their guitars, Mr. Morgan lingered near Lena's seat, waiting until the room had mostly emptied. Joe caught her eye on his way out, giving her a brief nod that seemed to say *I believe in you*, before disappearing into the hallway.

Now alone in the room with Mr. Morgan, Lena was still humming the melody of her song, the notes tumbling softly from her lips as she adjusted the tuning pegs on her guitar.

Mr. Morgan, leaning casually against the edge of his desk, crossed his arms thoughtfully. "Lena, you know you've got something special here, right?"

Lena looked up, surprised by his directness. "I don't know... I mean, it feels like it's the best thing I've written, but it's not finished yet."

Mr. Morgan smiled. "That's the beauty of it—songs like this, they're never really 'finished.' You'll keep tweaking it, finding new ways to express what you're feeling. But the bones are there. And it's... powerful."

He paused, then continued, his tone shifting into something more serious. "Have you ever thought about recording a demo?"

Lena blinked, her heart skipping a beat. "A demo? You mean, like, in a studio?"

Mr. Morgan nodded. "Yeah. You've been working hard, honing your sound, and I think you're ready to take it to the next level. It would be a great way to put yourself out there, get some feedback from people in the industry. I know someone—a producer in New York. He listens to a lot of new talent, especially up-and-coming songwriters."

New York. The word hit Lena like a lightning bolt. The thought of her music traveling all the way to New York—being heard by a real producer—felt both exhilarating and terrifying.

"But... how would I even do that?" she asked, her voice soft, unsure.

Mr. Morgan smiled reassuringly. "We can set something up. There's a studio in town I can help you get into. We'll record a clean version of 'Pieces of Me' and any other songs you want to include. I'll make sure it gets into the right hands."

Lena could hardly believe what she was hearing. This was a big step, bigger than anything she'd ever imagined. But as scary as it was, a small, fiery part of her wanted it—wanted the chance to share her music beyond her hometown, beyond the walls of her high school.

"New York..." she murmured, more to herself than to Mr. Morgan. The city seemed so far away, so distant and unreachable. But maybe it wasn't impossible.

Mr. Morgan watched her carefully, sensing her apprehension. "I'm not saying it'll happen overnight," he said gently. "But if this is what you want—to really pursue your music—you've got to take that leap at some point."

Lena swallowed hard, her mind swirling with the possibilities. "I want it," she said, her voice steady despite the whirlwind of emotions inside her. "I do."

Mr. Morgan nodded, his smile warm. "Good. Then let's make it happen."

As Lena left the music room, her heart raced with a mixture of excitement and fear. She couldn't stop thinking about New York, about the idea of someone outside of Janesville hearing her music—her words, her thoughts, her dreams. It felt surreal, like she was on the verge of something big, something life-changing.

As she walked home with her guitar slung over her shoulder, the crisp evening air cooled her flushed cheeks. She knew the road ahead would be challenging, but for the first time in her life, it felt like she was moving in the direction she was meant to go.

Recording a demo, sending it to New York—it was a chance to take her music beyond the small, safe world she had always known. And while the uncertainty scared her, it also made her feel alive.

The melody of "Pieces of Me" played softly in her head, the chorus swirling with renewed meaning. This was her moment, her turning point.

No matter the price, no matter the cost...

She would take that leap. And whatever came next, she would face it head-on, knowing that she was finally gathering the pieces of herself—one song at a time.

42

The late afternoon sun filtered through the thin curtains of Lena's room, casting golden light that danced over the walls. The room felt smaller somehow—claustrophobic with the weight of everything she wasn't saying, everything she couldn't say.

Lena sat on the edge of her bed, her guitar resting on her lap. She strummed idly, her fingers searching for something she hadn't yet found. Her notebook lay open beside her, filled with scribbles—half-finished lyrics, words crossed out, ideas abandoned. She paused, staring down at the mess of ink as if it could somehow tell her what to do.

The chords she played weren't coming together. Nothing was coming together.

Then she heard it—the knock at the front door, followed by the low murmur of voices. Her heart jumped. Tommy.

She set the guitar aside, smoothing her skirt with trembling hands as she stood. A moment later, her bedroom door creaked open, and there he was.

His shoulders were squared, but Lena saw the tension in them. His Sunday best jacket—pressed, neat—hung in the crook of his arm, but he wasn't in uniform yet. He was still just Tommy, her Tommy. And yet... he wasn't.

Not anymore.

"Hey," she said softly, searching his face.

"Hey."

The word fell flat between them. Tommy lingered in the doorway for a beat before stepping inside and shutting the door behind him.

Lena swallowed hard. She wanted to reach for him, to close the distance that had grown between them, but her feet wouldn't move.

Tommy broke the silence first, running a hand through his hair, disheveling it in that way she loved. But this time, it wasn't charming—it was anxious.

"The waiting..." He let out a breath, his voice tight. "It's killing me, Lena."

Lena's heart twisted.

Tommy paced to the window, his hands shoved into his pockets, staring out at nothing. "I thought it'd get easier, you know? That once I went to Madison, it'd stop feeling like... like I was dangling off the edge of a cliff." He turned back to her, and the vulnerability in his eyes stole her breath. "But it didn't. It got worse. No one told me anything then. No one can tell me anything now."

Lena bit her lip, unsure of what to say.

"I just keep thinking about it," Tommy continued. "About what comes next. About the plane or bus I'll take to basic, the drills, the shouting, the uniforms. About the heat and the dirt and the goddamn jungle." His voice cracked, and Lena flinched. "And about you."

"Tommy..."

"I needed you, Lena," he said, stepping closer now, his voice low and raw. "And I know—I know I've been pushing you away. But you've been doing it too."

Lena blinked, tears burning at the edges of her vision.

"We've wasted this time," he said, his voice breaking. "We could've spent it— really spent it. Instead, we've been afraid. Like if we didn't get too close, it wouldn't hurt as much." He laughed bitterly. "But it does. It already does. It hurts so damned much I can't breathe sometimes."

Lena's breath hitched, and finally, finally, she moved. She crossed the room and reached for him, wrapping her arms around his neck as the tears spilled over.

"I'm scared too," she whispered against his shoulder. "I'm scared of losing you. I'm scared of what this war could do to you. I'm scared of... everything."

Tommy pulled her closer, his arms tight around her. "I don't want to waste any more time, Lena. Not a second."

She nodded into his chest, letting herself sink into him, letting the walls she'd built crumble.

After a long moment, Tommy pulled back just enough to look into her eyes. "What were you working on?" he asked, glancing toward her guitar.

Lena wiped at her cheeks, letting out a shaky breath. "A song. But it's... not finished."

Tommy took her hand and led her to the bed, sitting beside her. "Play it for me?"

She hesitated, then picked up the guitar, the strings feeling foreign beneath her fingers. But when Tommy's hand covered hers briefly, giving her a reassuring squeeze, she began to play.

We'd walk along the old dirt road
Your hand in mine, we took it slow
The world was quiet, the stars were bright
With you beside me, everything felt right
You'd talk about the future, you had it planned
But you never asked if I could stand
Still in this town, in this quiet life
You saw me as your future wife.

The last chord hung in the air as Lena's voice faltered. She couldn't go on.

Tommy's fingers brushed her arm. "That's beautiful, Lena."

She shook her head. "It's not done."

"It doesn't have to be." He took the guitar from her, setting it aside before turning back to her. "It's enough."

Lena stared into his eyes—those brown eyes she'd memorized long ago—and saw the truth in them.

But she also saw the fear.

"I don't want to lose you," she whispered.

"You won't."

"You can't promise that."

"No," he said quietly. "I can't. But I can promise this—I'll fight like hell to come home to you. To this." He took her hand, brushing his thumb over her knuckles. "We'll figure out the rest later. But right now... right now, I just need you."

Lena swallowed hard and leaned in, pressing her forehead against his.

"I need you too."

And for the first time in weeks, Lena let herself believe in the possibility of later.

Even if it was fragile. Even if it was fleeting.

She held on.

43

The late afternoon sun streamed through the windows of Lena's house, casting long shadows on the hardwood floors as she paced back and forth in the living room. It was almost Thanksgiving, but the air still felt unusually warm for November. The leaves, which had held on far longer than usual, were now crisp and golden, rustling outside in the light breeze. Lena could hear her mother in the kitchen, preparing something for the upcoming holiday feast, the familiar clatter of dishes and the hum of an old Doo-Wop record playing faintly in the background.

But Lena's mind was elsewhere. On her music. On Tommy. There had been a night, just a week ago, when Tommy had come to her room after dinner. He'd knocked softly, his expression a mix of nervousness and something deeper when she opened the door. They'd spent hours lying side by side on her bed, his hand tracing gentle patterns on her arm as they whispered about everything and nothing. His kisses had been like promises, warm and lingering at first, then growing insistent, almost desperate, as if trying to capture all the time they wouldn't have.

No matter how close they'd been, though, the thought of basic training had lingered like a storm on the horizon. It made their connection feel fragile, like a candle flickering against the wind. And now here she was, a week later, the days slipping by without either of them reaching out. She could feel the distance creeping in again, not because they wanted it but because life seemed to pull them apart no matter how tightly they held on.

She had just gotten back from checking the mailbox. Again. Every day she walked down the path to the street, her heart beating just a little faster, hoping—hoping against hope—that today would be the day she'd find a reply. A letter. A sign. Something from New York.

It had been a few weeks since she and Joe had recorded the demo. Mr. Morgan had made sure it was polished, crisp. Lena had been nervous—more than she thought she would be—standing in front of that microphone in the small local studio, pouring her heart into the song she had worked so hard to craft.

"Pieces of Me" had never sounded better. Lena had felt it in her bones as she strummed the final chords, her voice carrying the weight of everything she had been through, everything she was still going through.

When the recording was finished, Mr. Morgan helped her package it up, along with a short note introducing herself to the producer he knew in New York. She had been cautiously optimistic when they sent it off, but now, with every day that passed without a reply, her optimism was beginning to fray at the edges.

She couldn't help but feel that she was at a crossroads, her life balanced on the precipice between what had always been expected of her and what she truly wanted. With Thanksgiving around the corner, her extended family would soon arrive for their usual gathering. The thought of having to sit around the table, smiling and nodding through conversations about her future—when all she could think about was Tommy and music—felt suffocating.

School had been a blur lately, with basketball season now in full swing. Bill was on the team, of course, his natural athleticism making him just as much a star in basketball as he had been in football. The games were exciting, and Sarah never missed one. Lena attended a few, sitting beside Sarah in the crowded gym, but her mind was always somewhere else—on Tommy, back in the studio, back in that mailbox, waiting for the reply from New York.

Tommy's arms around her were the safest place Lena had ever known. When he held her close, it was as if the rest of the world fell away—her music, her family's expectations, even the war that loomed over them. His lips, soft and lingering, carried a quiet urgency, like he was trying to memorize her with each touch. She'd leaned into him, matching his intensity, as if she could somehow capture the moment forever.

But even in those moments, when their bodies fit together like puzzle pieces, the weight of his absence was already there. It clung to the edges of their closeness, unspoken but undeniable. Every kiss felt like a plea, every embrace a fragile shield against the inevitable. The war hovered between them like a shadow, something neither of them dared to name. They had time now, but not enough, and they both knew it.

She found herself drifting in and out of her classes, even in Music Appreciation, where she'd once been so fully engaged. Joe had noticed, of course. He always seemed to know when something was off with her. The day they recorded the demo had felt like a breakthrough—like they were on the verge of something big. Joe had been with her every step of the way, pushing her when she doubted herself, reminding her that her music mattered.

But now... the waiting was unbearable.

Lena's mother had already begun planning for the big family gathering. She was fussing over the menu, talking about how they'd need extra chairs for the relatives coming in from out of town.

"Lena, did you hear me?" her mother's voice called from the kitchen.

Lena snapped out of her thoughts. "Sorry, Mom, what was that?"

Her mother appeared in the doorway, wiping her hands on a dishtowel. "I was asking if you could help me with the pies tomorrow. We're making apple and pumpkin—your grandpa's favorite." She paused, studying Lena's face with concern. "You've been so distracted lately. Everything okay?"

Lena forced a smile, nodding. "Yeah, just... you know, school stuff."

Her mother didn't look convinced but didn't press further. "Well, your father and I are proud of you. We know it's a big year with graduation coming up, but you're doing great."

Graduation. Another looming expectation. The closer it got, the more suffocating it felt. College or job applications, settling down, staying in Janesville. The future her parents saw for her wasn't the one she wanted, and it felt like every day was a countdown to having to make some monumental decision.

She thanked her mom, but her mind was already back on her demo tape, back on the reply that might never come.

Later that day, after school, Joe walked with her. It had become part of their routine now—a quiet time where they could talk without the others around. Sarah and Bill were always caught up in the whirl of school sports and future plans, but Joe and Lena... they had their music.

"Any news?" Joe asked, nudging her gently as they walked.

Lena shook her head, letting out a sigh. "Nope. I'm starting to think maybe I shouldn't have sent it."

Joe frowned, his eyes narrowing with determination. "Don't do that. That demo is good, Lena. It's really good. You know these things take time. You've got to have a little patience."

She gave him a half-hearted smile, but it didn't reach her eyes. "What if it doesn't happen, Joe? What if I'm just... wasting my time? I'm supposed to be thinking about college or jobs, about my future. And all I can think about is that tape."

Joe stopped walking, turning to face her. "You're not wasting your time. That's your future, Lena. Not college, not staying in Janesville, not doing what everyone expects you to do. This—" he gestured to the guitar case slung over her shoulder, "—this is it. You can't give up on that just because you haven't heard back yet."

Lena looked down at the pavement, his words sinking in. "I know. It's just... hard. All of it. The waiting, the not knowing."

Joe nodded, his expression softening. "Yeah, I get that. But we're in this for the long haul, remember? You've got to keep going, no matter what. You're gonna hear back from New York. I know it."

Lena exhaled slowly, glancing up at him. "Thanks, Joe. For... for always believing in me. Even when I don't."

His mouth quirked into a crooked grin, but there was something in his eyes she couldn't quite read. "That's what friends are for." He gave her a playful nudge on the arm. "Now go write something genius, okay?"

She laughed lightly, shaking her head. "Okay."

As they parted ways, Lena turned back once, catching Joe watching her. He raised his hand in a small wave before shoving it into his jacket pocket, his figure retreating down the sidewalk.

When she reached her house, the sun was beginning to dip in the sky, casting a warm golden glow over the street. The guitar case felt heavier on her shoulder, but her steps felt lighter, even if just by a fraction. Joe's words stayed with her, echoing in her mind like the fading notes of a song: *You're gonna hear back from New York. I know it.*

Still, the weight of the waiting game pressed against her chest. The hope he'd given her burned like a fragile ember—something she was scared to stoke too hard in case it went out.

With Thanksgiving only a few days away, more family pressure and questions about her future awaited her. But even as those worries loomed, she held on to Joe's words.

As she reached for the mailbox, her heart fluttered again with the familiar hope. She opened it... and for a moment, everything seemed to still. There, mixed in with the usual flyers and bills, was a letter addressed to her. From New York.

Lena's breath caught in her throat.

The wait was over.

44

Lena stood frozen on the front steps, the letter from New York trembling slightly in her hands. Her heartbeat thundered in her ears. This was it—the moment she had been waiting for, the reply that could change everything. She was just about to tear open the envelope when the sound of a familiar engine rumbled down the street.

Lena's head snapped up as Tommy's car pulled into the driveway, the sleek, turquoise-and-ivory 1957 Chevy Bel Air gleaming in the late afternoon sun. Her heart sank. She hadn't seen him much lately—hadn't made enough time for them as a couple. The guilt crept in as she shoved the letter into her back pocket, forcing a smile as Tommy stepped out of the car.

But even from a distance, she could tell something was off. His face was tense, his usually warm eyes clouded with frustration.

"Hey," she called out, waving slightly.

Tommy gave her a nod, shutting the car door behind him with more force than usual. As he walked toward her, the weight of the past few weeks hung in the air between them, unspoken but heavy.

When he reached her, he didn't wrap her up in the usual hug, didn't offer his usual easy grin. Instead, he stood there for a moment, hands shoved into his jacket pockets, staring down at the ground before meeting her eyes.

"We need to talk," Tommy said, his voice low but firm.

Lena's heart skipped a beat. "Okay... let's talk." She could feel the tension rising, the space between them thick with everything that had gone unsaid.

Tommy glanced around, then motioned to the porch steps. "Let's sit."

They both sat down, side by side but with a noticeable distance between them. Lena stared down at her hands, her thumb absentmindedly tracing the edge of the letter tucked into her back pocket. She had a feeling she knew what this was about. She had been distracted lately—distant—and she knew Tommy had been feeling it.

"You've been preoccupied, Lena," Tommy began, his voice quieter now but tinged with frustration. "It's like you're... somewhere else. And I get it, your music's important to you. But it feels like we're... drifting. And I don't want that. How do we keep getting back to the same place all the time? It's like the whole world is against us—like even we are against us."

Lena turned to look at him, her eyes stinging. "That's not true. I'm not against us."

Tommy shook his head, running a hand through his hair. "I don't mean you're doing it on purpose, Lena. I just... I feel like I'm fighting for us alone sometimes. And I know I'm not perfect. God knows I've been distracted too, with everything going on, but..." He trailed off, staring out at the street as if searching for the right words.

"It's like every time we try to get closer, something gets in the way," he said finally. "And maybe it's not just the world, Lena. Maybe it's us. Maybe we're the ones putting up walls without even realizing it."

The words hit Lena like a gut punch. She felt tears threaten to spill, but she blinked them back, her voice trembling. "I don't want walls, Tommy. I don't. But everything feels so... uncertain. You're leaving soon, and I don't know how to hold on when I'm scared of losing you."

Tommy's expression softened, and he reached out, his hand brushing hers. "I'm scared too," he admitted, his voice barely above a whisper. "Of leaving. Of what's going to happen to me. To us. But I can't do this alone, Lena. I need you to meet me halfway."

Lena looked down at their hands, his warm and steady against hers. "I don't know how," she said quietly. "I don't know how to hold onto you and still keep this part of me—the music, my dreams—alive."

Tommy exhaled sharply, leaning back slightly. "I never wanted you to choose, Lena. I've never asked that of you. But it feels like... maybe we're not meant to do this right now. Like no matter how hard we try, the pieces don't fit the way they used to."

Lena swallowed hard, guilt gnawing at her insides. She had known this was coming, had felt the distance growing, but hearing it out loud made it real. "I know," she whispered, her voice cracking slightly. "I've just had a lot on my mind. The demo, school, everything..."

Tommy's jaw tightened. "But what about us, Lena? Where do I fit into all of this? You're always talking about your music, and I support you, I do... but it feels like I'm an afterthought sometimes."

Lena felt tears prickling at the corners of her eyes. She didn't want to hurt him—she loved him—but it was hard to balance everything. The weight of his expectations for their future together clashed with the future she was starting to dream of for herself, and it felt like they were on two separate paths.

"Tommy, I'm sorry," she said, her voice barely above a whisper. "I never meant to make you feel that way. It's just... I'm trying to figure things out, you know? The music, what I want to do with my life... it's all happening so fast, and I'm scared."

Tommy turned to her, his eyes softening for a moment as he reached for her hand. "I get that, Lena. I really do. But I'm scared too. I'm about to be shipped off, and I don't know what's gonna happen when I'm gone. I need to know that we're still... us."

Lena squeezed his hand, the weight of his words settling over her. "You are everything to me, Tommy," she said, her voice thick with emotion. "But I also need to figure out who I am. I can't just stop chasing my dreams. I can't give up the music."

Tommy let out a long breath, his gaze dropping to the ground. "I'm not asking you to give it up. I just want to know where we stand. You're talking about sending demo tapes to New York, but... where does that leave me? When I come back from Vietnam, what's left for us?"

Lena felt a lump in her throat. She didn't have all the answers. She couldn't promise that everything would stay the same—because it wouldn't. But she didn't want to lose Tommy, not now, not when everything felt so uncertain.

"I don't know, Tommy," she admitted, her voice trembling. "I can't promise what the future will look like. But I do know that I love you. I want you in my life. I just... I need you to understand that I'm changing. I can't be the girl who stays in Janesville, who just waits around. There's more I want to do, more I need to explore."

Tommy's shoulders slumped, and for a long moment, he didn't say anything. The silence stretched between them, thick and heavy with the weight of possibility. Lena's heart hammered in her chest, waiting for his response, terrified of what he might say next.

Finally, he turned to her, his voice quieter now, almost resigned. "I don't want to hold you back, Lena. I never have. But I also don't want to lose you."

Lena's chest tightened. "You're not going to lose me," she whispered, leaning in closer, her forehead resting against his. "But I need you to be okay with the fact that I might be different when you come back. We both might be."

Tommy let out a shaky breath, nodding slightly. "Yeah... yeah, I get that." He pulled her in closer, his arms wrapping around her in a tight embrace. They stayed like that for a long time, the warmth of his body comforting, grounding her.

Lena felt a tear slip down her cheek, but she wasn't sure if it was from relief or sadness. Maybe both. The truth was, they were on the edge of something new—something unknown—and neither of them could predict what would happen next.

But for now, in that moment, they were still together. And that was enough.

After a while, they both pulled back, the tension between them easing slightly, though the uncertainty lingered.

Lena smiled softly, wiping the tear from her cheek. "You know you're still invited to Thanksgiving, right? My parents are looking forward to seeing you."

Tommy chuckled, the tension breaking just a little. "I wouldn't miss it for the world. Your mom's pumpkin pie is worth sticking around for."

Lena laughed, feeling the knot in her chest loosen. "Yeah, well, I'll save you a seat."

They sat there for a little while longer, the earlier argument fading, replaced by a tentative sense of understanding. It wasn't perfect, but it was something. They both knew the future was uncertain, but for now, they had each other.

After Tommy left, Lena sat on the porch for a few moments longer, her thoughts swirling. She loved him—she did—but his vision of their future together was still so different from the one she was starting to imagine for herself. She had no idea how they were going to make it work, but she hoped—prayed—that somehow, they could figure it out.

With a deep breath, she finally remembered the letter tucked in her back pocket. Slowly, she pulled it out, staring down at the New York return address.

Her hands trembled as she tore open the envelope, her heart racing as she unfolded the letter inside.

Whatever was written there would change everything.

But for now, she would take it one step at a time. One song at a time.

45

Lena sat on the front porch steps, staring at the letter in her hands. The envelope felt heavier than it should, as if the weight of all her dreams had been crammed inside. Her fingers trembled as she unfolded the crisp paper, her eyes scanning the neatly typed words that followed the familiar salutation: Dear Miss Carter...

We want to thank you for sending us your demo. It's clear you have a deep passion for music and songwriting, and we appreciate the vulnerability and emotion in your work.

However, at this time, we feel that your material isn't quite ready for production. We encourage you to keep honing your craft, continue writing, and developing your voice. With time, we believe you have the potential to truly break through.

We wish you the best of luck on your musical journey and look forward to hearing how your sound evolves.

Sincerely,
West 46th Street Records, New York

Lena's breath caught in her throat as the words blurred on the page. *Not quite ready...* The words echoed in her mind like a cruel taunt. After everything she had poured into that demo—her heart, her soul—it wasn't enough. She wasn't enough.

Tears welled in her eyes, spilling over as she clutched the letter to her chest. She couldn't bear the thought of going back inside and facing anyone, not after this. The rejection was too much, a crack in the fragile hope she had been holding onto for so long.

In one swift movement, she pushed herself up and rushed inside, heading straight for the sanctuary of her bedroom.

Lena slammed the door shut behind her, her chest heaving as sobs began to wrack her body. She threw the letter onto her bed, staring at it as if it had betrayed her. All those late nights, all the songs she had scribbled in her journal, the recording she and Joe had worked so hard on—it had all been for nothing.

She collapsed onto the bed, burying her face into the pillow as her tears soaked into the fabric. It felt like the world had come crashing down around her.

The door creaked open slightly, and Lena didn't even have the strength to lift her head.

"Lena?" her mother's soft voice called out, worry laced in every syllable.

Lena didn't respond. Her sobs only grew louder, her body trembling as the rejection consumed her.

Her mother stepped into the room, concern etched on her face. "Sweetheart, what happened? Is it Tommy? I saw him leave earlier. Did you two have a fight?"

But it wasn't Tommy. It wasn't about him at all.

Lena shook her head, her voice breaking through the sobs. "It's not him. It's... it's everything."

Her mother knelt beside the bed, gently rubbing Lena's back. "I'm here, honey. Whatever it is, we'll figure it out together."

But Lena couldn't explain it, couldn't put into words the depth of the hurt she felt. Her mother didn't understand her music the way Lena did. She had always been proud of Lena's talent, but music wasn't part of her world—it wasn't her dream.

Lena felt her mother sit down on the edge of the bed, sighing softly. "I wish you would talk to me, Lena. It hurts to see you like this."

Lena's tears only intensified. She wished she could explain it, but the rejection felt like a personal failure—something too raw to share.

Her mother, not knowing how to comfort her, quietly left the room, leaving the door slightly ajar.

Not long after her mother left, there was a soft knock on the bedroom door. Lena, still curled up on her bed, barely lifted her head.

"Lena?" Sarah's voice filtered through the door, gentle and tentative. "It's me... can I come in?"

Lena didn't have the strength to answer, but the door slowly creaked open, and Sarah stepped inside. She looked at her best friend, her heart sinking at the sight of Lena's tear-streaked face and red-rimmed eyes.

"Your mom called me," Sarah said softly, closing the door behind her. "She's worried about you... and so am I."

Lena tried to speak, but her voice came out in a broken whisper. "It's over, Sarah. My music... everything... it's all over."

Sarah's eyes widened, and she immediately rushed to the bed, sitting beside Lena. "What are you talking about? What happened?"

Lena reached out, pointing at the crumpled letter on the bed. Sarah gently picked it up, her brow furrowing as she read through the words. When she finished, she let out a deep sigh.

"Oh, Lena... I'm so sorry."

Lena buried her face in her hands again, the tears starting fresh. "I tried so hard, Sarah. I thought... I thought maybe I could do this. That I was good enough. But I'm not."

Sarah didn't hesitate—she pulled Lena into a tight hug, holding her as the sobs came pouring out. "That letter doesn't mean it's over, Lena. It's just one letter. It doesn't mean you're not good enough. You have to keep going."

But Lena shook her head, her voice shaky. "I don't know if I can. What if they're right? What if I never make it?"

Sarah pulled back slightly, looking Lena straight in the eye. "Listen to me. You are one of the most talented people I know. You've been writing songs since we were kids, and you've never let anything stop you. This is just a setback. It's not the end. You can't give up now."

Lena sniffled, wiping her face with the back of her hand. "It just... it hurts so much. I don't know how to handle it."

Sarah nodded, her own eyes misty with empathy. "I know. But you don't have to handle it alone. You've got me, and Joe, and even Tommy. We all believe in you. And you're gonna bounce back from this. I know you will."

They sat in silence for a while, the weight of the rejection still heavy, but with Sarah's presence, it didn't feel quite as unbearable.

"Maybe you're right," Lena said quietly after a long pause. "I just need to... process this. It's not the end. It can't be."

Sarah gave her a reassuring smile. "It's not the end, Lena. It's just the beginning."

Lena took a deep breath, feeling a sliver of hope break through the darkness. Maybe Sarah was right. Maybe this wasn't the end of her dream. Maybe it was just a hurdle she had to overcome.

But after Sarah left, the doubt crept back in. It wouldn't be until later, much later, that Lena would realize her obsession with the letter from New York had as much to do with the letter Tommy was waiting for as anything else. Perhaps more. Every day she checked the mailbox, it felt like a cruel twist of fate: her rejection intertwined with his inevitability, their futures bound by forces beyond their control.

Lena's fingers hovered over the rotary dial of the phone on her nightstand, trembling as she forced herself through each number. The familiar rhythm of the clicks felt like a lifeline, pulling her out of the swirling despair that had taken hold. The line rang once, twice, three times before his voice came through, slightly breathless, as if he'd been pacing.

"Lena?" Tommy's tone was sharp with concern. "What's wrong?"

The words wouldn't come at first, just the sound of her uneven breathing filling the silence.

"Lena?" Tommy's voice softened. "Talk to me."

"I need you," she finally whispered, the words cracking under the weight of her emotions.

"Where are you?" he asked without hesitation.

"At home," she managed. "I just... I just need you here."

"I'm on my way," he said firmly, and the line went dead.

Lena sat back on the edge of her bed, staring at the phone in her lap. It was only a few minutes later that she heard the low rumble of his car pulling into the driveway. She barely made it to the front door before he was there, standing on the porch with worry etched into every line of his face.

"Lena," he said, stepping closer, his hands reaching for her. "What happened?"

She didn't answer, just threw her arms around him, burying her face in his chest. The tension in her body melted the moment he wrapped his arms around her, holding her like he could shield her from the weight of the world.

"It's okay," Tommy murmured against her hair, his hand rubbing gentle circles on her back. "I've got you. Whatever it is, I'm here."

Lena didn't remember the drive to the lake. She didn't know how long they'd stayed like that, lying on the old quilt in the back of Tommy's car, his arms wrapped around her. The stars above them were bright, the air crisp and cool, and she felt the rough fabric of his jacket under her cheek as his hand rested lightly on her waist. His kisses were softer that night, slow and unhurried, like they had all the time in the world. But Lena knew better. She could feel the tension in his body, the way his fingers lingered at the edge of her shirt but didn't move further, like he was holding himself back—not just from her, but from the thought of leaving her. Every touch carried a quiet promise, but it was the kind of promise neither of them could keep.

Tommy exhaled deeply, his breath warm against her hair as he pulled her a little closer. "I don't want this to end," he murmured, his voice barely above a whisper.

Lena tilted her head up to meet his eyes, her heart aching at the vulnerability she saw there. "It doesn't have to. Not yet."

His lips curved into a small, bittersweet smile. "Every time I'm with you, it feels like the world stops for a little while. Like nothing else matters."

"But it does," Lena said softly, her fingers tracing the edge of his collar. "The world doesn't stop, Tommy. And it keeps pulling at us, no matter how much we want it to let us be."

His jaw tightened, and he looked away, his gaze drifting to the stars overhead. "I wish I wasn't going. That I could just... stay here. With you. Forget about everything else."

Lena's hand moved to his cheek, gently guiding his face back to hers. "You can't think like that. You're doing what you think is right. What you have to do."

The silence stretched between them, heavy and full of things they couldn't say. Finally, Tommy spoke, his voice rough but steady. "I'm scared, Lena. Not just about going, but about losing this. Losing you."

"You won't," she said firmly, even as her own fears clawed at her. "You'll come back, Tommy. And when you do, we'll figure it out."

His forehead rested against hers, his eyes closing as if he could will her words into truth. "Promise me something," he said after a long moment.

"Anything."

"Don't let this place take you. Don't let Janesville keep you here if I don't come back. You've got too much to give, Lena. Too much to be."

The tears she had been holding back slipped free, and she nodded, her voice breaking as she answered, "I promise. But you have to promise me something too."

"Name it."

"Come back to me," she whispered. "No matter what. Just... come back to me."

Tommy cupped her face, his thumbs brushing away her tears as his lips met hers again, slow and tender, as if sealing the promises they'd just made.

They stayed that way until the chill of the night crept in, and even then, Lena didn't want to let go. Every moment with Tommy felt fleeting now, and she clung to him, hoping that somehow, it would be enough to last until the next time.

46

Wednesday blurred into a rush of school and then Thanksgiving preparations, the house bustling with activity. Lena's mother moved between the kitchen and the dining room, setting out dishes and finalizing plans for the following day's family gathering. Thanksgiving was always a big event at the Carter household, with relatives coming in from all over. The living room was being arranged for the expected onslaught of cousins, aunts, and uncles who would soon fill every corner of the house.

Lena arrived home to find her mother in full hostess mode, hands deep in flour as she prepared pie crusts, her mind whirling with thoughts of table settings and side dishes.

"Lena, darling, can you peel these potatoes?" her mother asked, barely pausing to look up as she rolled out another crust for pumpkin pie.

Lena nodded, grabbing the peeler and setting to work, though her mind was elsewhere—lost in the weight of the rejection letter she'd received just a few days ago. The sting of it still clung to her, but it had dulled with time. She was trying to move forward, focusing on her music and her friends. But every time she thought about it, the disappointment crept back in, gnawing at the edges of her thoughts.

The clattering of pans, the hum of the radio playing softly in the background, and the occasional call from her father asking about where something was filled the house with a comforting sense of routine. This was how things always were at Thanksgiving—chaotic, loud, and warm.

Just as Lena finished peeling the last potato, a sharp knock at the door startled her. The sound carried through the house, cutting through the clatter of dishes and the faint strains of her mother's favorite Doo-Wop record. Before anyone could answer, Tommy let himself in. The brisk November air followed him inside, chilling the warmth of the kitchen as his heavy boots thudded against the hardwood floor.

Lena turned, her heart catching at the sight of him—but her relief was short-lived. The look on Tommy's face wasn't the easy smile she'd come to expect. His jaw was tight, his eyes shadowed with something dark and heavy, and it hit her like a cold wind.

"Tommy?" she asked, drying her hands on a dish towel. "What's wrong?"

He didn't answer right away, just stood there, his shoulders rigid, his hands deep in his jacket pockets. The silence stretched unbearably until, slowly, he pulled something out. A letter. It was creased and worn, as if it had been folded and unfolded a hundred times.

"I got this... a while ago," he said quietly, his voice almost swallowed by the clatter of the kitchen. "I didn't know how to tell you. I didn't know how to..." He exhaled sharply, the sound heavy with guilt and dread.

Lena's stomach sank. She didn't need to see the letter to know what it was.

"No," she whispered, shaking her head as if sheer denial could hold off what was coming. "Not yet. Not now."

But Tommy nodded, his expression grim. "It's real, Lena. I have to report to Madison on Monday. Processing. Then basic training."

The words knocked the breath out of her. The warmth of the kitchen, the familiar smell of roasting turkey and spices, the faint laughter coming from the next room—all of it faded into a dull hum. Her world narrowed to the letter in his hand and the unbearable weight of what it meant.

With trembling fingers, she reached for the paper. The bold type swam before her eyes as she skimmed the words: Order to Report for Induction... Military Entrance Processing Station... Madison... Monday...

Lena's chest tightened, nausea rising as the room spun. "Why didn't you tell me?" she rasped, her voice breaking. "Why didn't you tell me sooner?"

Tommy looked down, guilt etched into every line of his face. "Because I didn't know how. I didn't want to ruin... us. I didn't want to ruin Thanksgiving. But I couldn't keep it from you anymore."

The anger and pain surged all at once, sharp and overwhelming. "You didn't want to ruin us? Tommy, this... this changes everything!" The words came out louder than she intended, cracking like a whip.

He flinched, taking a step back. "I know it does. Don't you think I know that?" His voice rose, matching hers in intensity. "But I can't change it, Lena. I don't have a choice!"

Lena's breath hitched as she tried to steady herself, but the tears came anyway, hot and unstoppable. "How am I supposed to do this? How am I supposed to just... watch you leave? Pretend it'll all be okay when I don't know if—" She couldn't finish the sentence, couldn't bring herself to say the words that haunted her: if you'll come back.

Tommy's face softened, his frustration melting into anguish. "I don't know, Lena. I don't have any answers. All I know is I need you to believe in us. I need to know that when I come back, you'll still be here."

Her heart clenched at the quiet desperation in his voice. She wanted to say yes, to give him the reassurance he needed. But the truth was, she didn't know if she could.

"Tommy, I—" Her voice faltered, the weight of her fears silencing her.

He stepped closer, his hands finding hers, his grip warm and steady despite the trembling in his fingers. "I know it's not fair. I know this is asking too much. But Lena, I need you. You're the only thing keeping me together right now."

The room felt impossibly small, the air thick with everything unsaid between them. Lena stared up at him, the love she felt warring with the doubt and fear that threatened to consume her.

"I don't know how to do this," she admitted, her voice barely above a whisper. "I don't know how to wait for you, how to be here while you're... there."

Tommy cupped her face gently, his thumbs brushing away the tears on her cheeks. "You don't have to know, Lena. We'll figure it out, one day at a time. Just... don't give up on me. Don't give up on us."

His words broke something in her, and she leaned into him, wrapping her arms around his neck as her sobs wracked her body. "I don't want to lose you," she choked out.

"You won't," he whispered, his lips pressing softly against her temple. "I promise, Lena. I'll come back to you."

They stayed like that for what felt like forever, holding on to each other as if sheer willpower could keep the world from tearing them apart.

47

Deep down, Lena knew that nothing would ever be the same after this.

As Tommy finally left, the weight of his news pressed down on her, suffocating in its enormity. She watched his car disappear down the street, her chest tight as though her heart was physically fighting against the truth. For a long moment, she stood frozen in the entryway, her hand still clutching the edge of the doorframe.

Voices carried from the kitchen—her mother humming along to the record, the faint clatter of dishes, her father's low laughter as he relayed some story. The warmth of home had never felt more out of reach. Lena turned away and headed for the stairs, her legs heavy as if wading through a thick, invisible current.

In the sanctuary of her room, she shut the door behind her, leaning against it as though it might keep out the weight of the world. Her eyes fell on the familiar corners of her space—the guitar propped in the corner, the open journal on her desk, pages filled with scribbled lyrics, dreams, fragments of a self she no longer recognized.

She crossed the room and sank onto her bed, the springs groaning softly beneath her. Her fingers traced the edge of her comforter as she tried to focus, to breathe, but her mind was a whirlwind of images and emotions.

Tommy holding that letter. His voice breaking. The way his hands trembled when he reached for hers.

Lena lay back, staring at the ceiling. The peeling star stickers from her childhood caught the faint light, their edges curling with age. She used to stare at them and dream of all the places she'd go—New York, San Francisco, anywhere but here. But now, the stars felt like a taunt, mocking her with a future she wasn't sure she could hold onto.

Tommy was going to war.

War.

The word echoed in her mind, foreign and terrifying, carrying with it all the worst possibilities. She imagined him in a uniform, his face drawn and weary. She imagined him in some faraway jungle, surrounded by danger, the kind of place he might not return from.

And the worst image of all—the one she couldn't banish, no matter how hard she tried—was a folded flag, handed to his mother.

The tears came before she could stop them, hot and heavy as they slipped down her cheeks. She pressed her palms to her eyes, as if she could block out the thoughts that wouldn't stop racing through her mind.

What am I supposed to do?

Her guitar caught her eye, but the thought of picking it up—of singing, of writing—felt impossibly distant. Music had always been her refuge, her way of making sense of the world, but now it seemed so small, so powerless against the enormity of what was happening. What good was a song when the person you loved was being sent off to fight in a war you didn't believe in?

Lena sat up, her breaths shallow and uneven. Her journal sat open on the desk, her handwriting looping across the pages in fits and starts, the lyrics half-formed. She reached for it without thinking, her fingers brushing the edge of the paper.

The words stared back at her:

Fragments scattered in the wind,
Lost reflections deep within.

Her own handwriting felt foreign, like it belonged to someone else—a girl who still believed her biggest battle was convincing people to hear her songs. That girl didn't know what it felt like to hold a letter from the draft board or to see the fear in Tommy's eyes.

Lena slammed the journal shut and pushed it away.

She stood and began pacing the small room, her hands twisting nervously. Her thoughts circled back to Tommy's words: *We'll figure it out. We have to.*

But how?

How could she focus on her music, her dreams, when Tommy was being torn away from her? How could she sing about love or hope when her heart felt like it was breaking?

Her legs gave out, and she sank to the floor, her back against the side of the bed. She wrapped her arms around her knees, the tears falling freely now. "I don't know how to do this," she whispered to the empty room.

She thought of Sarah and Joe, of their unwavering support, but even that felt hollow. Sarah's encouragement couldn't change the fact that Lena's dreams were slipping through her fingers. Joe's passion for rebellion and change couldn't protect Tommy from the realities of a war they both hated.

The clock on her nightstand ticked relentlessly, each second dragging her closer to Monday. Too soon. Too real.

A soft knock on her door broke the stillness.

"Lena?" Her mother's voice was gentle, hesitant.

Lena didn't respond.

"Honey, are you okay?"

"I just... I need a minute," Lena managed, her voice hoarse.

There was a pause, then the sound of retreating footsteps. Lena let her head fall back against the bed, exhaustion weighing her down.

Her gaze drifted to the window, where the bare branches swayed against the deepening twilight. She thought of Tommy, of the way he had held her in the kitchen, his embrace tight and desperate, like he was trying to hold her together even as he was falling apart himself.

I'll come back to you.

But what if he didn't?

The thought made her chest ache, the uncertainty of it threatening to consume her. Lena closed her eyes, trying to focus on the steady rhythm of her breathing, but it did little to calm the storm inside her.

This can't be the end, she thought desperately. *This can't be where it all falls apart.*

But deep down, she wasn't sure anymore.

48

The crisp November air carried the scent of roasted turkey, sweet potatoes, and freshly baked pies through the house as family members slowly trickled in from all over the state, filling the Carter household with noise, laughter, and a comforting chaos that signaled the start of Thanksgiving. The kitchen bustled with energy—dishes clattering, the oven humming, and voices overlapping in lively chatter. But even in the warmth of the family gathering, Lena felt a cold, hollow pit in her heart, gnawing at her thoughts. Tommy's news about reporting for induction on Monday was like a dark cloud hanging over her, shadowing everything.

Lena stood at the counter, chopping vegetables, her mind elsewhere as her mother flitted around, coordinating the meal. Her parents' house, already cozy and warm, seemed to shrink as relatives began to fill every room.

"Lena, sweetheart," her mother, Evelyn, called from the dining room, "Can you check the rolls? And don't forget, Uncle Ned's bringing that cranberry sauce that needs to be reheated."

"Yeah, I've got it," Lena replied absentmindedly, though her thoughts were far from the kitchen.

Just then, the front door creaked open, and the sound of boots stomping on the porch echoed through the house.

"Ned's here!" her father, Robert, called from the living room, already half-watching the pre-game football commentary on TV.

Uncle Ned, her father's brother and the straight shooter of the family, strode in with his wife, Darlene, trailing behind, trying to corral their three rambunctious grade-school-age kids. They were already darting into the house, laughing and running circles around the dining table.

"Whoo-wee, it's cold out there!" Ned boomed, giving Robert a hearty handshake. "You keeping warm, big brother?"

"Just about," Robert chuckled, his eyes crinkling in that quiet way of his. "Come on in, grab yourself a drink. We've got some bourbon in the cabinet."

Ned's voice carried across the house, loud and unmistakable. "Don't mind if I do! Darlene, keep those kids out of the kitchen, would ya? Don't want 'em burning themselves on the stove."

Darlene, her cheeks flushed from the cold, sighed and waved the kids away, pulling off her gloves. "Don't you worry, I'll keep 'em in check," she said, glancing at Lena and offering a sympathetic smile. "How's school, Lena? You still writing those songs?"

Lena nodded, forcing a polite smile, though her heart wasn't in it. "Yeah, still writing. Trying to, at least."

Darlene leaned in a little closer, her voice dropping conspiratorially. "You know, Ned doesn't get it, but I think it's amazing. Keep it up, okay?"

Lena offered a genuine, if small, smile this time. "Thanks, Aunt Darlene. I will."

As Darlene wandered off to join Evelyn in the kitchen, more relatives arrived in waves—Gramma Enid and Grandpa Wally from Green Bay, their old station wagon pulling up out front as they carefully made their way inside, both bundled up in thick winter coats. Grandpa Wally, a war vet like Lena's dad, slapped Robert on the back as he stepped in, his gait slower these days but still proud.

"How's my favorite granddaughter?" Grandpa Wally said with a wink as he spotted Lena in the kitchen. "You keeping these young ones in line?"

"I'm trying, Grandpa," Lena replied, offering him a quick hug. "You want me to get you some coffee?"

"That'd be swell," Wally said, sinking into an armchair.

Then came Aunt Colleen and her husband Jim from Milwaukee, with their twin girls, Betty Sue and Linda Ann, practically bouncing through the door in matching coats. The two girls, far younger than Lena's cousin Missy, wasted no time before dashing off to find her—no doubt to spill some big secret or share the latest excitement. Colleen and Jim greeted everyone warmly, helping set up some last-minute dishes in the dining room.

Aunt Eileen, Evelyn's spinster sister, was the last to arrive, with her quiet but perceptive demeanor. She gave Lena a gentle pat on the arm, her eyes soft behind wire-rimmed glasses.

"You doing alright, dear?" she asked softly.

Lena nodded. "I'm fine, Aunt Eileen. Just... lots on my mind."

"I can tell," Eileen said quietly. "If you ever need to talk, you know where to find me."

Soon, the smell of turkey, gravy, and mashed potatoes filled the house, creating a comforting warmth that mingled with the voices and laughter of Lena's family as they sat around the long dining table. The plates were piled high with Thanksgiving dishes: turkey legs and wings, bowls of cranberry sauce, green beans, stuffing, and buttery rolls passed from hand to hand. The chaos of the meal made it feel like every other year, but for Lena, this year was different.

She sat between Missy and Tommy, her mind heavy with the weight of the conversation they had shared the day before. *Monday.* It echoed in her mind like a drumbeat. He would be leaving for his induction at MEPS in Madison, and the reality of what that meant loomed over her, almost too big to comprehend. She hadn't told anyone yet—hadn't even figured out how to say it out loud to herself.

But here he was, sitting beside her like it was any other Thanksgiving, smiling politely, exchanging small talk with her father and uncles. She could feel his leg brush against hers under the table, a gentle, grounding reminder that he was still there.

As Tommy leaned closer to her, his voice barely above a whisper, he said, "Don't let this ruin Thanksgiving. It's gonna be okay. Just... enjoy today, alright?"

Lena swallowed hard, nodding, though her stomach was in knots. She wanted to tell him it wasn't that simple, that she couldn't just forget what was happening, but she held her tongue. Instead, she forced a smile, tried to engage in the conversations buzzing around her, though her thoughts kept slipping away.

Uncle Ned sat at the far end of the table, his booming voice carrying over the clatter of silverware. "I'm tellin' ya, Robert, that last hunting trip we took? You shoulda seen the size of the buck I got. Biggest one yet. You remember that, Wally?" He glanced at Grandpa Wally, who was slowly working his way through his plate.

"Big as a house," Grandpa Wally grumbled in his slow, deep drawl. "But you still missed half your shots."

Laughter erupted from around the table, especially from Aunt Colleen's twin girls, Betty Sue and Linda Ann, who were busy sneaking bites of whipped cream from the dessert table. Missy tried her best to get in on the conversation too.

Lena's father, Robert, joined in the laughter, though his eyes occasionally flicked to Tommy. He was proud of him, everyone knew that, proud of Tommy's sense of duty and what lay ahead for him. But there was a subtle weight in Robert's eyes, the understanding that war was not the adventure people made it out to be. He'd fought in WWII, after all. He knew better than most.

"You sure you don't need another drink, Tommy?" Robert asked, reaching for the bottle of bourbon on the sideboard. "You've earned one, haven't you?"

Tommy smiled, shaking his head. "Thank you, sir. I'm alright for now."

Robert grunted approvingly. "Good man. Can't have you too full before we head out to the porch later for that man-to-man talk, huh?"

The mention of a talk sent a flutter of nerves through Lena, but she kept her face neutral, pushing a bite of stuffing around her plate as the conversation continued.

Across from her, Aunt Eileen chatted quietly with Lena's mother, Evelyn, both of them discussing the upcoming church events and how the Carters always did Thanksgiving just right. Aunt Eileen was the quieter of the sisters, always offering gentle smiles and knowing glances, while Evelyn took charge of every holiday with a level of perfection only she could maintain. She smiled warmly at Lena across the table, giving her a look of comfort, though unaware of the storm brewing inside her daughter.

"Lena, sweetheart," Evelyn said as she leaned over, placing another piece of turkey on her plate. "Make sure you eat up. You barely touched your food."

"Thanks, Mom," Lena muttered, taking a small bite but barely tasting it.

The food, the noise, the warmth of family—it should have been enough to drown out the dread in her stomach. But it wasn't. Tommy's quiet presence beside her, the looming knowledge of his departure, seemed to overshadow everything. She glanced over at him, watching him nod along to the chatter, but she could see it in his eyes too. The same weight.

At the kids' end of the table, her three rambunctious cousins were up to their usual antics, giggling as they made faces at Betty Sue and Linda Ann when the adults weren't watching. The three kids always found a way to add chaos to every family event.

"We're gonna sneak out after dinner," Linda Ann whispered to Missy, grinning.

"Sneak out where?" Missy whispered back, eyes wide.

"Down to the creek, duh! Like last year," Betty Sue chimed in, licking the whipped cream off her spoon.

Missy looked unsure, glancing toward Lena, but Lena was lost in her own thoughts, her mind already drifting to Monday. Missy shrugged, her excitement dimmed, but the twins pressed on with their plan.

As the meal stretched on, conversations swirled around football, Christmas plans, and stories from the past. Tommy chimed in now and then, answering Robert's questions about work and what he might do after his military service—though the future they spoke of felt farther away than it had just a few days ago.

The table felt like a world unto itself—warm, safe, and sheltered from the chaos outside. But the longer the meal went on, the harder it became for Lena to hold onto that illusion.

More turkey was carved, more rolls passed, and the pies set out as dessert. Coffee was poured, and Uncle Ned was already on his second helping of everything. Lena, though, could barely manage a few bites of apple pie.

At one point, Tommy squeezed her hand under the table, his thumb brushing over her knuckles in a way that was supposed to be comforting. And it was, in its own quiet way. But it was also a reminder—a reminder of what they were trying not to talk about. What they couldn't avoid for much longer.

Lena glanced up, meeting his eyes. The look they shared said everything words couldn't. Monday was coming, and they'd face it—together, somehow. But for today, they were here. Together. And for now, that had to be enough.

"We'll figure it out," Tommy whispered softly, just loud enough for her to hear, his eyes steady on hers.

Lena nodded, forcing a small smile even as her heart ached. "Yeah. We will."

The meal continued, a warm blur of family and food and chatter, but Lena's thoughts kept circling back to the one thing she couldn't push away. Monday.

49

The hum of post-dinner activity filled the house as the women cleared plates from the long dining table, the soft clatter of dishes and running water blending with the low murmur of football commentary drifting from the living room. Lena moved between the two worlds—helping her mother and aunts with the cleanup but constantly stealing glances toward Tommy, who sat quietly on the couch beside her father.

Frank Sinatra's "I've Got You Under My Skin" played softly in the background, mixing with the sounds of the television and murmured conversation. But even as Lena carried dishes to the sink and dried the silverware, her mind was elsewhere. She felt like she was holding her breath, waiting for something to happen—something that felt both inevitable and out of her control.

As she wiped down the counter, she glanced through the open doorway into the living room. There was Tommy, nodding along politely to something Uncle Ned was saying about football—something about Vince Lombardi and the Packers. Tommy smiled and laughed at the right moments, but Lena could see the tension in his jaw, the way he kept flexing his hands in his lap. He hadn't let go of that letter all night.

Her father leaned over to Tommy, saying something too low for her to hear. Then, she saw her father get up, pulling on his heavy coat, and gesture for Tommy to follow him. Tommy hesitated for a moment, but then stood up and grabbed his own coat from the arm of the couch. Lena's heart skipped a beat as she watched them head toward the front door.

"I'll be back in a minute," she muttered to no one in particular, handing the dishrag to Aunt Colleen.

She followed them through the dining room, slowing her pace as they stepped out onto the porch. The screen door creaked as it closed behind them, leaving her standing just inside, half-hidden behind the door frame. She stood there quietly, barely breathing, as the cool evening air seeped through the cracks in the door, chilling her skin.

From her hidden spot, Lena could see the two men through the thin mesh of the screen door. Her father and Tommy stood side by side, leaning against the porch railing. The moonlight cast long shadows across the yard, and their breath rose in small clouds in the chilly November air. The street was quiet— no sounds but the faint rustle of leaves and the distant hum of the town settling in for the night.

Lena's father was the first to speak, his voice steady but low.

"I know your father's already talked to you about what's coming," Robert began, his hands shoved deep into the pockets of his heavy wool coat. "But I feel like I need to say a few things myself, Tommy. You're practically family now. You've been good to Lena, and that makes you my responsibility too."

Tommy nodded, his gaze fixed on the ground, his hands gripping the porch railing tightly.

"Yes, sir," Tommy said quietly.

Lena could hear the seriousness in her father's voice, a tone she'd only heard a few times in her life—usually when he talked about the war. Her father didn't often speak about his time in WWII, at least not in any detail. There were vague references to "the boys" he served with, and the occasional story about basic training or his time in Europe, but rarely anything more.

Tonight was different. Tonight, Lena knew her father wasn't just speaking as her protector or Tommy's future father-in-law. He was speaking as one soldier to another, passing on knowledge he wished he didn't have to.

"War's not what they make it look like in the movies, Tommy. You're not going over there to be a hero." He paused, glancing at Tommy, who kept his eyes down. "You're going over there to survive. Keep your head down. Watch out for your brothers. And get home safe. That's the only thing that matters. Coming home."

Tommy swallowed hard, nodding. Lena could see the tension in his shoulders, the way his body seemed to hold the weight of the words pressing down on him. She pressed her hand against her mouth, feeling her chest tighten.

Her father continued, his voice thick with the kind of emotion Lena wasn't used to hearing from him.

"There's gonna be times when you think you have to step up. To save somebody. To be the hero. But trust me, son... It's not worth it if you don't make it home. Don't try to be something you're not. Don't try to prove anything. Just do your job, and come back to the people who love you."

Lena's heart clenched. She didn't think she'd ever heard her father speak so openly, so rawly about his experiences. And to hear him tell Tommy, the boy she loved, not to be a hero... It broke something inside her.

"You mean a lot to Lena, Tommy. More than I think she even realizes yet. And you mean a lot to me too. So promise me you'll remember what I said. Don't go looking for glory. Just come home safe."

There was a long silence. Lena watched as Tommy nodded again, this time more firmly.

"I promise," Tommy said softly. "I'll come back. For Lena. For all of you."

Her father reached out, gripping Tommy's shoulder in a gesture that was both strong and tender. Lena could see the respect in her father's eyes, the way he looked at Tommy not just as a boy anymore, but as a man—someone who was about to face the same things he had faced decades ago.

And then, unexpectedly, the tears came. Lena pressed herself against the door frame, willing them to stop, but it was no use. Silent tears slipped down her cheeks as she listened to the man she loved promise to come back from a war that had already claimed too many. Her father's words echoed in her mind, haunting her with the weight of what was to come.

She wiped her face quickly, trying to pull herself together, not wanting to be caught eavesdropping on such a private moment. But she couldn't move. She couldn't tear herself away from the sight of them—her father and Tommy, standing together in the cold night air, connected by something deeper than she could fully understand.

The porch light flickered above them, casting a soft glow over the scene. Her father patted Tommy's shoulder one last time before stepping back, his hands going back into his pockets.

"Come on," he said gruffly, his voice a little thicker than usual. "We've got family inside. Let's not keep 'em waiting."

Tommy nodded, wiping at his eyes briefly, and followed her father back toward the door. Lena barely had time to duck out of sight, retreating into the shadows of the hallway as the screen door creaked open and the men stepped back inside.

Her heart felt heavy in her chest, weighed down by the reality of what was happening. But as she watched her father and Tommy rejoin the family, she knew that something had shifted between them. Her father had given Tommy the talk—one soldier to another—and somehow, that made everything feel more real.

Monday was coming.

50

The night had settled fully over Janesville, a deep chill accompanying the fading remnants of the Thanksgiving feast. The once bustling house was now quieter as the relatives trickled out, arms laden with Tupperware filled with turkey, mashed potatoes, and pies, courtesy of Lena's mother, who made each of them promise to return the containers at Christmas.

"Now don't forget to bring those back, alright?" her mother called after Aunt Colleen, who waved off the reminder with a laugh.

Gramma Enid and Grandpa Wally settled themselves on the couch, grateful for the chance to sit back and rest after the long trip from Green Bay, while Lena's father made one last trip to the garage to grab something for them.

Lena slipped on her coat, feeling the cold as it seeped through the windows. The warmth of the house had already started to fade now that the ovens were off and the door was constantly opening and closing.

Tommy was at her side, zipping up his jacket and tugging on his gloves. They had barely spoken since dinner, their exchanges quiet and heavy with the weight of everything unsaid.

"Let's go for a walk," he suggested softly, his breath visible in the cold air. "Just you and me."

Lena nodded, and together, they stepped out into the night, the crunch of frost underfoot the only sound in the stillness. The cold hit her immediately—sharp and unforgiving—but it was a welcome distraction from the gnawing ache that had been sitting in her chest since Tommy showed her the letter.

As they walked, the town felt empty, almost abandoned. The streets were quiet, houses glowing faintly from within, but no one was out. The cold had driven everyone indoors, wrapped up in the warmth of family and firesides. But here they were, walking through the cold, with only the sound of their footsteps and the occasional gust of wind to fill the silence.

Lena pulled her coat tighter around herself, shivering despite the layers. Tommy's hand found hers, warm and solid in the chill, and for a moment, she let herself lean into that comfort.

"I can't believe how fast it's gotten cold," she said, her voice barely more than a breath against the biting wind.

Tommy chuckled softly, his breath misting in front of him. "Yeah... feels like winter's already here."

The streetlamps cast long shadows on the road, the frost shimmering under their light like tiny diamonds scattered across the pavement. Lena tugged her scarf tighter around her neck, trying to block out the cold, but it wasn't just the weather that left her shivering. The weight of Tommy's news loomed over her, a silent companion to their walk.

Everything looked so still, so peaceful tonight. And yet, inside, Lena felt like she was splintering.

Tommy walked beside her, his thumb absently brushing over the back of her hand. The gesture was familiar, comforting, but it wasn't enough to still the storm churning in her chest. He was quiet for a while, his breath clouding in the frosty air, and Lena felt the tension between them growing heavier with each step.

Finally, Tommy broke the silence. "Lena," he said, his voice softer than usual. "I've been thinking a lot about... what happens when I get back. After the war."

Her heart squeezed painfully at the words, at the ease with which he said them, as if coming back was guaranteed. She wanted to believe that too, more than anything.

"What have you been thinking about?" she asked, her voice almost too quiet.

Tommy's grip on her hand tightened as they walked. "I want... I want a life with you, Lena. I've been thinking about it a lot. After the war, after I come home, I want us to settle down. Get married, build a home, start a family."

Her steps faltered for just a second, her breath catching. He kept walking, oblivious to the turmoil rising inside her.

"I've thought about getting a steady job," he continued, his tone gaining confidence. "Maybe at the GM plant, like your dad. It's good work—honest work. We could get a little house, something cozy. I don't need anything big. Just you. And maybe..." He hesitated, then smiled softly, as if picturing it in his mind. "Three kids."

"Three?" Lena asked, trying to keep her voice light, though her chest felt tight.

"Yeah. A boy first, you know, someone to carry on the family name. And then two little girls who look just like you. Beautiful, smart, and..." His eyes softened as he turned to her. "Someone who can light up a room the way you do... I can see it so clearly, Lena. Us. A real future."

His words painted a picture so vivid, so beautiful, it made Lena's throat ache. She could see it too—Tommy coming home after a long day at the plant, their children laughing in the yard, the smell of dinner in the oven. It was a good dream. A safe dream.

But it wasn't hers.

The realization struck her like a sharp wind, leaving her breathless. She bit her lip, trying to hold back the words she knew she needed to say.

"Tommy, I..." She trailed off, unsure how to begin. How could she shatter this dream of his, this hope he was holding onto so tightly? Especially now, with so much uncertainty hanging over them.

"You'll be amazing, Lena," he said, his voice warm, earnest. "An amazing wife, an amazing mother. I know it. And I'll take care of us. You'll never have to worry about anything."

Lena stopped walking, her hand slipping out of his. The cold stung her face, her breath coming in short, visible bursts as she looked at him. "But what about my music?" she asked, her voice trembling. "What if I'm not ready to settle down? Not yet."

Tommy turned to face her, his brow furrowing in confusion. "You'll still have your music, Lena. I'm not saying you have to give it up. But maybe it doesn't have to be everything. You can still play, still write, but... after we've built our life together."

The sincerity in his voice was almost her undoing. He wasn't asking her to give up her dreams, not in his mind. But he didn't understand.

"It doesn't work like that," she said, her voice breaking. "Music isn't just something I do, Tommy. It's who I am. It's... everything. I can't just put it on hold. I can't—" She stopped, her chest tightening as the words spilled out.

Tommy's face fell, the smile fading as he searched her eyes. "I love you, Lena," he said quietly. "I want a life with you. I just don't understand why this music thing has to be more important than us."

"It's not more important," she said quickly, the words rushing out. "It's not... but it's part of me. And I don't know how to give that up without losing myself."

He looked away, his jaw tightening. The silence stretched between them, thick with everything they couldn't say.

Lena's hands clenched into fists at her sides. She wanted to scream, to cry, to tell him that she loved him more than anything, but it wasn't enough. It wasn't enough to give up the part of her that had kept her going all these years.

"Tommy," she said softly, stepping closer to him. "I want you to have this dream. I want you to hold onto it, especially now. But I can't promise you that I'll be ready for that life when you come back."

His eyes snapped back to hers, filled with pain. "Why not?" he asked, his voice cracking. "Why can't we both have what we want? Why can't you have your music and me?"

Her breath hitched. "Because I don't think you'll ever see my music the way I do. And I don't think I can give up enough to fit into the life you're imagining."

Tommy stared at her, the hurt in his expression cutting deeper than any words ever could. "So that's it?" he asked, his voice raw. "You're giving up on us before I've even left?"

"I'm not giving up," Lena said, tears slipping down her cheeks. "But I can't lie to you, Tommy. I can't promise you something I'm not sure I can give."

They stood there in the cold, the world around them eerily still. The space between them felt insurmountable, the dreams they'd once shared splintering into pieces.

Finally, Tommy spoke, his voice low. "I just wanted to believe we could have it all."

"So did I," Lena whispered.

They walked back in silence, the warmth of their hands in each other's replaced by the icy distance that had grown between them.

51

The muffled laughter from downstairs echoed up through the floorboards, mixing with the distant sound of what Lena could only guess was the shuffle of feet—her grandparents maybe dancing again, like they used to when she was a little girl. The warmth of that laughter and the rhythm of life below tugged at her heart, reminding her of the fullness of love and joy that existed within the walls of this house.

Her parents and grandparents were still so full of life, even after all these years. Her grandparents, Gramma Enid and Grandpa Wally, had been through so much—yet here they were, celebrating, laughing, dancing, despite all the weight of their past. Her parents, too, after so many years of hard work, still found moments of quiet joy together, the kind that comes from a shared life and love.

It made her question everything.

Lena stood by her window, looking out at the darkened street. The frost had settled on the ground, glistening under the moonlight. She could still feel

Tommy's kiss lingering on her lips, the warmth of it fighting against the cold night air that had chilled her during their walk. But even that kiss—the way it had felt both so right and so wrong—made her feel torn inside.

She loved him. She knew that. But love wasn't enough, was it? Not when her heart was pulled in two different directions. On one hand, there was Tommy—his dreams of a quiet, settled life, the house, the kids, the future he so desperately wanted to build with her. And on the other hand, there was her music, her restless spirit, the part of her that longed for something more than what Janesville could offer.

Her guitar sat in the corner, perched on its stand like it was waiting for her, its strings gleaming in the dim light of the room. Her music journal lay beside it on her desk, the pages filled with half-finished songs and scribbled-out lyrics. "Pieces of Me" had been one of the songs on her failed demo. New York—those dreams of making it as a songwriter in the big city—seemed so distant now, especially after the rejection letter. The sting of it still lingered, sharp and deep, as though someone had torn her dreams apart.

She thought back to the "Pieces of Me" outro that had come to her so clearly on the day she recorded the demo:

As the pieces start to fall in place,
I embrace the journey, I find my space.
Whole and free, I finally see,
The pieces of me were meant to be.
The woman I've been searching for—me.

It had been one of her favorites, and yet it felt... unfinished somehow. Like there was still a piece missing—something she couldn't quite name but that left the song feeling incomplete. Just like her.

Lena sighed and crossed the room to her guitar, her fingers brushing against the smooth wood as she picked it up. She sat down on the edge of her bed, cradling the instrument in her arms, her fingers finding the familiar chords of "Pieces of Me." But as she strummed the opening notes, the sound wasn't right. She pressed harder, but there was an unmistakable twang as one of the strings snapped, the sudden break echoing in the stillness of the room.

"Damn it," she muttered, her frustration bubbling up. It felt like everything in her life was breaking lately—her dreams, her relationship with Tommy, her music. Now even her guitar was falling apart.

She set the guitar down gently on her lap and started to replace the broken string, her hands working mechanically as her mind wandered. The rejection letter. Tommy's induction notice. Her family downstairs, still laughing and dancing as though nothing in the world could touch them. But here she was, sitting alone in her room, with nothing but a broken guitar and a head full of doubt.

As she tightened the new string, something stirred inside her—a melody, faint at first, but persistent. It tugged at the edges of her mind, pulling her back to the place where her songs came from. It wasn't "Pieces of Me." No, this was something different.

The words began to form slowly, haltingly, as though they were trying to find their way through the fog that had been clouding her thoughts. She strummed a few tentative chords, and the melody started to take shape. It wasn't perfect, not yet, but it was something.

I sit here with my guitar, fingers pressing down
Notes that don't belong to the song I feel inside.
The words are trapped, tangled in chords that won't come together,
And I wonder if they'll ever find their way to air.

The lyrics came to her in fragments, like pieces of a puzzle she didn't know how to put together yet. But there was something in them—something real, something raw. She couldn't finish the song tonight, she knew that much. It would take time, time she wasn't sure she had, but for now, just getting the words out was enough.

She closed her eyes, the song still playing in her head as she gently set the guitar back on its stand. It would take work but this song felt like it mattered. Like it was the beginning of something new. Something she hadn't yet discovered about herself.

Lena let herself lie back on her bed, the ceiling spinning as she thought about everything: the future she was trying to find, the past she couldn't let go of, and the present that seemed to be slipping through her fingers. She didn't know what tomorrow would bring, or the day after that. But for tonight, she had her music.

52

The smell of bacon, eggs, and fresh coffee filled the kitchen, weaving together with the warmth of family. Lena sat at the breakfast table with her parents and grandparents, her guitar resting quietly in the corner, forgotten for the moment as the cheerful chatter flowed around her. The tension from the previous day had eased a little, and the coziness of the moment made it easy to forget, if only for a short while, about the weight that had been pressing down on her heart.

Grampa Wally was in the middle of one of his legendary stories—this one about his days working on the docks back in Green Bay. His voice was gravelly but animated, his eyes twinkling with mischief as he recounted a tale that had them all in stitches.

"...so there I was, knee-deep in fish guts, and who walks up behind me but the mayor! And I didn't even notice at first, I'm so busy cursing at the pile of nets that just tore. Next thing I know, there's a hand on my shoulder and I'm turning around, smelling like a dead mackerel, and the mayor's looking me dead in the eye, saying, 'Son, I think you're missing your calling!'"

Laughter erupted from everyone at the table. Gramma Enid swatted him playfully on the arm, shaking her head with an amused sigh. "Wally, you've been telling that story for years, and it gets more ridiculous every time."

Lena's dad chuckled, his usual stern demeanor softened as he leaned back in his chair. "I'm still not sure I believe half of what comes out of your mouth, Dad."

Grampa Wally grinned, unapologetic. "Well, you don't have to, Robert. The fish guts were real enough. That's all that mattered that day."

Even Lena's mom, always the proper one, was giggling into her napkin. There was something magical about mornings like this—where no one had to rush off anywhere, where her dad didn't have to work, and the whole family could just be together. For a few precious hours, the world outside didn't matter. It was just the warmth of home, the love of family, and the joy of shared stories.

Lena watched her parents exchange looks across the table, their quiet connection, the easy way they moved around each other. Her father reached for the butter at the same time her mother passed it to him, a silent choreography that spoke of decades together. Her heart squeezed at the sight, torn between admiration and fear. Was this what she wanted? This kind of simple, quiet life, rooted in love and routine? Or was she meant for something else, something bigger?

As the laughter died down, Gramma Enid leaned in toward Lena, her soft eyes crinkling at the edges. "You're awfully quiet this morning, Lena girl. You've got something on your mind?"

Lena smiled softly, shaking her head. "Just thinking, Gramma. That's all."

"Good thinking or bad thinking?" her grandfather teased, winking at her from across the table.

"Somewhere in between," Lena admitted, glancing at her guitar for a moment. "I guess a bit of both."

Before anyone could respond, the sharp ring of the phone cut through the kitchen. Lena's mom was up in an instant, wiping her hands on her apron before picking up the receiver. "Carter residence... Oh, hello, Sarah dear."

Lena perked up, hearing her best friend's name. Her mom turned toward her, a smile spreading across her face. "It's for you, Lena."

Lena quickly took the phone, curiosity bubbling up inside her. "Hey, Sarah. What's up?"

On the other end, Sarah's voice was breathless with excitement. "Lena, you have to come over to my house. I've got the most exciting news, and I can't wait to tell you! Like, right now! Get over here as soon as you can!"

Lena could practically see Sarah bouncing with energy on the other side of the line. She glanced at her parents, still sitting around the table, her dad picking at the last of the scrambled eggs, her mom tidying up the dishes. "Okay, I'll be over in a few. What's going on, though? Give me a hint."

Sarah giggled, clearly enjoying the suspense. "Nope, no hints! Just hurry up. You'll die when you hear this."

Lena laughed softly. "Alright, alright. I'm on my way."

She hung up the phone and turned to her family. "I'm going over to Sarah's. She's got some... exciting news, apparently."

Her dad gave her a half-teasing, half-serious look. "Better not be any trouble, you two."

Lena rolled her eyes. "Dad, it's Sarah. The only thing we get in trouble for is staying up too late watching movies."

Her mom smiled knowingly, wiping her hands on her apron. "Well, you be back in time to help with dinner later, alright? We're still going to need you."

"Yes, ma'am," Lena said with a grin. She grabbed her coat and slipped out the door, her mind already buzzing with possibilities about what Sarah could have to tell her.

As she walked, her thoughts still swirled in a thousand directions—her music, Tommy, Thanksgiving, and now this new piece of excitement from Sarah. Whatever it was, Lena knew it was bound to make the day even more interesting.

The crisp air seemed to nip at Lena's skin as she approached Sarah's house, her steps slow and deliberate. Her heart felt heavy, a familiar ache twisting in her chest. She hadn't told Sarah about Tommy leaving yet, and the weight of it was almost unbearable. But today wasn't about her—at least, not yet. Sarah had called with news so exciting she could barely contain it, and Lena didn't want to ruin her friend's joy, no matter how much she was hurting inside.

She knocked gently on the door, her breath hanging in the air as she waited. A moment later, the door swung open, and Sarah's mom appeared with a warm smile.

"Well, if it isn't Lena! Come on in, sweetheart. Sarah's been bouncing off the walls waiting for you."

Lena forced a smile, stepping into the familiar warmth of Sarah's house. "Thanks, Mrs. Mitchell," she said, her voice softer than usual.

"She's upstairs in her room. You know the way," Sarah's mom said, giving Lena's shoulder a gentle pat before turning back to the kitchen. The sounds of pots clattering and the faint aroma of leftover Thanksgiving pies lingered in the air, but none of it made Lena feel at ease.

With a quiet sigh, Lena made her way up the stairs, her heart heavier with each step. She hadn't even had the chance to completely process Tommy's news herself, let alone figure out how to tell Sarah. But she shoved those thoughts down for now, knowing she had to be there for her friend.

Sarah's bedroom door was slightly ajar, and Lena could already hear the excitement in her voice before she even entered.

"Is that you, Lena? Come on in!" Sarah's voice rang out, bubbly and bright.

Lena pushed the door open, and there was Sarah, practically glowing as she sat cross-legged on her bed, her eyes wide with excitement. "Lena, I've been dying to tell you!"

Lena gave a small, hesitant smile, stepping inside and closing the door behind her. "You said you had some exciting news," she said, trying to match Sarah's energy but feeling like her own heart was miles away.

Sarah grinned from ear to ear, clearly savoring the moment, as she always did with her stories. She was a natural storyteller, always giving everything a big wind-up before getting to the point. "Okay, so picture this," she began, her hands gesturing wildly as she set the scene. "It's Thanksgiving dinner, and we're all sitting around the table. Bill's mom made the best stuffing ever, and his dad, of course, is talking about the Packers—what else is new, right? Anyway, dinner's winding down, and Bill—he's been acting a little weird all night, you know? Like, super quiet, which is so not like him."

Lena nodded along, trying to keep up with the enthusiasm, even though her mind was spinning with everything she hadn't said yet.

"So, everyone's getting ready for dessert," Sarah continued, her voice growing more animated, "and then Bill's mom brings out the pie—pumpkin, my favorite—and just as I'm about to dig in, Bill stands up. He's all serious, right? Like, way too serious for a Thanksgiving dinner. And I'm thinking, 'What the heck is going on?' And then—" Sarah paused dramatically, her eyes sparkling with delight, "—he pulls out this little box from his pocket."

Lena's stomach twisted, and she knew exactly where this was going. But she said nothing, letting Sarah have her moment.

Sarah giggled, her cheeks flushing as she reached for the tiny box sitting on her nightstand. "He opened it, Lena, and inside was this gorgeous ring. I thought

I was gonna pass out!" She held up her left hand, the delicate silver promise ring twinkling in the afternoon light.

Lena blinked, forcing another smile, but inside, her heart clenched. "Wow, Sarah," she whispered, her voice tight. "It's beautiful."

Sarah was practically vibrating with excitement. "Isn't it? He said it's a promise, you know? That after we graduate, we're gonna be together forever. Like, really together. We talked about it all last night—our life, our future... everything."

Sarah sighed dreamily, leaning back against her pillows. "Three kids, a house with a picket fence, just like we always talked about, Lena. I'm gonna be Mrs. Bill Thompson someday."

Lena's throat tightened as Sarah continued to talk about the life she and Bill were going to have. Three kids. The same thing Tommy had talked about the night before. A life Lena could barely imagine for herself—no matter how hard she tried. But she didn't say anything, not yet. She couldn't.

"Bill's so sweet," Sarah went on, her eyes far away with dreams of the future. "He even said we could name one of the girls after my grandmother. Isn't that perfect?"

Lena swallowed hard, trying to keep herself together. "It's... perfect," she managed, her voice almost a whisper. But her heart was pounding, and all she could think about was Tommy's news, the letter that was sending him off to war, the way her world felt like it was falling apart while Sarah's was falling perfectly into place.

Sarah noticed Lena's quietness, her smile faltering just slightly. "Are you okay, Lena?" she asked softly, sitting up straighter. "You've been kind of... off today. Did something happen with Tommy?"

Lena looked down at her hands, her fingers twisting nervously in her lap. She didn't want to ruin Sarah's joy, didn't want to be the one to darken her perfect moment. But she couldn't keep it in any longer. Her voice was soft, barely above a whisper. "Tommy's leaving, Sarah."

Sarah's eyes widened, her smile fading as the weight of Lena's words sank in. "What do you mean... leaving?"

Lena bit her lip, tears welling in her eyes. "He... he got his letter. He has to report for induction on Monday. He's leaving for basic training and then Vietnam."

The room fell silent, the air suddenly heavy with the reality of Lena's words. Sarah's hand flew to her mouth, her eyes brimming with shock and sadness. "Oh, Lena," she whispered, her voice cracking. "I... I didn't know."

Lena shook her head, tears finally spilling over. "I didn't know how to tell you. I didn't want to ruin your news."

Sarah reached out, pulling Lena into a tight hug, her own eyes filling with tears. "Lena, I'm so sorry. I can't even imagine what you're going through."

For a long moment, they just held each other, the weight of Tommy's departure settling between them. Lena knew that no matter how much they dreamed of their futures, everything was about to change. And as much as she wanted to be happy for Sarah, all she could feel was the growing hole in her heart where Tommy had been.

53

Lena stepped out of Sarah's house with a forced smile, waving goodbye as Bill arrived, his usual confident stride carrying him up the front steps. She didn't want to intrude on their time together—especially not after Sarah's big news about the promise ring. The weight of her own reality was too much, and the last thing she wanted was to be the third wheel in her best friend's glowing romance.

She made up a quick excuse, telling them she was meeting Tommy at the soda shop, but the truth was, she just needed to clear her head. To be alone with her thoughts for a while.

The cold bit at her skin as she walked down the quiet streets of Janesville, but as the sun started to rise over the horizon, its rays slowly chased away the chill. Her breath puffed out in little clouds, the soft crunch of her boots on the frosted ground the only sound around her. The world felt still—too still, considering the storm swirling inside her.

She couldn't stop thinking about Tommy. About Monday. His induction. His departure. The way everything felt like it was slipping through her fingers, no matter how hard she tried to hold on. Her music, her dreams... it all seemed so small compared to the reality of losing him to the war.

The soda shop loomed ahead, its windows fogged up from the warmth inside. She stopped outside, not sure if she really wanted to go in. The street was empty except for a figure leaning against the wall near the shop's entrance—someone familiar.

Joe.

He was bundled up in his worn jacket, a cigarette dangling between his fingers, the tip glowing faintly as he took a slow drag. His eyes flicked up as she approached, and for a moment, they just stared at each other, the silence stretching between them.

"Lena," Joe said, exhaling smoke into the crisp morning air. "Didn't expect to see you out this early."

Lena pulled her coat tighter around herself, offering a faint smile. "Yeah, well... needed to get out. Clear my head."

Joe pushed off the wall, stamping out the cigarette beneath his boot. "Something tells me you've got more than just a little thinking on your mind."

She hesitated, her eyes drifting down to the sidewalk. "Tommy's leaving on Monday."

Joe's expression softened, his usual rebellious edge melting away. "Yeah... I figured it'd be soon." He stuffed his hands into his pockets, stepping closer. "That's rough, Lena. Really rough."

Lena swallowed hard, fighting back the tears that threatened to spill over. "It feels like everything's falling apart. I don't even know what to say to him anymore. He's got his life all planned out—marriage, kids, the whole thing. And here I am... still trying to figure out who I am."

Joe studied her for a long moment, his brow furrowing. "And that's okay, you know? Not having it all figured out. You don't have to have all the answers right now."

She looked up at him, searching his face for something—anything—that might make her feel less lost. "But what if I don't fit into his plan, Joe? What if... what if I'm not enough?"

Joe's eyes softened even more, and he shook his head. "You're more than enough, Lena. You always have been. But the thing is... you gotta figure out who you are first. Not who Tommy wants you to be. Not who your parents want you to be. You."

Lena let out a shaky breath, the weight of his words settling over her. "I don't even know where to start."

Joe smiled faintly, his usual cocky grin replaced with something gentler. "You're already starting. You've got your music. That's something most people don't have—a voice. And it's a damn good one, too."

Lena's gaze dropped to the guitar case slung over her shoulder, the one she'd almost forgotten she was carrying. "Yeah, but... it feels so small. Compared to everything else. Compared to what Tommy's about to go through."

Joe tilted his head, studying her with those sharp eyes of his. "Your music's not small, Lena. It's yours. It's who you are, even when everything else around you feels like it's falling apart." He paused, his voice softening even more. "And maybe it's exactly what you need right now."

Lena's heart thudded in her chest, her fingers tightening around the strap of her guitar case. Joe always had a way of cutting right to the heart of things, of saying what she needed to hear even when she didn't realize it.

"You know," Joe added after a moment, "I've been thinking... maybe it's time we got out of here. Just... hit the road. See what's out there. New York. San Francisco. Somewhere bigger than this place."

Lena blinked in surprise, her breath catching in her throat. "You... you want to leave Janesville?"

Joe shrugged, his hands still deep in his pockets. "I've been thinking about it for a while now. This town... it's too small. Too... narrow. You feel it, don't you? Like it's holding you back?"

Lena nodded slowly, the idea of leaving—of running away—stirring something deep inside her. A part of her wanted to say yes, to pack up her guitar and hit the road with Joe, to chase the dreams that felt so far out of reach here in Janesville. But there was still Tommy. Still everything else she couldn't quite leave behind.

"I don't know, Joe," she whispered. "I don't know if I can just... go."

Joe gave her a small, understanding nod. "I get it. But just... think about it, okay? You've got something special, Lena. Don't let this place—or anyone— keep you from finding out just how far you can go."

Lena didn't know what to say, so she just nodded, her heart feeling heavier than ever. The idea of leaving felt impossible, but so did staying. And in that moment, standing there on the sidewalk outside the soda shop with Joe, everything felt like it was hanging in the balance.

54

Lena sat at the corner booth of the soda shop, her fingers tracing idle patterns on the checkered tabletop. She stared into the half-empty glass of soda in front of her, the ice melting slowly, droplets forming on the outside of the glass. The warmth of the place contrasted with the cold that clung to her thoughts, her mind still spinning from the conversation with Joe and the overwhelming weight of Tommy's looming departure.

She could hear the faint hum of conversation around her, the clatter of dishes from the kitchen, and the soft sound of the jukebox in the background, but it all felt distant—muted. Her eyes drifted toward the window, catching the sight of Joe walking down the street with Carly, his arm draped casually over her shoulders. She watched as they disappeared into the cold, leaving her alone with her tangled thoughts.

Everything felt so heavy—Joe's words, Tommy's news, the rejection letter, her music, all swirling together in a haze of uncertainty. Lena felt like she was standing at a crossroads, not knowing which way to turn. Every path seemed fraught with choices she wasn't ready to make.

Suddenly, the bell above the soda shop door jingled, and she looked up to see Tommy walking in, his tall frame silhouetted against the bright light outside. He spotted her immediately and made his way over, a smile tugging at the corners of his lips. Lena straightened in her seat, trying to push aside the weight in her chest.

"Hey," Tommy said softly as he slid into the booth across from her. His eyes searched her face, and there was a gentleness in his expression that made Lena's heart ache even more.

"Hey," she replied, trying to smile. But she knew it didn't quite reach her eyes.

"Joe said you might still be here," Tommy added, leaning forward slightly, his voice warm. "I'm glad I caught you."

Lena nodded, wrapping her fingers around the cool glass in front of her, hoping the physical act of holding onto something would ground her. "Yeah, just... needed some time to think."

Tommy's smile faltered slightly, and she could tell he knew something was off. He reached across the table, taking her hand gently in his, his thumb brushing over her knuckles. "I know it's been a lot lately. I just wanted to... make today about us. Give you a break from everything."

Lena's heart clenched at his words. He was trying so hard, and she could see it in his eyes—the love, the care. But that only made the ache in her chest deepen. How could she tell him that everything felt like it was slipping through her fingers? That she wasn't even sure what she wanted anymore?

But she didn't say any of that. Instead, she smiled softly, squeezing his hand. "That sounds nice, Tommy."

His face lit up at her words, the worry fading from his expression. "Good. I've got the whole day planned out for us. We'll start with ice skating at that big indoor rink in Madison—got it all cleared with your parents so they won't worry."

Lena's eyes widened in surprise. Ice skating? In Madison? He really had planned something. "You... cleared it with my parents?"

Tommy nodded, grinning. "Yep. Your dad even cracked a joke about how I better keep you from falling on the ice. And your mom, well... she gave me enough warm scarves and mittens to outfit an army."

Lena laughed despite herself, the image of her mother fussing over her and Tommy before sending them off to Madison warming her heart. For a brief moment, she let herself feel the lightness of it, the simplicity of just being together without the weight of everything hanging over them.

"That sounds... perfect," Lena said, her smile more genuine now, though the knot in her stomach remained.

"Good." Tommy's grin widened as he stood up, holding his hand out to her. "Let's get going before it gets too late."

Lena hesitated for just a second, looking down at her hand still wrapped in his. She could feel the weight of the things she hadn't said, the uncertainty that still loomed over them. But Tommy was here, and he was trying to give her a day— a day where they could pretend, just for a little while, that everything was okay.

She stood up, slipping her hand into his fully, and let him lead her out of the soda shop. As they stepped into the crisp air, she glanced up at the sky, the sun shining brighter now, chasing away the lingering morning chill.

Tommy wrapped his arm around her as they walked toward his car, his touch familiar and warm. Lena leaned into him, her head resting against his shoulder.

"Thank you, Tommy," she said softly.

"For what?" he asked, glancing down at her, his brow furrowed slightly.

"For today. For everything."

Tommy smiled softly, pressing a kiss to the top of her head. "Anything for you, Lena. Always."

But as they reached the car and Tommy opened the door for her, Lena couldn't help but feel that the words hung between them like an unspoken promise she wasn't sure she could keep.

55

The chill of the ice rink greeted Lena as she stepped inside, the cold air wrapping around her like a familiar winter coat. The rink was large, the kind where you could get lost in the open space. A few families and couples glided effortlessly across the ice, their laughter echoing through the cavernous arena. Tommy led the way, a wide grin plastered across his face.

"This place brings back memories," he said, slipping his hand into hers as they walked toward the rental booth.

"You used to come here a lot?" Lena asked, her breath visible in the cold air. She fumbled with the skates, lacing them up tightly.

"Yeah, played ice hockey all through middle school," Tommy replied, sitting down next to her and finishing the laces on his skates with ease. "But this... this is different. Not used to going slow."

Lena chuckled. "Well, you might have to go even slower. I've barely skated before. Don't let me fall."

"I won't," Tommy said, standing up and offering her his hand. "Promise."

They shuffled their way onto the ice, and immediately, Lena could feel the uncertainty in her legs. She wobbled, clutching Tommy's hand tightly, trying to balance herself. He laughed, steadying her, his strong arms pulling her close to him.

"Easy, easy. You're doing fine," he said, his voice warm with encouragement.

Lena looked up at him, feeling a blush rise in her cheeks as she tried to focus on not toppling over. "This isn't as easy as it looks."

"You just need to trust the ice," Tommy said, gliding effortlessly beside her, his movements smooth and practiced. "Don't fight it."

As they circled the rink slowly, Lena began to relax, her grip on Tommy loosening as she found a rhythm. It wasn't perfect—she wobbled and stumbled now and then—but with Tommy by her side, the fear of falling seemed to melt away.

They laughed together, Tommy occasionally pulling her into a playful spin, her arms flying out as she squealed with surprise. It felt like old times, when everything between them had been easy and light.

"Remember the first time we came to Madison?" Tommy asked as they glided along, the cold air biting at their cheeks.

Lena smiled. "Yeah, we were so excited just to be out of Janesville for a day. We didn't even know what we wanted to do."

Tommy laughed. "We ended up getting lost downtown, wandering around until we found that record store. Spent hours in there just looking at records and books we couldn't afford."

Lena's heart swelled with the memory. That day had felt like the beginning of something, the first time she'd seen Tommy's softer, dreamier side, the boy who loved music almost as much as she did.

"Do you ever think about what could have been different?" she asked softly, her words hanging in the cold air as they skated together.

Tommy glanced at her, his brow furrowing slightly. "What do you mean?"

Lena hesitated. "I mean... if things were different. If you weren't going away."

The weight of her words seemed to settle over them both, and for a moment, they skated in silence, the only sound the soft swish of their skates against the ice.

"I try not to think about that," Tommy said finally, his voice low. "Because it doesn't change anything. But I do think about what happens when... when I get back."

Lena nodded, feeling the familiar ache in her chest. "Yeah. When you get back."

Tommy squeezed her hand gently, guiding her off the ice as they finished their last lap around the rink. "Come on. Let's go for a walk by the lake. Get some fresh air."

She nodded, her cheeks flushed from the cold and the quiet joy of the afternoon. For a moment, the world felt lighter—like it was just the two of them and nothing else. They paused only long enough to exchange their skates for boots before stepping out into the crisp air.

The sun hung low in the sky, painting the lake in shades of gold and silver. The water shimmered in the fading light, and the stillness around them felt almost sacred. Lena leaned into Tommy's side, his arm draped around her shoulders, and let the quiet envelop them.

"Feels good to just... talk like this," Tommy said, his breath visible in the cold air. "Without all the heavy stuff weighing us down."

Lena nodded, but the weight was still there, lingering just beneath the surface. The memory of his induction notice, the unspoken countdown to his departure—it clung to her thoughts like a shadow. But she let herself stay in this moment, matching her steps to his, the sound of their boots crunching softly against the frozen ground.

"Let's skip the part where we fight," Tommy said suddenly, his tone light but tinged with something deeper. "And agree for a moment there'll always be an us."

Lena stopped, caught off guard by the vulnerability in his voice. She looked up at him, her brow furrowing slightly. "Tommy..."

"I'm serious," he said, squeezing her hand. "Let's just... imagine it, okay? No war. No distance. Just you and me. Do you ever think about what you'll do... you know?"

"You know what?" she asked, though she knew what he meant.

"When we're married," he said softly, his words hanging in the cold air between them. "When I come back."

Her heart clenched at the certainty in his tone. He always spoke about the future with such conviction, as if he could will it into existence just by saying it out loud. And for a fleeting moment, she wanted to believe it too.

"What about your music?" Tommy continued, his voice hesitant. "How does that fit into everything in a way that works? In a way that fits us?"

Lena looked away, her eyes tracing the frozen edge of the lake. She wanted to give him an answer, something that would make everything easier, but the words didn't come. She could tell this was something he had thought a lot about. Still, it didn't make it any easier.

"I don't know," she said finally, her voice barely above a whisper. "I want both. I want you and my music. But sometimes it feels like... like I can't have both."

Tommy stopped walking, turning to face her. His brow furrowed, the familiar lines of frustration appearing on his face. "Why not? We'll make it work, Lena. I'll get a good job, maybe at the factory or something. You can play music in the evenings, or weekends—whatever you want. We'll have a family, and you can still do what you love. Everything will work out."

His words were so sure, so steady, and for a moment, Lena felt like she was the one doubting something she shouldn't. But deep down, she knew. She knew that the life Tommy was describing wasn't the life she'd imagined for herself.

"Tommy," she started, her voice trembling. She wanted to tell him the truth, to explain how much music meant to her, how it wasn't just something she did but something she was. But the look in his eyes stopped her. He wanted this so badly—this dream of theirs, this promise of a future together. How could she take that away from him?

Instead, she bit her tongue, forcing a smile. "Maybe you're right. Maybe it will work out."

Tommy smiled back, relief softening his features. "See? We'll figure it out, Lena. We always do."

But the knot in her chest only tightened.

They walked on in silence for a while, the sound of the lake lapping gently against the shore filling the quiet. The unspoken tension between them pressed harder with every step, and Lena's mind raced with everything she wasn't saying.

Finally, Tommy broke the quiet, his voice lighter now. "You know what? Let's get something warm to drink. I think we've earned it after skating like pros today."

Lena let out a small laugh, grateful for the shift in tone. "Hot chocolate?"

"Hot chocolate," Tommy confirmed with a grin.

As they turned toward the diner, Lena slipped her hand into his again, the warmth of his touch grounding her for the moment. But as much as she wanted to hold onto it, the truth lingered in the back of her mind like the cold wind against her skin.

Maybe we'll figure it out, she thought. But what if we don't?

The diner was a welcome relief after the cold walk by the lake. They found a booth by the window overlooking the water, the dim lights inside casting a soft glow over the room. The smell of fresh pastries and hot chocolate filled the air, and Lena felt a sense of comfort settle over her.

Tommy ordered for them both—hot chocolate with whipped cream and two warm pastries. As they waited for their food, they fell into an easy conversation about music, just like they used to.

"Have you been working on anything new?" Tommy asked, stirring his hot chocolate.

Lena nodded, her thoughts drifting back to the song she'd been writing. "Yeah, there's this new one. It's... it's about finding myself, I guess. About trying to piece together who I am, who I want to be."

Tommy smiled. "I'd love to hear it."

Lena hesitated. She wasn't sure how to tell him that the song—like all her songs—wasn't just about her, but about the things she couldn't say to him. About the parts of herself she was still trying to figure out.

"Maybe soon," she said softly.

They sat in silence for a while, sipping their hot chocolate, the warmth of the diner wrapping around them. Outside, the lake shimmered in the distance, the cold air still lingering just beyond the window.

And for a moment, it was enough—just being here, together, talking about nothing and everything, like the world outside didn't exist. But deep down, Lena knew that their time was running out.

56

As Tommy's car pulled up in front of Lena's house, the fading light of the sun cast long shadows over the front yard. The warmth of their day together still lingered in the air between them, but the reality of time slipping away started to settle in.

"I had a good time today," Tommy said, turning the engine off but leaving his hand on the keys. His voice was soft, thoughtful, like he was trying to savor every last moment.

Lena smiled, though her heart felt heavy. "Me too. It felt... normal, you know? Like everything was the way it used to be."

"Yeah," Tommy said, glancing at the house. "But it's not, is it?"

Lena didn't answer, but her silence spoke volumes. She looked at Tommy, studying the lines of his face, the way his eyes held that quiet strength, the way he tried to reassure her even when they both knew what was coming.

"I should get inside," Lena said, unbuckling her seatbelt, though she made no move to leave just yet. "I promised I'd help with dinner."

Tommy nodded, his hand slipping from the keys to rest gently on her arm. "I'll see you tomorrow?"

"Yeah," Lena said, her voice catching in her throat. "Tomorrow."

She opened the car door and stepped out, the cold air hitting her like a reminder of reality. Before she could take more than a few steps toward the house, the front door swung open, and her father appeared, his broad frame silhouetted by the warm light inside.

"Tommy! Come on in, son," her dad called out, waving him inside. "It's almost dinner time. You're not gonna just drop Lena off and disappear, are you?"

Tommy smiled, but Lena could see the hesitation in his eyes. "Thanks, Mr. Carter, but I've got to get home for dinner with my folks."

"Nonsense," her father insisted, stepping out onto the porch. "I'm sure your parents won't mind you being a few minutes late. Come say hello to everyone."

From inside the house, Lena could hear her mom's voice chiming in. "We've got plenty of food, Tommy. Don't be a stranger!"

Lena's grandparents, too, were likely seated in the living room, waiting to see Tommy. Her grandfather had taken a liking to him over the years, always eager to chat with the young man who reminded him of his own youth—strong, steady, and ready to serve his country.

But Tommy shook his head, gently refusing. "I really appreciate it, but I should get home. My mom's already got dinner on the table, and she'll have my head if I'm late."

Her father laughed. "Alright, alright. But don't be a stranger, you hear? You're family now."

Lena's heart squeezed a little at her father's words. Family. It sounded so final, so certain, like everything was already decided.

"I'll see you soon, Mr. Carter," Tommy promised, flashing his easy smile before turning back to Lena. "I'll call you later, okay?"

"Okay," Lena said, stepping up onto the porch as Tommy backed out of the driveway. She waved as he drove away, the sound of the engine fading into the quiet evening.

For a moment, she stood there, watching the car disappear down the road, feeling a pang of longing, a mix of everything—love, fear, uncertainty— tangled up inside her. She wanted to run after him, to hold onto him and make everything stop, to freeze this moment and keep things just the way they were before everything changed.

But she couldn't. Tommy was going, and there was nothing she could do to stop it.

"Lena?" her mother called from inside, pulling her from her thoughts. "Come on, sweetheart, we need to get started on dinner."

Lena took a deep breath, brushed the cold air from her arms, and stepped inside, closing the door softly behind her.

The warmth of the kitchen was immediate, the smells of roasting meat and simmering vegetables wrapping around Lena like a comforting embrace. Her grandparents were already seated in the living room, her grandfather laughing loudly at something on the TV, while her grandmother chatted with her dad at the table.

"Lena, dear, you're just in time," her mom said, wiping her hands on a dishtowel as she bustled around the kitchen. "I've got the potatoes boiling, but we still need to set the table. Can you help with that?"

"Of course," Lena said, stepping over to the kitchen counter where the dishes were stacked.

As she moved through the familiar motions of helping with dinner—setting the table, checking on the food—it all felt surreal. Her mind kept drifting back to Tommy, to the day they'd spent together. She wasn't sure what hurt more: the fact that he was leaving or the fact that there was nothing she could do to change it.

"Lena?" her grandmother's voice broke through her thoughts.

Lena blinked, realizing she'd been standing still with a spoon in her hand for the last few moments, lost in her thoughts.

"You alright, dear?" her grandmother asked, concern creasing her brow.

"Yeah," Lena said quickly, forcing a smile. "Just thinking."

Her grandmother nodded knowingly, her eyes soft with understanding. "You've got a lot on your mind these days, don't you?"

Lena swallowed hard, unsure of what to say. Her grandmother had always been able to read her like an open book, and tonight was no different.

Before she could answer, her father's booming voice cut through the room. "Dinner's ready, everyone! Let's gather around."

As the family moved to the table, the usual chatter began, everyone settling into their familiar roles. Her dad and grandpa joked about the football game on TV, her mom and grandma talked about the next family gathering, and for a moment, everything felt normal.

But normal felt fragile to Lena. She joined in the conversation as best she could, her smiles and nods masking the unease simmering beneath the surface.

After dinner, she excused herself early, retreating upstairs to the sanctuary of her room. She sat cross-legged on her bed, her guitar resting in her lap. The room was dim, illuminated only by the soft glow of the bedside lamp casting long shadows across the familiar space. Her fingers idly plucked at the strings, but the notes didn't come easily tonight.

Her music journal lay open beside her, half-filled pages of lyrics she had scribbled down over the past few weeks. Songs about hope, about resilience, about finding herself in the midst of everything. But tonight was different. Tonight, the melodies were sadder, the lyrics harder to grasp.

She felt like something inside her had shifted—maybe it was Tommy leaving soon, maybe it was the weight of the rejection letter, or maybe it was the realization that she wasn't ready to say goodbye to the life she knew, even as she longed for something more.

The familiar first few lines of the new song flowed softly from her lips as she gently strummed her guitar.

The summer sun would kiss my face
Running barefoot through the endless grass
The lake was quiet, the air was sweet
With every breeze, I'd feel alive
Home was simple, love was kind

Her voice trembled, the words coming slowly as though each one weighed heavy in her throat. She tried to keep going, tried to make sense of the swirling emotions inside her, but the tears she had been holding back since Tommy dropped her off finally began to slip free.

Lena set her guitar aside, the unfinished melody lingering in the air. She picked up her pen, scribbling down part of the chorus, though it still didn't feel right.

The shadows of yesterday follow me
Like echoes in the wind, like whispers in the trees
I chase the light, but it fades and fades
And all I'm left with are the shadows of yesterday...

She stopped, her hand hovering over the page. The tears flowed more freely now, staining the edges of the paper as she wiped at her cheeks with the back of her hand.

She didn't want to cry—didn't want to feel this lost, this unsure of herself. But everything felt so heavy, like the weight of her future was pressing down on her, suffocating her dreams. It was all too much: the rejection letter, Tommy's impending departure, the uncertainty of what her own life would be like once he was gone.

A soft knock sounded at the door, breaking through the quiet.

"Lena?" her mother's voice came from the other side, gentle but full of concern. "Can I come in?"

Lena quickly brushed the tears from her cheeks, taking a deep breath before answering. "Yeah, Mom. Come in."

Her mother opened the door slowly, stepping inside with a tenderness that showed she already sensed something was wrong. She crossed the room quietly, taking in the sight of Lena sitting there with her guitar, her music journal open on the bed.

Her mother sat down beside her, her hand resting lightly on Lena's shoulder. "You've been so quiet all night, sweetheart. I just wanted to check on you."

Lena's throat tightened, the tears threatening to spill over again. She didn't know how to explain everything that was weighing her down—how the rejection letter had shattered her confidence, how Tommy's news had left her feeling hollow, how her dreams felt distant and unreachable.

"It's just..." Lena began, her voice barely a whisper. "Everything feels... wrong. Like I'm trying to hold onto something, but I don't even know what it is anymore."

Her mother's hand moved to gently stroke her hair. "Is this about Tommy?" she asked softly, her eyes searching Lena's face for clues.

Lena shook her head. "Not just Tommy. It's everything. The music, the future... I don't know what I'm supposed to do. I thought I had it all figured out, but now..." Her voice broke, the weight of her uncertainty crashing down around her. "I just don't know."

Her mother didn't say anything right away. She simply sat there, holding Lena close, giving her the quiet support she needed. After a long moment, she spoke in her soft, reassuring voice.

"You don't have to have it all figured out right now, Lena," she said gently. "Life doesn't work like that. It's messy, and sometimes it throws things at us we're not ready for. But that doesn't mean you're lost. You'll find your way."

Lena rested her head on her mother's shoulder, letting the warmth of her presence calm the storm swirling inside her.

"And your music..." her mother continued, her voice filled with quiet admiration. "It's beautiful, Lena. I know how much it means to you, and I believe in you. Maybe that letter from New York wasn't what you wanted to hear, but that doesn't mean it's the end. You'll write another song, and then another. You'll keep going."

Her mother's words washed over her, soothing the ache inside her heart.

"I'm just so scared," Lena whispered, her voice trembling. "Scared of what's going to happen to Tommy... scared of what's going to happen to me if I don't figure this out."

Her mother pulled her closer, pressing a soft kiss to the top of her head. "We all get scared, sweetheart. But you're stronger than you think. And no matter what happens, you'll find a way through this."

Lena let the words sink in, feeling the knot in her chest slowly loosen, if only a little. After a while, her mother stood, giving Lena's shoulder one last reassuring squeeze before heading for the door. "If you need anything, you know where I am," she said softly before slipping out of the room.

Lena sat there for a few more moments, her thoughts still tangled, but something had shifted. She picked up her guitar again, her fingers brushing over the strings. She wasn't sure if she had the words yet, or if they would come at all tonight, but she knew one thing: she would keep searching for them.

She would keep writing, keep dreaming.

Even when the shadows of yesterday loomed large, she would keep going.

And somewhere, in the midst of all the confusion, she would find herself again.

57

Saturday passed in a blur of Tommy.

They'd spent the day together, stealing moments as though time owed them something—long drives on quiet backroads, the hum of the radio filling the silences, the crackle of leaves underfoot as they wandered through the park. They hadn't done much, really, but it was everything.

Tommy had taken her to a diner in Whitewater for lunch, insisting she try the pie he swore was the best in town. They'd laughed as she teased him for getting crumbs on his jacket, and he'd retaliated by smearing whipped cream on her nose. It had felt so normal, so ordinary, that for a little while, Lena let herself believe they could stay in that moment forever.

But then there had been the quiet moments too—those heavy silences where Tommy's eyes turned distant, and she could almost hear the thoughts he wasn't saying. She'd wanted to ask him, to press him to share what was weighing on him, but the words stayed trapped in her throat. She didn't want to shatter the fragile peace of the day.

Now, sitting on the edge of her bed, Lena brushed her fingers absently over the guitar strings, the soft hum of the notes filling the stillness of the room. Her grandparents had gone to bed hours ago, and the house had found its usual quiet rhythm.

Her thoughts drifted back to Tommy—the way his hand had lingered on hers when he dropped her off, the way his eyes had searched hers like he was trying to say something without words. She'd felt it all day, that undercurrent of urgency, of time slipping away faster than either of them could catch it.

She should have said something, she thought. Should have asked him what was going through his mind, about the weight he carried that he seemed determined to shoulder alone. But something had held her back—a fear, maybe, that if they spoke the truth aloud, it would only make the inevitability of Monday more real.

Lena sighed, her fingers stilling on the strings as she stared at the open journal. The words on the page were half-formed, fragments of songs that didn't feel finished. Much like her day with Tommy—beautiful but incomplete, full of things left unsaid.

As if on cue, the phone rang, its sharp trill cutting through the silence of her room. Lena jumped slightly, startled, but quickly reached for it, knowing instinctively who it was.

"Hey," Tommy's voice came through the line, soft and familiar. "I didn't wake you, did I?"

"No," Lena replied, her heart picking up pace at the sound of his voice. "I was just... thinking."

"About today?" he asked, his tone casual, but there was an underlying tension there. She could hear it.

"Yeah," Lena admitted. "And... about tomorrow too."

There was a pause on the other end, long enough for Lena to wonder if Tommy was hesitating, choosing his words carefully.

"My parents are going to the Henderson's tomorrow for the day," Tommy finally said, his voice dropping a little, becoming quieter, more intimate. "So... it'll just be us. At my house."

Lena's heart skipped a beat. She didn't know why, but the way Tommy said those words—just us—left her feeling... something. Uncertainty, excitement, maybe even fear.

"Oh," she breathed, trying to keep her voice steady. "Okay."

Another pause. Longer this time.

"Don't worry," Tommy added, as if sensing her hesitation. "I just thought it'd be nice. You know, to spend the day together, just the two of us. No interruptions. We've barely had any time alone lately."

"Yeah," Lena replied, though the words felt a bit distant, like they didn't fully reach her. She didn't know what Tommy expected from the day. Maybe he didn't expect anything, but there was something in his tone—something in the way he emphasized just the two of us—that made Lena's mind race with possibilities.

"Sounds good," she said, forcing herself to relax. But inside, her thoughts were anything but calm.

Tommy's voice softened. "I'll pick you up around ten, okay? We'll have the whole day."

"Okay," Lena echoed, though the uncertainty in her chest only grew. "I'll see you then."

"Goodnight, Lena," Tommy said softly, and there was a warmth in his voice that made Lena's heart ache, even as confusion swirled inside her.

"Goodnight, Tommy," she replied before hanging up the phone.

Lena sat on her bed for a long time after the phone call ended, staring at the handset as though it held all the answers she needed. But there were no answers—only more questions. What did Tommy expect of her tomorrow? Was he thinking the same things she was? And what did just us really mean?

She lay back against her pillows, staring at the ceiling as her mind wandered. Tommy had always been good to her—sweet, caring, and steady. But tomorrow felt different. There was something in his voice tonight that had unsettled her, a kind of longing that she didn't know if she was ready to face.

Tommy had never pressured her—he wasn't like that—but did he expect them to take the next step in their relationship? Was that why he wanted to be alone with her all day, away from prying eyes and the watchful presence of family?

Lena's heart raced at the thought. She wasn't sure if she was ready for that kind of intimacy, not with everything going on. *But what if it's not about that?* she reasoned with herself. *What if Tommy just needs comfort? Someone to be there with him, to help him through all of this?*

She sighed, feeling the familiar tug-of-war inside her—between what she wanted and what she thought she should want. Between the love she had for Tommy and the dreams she had for herself. It wasn't that she didn't love him. She did. Deeply. But it was the future he envisioned for them—a simple life, a home, children—that scared her.

What if I lose myself? she thought, the question echoing in her mind.

But it wasn't just about losing herself in Tommy. Father Michaels' words from last Sunday's sermon echoed in her mind: *The sacred bond of marriage is a covenant, blessed by God. To step outside of that before you're ready, before you've made that commitment in His eyes, is to carry a burden that weighs on your soul.* Lena had squirmed in the pew then, feeling the familiar weight of expectation pressing down on her shoulders.

She could still picture her mother nodding along in agreement, her father listening with his usual stoic expression. Father Michaels had looked right at her, or at least it felt like it. His words lingered now, sharp and certain, cutting through her racing thoughts.

What if tomorrow led to something she wasn't ready for? Something that would make her question everything she believed?

Lena hugged her knees to her chest, guilt and confusion swirling together. It wasn't that she didn't love Tommy. She did. And sometimes, when they were alone, when he kissed her with that quiet urgency, it felt so easy to imagine letting herself go, surrendering to the pull between them. But then, her conscience would creep in, heavy with the weight of everything she'd been taught—what she owed to herself, to Tommy, to God.

Was it wrong to want to hold onto both her faith and her love for him? Could she find a way to honor both, or would she always feel this push and pull, torn between the life she was raised to lead and the one she longed to create?

Her eyes drifted to her guitar, sitting silently in the corner of the room. Her music had always been her refuge, the place where she could let go of everything and just... be. But now, even her music felt distant. The rejection letter still weighed on her heart, making her doubt herself, her talent, her dreams.

She pulled her covers up to her chin, curling into herself as her thoughts continued to swirl. She didn't know what tomorrow would bring—if it would be a turning point for her and Tommy, or if it would only make the distance between them more apparent.

One thing was certain: whatever happened tomorrow, it would change things.

Lena wasn't sure she was ready for that kind of change.

With a heavy heart and a mind full of questions, she closed her eyes and slowly drifted off to sleep, the soft whisper of her music journal and the weight of her choices pressing down on her, even in her dreams.

58

The house was full of warm, lingering goodbyes as Lena stood on the porch, watching her grandparents gather their things. Gramma Enid tucked a scarf tightly around her neck, while Grandpa Wally was already at the car, loading up the trunk with bags and leftovers.

"You'll write, won't you, Lena?" Gramma Enid asked, her eyes twinkling as she pulled Lena into a tight hug. "Tell me all about that music of yours."

Lena smiled, nodding as she hugged her grandmother back. "Of course, Gramma. I'll write."

"Good girl," Enid whispered, before pulling back, her eyes full of warmth and pride. Grandpa Wally came over and ruffled Lena's hair the way he had since she was a little girl.

"Take care of yourself, Lena. And take care of your folks," he said with a wink.

"I will, Grandpa."

With that, they were off. Lena stood with her parents, waving as the old sedan backed out of the driveway and began the long journey back to Green Bay. The house felt suddenly quieter, emptier.

Her mother sighed beside her, adjusting the collar of her sweater. "It's always so nice to have them, but it's good to get the house back too."

Lena nodded absently, her thoughts elsewhere, already anticipating the day ahead. Just then, the low rumble of an engine cut through the quiet. Tommy's car pulled up, and Lena's heart quickened as she saw him step out, smiling shyly in her direction.

"Tommy's here," Lena's father remarked with a hint of approval in his voice. He waved casually at Tommy, who returned the gesture before leaning against his car and waiting for Lena.

"Go on, honey," her mother said with a knowing smile. "Have a good day."

Lena grabbed her coat, kissed her mom on the cheek, and hurried down the steps. "See you later," she called, making her way toward Tommy's car.

As she slid into the passenger seat, Tommy gave her a gentle smile, and they pulled away from her house.

The drive to Tommy's house was short but quiet, the kind of easy quiet that had always come naturally between them. Lena's mind raced with thoughts, unsure of what to expect from today. Tommy hadn't shared much, just that they would have the day to themselves.

When they pulled up to his house, Tommy parked the car, turning to Lena with a grin. "I've got something special planned."

Lena raised an eyebrow, curious but still slightly wary of what Tommy had in store. As they stepped inside, the warmth of the house immediately greeted them, and Lena noticed something different right away. The air smelled clean, almost fragrant, and the living room looked... well, it looked like Tommy had really put in an effort. Everything was tidy, the coffee table clear except for a few carefully arranged records sitting on top.

Lena's eyes were immediately drawn to the records Tommy had laid out: Otis Redding - The Great Otis Redding Sings Soul Ballads, Simon & Garfunkel - Parsley, Sage, Rosemary and Thyme, and Frank Sinatra - Strangers in the Night. Her heart softened as she realized Tommy had picked these out for her, knowing her love for music.

"You... you did all this?" Lena asked, her voice soft with surprise.

Tommy shrugged, a little bashful, scratching the back of his neck. "Yeah, I thought... you know, we could listen to some records, maybe cook something together. Nothing too fancy, but... I wanted today to be about us."

Lena's eyes scanned the room again before they followed Tommy into the kitchen. That's when she saw the next surprise: the ingredients for a homemade tuna noodle casserole neatly laid out on the counter—egg noodles, canned tuna, cream of mushroom soup, and a bag of mixed peas and carrots, plus a small bowl of potato chips ready to be crushed for the topping.

Lena smiled, feeling a strange mix of emotions. On the one hand, she was touched by the effort Tommy had gone through to make the day special. But there was also an underlying sadness—knowing that this was his way of trying to hold onto the normalcy of their relationship, even as everything around them was changing.

"This... this looks great," Lena said, turning to Tommy. "You've really thought of everything."

Tommy stepped closer, his hands gently resting on her arms. "I wanted to make today special. Before... you know, everything changes."

Lena nodded, swallowing the lump in her throat. Everything was about to change, and for a moment, she felt that familiar tug inside her—between the life Tommy imagined for them, and the path she wasn't sure she was brave enough to follow.

But for now, standing in Tommy's kitchen, surrounded by his thoughtfulness, Lena was determined to make the most of the day.

"Let's make that casserole," Tommy said with a grin, breaking the tension with a playful nudge toward the kitchen counter. "You can be in charge of the chips."

Lena smiled back, grateful for the lightness he brought to the moment. She grabbed the potato chips and got to work, crushing them between her hands, the noise loud and satisfying in the quiet kitchen. Tommy moved beside her, boiling the noodles and mixing the tuna and vegetables into the creamy sauce.

It was a simple task, cooking together, but it felt like more. It felt like a way to hold onto each other, to hold onto the present, even as the future loomed over them.

Lena stole a glance at Tommy as he stirred the casserole, his expression focused but content. She couldn't shake the thought that he was trying so hard to keep things the same—to keep them the same—when everything was about to shift. But for now, she decided to let that thought rest, to simply be here with Tommy, to share this moment and not let the future steal it away.

When the casserole was finally assembled and slid into the oven, Tommy leaned against the counter, wiping his hands on a dish towel. "It's not exactly gourmet," he joked, "but I think it'll do."

Lena chuckled softly, brushing stray crumbs from her fingers. "It's perfect," she said, and she meant it. The effort, the thoughtfulness—it was everything. For a moment, it felt like the world outside didn't exist—like there was only the warmth of the kitchen and the shared effort to create something, however small, together.

Soon, the tuna casserole sat steaming on the table, its golden crust of crushed potato chips crackling as Tommy dished out servings onto their plates. The kitchen was filled with the warm, comforting scent of food, and though the meal was simple, it felt special—like a snapshot of a future Tommy was already imagining.

Lena sat across from him, watching as he took his first bite, his eyes lighting up with satisfaction. "Not bad, huh?" he said, grinning as he chewed.

Lena laughed softly, taking a bite herself. "I'll admit, I didn't think you had it in you, Tommy. But this is... pretty good."

Tommy winked, sitting back in his chair, content. "Stick with me, Lena. There's more where that came from."

They ate without saying anything for a while, the soft hum of Otis Redding playing in the background. Lena let herself relax, the weight of the world lifting just slightly as they talked about little things—the kind of mundane, sweet conversations that filled long afternoons.

"What do you think about Simon & Garfunkel's new album?" Tommy asked, nodding toward the record player, where Parsley, Sage, Rosemary and Thyme sat ready to play next.

Lena smiled, setting down her fork. "I love it. Their lyrics are like poetry... it's hard to believe two people can harmonize like that, you know? It's almost like they were meant to sing together."

Tommy leaned forward, his eyes catching hers across the table. "Kinda like how you and I were meant to be together?"

Lena's heart skipped a beat. There was something about the way he said it, so sincere, so sure of himself, that made her want to believe it too. But the weight of her dreams, her music, her uncertainty about the future pressed at the edges of her heart. She forced a smile, not quite ready to dive into that conversation yet.

"Maybe," she said softly, letting the word hang in the air.

After dinner, Tommy cleared the dishes, refusing to let Lena help. "You relax," he insisted, turning up the music a bit as he moved about the kitchen. "I've got this covered."

Lena wandered into the living room, sitting down on the couch as the rich tones of Frank Sinatra filled the room. She closed her eyes for a moment, letting the smooth melody wash over her, pulling her into a world where things felt simpler, where the future wasn't so uncertain.

A few minutes later, Tommy joined her on the couch, pulling her close as they both sank into the music. The midday sun was casting a warm glow through the windows, and for a moment, it felt like they were in their own little world—just the two of them, wrapped up in each other.

"This is nice," Lena whispered, her head resting on Tommy's shoulder.

Tommy's hand found hers, lacing their fingers together. "It's more than nice," he said softly. "It's perfect."

They sat like that for a long time, the conversation flowing freely, touching on everything from childhood memories to silly dreams for the future. Lena found herself laughing more than she had in days, her worries momentarily forgotten as they shared stories and jokes.

As the evening settled in, Tommy stood up and disappeared into the other room. When he came back, he had a small box in his hand, his expression suddenly serious.

Lena's heart skipped again, a mixture of excitement and anxiety bubbling up inside her.

"What's that?" she asked, though she already knew.

Tommy knelt in front of her, opening the box to reveal a delicate silver ring with a tiny heart-shaped stone in the center. "I know things are... complicated right now," he began, his voice steady but emotional. "But Lena, I love you. I've always loved you. And I don't want to wait any longer to show you how serious I am about us."

Lena's eyes welled up with tears, her breath catching in her throat as she looked at the ring. "Tommy..."

He took her hand gently, slipping the ring onto her finger. "This isn't a proposal... not yet. But it's a promise. A promise that I'm coming back for you. That we're going to build a life together—just like we talked about."

Lena blinked back the tears, overwhelmed by the gesture, by the weight of what Tommy was offering her. It was beautiful, romantic, and everything she knew he wanted. But part of her heart was still tugging toward something else, something she couldn't quite name.

Still, in this moment, with Tommy's hands holding hers, she couldn't think about that. She didn't want to think about it. All she wanted was to hold onto this feeling, to believe, even if just for tonight, that everything could be as simple and perfect as Tommy imagined.

"I love you too," Lena whispered, her voice thick with emotion.

Tommy smiled, pulling her into a soft, slow kiss. The world outside disappeared, and for now, there was only them—two people in love, holding on to each other as tightly as they could.

The promise ring glinted softly on Lena's finger, catching the last light of the day as the sun dipped below the horizon.

59

Lena sat on the couch, her hand resting gently on Tommy's. The weight of the promise ring on her finger felt heavier than she expected, not from its physical presence, but from everything it symbolized. She stared at the small stone, the delicate silver band that now encircled her finger, and for the briefest moment, the world felt like it had stopped. Tommy's words echoed in her mind—his love for her, his unwavering belief in their future together.

But deep inside, Lena was a storm of emotions. She had spent so long torn between what Tommy wanted, what her family expected, and her own yearning to break free, to find herself through her music. Yet tonight, all of that seemed far away, lost in the warmth of the moment. Here with Tommy, the only thing that seemed to matter was him—his steady love, his belief in their future, and the promise of a life together.

Tommy's hand squeezed hers gently, pulling her from her thoughts. He turned to her, eyes soft and full of that familiar tenderness. "Lena," he whispered, his voice low and gentle, "I know everything's been hard, but I need you to know that I'm here... with you. And no matter what happens, we'll be okay. I'll come back for you."

Lena looked up at him, her chest tightening. She could feel the weight of his words, the finality in them. Tomorrow, the world would change. Tomorrow, Tommy would leave, and nothing would be the same again. The thought of it made her heart ache, made the future feel like an impossible mountain to climb.

But tonight... tonight was theirs.

Without thinking, Lena leaned forward, pressing her lips to his. The kiss was soft at first, a tentative meeting of lips, but soon it deepened. She felt herself melting into Tommy, into the warmth of his arms, into the safety of the moment. Her hands slid up to his face, fingers tracing the familiar lines of his jaw as she kissed him again, more urgently this time, as if she could capture this feeling and make it last forever.

Tommy responded, his arms wrapping around her, pulling her closer. They fell back onto the couch together, their bodies pressed tightly against each other as the kiss grew more passionate. Lena's heart raced in her chest, every beat a reminder of how much she loved him, how much she wanted him. She let herself get lost in the moment, in the feel of Tommy's hands on her skin, in the way his touch made her forget everything else.

The world outside fell away. There was no war, no uncertainty, no Father Michaels, no far-off dreams of New York. There was only them—Tommy and Lena, wrapped up in each other, desperate to make this moment last. It was raw and real, and it was everything Lena hadn't let herself want—everything she didn't know she needed until now.

As the night deepened, they moved together slowly, carefully, as if they both knew this was more than just a night. It was a goodbye, a promise, a way of holding on to each other even as the world around them was pulling them apart. Lena's breath caught in her throat as she gave herself to him, her heart heavy and light all at once.

Every touch, every kiss, every whispered word felt like a thread tying them together, a bond that neither time nor distance could break. Lena clung to him, her body trembling with the weight of her love for him, with the fear of what was to come.

Tommy held her close, his hands gentle but firm, his touch reassuring. "I love you, Lena," he whispered against her skin. "I always will."

Tears welled up in her eyes, but she didn't let them fall. Instead, she buried her face in his chest, letting the sound of his heartbeat lull her into a sense of calm, even as her mind raced with everything she wasn't ready to face.

The night stretched on, and as they lay together in the quiet aftermath, Lena felt both closer to Tommy and further from him than she ever had before. The weight of the promise ring on her finger was a reminder of the life he wanted for them, a life that felt both beautiful and terrifying. But for now, in this moment, she let herself believe in it. She let herself believe that love could be enough to bridge the gap between their dreams, that they could find a way to make it all work.

But even as she lay in Tommy's arms, her body still warm from their shared intimacy, a small voice inside her whispered that this night was the beginning of something much bigger—a journey she hadn't even begun to understand yet.

Tommy kissed the top of her head, his hand resting on the curve of her waist as they drifted off into the quiet of the night, wrapped in each other and a fragile hope for the future.

Thank you for reading…

Songbird in the Rain

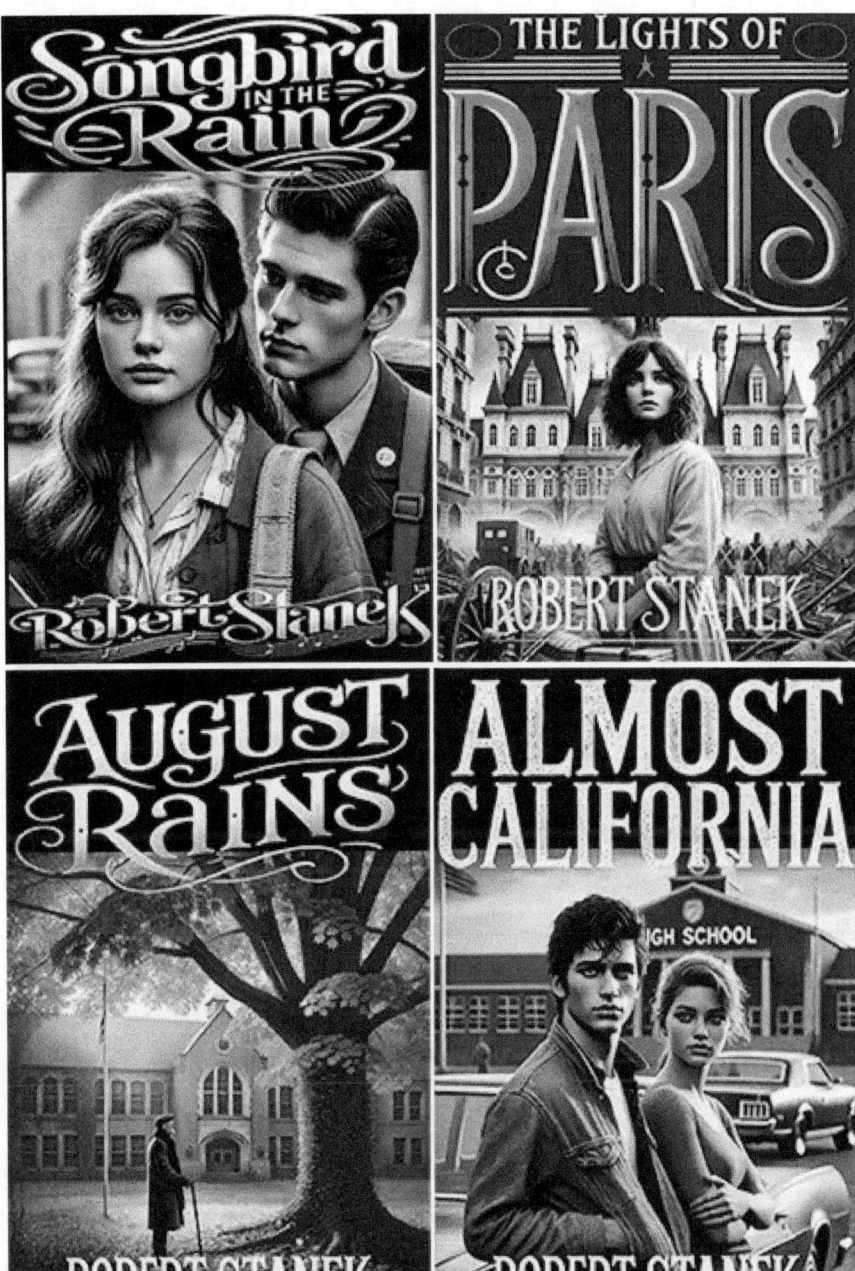

About the Author

Robert Stanek grew up in Wisconsin, not far from the town of Janesville, the heart of *Songbird in the Rain*. His Midwest roots have shaped his love for small-town stories filled with vibrant characters and emotional depth. As an author, Stanek has a gift for weaving rich, evocative tales that explore the human condition through the lens of history, music, and personal transformation.

With a lifelong appreciation for music and storytelling, Stanek often draws inspiration from his own experiences and the changing cultural landscapes he's observed. His novels explore themes of love, resilience, and the fight to break free from expectations, resonating with readers who seek emotionally charged, character-driven narratives.

In *Songbird in the Rain*, Stanek takes readers back to the transformative 1960s, crafting a story that is as much about the social and cultural upheavals of the time as it is about Lena's deeply personal journey. His portrayal of the Vietnam War era, the rising counterculture, and the timeless struggles of love and identity will captivate readers who enjoy historical fiction and coming-of-age tales alike.

When he's not writing, Robert Stanek spends time exploring the natural beauty of the world, seeking inspiration for his next project, and connecting with readers who share his love for heartfelt storytelling.

Robert Stanek lives in the U.S. Pacific Northwest with his family and is hard at work on his next novel. Readers can visit his website robert-stanek.com to learn more about his work, find updates on upcoming releases, and delve into behind-the-scenes insights into his creative process.

www.ingramcontent.com/pod-product-compliance
Lightning Source LLC
Chambersburg PA
CBHW060308100726
47907CB00002B/337